REVIVER

SETH PATRICK

REVIVƎꓤ

Thomas Dunne Books
St. Martin's Press
New York

THOMAS DUNNE BOOKS.
An imprint of St. Martin's Press.

REVIVER. Copyright © 2013 by Seth Patrick. All rights reserved. Printed in the United States of America. For information, address St. Martin's Press, 175 Fifth Avenue, New York, N.Y. 10010.

www.thomasdunnebooks.com
www.stmartins.com

Library of Congress Cataloging-in-Publication Data

Patrick, Seth.
  Reviver : a novel / Seth Patrick. — 1st U.S. edition.
      p. cm.
  ISBN 978-1-250-02170-0 (hardcover)
  ISBN 978-1-250-02169-4 (e-book)
  1. Police—Fiction. 2. Journalists—Crimes against—Fiction. I. Title.
  PR6116.A8455R48 2013
  823'.92—dc23

                                                          2013009949

St. Martin's Press books may be purchased for educational, business, or promotional use. For information on bulk purchases, please contact Macmillan Corporate and Premium Sales Department at 1-800-221-7945 extension 5442 or write specialmarkets@macmillan.com.

First published in Great Britain by Tor, an imprint of Pan Macmillan, a division of Macmillan Publishers Limited

First Edition: June 2013

10 9 8 7 6 5 4 3 2 1

For Laura

(No pressure)

Acknowledgements

Thanks first to my agent, Luigi Bonomi, for his support and enthusiasm; to Peter James for his encouragement; to my editor, Julie Crisp, for her guidance and for taking a chance on a first-timer; to everyone at Pan Macmillan; and to Brendan Deneen at Macmillan Films for making the movie deal happen.

Also to those who read early drafts and whose feedback was so useful, including Dorothy Fawcett, Mark Sutherns, Ross Manton, and Scott Pitkethly of Unicorn Power. Special mention goes to Doctor Tim Gosling and Doctor May Yee Yong, who read every draft I threw their way with diligence and speed, and whose suggestions made the finished book so much stronger.

And of course, to my wife and children for putting up with me no matter how distracted I was.

Final thanks go to Edgar Allan Poe. It was the discovery that I shared a birthday with Poe that led to *Reviver*, as it brought to mind two of his stories I'd read years previously. First, *The Facts in the Case of M. Valdemar*, in which Monsieur Valdemar dies under hypnosis but his corpse speaks, the tongue vibrating hideously in the dead mouth. Second, *The Murders in the Rue Morgue*, widely regarded as the first modern detective story. These tales collided in my head, and – with the image of Valdemar being questioned by Poe's detective, Dupin – *Reviver* was born.

1

Sometimes Jonah Miller hated talking to the dead.

The woman's ruined corpse lay against the far wall of the small office. The killer had moved her from the centre of the room; she had been dragged to the back wall and left propped up, slouched with her head lolled to one side.

Forensics had been and gone, leaving him to get what he could. They had been eager to leave. Jonah sympathized. Hearing the dead bear witness to their own demise was never pleasant.

He was wearing the standard white forensic coverall, as much to protect his own clothing as to prevent contamination of the scene. Gloves on his hands, covers over his trainers. He took a slow deep breath, ignoring the dull tang of blood in the air. It was a familiar smell.

The heavy wooden chair had been discarded next to the window, after the killer had used it to bludgeon the life out of the woman. Blood spatter was everywhere, clear swing patterns on the walls and ceiling.

The woman's corpse had almost been pulped by the frenzied attack. Her limbs had been broken, her torso ripped and distorted, the back of her skull torn apart. However, the throat seemed undamaged; the lungs, from what could be seen of them, appeared intact. That was the important thing. Three cameras were placed around the room, ready to record everything that happened. It was vital to have the words spoken aloud.

The duty pathologist had not moved her. Disturbing the body would make revival more difficult, reducing the chance of success. Time of death had been estimated at around nine the previous evening, almost twelve hours before.

Her name was Alice Decker. She was a clinical psychologist, and this was her office; a family picture in a mangled frame lay on the floor, Decker smiling beside her husband and two teenage daughters.

With care, Jonah stepped around one tripod-mounted camera, his paper suit rustling as he tiptoed between cable and bloodstain. He knelt by Alice's body and removed the latex glove from his right hand. Direct contact was an unpleasant necessity.

'Everything ready?' he asked, looking into the lens of the nearest camera. There was a brief confirmation in the earpiece he wore. The red indicators on the cameras went green as recording commenced.

Jonah took the victim's shattered hand. 'Revival of subject Alice Decker. J. P. Miller, duty reviver,' he stated. He focused, the cameras recording in silence. Minutes passed. His eyes closed. His face betrayed nothing of his work's difficulty, but it was *this* part that he hated most, this plunge into the dark rot to bring his subject back.

A violent death was harder, and Jonah was always dealing with violent deaths.

The violence also limited the time he would have. When he brought Alice back, he expected five minutes of questioning at most, perhaps far less. He would release her as quickly as he could, once there was nothing more to be learned. After the indignation of death, and the sacrilege of resurrection, it was the least he could do.

He opened his eyes and breathed deeply. He'd been going for twelve minutes and was close to success, the worst of it over, but he needed a moment to prepare for the final effort.

Her open eyelids flickered, an early indication. For a moment, his gaze stayed on her left eye, which had been punctured in the attack and had spilled slightly onto her cheek, leaving the eyeball

2

surface subtly wrinkled. The tip of the bone shard that had caused the wound was visible in the fractured mess surrounding the eye, retreated now that the damage was done.

Above her left ear he saw a flap of Alice's scalp that had been lifted in the assault. The severe damage underneath was a confusion of colour – whites, greys and reds mingled with Alice's blonde hair. The worst of the damage to the head was at the back, pressed to the wall and not visible.

Ready at last, Jonah closed his eyes and continued with the revival. Moments later, her throat quivered briefly. A dozen more seconds passed, and then he had her.

'She's here,' he said.

The corpse inhaled, an unpleasant wet rasping coming from the chest. Jonah couldn't help noticing how unevenly the chest rose, open in places, jagged lines clear through clothing. Low cracks of bone and gristle were audible under the groan of air entering the dead woman's lungs. Her vocal cords started to move, creating a gentle wail.

Full, her chest halted.

'My name is Jonah Miller. Can you tell me who you are?' Jonah tensed, waiting. It was far from certain that she would be able to respond at all, let alone audibly.

A low sigh rose from her, the grim bubbling from her lungs distressingly loud in comparison.

Then a word formed. 'Yesss . . .' she said. 'Alice . . .'

To the cameras, her voice was a whisper, monotone and distant. To Jonah, it was as if the corpse spoke directly into his ears, with a terrible clarity. This clarity was equally true of the emotional state of the subject, laid bare to the reviver. With murder, the emotion was often anger. Anger at being dead. Anger at being disturbed.

Gripping her hand, Jonah leaned in. He steeled himself and made full eye contact. The dead couldn't see, but if he avoided looking his subject in the eye, he felt like a coward.

'You're safe, Alice,' he said. His voice was calm and warm.

The chest fell as Alice exhaled. Sounds of popping, and of tissue coming unstuck, came from her. She inhaled again.

'No . . .' she said. Her voice was full of despair, and this was a bad sign. He needed indignation, not self-pity.

He paused, uncertain whether she was aware of her situation. It was more common in adult subjects; sometimes they simply didn't know they were dead. A refusal to accept it could bring the revival to an abrupt end, a rapid onset of incoherence, then silence.

'Do you know where you are, Alice?' he asked.

'My office.' Her tone, her sense of loss. He could tell: she knew what had happened, and was understandably afraid.

'Please, let me go,' she said. Jonah halted, a painful memory surfacing. He had heard those words often enough since, but they still made him pause.

'I will, but there are questions I have to ask. What happened here, Alice? What happened to you?'

Alice exhaled, but said nothing. Precious seconds slipped past. Jonah knew how agitated the observers would be, watching their key witness flounder, knowing time was short, but he was patient. At last, the chest moved again, and she inhaled.

'Please, let me go,' she said.

Jonah considered his options for a moment, then chose another tack. He made his voice cold, stern.

'Tell me what happened, Alice. Then I'll let you go.'

Another pause.

'We want to catch who did this, but you need to help me.'

Still no reply. He decided to risk scolding her.

'Don't you care what's been done to you?'

He sensed anger forming, outrage congealing from her despair.

'I was alone,' she said. 'The building was empty. I was working. The door opened.' She inhaled, then paused. With each breath she took, with each pause she had now, there was a risk of it being a final silence. He needed her to keep talking, her breaths momentary delays. Time was running out.

Yet he had to take care, not push too hard. He waited a few seconds before prompting. 'What time was it?'

'Eleven. Just after. I asked him what he was doing here.'

'Who was it, Alice?'

'He said George had let him in but George had gone hours ago.'

'Who was it, Alice?'

'He'd been crying, I could tell; blood on his hand, he saw me notice and hid it behind his back.'

'Who was the man, Alice?' He was anxious to get the name, in case she stopped. The details could wait.

'I said something about the door, to distract him. He looked away, and I tried to use the phone. I knew I was in trouble.'

She stopped, not inhaling this time.

'Who was the man, Alice? What's his *name*?' He heard one of the observers swear, and felt like doing so himself. Then Alice inhaled again, more deeply than before. Her back slid several inches along the wall, making Jonah flinch.

Reluctant, he moved closer, and reached around with his right arm to cradle her. He pushed his knee hard against her legs, supporting her enough to prevent her slipping out from the wall. He was brutally aware of her injuries now. A splinter of rib dug painfully into his forearm. He could feel her breath on his face as she spoke.

'He saw my hand on the phone. He moved fast, and wrenched it off the table. He hit me hard, the side of my head. I fell. He picked me up – threw me. The rage on his face, I asked him please, *please*.' And then, to Jonah: 'Please, let me go.' She stopped again.

'What was his name, Alice? *His name*.'

Jonah found himself holding his breath. Fifteen seconds passed. With a suddenness that made him start, she inhaled; he could feel the muscle tear, feel the bones grinding against each other.

'Roach,' she said, her voice fading now. She was losing focus, dissipating. 'Franklin Roach. He lifted the chair. I saw him swing it at my head. So much rage.'

Silence. His intuition told him there would be nothing else. Jonah waited a few moments before speaking to a camera.

'I think that's all we get.'

He got a confirmation that it was enough, and then the green camera lights went red as recording stopped.

He turned back to Alice. Silent as she was, she was still present. Release would come the moment he broke physical contact – the moment he let go of her hand.

'We'll catch him.' His voice was tender again. 'You can rest now.' He was about to release her when she spoke, a terror and an urgency in her voice.

'*Something's coming,*' she said. '*Please, let me go. There's something coming.*'

She was confused. Somehow, she had refocused, and Jonah was reluctant to let her go like this. He wanted to reassure her. The terror she was feeling was considerable, and Jonah had to work hard to keep calm; revivers sensed the emotions of the subject, and as those emotions grew stronger they could prove overwhelming.

'There's nothing coming, Alice. You can rest now. It's over. You can sleep.'

'Something's coming . . . please, let me go!'

'Alice, it's OK, it's OK. You're safe.'

'I can't see it! I can't see it!' Her lips barely moved, her voice fading, but to Jonah she was screaming.

'Alice, you're safe. Please, you're—'

'It's below me!' The fear surged, sudden and total. He was frozen now, bewildered and infected by her level of terror. He had an image of darkness beneath him, stalking, circling. 'Please, please, let me go! *Please*, it's . . .'

Jonah released her hand and lurched away from her. He scrambled back, staring, appalled that his inaction had led to such distress. She had simply been confused; her words were meaningless. He should have let her go at once.

And yet. It hadn't just been a desire to reassure her that had made him delay. He had felt something. He turned to a camera.

'Did you get any of that?' he asked, but there was no response. Nobody was watching. Then the red light on the camera faded and died. Jonah looked at it, puzzled, and saw movement reflected in the blank lens. Movement behind him. He turned back to the corpse. Alice's head, which had been lolled to one side for the duration of the revival, now twitched and rose. The eyes moved to look at him.

It wasn't Alice. Jonah had no idea what this thing was, staring back at him. It spoke.

'*We see you*,' it said, and then it was gone.

2

The knock on Daniel Harker's door came just after half past one.

The afternoon was hot and muggy. Daniel had been out of bed for only an hour, and wasn't in the mood for visitors. He'd heard the car tyres crunching on the gravel out front, and the footsteps approach his door. When the knock came he'd already decided what to do. He ignored it.

He sat alone in his kitchen, curtains still closed, eating a bland lunch of dry toast and tomato soup. It was all he could stomach. He looked at the two empty wine bottles on his sink drainer and vowed not to drink for several days. Or until evening, at least.

He knew he was drinking too much, but it was an annual pattern. Each year, the hated month of April would arrive. Each year, he would become withdrawn and uncommunicative, sinking into a depression that would have a tight hold until the end of June.

June was more than half gone now, and his daughter Annabel was coming home for the Fourth of July; home from her own career as a journalist in England.

He needed a week to straighten himself and the house out, make it presentable and welcoming. She knew about his dark times, certainly. She had as much of a share in them as he did, but she was young. She had her own way of dealing with things.

Her annual visit marked the end of Daniel's grief, at least until the following year. It gave him a deadline, something he always needed to focus his mind. Without her coming, he suspected he would rough it indefinitely. He knew his daughter thought the same. And every year, she gave him just long enough, and no more. Every year since her mother's death.

He missed Robin. God, he missed his wife.

She had been an elementary school teacher and had loved what she did, continuing to work even after Daniel's wealth and success had arrived.

'We're rich,' he told her time and again. 'We should be living it up, making the most of it.' Robin's answer was simple, and it shut Daniel's mouth at once. She would give up her job, if he gave up writing. And *that* wasn't something he would consider.

But it had not been his novels that had brought their wealth.

After leaving university with a degree in English literature, he had drifted, taking a year-long journalism course both to delay the need to find real work, and to give him a career he could use as backup while he toiled away on his novel.

Yet that book died, and he began another. He found work, meandering from newspaper to magazine, and earned a reasonable wage with a competence and dedication that made him a respected underachiever.

His pieces were well-crafted and punctual, but he lacked the luck and judgment of some of his peers. He lacked something else as well – the ability to spin, to distort, to *lie,* and expand the smallest nugget of truth into something bigger. So he broke underwhelming stories while his novel writing stuttered and failed.

But then, twelve years ago, he discovered Eleanor Preston. He found the first reviver.

*

A friend had passed a possible lead his way: a claim of a fraudulent medium, stealing from the bereaved.

Sixty-year-old Eleanor Preston had worked as an administrator in a hospice for twenty years, until Trudy Brewer's interference got her fired. Brewer's uncle had died at the hospice; Eleanor Preston had then, according to Brewer, offered her services to Brewer's parents for a significant payment. Daniel's first impressions of Trudy Brewer weren't positive. Her real concern seemed to be financial: her uncle and parents were relatively well off, and Daniel could see that any payment to Eleanor Preston would be coming out of Trudy Brewer's inheritance.

When Daniel spoke to her parents, the situation seemed innocent enough. They were coy about what Eleanor Preston had actually done for them, but they assured him that Preston had taken no payment. Daniel's interest waned, with the prospect of a meaty story – something he could actually *sell* – dwindling, but they had already arranged a meeting that Daniel felt obliged to accept.

'I didn't know what happened, the first time,' Eleanor Preston told him. The two of them were sitting on a bench in a park five minutes from her home. The sun was low, the November air cold. Daniel was hoping to be gone before dusk fell.

A little overweight and with a smile ingrained in her face, Preston was likeable. He felt sorry to be wasting her time.

'This was just shy of a year ago,' she continued. 'Maggie. A lonely woman, seventy-three. What was left of her family had made sure she was comfortable in the hospice, but hardly came to see her. I was in the habit of spending any spare time I had talking to those who were left alone more than I thought right, and for a few weeks I spent that time with her. I was the only one would see her through to the end, and we both knew it. It would be another two or three weeks, I thought, but one morning between early rounds and breakfast she died. They let me sit with her once she'd been pronounced. Left me alone with her awhile. I took her hand and told her I was sorry I didn't get to say good-bye. I didn't understand what I did next. Still don't, not really.'

Daniel shifted on the bench, the cold working its way through him. He rubbed his hands to warm them. He noticed Eleanor Preston's look, and tried to keep his impatience out of his voice when he spoke. 'So until a year ago, you didn't know you were a medium?'

Eleanor smiled. 'Oh, I'm no medium, Mr Harker. Quite honestly, I don't know *what* I am. I've helped five families since then. I take no money. And I knew it was just a matter of time before it all came out. But I'm no medium.'

Daniel asked what she meant, and Eleanor Preston told him every last ridiculous detail. The dead spoke to her, she explained. Physically spoke. *Not a medium*, Daniel thought. *Not even a con-woman. Just crazy.* The disbelief was written on his face, he knew, but Preston continued, watching him with a look of amused tolerance. She told him of another 'session' she would be doing the next night, one which the family was willing to let him observe and record.

She believes this, Daniel thought. He wanted to understand how an apparently rational woman could have deluded herself so badly. Perhaps that could be his story.

And so, thirty hours later, Daniel went to a funeral home with Eleanor Preston. In a small private room, a dead man lay on white sheets. The only others present were the man's wife and daughter. They greeted Daniel with such warmth that he felt his cheeks burn, knowing they were as deluded as Preston.

He was asked to take a seat, and he did. After fifteen minutes, he believed. Five days later, so did the rest of the world.

*

There was another knock on Daniel's front door. Why the hell they were being so persistent he didn't know, but he didn't feel like speaking to anybody. He'd only been out of the house twice in the past five weeks, barely managing to overcome his desperate need for solitude, and for what? The man he'd gone to meet hadn't even shown up the second time.

Whoever it was at the door could leave a damn note and let him alone. He took his plate to the sink and washed up.

Behind the sink, hung on the wall, were two framed covers that had transformed his life. First, the cover of *Time*, a modified reprint of the article he had written in a fugue twelve years before. 'Speaking to the Dead,' the title read, his name below it.

Beside it, the cover of his first published book, the source of his wealth – his, and Eleanor's too. It was in part an account of Eleanor's life, but the main focus was the Revival Baseline Research Group, the research effort that had been established in a blaze of public interest to investigate this new phenomenon.

He liked to look at those covers, because he was proud of what he'd written and the reaction his work had prompted – one of fascination, not fear.

Standing in Eleanor Preston's spare bedroom with a speaking corpse, Daniel had stared, frozen, trying to understand just how Eleanor could have faked such a thing. But the truth of it was undeniable, almost *visceral;* his cynicism was dispelled with each word that came from those dead lips. For a moment, he had been consumed with horror – knowing it was true, and terrified of what was to come. But as Eleanor Preston had spoken, prompting the dead man with gentle questions, Daniel's fears vanished, the atmosphere calming and softening as the deceased spoke to his family.

The exchanges were tender, personal. The man spoke of times he remembered, times he cherished; he made his wife and daughter promise to live their lives fully, and remember him with a smile. His family, in tears, repeated 'I love you' and 'I miss you.'

They said their good-byes, and were joyful.

Daniel's article had captured that moment.

*

The world reacted as it always does to the great truths. First, with ridicule; then, hostility; and finally, acceptance. The ridicule lasted for days after the story broke, but it faded faster than Daniel had expected. The footage he had taken retained much of the power he had felt that day, and accusations of forgery rang false to most of those who watched it. Those who declared it a hoax sounded more and more uncertain. When Eleanor Preston repeated the feat under close scrutiny, the world made up its mind. Revival was real.

Anger and fear followed. It was denounced by many as an abomination. Some of that anger found its way to Daniel. The fact that he had broken the story gave him some authority, but also part of the blame. Threats came by letter, by email, by phone; it was a difficult time. Eleanor fared less well, and Daniel watched on, feeling for her as she was put in hiding for her safety, her home gutted by arson.

It would have been so easy for the world to have turned against revival, but the rage subsided. In part, Daniel thought, it was due to the tone of his articles. Other journalists later focused on the macabre elements and played up the unease. Daniel always went the other way. Here was something new, he had said in that first article. Something that, in this case at least, was undeniably good.

Yet he knew the main reason for the anger dissipating was simple, and very human. Revival was evidence of a life essence that survived death. Different faiths interpreted the effect in their own ways, but any hint of evidence of an afterlife was embraced.

The angry rejections of revival were far outnumbered by those who wanted to know what it *meant*.

*

Eleanor Preston refused to deal with the media, except through Daniel. He would write her biography, and they would split the profits. She had plans for the money, she told him.

The government set up an investigative group to examine Eleanor's claims. She was wary; her only desire was to prove to the remaining sceptics that revival was real, and to get back to doing what she wanted to do – let the dead say good-bye and the living heal.

She agreed to the investigation, but with restrictions. She would only conduct revivals for the grieving. Everything the researchers wanted would have to be tailored to that: nonintrusive, respectful.

With agreement reached, the Revival Baseline Research Group was formed. It became known as Baseline. There was no shortage of scientists interested; funding was both American and international, governmental and private.

It was quickly established, beyond doubt, that revival was a genuine phenomenon.

Eleanor had always believed that revival was something new, and that more would have the same skill she had. She was proved right. People came forward; those who recognized part of themselves in Eleanor's descriptions of how she felt; those who experienced the feeling of cold when they touched people, a feeling that revivers would soon label 'chill.' Finding other revivers, who would not be bound by Eleanor's restrictions, was crucial to Baseline's investigations. And while most failed the ultimate test of an actual revival, some succeeded.

Eleanor left Baseline in their hands. Three months after being revealed to the world, the first reviver went back to her calling. Later, after the overwhelming success of Daniel's book, she used her money to set up the first private revival service, launching an industry that even became a common, if expensive, insurance option.

The world, meanwhile, waited for news from Baseline. Waited to find the ultimate truths they sought. What was the nature of revival? Why had it started to happen? What did it *mean*?

They would be disappointed.

Some discoveries were made, of course.

Eleanor's revivals had not been representative of the true success rate; revival after death from natural causes was much easier than after one involving physical injury.

It was not simply the brain being woken – severe head injuries made revival more difficult, yes, but not impossible, and the subjects were lucid, the damage to the brain irrelevant once revival was achieved.

There seemed to be no electrical activity at all, either in the brain or in the muscles that moved the lungs and vocal cords. However, the source of the movement could not be identified.

By the end of its first year Baseline had a stable of twelve revivers, and became focused more on the details of successful revival – how to make success more likely, how to extend its length – and less on what revival itself *was*.

What hostility remained gradually coalesced into a protest group called the Afterlifers, well funded from an uneasy collaboration of disparate religious interests who saw revival as desecration, an unacceptable disturbance of the dead. But loud as they were, they found their calls for a moratorium ignored. Direct action from more extreme members brought public disapproval. Their message of outright objection to revival took a backseat, replaced by more successful calls for greater control, rights for the dead, and a system ensuring revivers were licensed.

For many, Baseline was a failure. Even with its count of revivers increasing, with over one hundred revivers out of a worldwide tally of almost three hundred, it would get no closer to the mystery of where revival came from; find no smoking gun for anyone's preferred God.

Baseline would continue for another five years before being disbanded, public funding drying up as the certainty of discovery faded, transforming into an expectation that the truth would always be elusive. Many lines of research were discarded; some of the companies who had contributed brought teams back to their own facilities to continue, but it was the potential for profit in the burgeoning fields of both private and forensic revival that guided their work now, not the search for meaning.

For Daniel, with financial security beyond anything he'd expected, it was a new beginning. He and Robin bought a perfect home; he began to write fiction again, insisting on a pseudonym for his crime novels to see if they had wings of their own. Later, as forensic revival became accepted, he started the Revival Casebook series under his own name, case histories from real revivals with sensationalism kept to a minimum. He even took an executive producer role on the inevitable TV series until they started to take too many liberties with the truth.

He was busy. He was happy. For a time.

*

He heard a sound from the hall – a man calling his name from the front door, and another burst of knocking. *For Christ's sake, leave a card and go*, he thought, sitting back down at the kitchen table. Then he cursed again, annoyed with himself and his annual withdrawal from the world, his difficulty in breaking it.

Hanging on the wall to his left were two framed photographs. The larger of the two showed him and Robin, with a fifteen-year-old Annabel, on Myrtle Beach. He thought back to the camera, balanced precariously on a rock, himself running back to his family before the timer counted down. The image was his favourite of all their family pictures. Informal, a warm, natural smile on all three faces; taken two years after Preston's discovery, as his second crime novel was released and well reviewed.

Ten years ago, probably the happiest time of his life. Four years before Robin died.

He thought of the first time they met. He thought of her smile, the first thing he'd seen of her; of her accent, a soft English forged from a childhood first in Yorkshire in the north of England, and then Sussex in the south. It was an accent she would never lose.

'You came to America to do English. What the hell for?' he asked her. She was taking an English degree, but she'd chosen to come halfway around the world to do it. He hadn't meant to be cruel, but her face had fallen.

He'd sworn to himself to do what he could to make that smile return.

They married three years later, and it was good. Even with the financial pressures, and Daniel's frustration at his underwhelming career. Neither of them had close family; both were only children, with no surviving parents. It intensified what they meant to each other. When Annabel was born, despite money becoming even tighter, Daniel felt blessed. He also felt anxious, waiting for the bad luck that he seemed to have evaded since meeting his wife to finally track him down. When at last the money came, he thought his life was perfect.

*

Then one April, out of nowhere, Robin collapsed at work. She was dead by the time Daniel had reached the hospital. A brain haemorrhage.

His heart had been torn out, and he had not recovered. She had been part of his core, part of what made him who he was, and she was gone. Now six years had passed, and his grief for Robin was as sharp-edged and barbed as it had been on the day of her death.

Annabel had kept him alive. She was in her first year at university in England, and had returned immediately to find her father destroyed, barely able to talk. Robin had always planned for a private revival in the event of her death, but when the time came it proved too difficult for Daniel. He stayed away and left Annabel to attend alone. It was not something he ever expected Annabel to forgive him for, just as he would never forgive himself. Self-hatred swamped him over the following weeks; trapped in his despair, withdrawing from his life, from his own *daughter*.

Robin had been stronger than him, always, and Annabel had her mother's strength. Even though he was angry and uncommunicative, Annabel stayed with him for five months, putting her university studies on hold. When he eventually emerged from his despair, their relationship had changed; but damaged as it was, Annabel had not allowed it to wither, even as the pattern repeated.

For Annabel, April would always be her mother's death, but it was also the time her father grew dark and distant. He knew his behaviour made it so much worse for her, but every year – every

April – Daniel found himself plummeting, whatever he tried to do to distract himself. Unable to work, drinking heavily, alienating his daughter once again. And yet, always coming back.

She would be home soon. It was time, Daniel told himself, to once more call an end to the grieving. It was time to live up to Robin's memory, rather than collapse under the weight of loss.

It was a realization that came every year, but it was always hard-won. It marked the rebirth of his own life. Annabel – his little Annie – would be here soon enough, and he would smile and laugh with her, and repair what they had, and be happy again.

There was another knock at the door. He glanced at his watch. Whoever it was had been trying for ten minutes now, while he'd been ignoring them. Hiding from them, as he'd hidden from life for the past few months. Enough hiding, he thought, and stood.

Resolved to face the world, Daniel Harker walked to his front door and opened it. His body would be found twenty-five days later.

3

The Central East Coast office of the Forensic Revival Service was in an unremarkable three-storey building in the south of Richmond, Virginia, that was easy to overlook. Passers-by would come and go without glancing at it, or the muted nameplate for 'FRS (CEC)' on the wall by the door.

However, those who lived in the area, and those who worked in the other buildings in the same industrial estate, knew well what it was. Deep unease had accompanied its arrival. Protests from Afterlifer groups had focused on the building for the first year, until the Forensic Revival Service grew, and larger, higher profile offices opened across the country. Now, seven years later, it was regarded with a degree of pride.

It was a bright Monday morning, just past eight-fifteen; another hot day looming. Jonah Miller swiped his pass at the main entrance and walked through the empty reception area, up one flight of stairs and into the open-plan office. On a typical day there would be thirty revivers and twenty-two support staff, but this early there were only a handful of people. He headed to his desk, smiling as best he could at those who said hi.

He'd woken at six, restless and disjointed, and had set off for work intending to use the time to make a dent in the paperwork that had been building for weeks. But he was tired. Another bad night of fractured nightmares had left him with a head that felt full of gravel and dust.

He stared out the window beside his desk and his eyes drifted up to the clouds. He watched them and let his thoughts wander. Watching the clouds had always been his respite from the world, losing himself in a gentle, changing sight that had nothing to do with *people*. To look down, and watch those scurrying from place to place, would bring unwelcome thoughts into his head – thoughts of who these people were and what lay ahead of them. And in the end, it was death, sure as anything.

He smiled at his morbidity, but given his line of work it was hard not to think it. Most of the subjects he revived had been in the middle of just another day, when death stole up on them and pounced. The people heading into the bakery on the corner to collect their lunches; the cars nudging along in the heat of morning congestion. For every one of them, the day would come. Who would grieve them? A mother? A father? A wife? A child?

And from *that*, to this: Who would grieve for him? His friends would mourn, but true grief – the complete desolation he had both witnessed and experienced – needed family, and he had no family now. He hadn't even spoken to his stepfather in eight years.

He shook the thoughts from his head, wanting them gone.

Alice Decker's revival had left him with this exhaustion. Five days later, and he was still struggling to deal with it.

He'd been told it was all in his mind, but however much he tried, he couldn't dismiss it as such. It had struck deep, leaving behind an irrational fear and a feeling of being watched.

This paranoia was feeding into his dreams. The nightmares had been overwhelming. Alice Decker had stood in his living room, her face without skin, talking to him. The words had been gibberish, and *God*, he'd been scared. He'd woken to the dawn, certain he'd been in that dream for days.

Since then, every night but one had been disturbed by Decker's cackling face. The one night she didn't make an appearance he had dreamed of his mother's death. He had woken to darkness and tears, unable to go back to sleep.

*

The Decker revival had been made worse by the fact that nobody had been around – nobody he wanted to confide in, at least.

He had fled the scene without a word to the supervising officers, or even to J. J. Metah, the attending FRS technician. Only the cop on guard by the entrance to the floor of Alice Decker's office saw him leave, pale and hurried.

The next day had been Thursday. Jonah had spoken to J. J., expecting that some physical sign of the event must have been recorded.

'Did you see anything after the recording stopped, J. J.?' he asked, keeping it as casual as he could while his heart pounded loudly in his ear.

'No,' J. J. told him. 'The live feed was off. I was busy getting the footage ready for handover. What happened? You'd already gone when I came out.'

'I . . . just got a little dizzy,' he said, forcing a smile. 'Needed some air.'

He had really wanted to talk to Never Geary first, but Never had been at a conference in Vancouver, and was due back at work on Tuesday.

Jonah had called him by afternoon, even though he'd tried hard to resist, not wanting his friend to worry. But Never's familiar Northern Irish accent had been good to hear.

Jonah filled him in.

'They'll tell you it's overwork,' Never replied. There was a buzz in the background that Jonah assumed was conference-hall murmurs, until he heard the clink of glass nearby.

'Are you in a bar, Never?' Silence for a moment, but Jonah could swear he *heard* Never's grin.

'Might be. All finished for the day, I'm catching up with a few people. And don't change the subject. It *was* overwork. You know it was.'

Jonah hesitated, wanting to agree, to try to forget it, but he had too many doubts not to share them. 'That's the thing. I *don't* know.'

'What the hell else *could* it have been?'

Jonah knew the question had been meant rhetorically, but it still made him pause. 'I talk to the *dead* for a living, Never. There's plenty we don't know.'

'Talk it over with Jennifer.' Jennifer Early was the FRS counsellor. She was a busy woman.

'I don't want to make a big deal about it.'

'Talk it over with her, Jonah. Promise me.'

Jonah had promised.

*

By nine o'clock the office was busy, readying for the day ahead. As it was Monday, those who had worked over the weekend were passing on the details of the revivals that had taken place. Jonah listened with half an ear, but Sam Deering's morning meeting at nine-thirty would bring him up to speed if there was anything worth hearing. In the meantime, he was managing to concentrate enough on paperwork to make actual progress. Gossip could wait.

'Morning, Jonah.' Jonah looked up to see Sam smiling at him. When they had first met, almost twelve years before, Jonah had been a frightened boy of fourteen. Eleanor Preston had still been a novelty at the time, known to the world for less than six months. Sam had been fifty-two, looking much younger and with the energy to match. The energy was still there, but the years had finally caught up with his hairline.

Jonah smiled back. 'Hey, Sam.'

'How are you?' Sam's eyes were serious and concerned. It was a pointed question, not a nicety. After speaking to Never by phone, Jonah had finally gone to Sam and told him what had happened. Sam had sent him to the counsellor at once, but Jonah could see the disappointment, and he knew why it was there. They'd known each other a long time, ever since Jonah's mother had died and he'd stumbled into his revival ability in appalling circumstances. Sam and Jonah were close, yet it had taken twenty-four hours and a push from Never before Jonah had gone to him.

'I'm much better,' Jonah lied, but whether Sam bought it he couldn't tell.

'Good. I've spoken to Jennifer this morning. Can you come to my office later?'

'Sure,' Jonah said, managing a smile as Sam left but feeling sick inside. They were going to take him out of active duty for a while, he knew. Another break, to let him recoup.

Two years ago, Jonah had suffered from burnout. Overwork had led to erratic, self-destructive behaviour that had peaked in a breakdown after a bad revival experience. It had meant two months off work, something that had proved difficult. Painful, almost.

For Jonah, revival was all he had to offer, so he offered it completely. Revival wasn't a job. It was what he *was*.

*

Just after nine-thirty he joined everyone as they gathered near Sam's office. Sam stood outside his office door and raised his hand, waiting for the chatter to settle.

'Welcome, everyone. The start of a beautiful day, and so far a quiet one. First up, the Vancouver conference went well. Congratulations to all who gave talks. I see most of you are back, hopefully not too hung over.' He got scattered laughter at that; Jonah could see Pru Dryden as she shook her head with a rueful look, which turned into a sheepish smile.

'Most of the presentations were recorded,' Sam continued. 'We'll have them available on the intranet in the next few days. I think Never's back tomorrow . . . ?' He looked over to Jonah, and got a nod. 'He'll organize it and mail everyone the link. The weekend was busy as always, and North East are short and might ask for cover. Anyone with court appearances lined up this week, try and find out if they really need you. We can't afford to have our people hanging around court all day if they're not going to be called. We need all the people we can get. Any questions?' There were no takers. 'Then that's it from me. Good luck as always.' He caught Jonah's eye and inclined his head towards his office door with a questioning look.

Jonah nodded. Now was as good a time as any. He walked against the tide of people returning to their desks; as he was about to reach Sam, Hugo Adler, Sam's deputy, beat him to it and started to talk budget allocations.

'Go on in, Jonah,' Sam said, sounding like a condemned man. 'I'll be a few minutes.'

Jonah took a seat, and as he waited he glanced around the walls of Sam's office. Pictures featuring Sam, spanning his FRS career. That kind of picture would soon be no more, Jonah realized; Sam was retiring in two weeks.

It would be strange, the FRS without Sam Deering. Sam had practically invented forensic revival. He had been working for the FBI at the Quantico forensic lab when revival had emerged, and had been their man at Baseline. Initially there to observe and validate the methods being used, it hadn't taken him long to realize the potential and form a group of researchers whose focus differed from all the others. Rather than investigating the deeper meaning of the revival phenomenon, they would look instead at something far more practical.

And while the other research teams struggled, Sam's surged ahead, exploring the possibility of the forensic use of revival.

With time and care, two key facts were established: a revived subject knew no more and no less than they had while alive; and revivers had a clear feel for the emotional state of the subject, able to tell whether what was said was truth, lies or evasion. This second fact was the single most important development for forensic use.

To have the killer's name spoken aloud by a victim of murder, and the truth of it known beyond doubt, was breathtaking.

It took time for revival evidence to be accepted, but Sam and his team were patient and determined. The work paid off. And, as the number of revivers around the world increased, so did the viability of Sam's core idea – that forensic revival could become routine.

The first criminal application was in a simple murder case. The victim, stabbed in the heart, quickly identified his killer. Confronted with the video evidence of the corpse accusing him from the grave, the murderer confessed. Press response was dramatic, calling for widespread use of the technique; public opinion concurred.

Sam was asked to head up a small unit of revivers for a trial period at Quantico. A tiny office building housed Sam, five administrative assistants, four technicians, and the six best revivers he could steal from the various research groups at Baseline.

There were many who expected the trial to fail. Criminals would learn, they said. Sufficient damage to the body made revival impossible. Decapitation would become standard practice.

Those naysayers had missed the point. The true worth wouldn't be in targeting professional criminals. Yes, those in the know would take a little extra care, but they always *had*. Even before revivals, the best-planned murders had one thing in common – no one would find the body at all.

Revival would be best for the cases where murder had been poorly thought out, or where it had been badly executed; where it had been rushed, or where it had been spur of the moment. Inept, sloppy, complacent. And that covered most of them.

Sure enough, amateur killers who thought they knew how to prevent revival did their best, but even when they succeeded, the additional mess and complication often proved their downfall.

The public in general had a limited idea of what revivers could actually achieve. The more lurid novels and television dramas played fast and loose with the truth for narrative convenience, just as they did with every other area of forensic science. As a result, belief ranged from one extreme to the other – from thinking that any significant damage to a corpse stopped revival, to thinking that no amount of injury or putrefaction could prevent it.

The trial was a success. Sam's team moved to their current site in Richmond and established the Forensic Revival Service. Cases came to them from all over the country, even though transporting a body shaved a good 20 to 30 per cent off the revival chances.

While Baseline ground to a halt and closed down, the FRS grew rapidly. One office became five across the US; five became twelve. Overall management was moved to the largest of the regional offices, in Chicago. And Sam Deering was happy to remain, quietly excelling in what was now called the Central East Coast Forensic Revival Service.

'Sorry about that, Jonah,' said Sam from behind him.

Jonah turned his head and gave Sam a nervous smile. 'Problems?'

'Budgets. One thing I'll not miss when I go.' He sat behind his desk and typed at his keyboard, peering at his monitor as he reached for reading glasses and put them on. 'Jennifer sent her report through last night and discussed it with me this morning. Before we talk about it, though, I wanted to congratulate you again on the Decker case. It was a difficult job, and I hope you appreciate what you achieved. Did you hear any more about it?'

'Beyond what was on the news, no,' said Jonah. 'They didn't give many details, but they said a man had been caught. I presumed it was Roach. Since then, nothing.'

'I got word from a friend. They'll be making some of it public in a few days, but I thought you should hear it all. Roach was a weight junkie, had been for years. Steroid abuse. Whatever he'd been taking, it led to psychotic episodes. They got it under control, but then his wife left him and took their young son with her. He challenged for custody. Alice Decker had been part of the assessment panel that Roach blamed for losing his case, as if he ever stood a chance. Her opinion had been damning. Then Roach fell back into his old ways. He snapped, and went looking for some payback. Twenty minutes after you got the name, police were at his home.'

'They found him there?'

'No.'

'He went after the others on the assessment panel?'

'No. Decker was his first and only target from the panel. She was also the only woman, which I suspect is no coincidence. No. They found him at his ex-wife's.'

Jonah's face fell. This could be bad. 'Shit.'

Sam saw the look in Jonah's eye. 'Don't worry, she's fine. She wasn't there, wouldn't have been for another hour. But Roach was waiting inside the house when the police arrived. He'd broken in around back. When they arrested him he had a collection of pills that would kill an elephant. It wasn't a friendly visit.'

Jonah was quiet.

'Be proud, Jonah. Decker was rated a ten per cent chance. Even for you, that's impressive.'

Jonah nodded, but it was half-hearted. It had been a good result, sure, but he expected no less from himself. He was one of the best revivers in the country, at least as far as the difficult cases went. Overall, others performed better: a more natural instinct for asking the right questions; more consistent in getting everything that was needed; more effective in court appearances. But when conditions made success very unlikely, or when another reviver failed to bring a subject back, he was always first choice. All he could think of now was the result of Jennifer's report. 'OK, Sam, but can we get this over with?'

Sam sighed. 'All right. Jennifer has serious concerns about the way you're dealing with this. And I share them.'

Jonah was fidgeting. 'She said I was hallucinating.'

'You were, Jonah. Of *course* you were. You've been through it before. I don't understand your reluctance to—'

Jonah interrupted. 'It wasn't the same. This was lucid. I didn't lose consciousness, I didn't black out. This happened.'

'Jennifer mentioned your difficulty sleeping since the revival. And you mentioned a feeling of being watched.'

'I didn't hallucinate,' Jonah insisted. 'The camera powered down, I didn't imagine it. I didn't imagine *any* of it.'

'Nobody else saw anything.'

'Recording had stopped. They weren't looking at the feed from the camera.'

Sam skimmed his eyes over Jennifer's report again. 'After your problems two years ago, your workload was reduced. But over time, it's crept up. Your case load over the last four months averages out above your guideline maximum, and the peaks are unacceptably high. Too much for too long. You're overtired, overworked and experiencing clear symptoms of burnout again. You of all people should understand what that means.'

Jonah looked down to avoid Sam's eyes. Of course he knew, even before his previous episode. The toll the revival process could have was something all revivers understood well.

To be swamped with the emotions and memories of a revived subject left a mark, one that required careful monitoring. Eleanor Preston had experienced few symptoms, but all her subjects had been expecting both their death and their brief awakening. With those subjects who were not so prepared, robbed of life through accident or murder, it was much harder on the reviver and could lead to severe exhaustion and temporary loss of ability. The reviver could even be left with some of those extreme emotions and those memories; they were known as remnants, and they could hang around for days.

Rest periods were crucial to avoid these problems. Most revivers were what they called long-tail, a 'tail' referring to the length of time they had to wait after performing a revival before another could even be attempted. Too soon, and the chance of success was minimal. A typical reviver had to wait thirty-six hours before their chances recovered even by 50 per cent, and seventy-two hours for them to return to normal. Their rest periods were built in.

Short-tailers were those who recovered their ability faster than average. Jonah's was the shortest in the department, returning in full after twenty hours; partly why he was so vulnerable to over-work.

Jonah looked down. 'It felt real.'

'That's the thing, Jonah. It often does. Some of your colleagues have experienced exactly that. Stop talking about this as anything other than hallucination. It's not helpful. You've had them before.'

Jonah's voice rose a little in frustration. 'Not like this.'

Sam paused. 'Granted. But talk to Pradesh. Talk to Stacy. They've both had genuinely frightening—'

Jonah cut in. 'They both blacked out, Sam. People were there to see it.'

'I know. But they thought what happened was real. That's the point. Talk to them. And don't worry. It happens, and all it means is that you need a break.'

Jonah shuffled in his seat. 'What kind of break?'

'Well, we're short staffed, so you'll have to work most of the week. Jason's back from vacation on Thursday, which should let us arrange things better. But you're here to make up the numbers, understand? Spend a few days catching up on your backlog of paperwork. If absolutely necessary, you can handle a simple case, but only from Wednesday – any sooner and Jennifer would kill me. OK? Then you get a full week off work, no arguments. And no coming in just to see what we're up to. I know what you're like.'

Jonah said nothing in reply, and looked away.

Sam continued. 'After that . . . well, you know we have a group coming from San Diego.' Jonah nodded. Five new revivers and a dozen technicians were coming over for training. 'You were already going to be helping out, but I think you should focus on that and do as few revivals as possible. At least two months with week-long tails, then back to full workload gradually.'

Jonah's face crumpled.

'Sorry,' Sam added. 'But believe me, Jonah – there's nothing wrong with you that rest won't fix.'

Jonah looked up and sighed, resigned to it. 'OK, Sam. OK.'

*

Just after five, as the end of his working day approached, he headed to the office kitchen to make a coffee and kill some time. He heard Never Geary's familiar voice coming from within, and found Never speaking to Sam Deering.

'There he is,' Never said, a grin spreading. 'How are things?'

Jonah grinned back. 'What are you doing in? Thought you weren't back at work until tomorrow?'

'I'm just here to say hello.'

Sam said, 'I'll leave you to it. We'll talk more in the morning, Never, OK?'

'OK,' said Never. Sam left, and Never gave Jonah a conspiratorial smile. 'Sam wants me to babysit you until you go on leave.'

'He told you about that?'

'Of course. Now, how are you doing?'

'Stressed and tired.'

'I can understand it. It sounded extreme.'

'It was *different*, Never. Sam and Jennifer kept on about how it was overwork, and that I'd been there before. But it was different. And I wish you'd been there instead of J. J.'

'J. J.'s good,' said Never, raising an eyebrow.

'You keep the cameras running. J. J. cut them off the moment we got a result.'

Like J. J., Never was a revival technician, responsible for setting up and managing the hardware needed for the task. The three video feeds were only part of it; two additional audio recordings were made, and everything was recorded onto both flash drives and hard disk. Redundancy and careful design meant that problems during a session were rare, and hadn't yet proved disastrous. It was a system

Never was proud of – he had been key in the original design. Now a countrywide standard, it was also used by many forensic revival groups in the rest of the world.

Revival technicians needed their own skill set. Conscientious and precise, confident and resourceful, they had to be comfortable around revivers and able to stomach death. As the most senior in the office, Never was given the highest-profile and most difficult cases, which meant that much of his work was with the three best revivers – Jason Shepperton, Pru Dryden, and Jonah.

'When the coordinating officer gives the word, recording can stop,' said Never. 'The police are usually too keen to get hold of the footage to warrant the wait. If he'd kept recording, all the cameras would have seen is you freaking out over nothing.'

'And then I'd *know* it was all in my head. *You* record to the end, though. Always.' He looked Never in the eye.

'I do,' said Never. 'Force of habit.' Jonah's gaze was still on him, and there was no avoiding it. 'All right, all right. I'll have a word with the others.'

Jonah nodded and smiled. 'Thanks.'

'Now,' said Never, making a point of looking at his watch. 'Half an hour before you knock off, so let me check my mail and I'll hang around until quitting time. Then we can share a cab.'

Jonah narrowed his eyes. His apartment was a ten-minute walk away. 'Why would I want a cab, Never?'

'I need a drink. And you need several.'

*

It was the only sure-fire way, Never Geary knew, to get Jonah out for anything remotely social. Ambush.

When they first met, Jonah had been nineteen, Never a twenty-five-year-old hardware whiz who'd been working in the Quantico lab on forensic data recovery, then insinuated himself into Sam's trial forensic revival unit and realized he'd found his niche. To begin with, his and Jonah's relationship had been more of an older-brother thing, but it hadn't taken long for them to become friends.

And Never knew his friend well.

He fended off Jonah's request to shower and change, which he recognized for what it was – an excuse to return to his apartment and attempt to talk Never into having a quiet drink there. At last, they were sitting in a dim corner of one of the few bars Jonah liked. Not busy, especially on a Monday evening, and cosy. The kind of place you could go to and still hide, Never thought. Just the kind of place Jonah *would* like.

On the flight home that morning, Never had been worrying, not knowing what to expect. Jonah had always seemed fragile to him – especially after his breakdown. Here, in the wilds outside the haven of his apartment, he was quiet and withdrawn. *Not for long,* Never thought, buying the first round. Tray in hand, he returned to the table.

Jonah looked up at him and raised an eyebrow when he saw what was on the tray. A pint of Guinness each, and their favourite chasers – whiskey sour for Never, and a shot of tequila for Jonah.

'I wasn't planning on getting drunk,' said Jonah. 'We *do* have work tomorrow.'

'We're not getting drunk, we're getting relaxed. *This,*' he said, lifting his sour, 'is to knock down my jet lag. *That,*' pointing at the tequila, 'is to take the fucking frown off your face.'

Jonah shrugged and lifted his drink, and Never thought there was the ghost of a smile creeping onto Jonah's lips.

By the time the pair had started on their second round of drinks, Never was dishing out conference dirt.

'Pru got massively drunk on the first night,' he said, 'and by God you should have seen the fella she ended up with. Definite groupie.'

Reviver groupies were a bizarre breed, seeking out close encounters with reviver kind. Many of them had chill; apparently that was the point.

Chill, the sensation that most non-revivers got from the touch of a reviver, came in many degrees, depending both on the reviver and the sensitivity of the person. Typically, it was a moment of cold, like a hand plunged into icy water, fading as soon as contact was broken. At its worst, it was a bitter ache that filled every part of you, leaving behind it a taint of death and a deep fear.

Half of the FRS staff who weren't revivers didn't get chill at all, Never Geary being one. It meant he had no direct experience of how it felt, but Jonah certainly did; both the reviver and the person they touched experienced much the same thing. Some revivers wore gloves routinely to avoid it. Jonah's own level of chill was particularly severe. It wasn't something the light gloves revivers favoured could mask. He wore leather gloves when they wouldn't be conspicuous – in cool weather, when he was outside – but the rest of the time he found any kind of glove hot and restrictive. Instead, he preferred to be very careful.

The idea that anyone would seek out even the mild form of chill gave Never the creeps, but with Pru it would have been strong. Sufficiently drunk and she wouldn't feel it, but Never and Jonah both knew just how drunk that would mean.

Conferences were common enough – as a co-designer of the standard revival recording protocol, Never typically attended three or four a year. Pru Dryden attended even more. Overall, she was probably the best reviver they had. Not the same level of raw revival ability as Jonah, but she was unflappable in court and her revival questioning was always canny and precise.

Jonah avoided conferences if he could, but Never spent much of his waking life trying to get him to come along, convinced that many of Jonah's problems could be traced back to his reliable lack of sex. Conferences were a hotbed of that kind of extracurricular activity, particularly for revivers. Chill simply didn't happen between revivers, and with everyone else, you would know who had chill and who did not.

It was always handy, Never knew, to have Jonah around in an environment like that. While Never's accent and near-constant grin drew in the occasional admirer, Jonah was way up on the scale. Not that Jonah was aware of it, paying little attention to how he looked or what clothes he wore. He'd get his black hair cut as rarely as he could, meaning it varied between extremely short and its current tousled look, but it suited him either way.

It added up to a moth-to-the-flame effect that typically worked in Never's favour; more than once Never had found himself talking to a gorgeous woman who'd come over to get introduced to Jonah, only to find that Jonah had lost the power of speech.

This year, the International Forensic Revival Symposium was being held in Richmond, as a mark of respect for Sam Deering's retirement. Jonah had agreed to give a presentation, but it had been more than a year since Never had been able to get him to go further afield. In the one encounter Never had managed to engineer at the time, the woman in question had turned out to be complicated: married, confused, and highly strung. It didn't end well. Even so, Never thought it had been a success; that for one day at least, Jonah had pulled the broom out of his ass and relaxed.

They gossiped like old women until ten, when Jonah made noises about work. True to his word, Never agreed that it was time to call it a night. They left, Jonah laughing and unaware that, for the first time in five days, Alice Decker was not in his thoughts at all.

4

Wednesday morning was unusually quiet. Jonah found himself scything through his backlog of paperwork, after a solid night of sleep that had been welcome, if unexpected. His spirits were high – it had been seven days since the Decker revival, and the week-long tail Jennifer Early had insisted on was over.

Things got busier that afternoon.

Shortly after two, Sam leaned out of his door and called to the other side of the office, 'Pru, you're up. Traffic fatality outside Greensboro. Sort out your technician with Never and get there.'

Pru Dryden was twenty-nine years old. Her small size and good looks always drew confused glances when people saw her for the first time, arriving on the scene like some kind of revival fairy. She stood up from her desk and walked over to Sam without enthusiasm. 'Any details?'

Sam handed her a printout of the request form. 'Take a look.'

A request had come in for an in-situ revival at a traffic incident: a white van swiping a family's hatchback on a country road, sending it into a tree. The father, driving the car, had been killed; his wife was unconscious and critical, their two young sons injured but stable. In the van had been a man and his girlfriend, two rough pieces of work more concerned with the damage to their van. The man had been drinking, but their story had the girlfriend driving, the hatchback coming round a bend too far into their lane to avoid. Traffic fatalities were not routinely revived, but there were inconsistencies here and no other witnesses, and a clear suspicion that the girlfriend had not been driving as they claimed.

The dead father's testimony could resolve these issues. The severity of injury required a highly skilled reviver.

Pru lowered her voice. 'Boss, I have to be honest. I woke up with a migraine. I'm not feeling up to it.'

Sam looked at her. 'You're the only person who has much of a chance, Pru. Do your best.'

Pru trudged over to Never. He reached behind him and grabbed an orange plastic pack from a pile behind his desk; Revival Kits contained various items useful for the job, but it was the protective clothing and cleaning equipment inside that revivers found indispensable. To varying degrees, revivers were obsessive about cleanliness. It was something Never could understand, but some were damn near OCD. Nails trimmed past the quick, and hands scrubbed red.

He gave Pru the pack; she let out the strap and slung it onto her shoulder.

'A tough one, Pru,' he said.

'Tell me about it.'

'You'll be fine,' he told her. 'Take Ross on this one, he's down in the equipment room. Have fun.'

She grimaced and left, passing Jonah on the way.

'Good luck,' Jonah said, and she nodded. She looked anxious, and he didn't envy her. Even with his past, he took traffic fatalities. They tried to give them to the others – his mother's death was a raw wound, and the association risked affecting his performance – but sometimes there was just no choice. Two years before, he'd had a non-vocal revival that had involved reaching into the twisted wreckage and gripping the corpse's shoulder, unseen. It was one of the revivals that would stay with him; the only one he had ever performed where he couldn't even see the subject.

It would stay with him for other reasons too – it had started the deterioration that had led to his breakdown. Those around him thought the stress had been the biggest factor, and he had let them think it. The full story was something he kept to himself.

Half an hour later, a call came for another in-situ case. Handgun to the back of the head, it was one of the most challenging injuries for a reviver.

In his mind, Jonah was already there, but Sam sent Tunde. Wishing him luck, Never threw him a kit, then smiled as Jonah approached.

'Do I sit and do nothing all week?' Jonah asked him.

'If by "nothing" you mean the mountain of paperwork you always moan about, then yes. That's the plan.'

*

The plan came to an end the next morning.

Revival took a toll. Rules on workload were stretched in every way but one – after a revival, there was a thirty-six-hour minimum before another could be attempted. It didn't matter if revivers were short-tail and their ability would have returned in full before then, the thirty-six-hour rule was strictly followed.

The previous day's work had taken two of the best revivers out of play. Anything tricky would have to be handled by Jason Shepperton, back from vacation, or at a push, by Jonah.

In a normal week, there would be perhaps two or three cases in total requiring the highest-level revivers, so there was a good chance things would be quiet. But when Jonah reached his desk at eight-thirty to hear there was a possible murder, he knew that Sam Deering would send Shepperton. Jonah didn't mind this, necessarily – if the case profile gave Shepperton a similar chance of success, it was justified.

But Jonah disliked the way Shepperton did things. He was casual about death, and short on respect for the victims. He treated them, to Jonah's eyes, with disdain. That lack of respect may have been subtle, and certainly Shepperton did nothing that attracted official disapproval, but Jonah found his attitude intolerable.

How big a problem it would be for Jason to take this would come down to the nature of the case.

He saw Never emerge from the kitchen, bleary-eyed, nursing a mug. Jonah intercepted him on the way to his desk and asked about the case.

'Girl, nine years old,' Never said. 'Apparent burglary, kid walked in on it. Discovered dying by the father at four a.m.'

'Straightforward?'

'Not quite,' Never said, with a wince. 'Revival should be OK, though. Here . . .' He handed Jonah a few sheets of paper: the email requesting attendance, and a preliminary report covering the extent of the victim's injuries.

Jonah looked it over. It had happened in Manassas, a suburb of Washington, DC; it was usually the larger, North East office that dealt with cases in DC, but they were even more stretched than the Richmond office. They often relied on Richmond taking on the harder cases – after all, as the first FRS office to have been formed, Richmond had attracted the best, and as a result had quite a port-folio of skilled revivers.

Nikki Wood, the girl's name. Minor head trauma. 'Shit. She was unlucky to die from this. So why not straightforward?'

'There's some suspicion about the father.'

Jonah drew in a breath.

'Bob Crenner's the detective on it,' Never said. 'Good cop, I've worked with him before. The begging email's from him. If we can't send anyone immediately, North East will do it in-house the day after tomorrow.'

The unpredictable ebb and flow of revival work sometimes meant that on-site revivals were impossible to staff; all the FRS offices had revival suites, rooms where revivals could be done in-house in more controlled surroundings, with cold rooms to keep the body in good condition and observation areas for interested parties. It all took more time, of course, and the revival chances took a hit, but often there was no other option.

'And Sam's sending Jason?'

'Sam's not in until the afternoon,' said Never. 'So it's Hugo's call and he's not in yet either. I'm sure he'll send Jason. The only . . . Ah.' He stopped, recognizing Jonah's tone. 'The only options are Jason and you. And he won't send you.'

Jonah glanced around the office, a gentle bustle of morning coffee and gossip. His voice was low. Conspiratorial. 'Shepperton in yet?'

'No.' Never frowned. 'But any minute.' A brief pause, and the light dawned in Never's eyes. 'Uh uh,' he said, shaking his head. 'No way.'

Jonah smiled. 'With Sam and Hugo out of the office, the decision's left with the senior reviver and senior technician, right? Me and you.'

'I've been told to keep you away from anything tricky.'

'It's not severe trauma. Nothing to suggest it'll be a difficult revival.'

'Apart from the fact that it's a *nine-year-old girl*?'

'We're talking about a family who've lost a child, a child who may have been killed by her father. A father under suspicion who may be innocent. You want to send Shepperton into that?'

While Never didn't have quite as strong an opinion as Jonah about their colleague, he had been the technician for Shepperton many times. He knew that subtlety and compassion were not the reviver's strong points. The thought of Shepperton handling this case made him uneasy.

Torn, he took a swig of coffee and looked Jonah in the eye. 'Fuck it,' he said. 'You win.'

*

They took one of the six FRS cars, Never driving. Two hours later, they arrived at the scene, a cosy street of semi-detached homes, the road outside swamped by vehicles and a large white forensic tent.

They'd taken an angry call from Hugo Adler by then, but Jonah had talked him round.

It was ten-forty in the morning and the heat was already oppressive, the sunlight harsh.

A crowd of onlookers was being held at bay three houses back on both sides by metal barriers and tape, guarded by a handful of young uniformed cops.

Jonah observed the people watching with fear and intrigue as paper-suited investigators searched the front garden, and one by one, turning to see the dark green car with 'FRS' in discreet white lettering on the doors. A ripple of interest spread through the crowd, and more and more eyes were directed his way. They know, thought Jonah. They know what I am.

He met some of those eyes, and hated the look they gave him now, awe and fear combined. That look had changed little through the years. Public perception of forensic revivers had always been confused – intrigue and aversion battling it out with pragmatism – but up close the deep unease returned. He often thought it had been almost miraculous, how widely revival had been accepted, given the way people felt when it was right in front of them. He supposed it was just the same in other parts of life. People were fine with some things as long as they didn't *encounter* them.

He looked down to avoid the stares, but in his head he heard the words spoken by the corpse of Alice Decker, sudden and close: '*We see you.*'

His left hand gripped the side of his seat and squeezed. He tried to slow his breathing, feeling the rising panic in his chest that always preceded his work. It had hit early, brought on by the memory of those hissed words, and it was stronger than usual. He could hear the murmuring of the onlookers grow louder.

He closed his eyes and concentrated on his breathing, trying to shut out the noise, but it grew relentlessly, an overwhelming drone pounding at his head. Again he heard the words, buried in the din: '*We see you.*' He *knew* that if he opened his eyes and looked, Alice

Decker would be there outside the window, an inch from his face, grinning at him with bloody teeth – torn from his nightmares and thrust into the real world.

A hand gripped his shoulder. Startled, he looked up to see Never's concerned face. He realized that the car had stopped.

'You OK?' asked Never.

'I don't like crowds,' he said. 'Let's get inside.'

5

As they approached the house, Detective Bob Crenner came out of the side flap of the forensic tent; paper-suited, hand up in greeting, the sun glinting off his reddening bald patch. He was in his mid-forties and overweight, with a smile in his eyes that Jonah thought looked genuine – not every cop was keen to see the FRS arrive, even when they needed them. Like any snapshot of the population, there were even those with Afterlifer sympathies, especially since that organization had softened their message and their methods. Many cops saw revival as a necessary evil, and it wasn't unusual for their unease and dislike to be out in the open.

'Mr Geary,' Crenner said brightly. 'And Jonah. We're nearly ready for you. Like the office?' He gestured at the tent.

'Office?' said Never. 'We were wondering if the body had ended up outside the house.'

'No. The CSI unit put it up for some shade. They've been having trouble with their equipment sitting in hot vans. It's one of the only cool places in the vicinity, so make the most of it.'

Jonah peeked through the entrance flap. Equipment boxes were stacked by the back wall. There were a dozen people inside, and like Bob Crenner, almost everyone was in a paper suit. He nodded at Crenner. 'You must be cooking in that.'

'Stripped bare underneath.'

'You went commando?' Never grinned.

'Top half only,' said Crenner with a smirk. He led them in, and the cool shade was welcome. 'My partner as of six months ago, Ray Johnson,' he said, pointing to a young black man in the far corner. 'He's supervising the set-up. Ray!' he called.

Detective Ray Johnson was speaking to a young woman who was one of the few not wearing protective clothing – also not uniformed, Jonah assumed she was either another detective or with forensics. When Crenner called, Johnson wrapped up the conversation and headed over. The young woman glanced at Jonah and he looked away quickly, then back. She was smiling at him and nodded in greeting. Jonah felt his cheeks redden as she turned and walked out the far side of the tent.

Johnson reached out his hand to Never. 'Detective Ray Johnson. It's Never Geary, right? You're the revival technician?'

'Reputation precedes me, huh?' said Never, shaking Johnson's hand.

'I've seen you on another case, but I was in uniform then. This is only the second revival I've been involved in since I moved up in the world.' As he turned to Jonah, his hand was still outstretched ready to shake, but as he spoke he jerked his hand back. 'And you're the reviver?'

Neither Johnson nor Jonah was wearing gloves, a fact that presumably Johnson had only just noticed. Jonah wondered if the detective had made the mistake of shaking a reviver's bare hand in his last case. Not a mistake people tended to make twice. 'Jonah Miller,' he replied, with a smile.

'Fill them in on the case, Ray,' said Crenner. 'I think Fennell's forensics people will be done in the living room in ten minutes or so, and then it's all yours.'

Johnson took them to a corner, where they sat in green plastic chairs that looked suspiciously like garden furniture, presumably sourced from one of the neighbours. He leaned forward, speaking with a low voice.

'Victim is a nine-year-old girl, name of Nikki Wood. Nine-one-one call was taken at 3.50 a.m. She had no life signs when the paramedics arrived. They spent forty-five minutes trying to resuscitate her where she lay, but she was pronounced dead at the scene at five. Medical examiner's prelim suggests the attack would have been tens of minutes before she died, maybe up to an hour. Head wound is the apparent cause, but we haven't identified a weapon yet. No other injuries. The father says he found her after hearing a noise from downstairs. He *claims* there was an intruder.'

Jonah raised an eyebrow towards Never but said nothing. Johnson continued: 'Nikki had a known problem with sleepwalking; her father suggests she surprised a burglar, who struck out.'

'And you suspect the father,' said Jonah.

'Bob says not, but . . . Stu Fennell, the forensics lead, reckons things don't add up. He described it as "staged", and I can see what he means. There are signs of a scuffle – a coffee table was overturned, magazines scattered, but they're a little precise, a little arranged. Plus the guy seems too calm for someone whose daughter was murdered this morning. His statement was . . . well, *rehearsed*, maybe. Too clear. For me. Like I said, Bob disagrees.'

'Was anything stolen?' asked Never.

'Mrs Wood had several items of jewellery taken, family heirlooms. Overall about twenty grand.'

Hearing the figure, Never whistled. 'Strong motive for theft.'

'The items were kept in a box under a sideboard shelf. Anyone who knew about it could have just taken it and left, but if someone wanted to make it look like a burglar got lucky, they needed to mess the place up. Now if they did that, admittedly there'd be a risk of the mess looking the way it did. Sure, maybe someone knew about it. That's what the father's been saying. There was a broken pane of glass in the front door. But there's a problem . . .' He leaned closer. Jonah and Never found themselves leaning closer too. 'The glass was broken from the inside. So maybe it was no burglary. Something gets out of hand, father to daughter. He panics. Theft is the only story he can think of. If so, we'll find the jewellery dumped a street or two away. Or even hidden in the house.'

'But Bob Crenner doesn't agree?' said Never.

'No. He thinks the father's telling the truth.'

'Why do you think he might have killed her?' asked Jonah, but he had a feeling he knew where Johnson was headed.

'Maybe it was a pure accident and he's covering it up, but we haven't just pulled this out of thin air. There's a history. Two years ago Nikki ended up in the ER with a broken arm, blamed on falling down while sleepwalking. Last year she was back in the ER with two broken fingers, again blamed on sleepwalking. Social Services got involved; nothing came of it, but they were wondering about physical abuse, possibly sexual. And if I had to put money on it, that's what I'd go with.' Johnson looked across the tent. A cop had ducked through the door flap carrying a cardboard tray loaded with paper cups and cans. 'Good, the drink runner's back. Can I get you one?'

Jonah, despite the heat, wanted coffee, while Never opted for Coke. Ray Johnson went to fetch them.

'I don't like the sound of this,' said Jonah, when Johnson was out of earshot. 'If they want to throw some abuse questions at the girl, we lose either way.' A successful revival could be scuppered by a reluctant subject; getting the subject back, and past the disorientation – getting them to talk at all – was one thing. Getting a child to speak about something as painful as abuse was extremely difficult, and risked stubborn silence.

And if there was nothing in the allegation, even bringing the topic up would alienate the subject.

Jonah continued: 'If we found out Johnson is right, she'd be unlikely to talk about it explicitly. It'd be ambiguous.' Ambiguous, and contentious; with the subject avoiding explicit confirmation, the opinion of the reviver would be all that supported the claim in court. He didn't relish the prospect.

'Bob Crenner's a smart man,' said Never, shrugging. 'He'll not get you to ask anything clumsy. And if he's not keen on the theory, you might not even have to touch it.'

Ray Johnson came back with the drinks, handed them out, and tilted his head back to the small crowd that had descended on the drink runner.

'See the looker with the bracelets?' he said. It was the woman he had been speaking to when they'd first arrived. 'That's Nala George. She's the family liaison, victim support.' Jonah hadn't noticed the bracelets before, but her right wrist was overrun with them. He looked at her more carefully now that she wasn't aware of him; not uniformed, the norm for victim support these days, but wearing off-white jeans and a white short-sleeved shirt against black skin. He was uncertain if her features were more Caribbean or Polynesian, but he supposed it didn't matter either way. She was gorgeous, she'd smiled at him, and she would almost certainly find his touch repellent.

'She's pissed that we're thinking bad thoughts,' said Johnson.

'She got wind of it?' said Never.

'Yeah . . . I asked her how she thought the father was coping. She's sharp. She saw right through me.'

Jonah found himself watching Nala George with longing and sorrow. When she turned and saw him watching, she smiled and nodded at him, walking back outside. Jonah snapped his head round. 'We give the family the benefit of the doubt,' he said. 'If we play it carefully, we can find out without any risks.'

'Ten dollars says I'm right.'

Jonah glared at the policeman. 'This isn't a fucking game.'

Ray Johnson's eyes widened. 'OK, sorry . . .' He turned to Never. 'I'll go and see if they've cleared out of the room yet. Then like your friend says, we can find out.'

'Please try not to piss off people we work with,' Never said with a smile as Johnson hurried outside.

Jonah shook his head. 'The hell with him. All they have to do is keep an open mind for a while; instead, they're risking the father getting wind of their little theory.'

'I'm on your side,' said Never. He tried to change the subject. 'Nala George is cute, huh?'

'Who?'

'The victim support officer. You're fairly transparent. You know that, right?'

Jonah ignored the jibe. 'Yeah, she's cute. And what are my chances?' The chances of anything coming of it. The chances of her not getting chill.

'Fuck all,' said Never. 'But then that's about the same as my chances, so we're even.' He raised his can. 'Cheers.'

Jonah thudded his cup into it. 'Cheers,' he said.

*

Detective Johnson returned two minutes later to give them the go-ahead to begin setting up. Jonah and Never broke out their protective clothing and donned their paper suits and latex gloves in practised silence, putting shoe covers in their pockets, ready to put on before they entered the house. During the revival Jonah would only wear one glove, on his left hand. The right hand would be bare, ready to make contact with the victim, but he would wait until going into the house before he took it off.

Jonah sat where he was, nursing his coffee as Never led Johnson to the car. They took two cases of equipment each and went into the house.

It would take Never twenty minutes to complete the set-up and testing of all the equipment. Jonah reached inside his paper suit to his own trouser pocket and pulled out a small blue plastic box. Inside, there were four blister packs of pills, a necessary evil for a reviver's work. One was a nausea suppressant. One was an anti-emetic. One was BPV, a drug developed specifically for revivers to suppress the remnant effect. The fourth was plain old aspirin. He popped out one of each into his hand, and glared at them.

Vomiting during the initial revival was a common annoyance, and could even scupper the attempt; the nausea-suppressant and anti-emetic made that less likely, but the cocktail left him with a dry mouth and restlessness that lasted for several hours. The BPV gave him a suite of side effects including a headache, sometimes a bad one. That was why he always took the aspirin in advance.

He threw the lot into his mouth, washed it down with the coffee, and waited for them to take effect. He carefully avoided eye contact while he sat, wanting to escape any kind of interaction. Preparation time, he told himself – he needed to focus, not be distracted – but mainly it was his nature. Shy. Loner.

He found it difficult, sitting in the open, surrounded by people who were mostly strangers yet who knew what he did and what he was. It wasn't as bad as his days at court, but even the people who were used to being on the periphery of an onsite revival could be wary of the reviver.

His drugs were kicking in, and he could already feel the slight dizziness BPV sometimes brought with it.

'You OK?'

The voice startled him. He looked up. It was Nala George, the victim liaison officer. She nodded towards the chair beside Jonah.

'Go ahead,' he said automatically, avoiding her eyes. She sat.

'I was looking for you. I didn't recognize you with the protective clothing on. Did anyone pass on the attendance request?'

Jonah looked at her warily. Relatives of a subject could request attendance at the revival, but in 80 per cent of cases they didn't. Even when they did, it was at the discretion of the duty reviver, but Jonah understood the importance of saying good-bye. He always tried to accommodate it. Nonetheless, it was an additional complication.

'They want to attend?'

Nala George nodded. 'Uh huh. Try not to sound so enthusiastic.'

'Sorry.' He winced inside at being so easily read. 'I'll do my best. Are they sure?'

'They've been at a private revival before, when Nikki's grandmother died last year. Nikki was present. She'd even mentioned that she'd want to have the same opportunity to say good-bye if anything happened.'

He thought about the complications for a moment, then opted to be honest. He lowered his voice. 'You understand there's a question over the father?'

Nala shook her head, with a grimace. 'I know. It's bullshit. Someone raises the question, and then everyone starts treating the man differently. They just like to think the worst of people.'

Jonah nodded. Thinking the worst of people wasn't hard when you were exposed to the results – and the perpetrators – every day. 'All the same, there's a good chance the questioning will have to address it, so I'd rather they didn't attend the interview.' He saw Nala's face drop. Her mouth opened to protest, but he held up a hand to stop her. 'The girl's young, her injuries are minor. Chances are good she'll still be coherent after questioning. As long as the father's in the clear—'

Nala broke in, impatient. 'He *is*.'

Jonah nodded an apology. 'As long as he is, if Nikki's still coherent I'll give the word and they can come in. Would they be OK with that?'

'I'll ask them.'

'They have to understand, it's not a given. And Forensics wants us to keep the scene pristine, so you'll need to scrounge some protective clothing and keep them out here for the time being. If I give the go-ahead, they need to get inside quickly. They may not have long.'

'Understood.'

'If they agree, I'll want to talk to them before I start.'

Nala George smiled at Jonah. 'Thank you,' she said, placing her hand on Jonah's shoulder.

'You're welcome,' he replied, looking down at the ground. With his paper suit and clothing between her hand and his skin, she didn't feel it. Jonah was acutely aware, though, and the hint of chill was unmistakable. He felt himself deflate a little, the tension of being around her gone. She was, as expected, off limits. *Shame,* he thought. *I liked her eyes.*

Nala George walked away to find the parents, to ask them if they were ready to speak to their dead daughter.

*

The third camera was causing Never some trouble. Mounted in the corner of the room farthest from the door, it had a wide-angle lens and was the least critical of the three, but testing had shown some signal degradation. The revival would be observed from the dining room next door, and so the cables he had used were among the shortest he had with him. Degradation over that distance could only mean a fault, so he had opted to swap the cable for the next length up, and live with the spare five metres coiled beside his monitor console. As he plugged the gold connector into the camera, he was aware of Detective Johnson hanging around by the door, fidgeting.

'Nearly done,' Never said, quietly amused by the man's impatience. Perhaps it was a desire to get on with the revival and with the investigation; or it may have been his unease at being in the same room as a corpse. If it was the latter, Johnson would have to get used to it, if he wanted to continue working with Crenner on homicides.

The thought of the corpse reminded him it was there. Even though the cameras were trained on it, and he had spent the last ten minutes studying the live feed and checking recordings, it stopped being a body while he worked. It was just an image.

On first entering the room, he had spent a moment looking at the child, getting it out of his system. Children struck home with more power. Partly, it was their innocence and youth, but it would be naive to think that was all that made it harder. It was the *rarity*. He was in no doubt that, given enough dead children, he could become immune to the sight, just as he was to the sight of dead adults. He was grateful to find his eyes watering when he saw Nikki Wood's body for the first time. *Not immune to it yet,* he had thought.

He finished securing the connector to the camera, took a careful step back from it and looked again at the subject. Nikki Wood's body lay against the front edge of a light beige sofa. She lay as the paramedics had left her: on her back, her arms limp at her sides, her pyjama top pulled open. Her eyes were closed. The side of her head on the pale carpet lay in a small patch of dark blood.

She had been dead for seven hours now. Rigor mortis would be creeping in already, but revival was not always affected by early rigor; the forces involved were strong enough to stretch the muscle fibres that rigor had contracted, while leaving the muscle structure intact. Once rigor was too far advanced, this pulling would cause damage to the tissues severe enough to risk the continuation of vocal revivals, damage that would complicate the pathologist's job even more than normal. The choice was either to wait until it began to subside, possibly another twelve hours or more, or use a series of enzyme injections aimed at freeing up the muscle.

Neither option was ideal. A long delay would reduce revival chances and required the corpse to be kept cool to minimize degradation, either with use of an onsite cooling system, or relocation of the body – which again made revival harder. The enzyme alternative was a pathologist's worst-case scenario. Jonah's kit contained the enzymes, and he could overrule pathology concerns – making the ultimate decision to use it his – but it always led to friction with the pathology liaison. The liaison on this case was Sally Griggs from the North East office; as no issues had arisen yet, she was handling it by phone, but Never could imagine the dialogue that would result if Jonah had to call her to clear enzyme use. It wouldn't be pretty.

Movement to Never's side, and a subtle cough, snapped him from his thoughts. Time was pressing.

'I'll see if that's sorted it,' Never said, walking to the living room door. 'Then I'll run the final checks.'

'How long?' asked Johnson.

'Not long. Better go and get Jonah and your boss.' As he spoke, a crime scene officer walked past the doorway, and Never glared at his back. 'Aren't they supposed to be out of here? We don't want intrusions.'

Johnson nodded. 'I'll get the house cleared of everyone except those attending.'

'So who else'll be here?'

Johnson smiled ruefully. 'That's up to Bob. Pretty much everyone wants to observe. I think we could sell tickets for this one.'

Johnson left, and Never returned to the other room to see if the signal problem had been resolved. As he looked at the image of Nikki Wood's corpse, he thought of Jonah and found himself growing anxious for his friend. He knew the questioning would not be easy. But at least the initial revival should, he thought, be a simple one.

But how could it be? How could it ever be simple to bring back a child?

*

Barely two minutes had passed when Nala George returned to the tent. Jonah felt his meds settle, the dizziness short-lived this time, and mild.

Wordless, he looked the question at her, and she nodded: the parents had agreed. He stood and followed her out.

He squinted coming out of the shade. The sun seemed relentless, the skin on his face tender and sensitive to the harsh light, another BPV side effect. The heat was immediate, and for a moment he wished he'd done the same as Bob Crenner and taken his shirt off under the suit. But he rejected the idea at once – he felt exposed enough as it was during a revival.

They reached the tape marking the inner limit of the exclusion area. The onlookers were thinner on this side, the side on which the cul-de-sac lay; most of the gawkers on the other side presumably came from nearby streets. They ducked under the tape, and a uniformed cop moved one of the metal barriers, letting them pass.

Nala spoke, her voice low, 'Julie and Graham,' she said. 'They're staying with their friend Dawn Hannick. Number 30. Just ahead.'

Five doors down from the Woods' home, a lone female cop stood at the garden gate. She and Nala nodded at each other as they passed.

Nala knocked at the front door, and it opened to a woman who looked exhausted.

'Dawn,' said Nala. Dawn Hannick said nothing, merely turned and walked inside. Nala and Jonah followed, Jonah closing the door behind him.

Julie and Graham Wood were in the kitchen, sitting at a small table in one corner. They looked up – distraught, utterly adrift. Jonah had his doubts about their ability to understand what it was they were asking to do. He would have to rely on the victim liaison's judgment, and keep a close eye on the parents during the revival if it proved possible to bring them in.

Dawn Hannick walked over to the sink, busying herself. Wary and haggard, she seemed older than her friends, perhaps mid-sixties to their late forties, but at times like this age crept up on people.

Attendance cases were often difficult, but also worthwhile – illustrating how it was not just money that drew revivers into the private revival industry. Helping bring justice to bear gave Jonah a feeling of usefulness and a deep satisfaction in his ability; it was common for forensic revivers to dismiss the work of private operators as less important. The reality was that there were far more deaths than those Jonah and his colleagues dealt with each year. The majority were unexpected. Most were devastating.

Private revivals helped people deal with the aftermath. Yet standard private revival insurance could guarantee nothing, paying only for a chance of success. It was a simple problem of numbers;

how many revivers there were, at what levels of ability, against how many deaths. Inevitably the best of the best were reserved for the rich. The cheapest insurance bought you revivers with success rates of 10 per cent for uncomplicated cases. In contrast, even the worst forensic revivers had to be D3 rated, with 85 per cent success for the same case category.

There was certainly a steady trickle of defectors from forensic to private; for those revivers who had suffered all they could of vicious deaths, the appeal was obvious. Private revival work was easier in so many ways. Jonah didn't share the disdain for it that many of his colleagues did, and could easily understand how people might be tempted by the better pay and working conditions of private revival, but he also understood that it wasn't only the money, or the reduction in stress.

More than once, he had considered swapping the satisfaction of justice for the satisfaction of helping the bereaved – what Eleanor Preston had regarded as her calling. Sometimes, though, he could do both.

Nala walked over to the Woods and sat at the table. The couple were red-eyed and horribly gaunt, as though the trauma of their daughter's death had physically eaten away at them. Julie Wood was wearing a dressing gown over a nightshirt, sandals on her feet; Graham an old tee shirt, jogging pants, trainers.

Jonah remained standing, knowing he had to avoid contaminating his protective clothing. He stood beside Nala, feeling awkward.

'This is the reviver. His name's Jonah.' Nala's voice was gentle and supportive. Julie Wood replied first, addressing her response directly to Jonah.

'Thank you. For letting us speak with our daughter. We just want to say good-bye.' Her voice was flat, defeated. Graham Wood nodded silently, blank and lost.

Jonah crouched down to make them feel more at ease. 'I'll question Nikki first. You'll be outside for that. The duration of a revival is difficult to know, but if we complete questioning and I think Nikki can cope with it, I'll send for you. Be quick, but be careful. Mind your step. I'll be passing on what you want to ask – Nikki won't be able to hear you directly. You can either watch from the room next door or be in the living room with Nikki. Do you know which you'd rather do?'

The couple shared a look and nodded to each other.

'With her, please,' said Julie Graham. She raised a tissue to her face and dried her eyes.

'OK. We'll suit you up, like me. Touch nothing, be careful of the equipment. Think about what you want to say. Keep it short and simple. When you're done, tell her good night. They prefer good night to good-bye. Leave when I tell you. Do you understand?' They nodded. 'I can't emphasize enough, this will be difficult. If you feel you can't do it, tell Nala at once, and don't be ashamed to say it. Understand that there's a significant chance we'll not complete questioning before the revival ends. If I think that's happening, I'll give her a message from you, so think about what you—'

Julie Wood interrupted, fresh tears flowing. 'Tell her we love her.'

Jonah nodded. It was always that. In the end, what else was there?

6

In one corner of the dining room, Never had set up his monitoring console. A laptop PC controlled everything; a second laptop beside it was there as a backup, and control could be switched to it instantly if necessary. Both machines showed the same display: a row of windows with the feed from each camera. In the central image, Nikki Wood's face stared out at him, silent for now.

The laptops were on a small portable table, while Never sat on a camping stool, one he'd found to be more comfortable than any chair he'd used over the years.

'I like your seat,' said Bob Crenner as he came in.

Smiling, Never indicated one of the equipment bags he and Johnson had brought from the car. 'There's a spare if you want it.'

'I'll stand.'

'Suit yourself. Detective Johnson suggested we'd have a crowd,' Never said, looking around the conspicuously empty room.

'What people want and what people get are two different things. We're bare bones on this. Senior officer, revival co-ordination officer. Nobody else.' That meant just Crenner and Johnson. 'Unless Jonah gives the word for attendance. Have you heard?'

He nodded. Jonah had put his head around the door briefly to let him know, and Never had been somewhat put out by the added complication. Still, he had no intention of letting Bob Crenner see that. 'Yeah, shouldn't be a problem.' Usually it wasn't, although Never always found himself tensing when relatives entered the scene. Particularly as they stepped over his cabling. Nobody had ever tripped, nobody had ever knocked over a camera, but he still fretted.

After telling him about the parents' attendance request, Jonah had left to psych himself up for the revival, and Never knew the routine. Jonah tended to get panicky about now, sometimes to the point of throwing up, even with his medication. A lot like stage fright, Never thought, and he supposed it served a purpose – emptying the stomach in advance, when it wouldn't really matter.

Detective Johnson entered a moment later. Jonah followed, pale and anxious.

'How're you doing?' called Never.

'Ready to go,' Jonah said. 'The parents are waiting with Nala George in the forensic tent outside.'

Johnson was holding a radio in his hand. He waved it. 'I'll let her know if Jonah gives the go ahead.'

'OK,' said Crenner, then he turned to Jonah. 'When you bring her back, we get her statement first. Standard stuff, then we'll play it by ear. But there's a complication . . .'

Jonah nodded. 'The abuse allegation? Ray mentioned it. He also said you don't think there's anything in it.'

'No, but the question's been raised and there's enough to warrant taking it seriously. We'll have to deal with it. Tread carefully.'

'I will.'

'Good luck, Jonah. You ready, Never?'

'Few more seconds.'

Jonah, Crenner and Johnson fell into silence, finding themselves looking at the screens on Never's table, the face of the dead child looking back. The only sound was from Never's fingers on his laptop keyboard, finishing his preparations. At last the sound stopped.

'I'm all set,' Never said.

Jonah's earpiece sat on Never's table. Wordlessly, Jonah picked it up and left the room, closing the door behind him. A moment later, he was visible on the wide-angle shot of the living room as he entered. He closed that door too, stepped carefully to Nikki Wood's body, and knelt.

Thinking of her parents, he pulled the sides of her pyjama top together. Some of the buttons had been torn free when the paramedics had opened it, but there were enough left to hold it in place.

His practised hands ran over her throat, palpating the flesh to determine the extent of rigor. It was present, but not yet a problem. He removed the glove from his right hand and put the earpiece in place, then looked at the camera ahead of him. The flow of adrenaline was stirring up nausea and panic. He took some long, steadying breaths until he had settled again.

'Ready,' he said. The red light on the camera went green. 'Revival of subject Nikki Wood. J. P. Miller, duty reviver.'

*

Jonah shifted his weight. His left knee, on the carpet, had started to ache a little. He decided to change position. The right knee stayed where it was, the left leg came up onto the foot. It felt better; better able to respond.

Better able to *run*.

The realization triggered a sour smile. This was his first revival since Alice Decker. Perhaps it was natural.

He had wondered aloud to the FRS counsellor how he would handle his next case, whether he would feel the same terror emerge in a difficult moment and disgrace himself by fleeing. Now, holding this dead girl's hand, the time had come to find out. Part of him was trying to believe in the hallucinatory nature of the entity that had spoken to him through Alice Decker's corpse; the rest of him was content with the thought that if it returned, Never would witness it. Scant comfort, maybe, but it seemed to be enough to let him get on with it.

He relaxed, shifted his weight again.

He began by watching the body, studying the face. There was so little injury visible, only the stain on the carpet under her head marking the damage. Her eyes were open, her expression blank. He looked at her hair, dark brown and cropped short.

Hanging in the room were several family portraits. One was of the two parents together; another was of them with Nikki, their only child. And one was of Nikki, on her own in a school uniform, hair longer, broad smile and eyes full of life. He turned back to the dead eyes beside him. He had to find that life, wherever it was.

He slowed his breathing and closed his eyes. The ambient noise from the room faded, as his awareness focused.

What he did next felt simple enough, natural enough; but to talk of reaching for the dead in the air around you – or in some vast space beyond – begged questions of the nature of that space, the nature of that reach, and those questions had no answers. Ultimately there was only reaching, and bringing back.

He sensed her. He braced, and felt himself shoot forward, pulled by the grasp that held him. He was within the corpse now, sensing every part of it; aware of the earliest signs of decay that had crept in since death, and of the tiny clotted lump in her brain that had eventually killed her. This was the first stage of any revival: the *reversal*. Feeling what damage was done that had led to their death; feeling the degradation that had followed. Getting close to them, a part of them, death surrounding him. And to get anywhere, he had to embrace it. He had to let it *fill* him, *engulf* him. And as they came back, in his mind the death and injury left them. The harder the case – the more damage, the more decay – the longer it would last, and the more severe it would be.

In the darkness he stretched, somehow; turned over until he felt more at ease. He sensed the corpse as his own body now; as if he were dead, lying in its place on the carpet. The odour of death was slight, and it dissipated as the decay slowly reversed, the initial processes of degradation – the beginnings of rot – turning back, the muscles becoming fresh. He felt the clot disperse, tissues reconnecting. He felt the skin sealing around the wound.

It had taken less than ten minutes, and the reversal was complete. He waited for the second stage to come: the *surge*.

The surge was the moment before they came back to him – a flood of image, sound and emotion. It was as if they screamed their *life* at him. Out of his hands; all he could do was endure it, however extreme it became, knowing that if he threw up or pulled out, he might have to start the revival all over again.

After one attempt at revival, time was critical. The reviver who'd made the attempt would be weakened and have less chance of success than before. A second attempt would have to be made within two hours, ideally with a different reviver. Any later, and it was as impossible as bringing someone back twice.

Jonah was always scared of the surge, unsure what to expect. A reviver couldn't know in advance how difficult it would be. So much depended on the subjects. They could show indignation. Surprise. Anger. Fear. The emotions around their death could magnify the surge in unpredictable ways. Something that he expected to be simple could overwhelm him, too much too fast, a gut-wrenching feeling of a ride he couldn't afford to get off. And all the while, having to be ready to talk to the subject the instant it stopped.

An image flashed: a bright sky from a summer long before. He tensed, waiting to see how the surge would go. Another image sparked, long grass in sand, a strong smell of the sea.

And then it came in full and swamped him: pain, at first; anger there, but outweighed by the sorrow. Confusion, too. The surge grew, pictures and sounds and feelings, compressed and hurled at him. He felt his stomach lurch at the sense of speed, plunging down through the child's mind. *Not so bad*, he thought and hoped, *not so bad this time*, and he held on as it peaked and fell away.

His realized he'd been holding his breath. He let it go, and breathed deeply.

He opened his eyes to find himself kneeling over the unchanged corpse of Nikki Wood. It was done.

'She's here,' he said to a camera. Nikki's corpse inhaled quietly

– none of the dramatics of Alice Decker's revival, just a trace of mucosal sounds. Jonah sensed nothing *else* with her – no other presence. He grimaced and put the thought from his head. His work could proceed.

'My name is Jonah Miller, Nikki. Can you hear me?'

An instant response, heartbreakingly gentle. 'Yes.'

'Do you know where you are?'

'I died.' Jonah was thrown for a moment by Nikki's frankness. Children accepted this at least as readily as adults, their grasp of the situation often immediate, without denial or evasion.

'That's right, Nikki. I'm here to ask you some questions about how you died. Do you understand?'

'Like Granny Mo.' Her grandmother; the revival her parents had mentioned.

'Yes, Nikki. Like Granny Mo. Can I ask you some questions?'

'Yes. Is Mom here?'

'You can talk to her when you've answered our questions. I promise.' A promise he might not be able to keep.

'OK.'

He sensed she was disappointed. 'Tell me what happened. Why did you come downstairs?'

'I was asleep. I must have been sleepwalking again. I hate that, I wish I didn't do that . . .' She halted, silent. Jonah waited ten seconds.

'Nikki?' he said, a small prompt, and Nikki's chest rose at once.

'I woke up, standing in the living room. A man was going through the drawers in the sideboard. It was dark, he had a flashlight. He wasn't even looking at what was in them. He just pulled out each drawer, took out the things inside and put them on the floor. He turned the drawer over and set it down too. Then he did the same with the next. I was afraid. He was being so quiet, I didn't understand. I backed away.'

She stopped but stayed silent. Jonah sensed it was fear, fear of the events that followed.

He prompted her again, trying for warm authority. 'Please, Nikki. Continue.' A few seconds passed before she inhaled.

'He heard me. I didn't know what to do. He pointed the flashlight at me and said he would kill my parents if I made a noise. He told me to stand in the corner of the room and face away from him. I did. I heard him take another drawer out. I was crying. I tried to be quiet, but I peeked. He'd found my mom's jewellery box. I didn't want him to have it. It was Granny Mo's. It's very important to Mom.'

She fell silent again.

'You're doing so well, Nikki. We're nearly done.'

'I told him to put it back, that it was important. He told me to be quiet. I was crying. He told me to stop, and it made me cry more. He stepped towards me and I was frightened and I went to run. He caught me and I tried to shout but his hand covered my mouth. I kicked out and he threw me. I hit my head hard on the wall.'

Jonah heard Crenner whisper something to Ray Johnson: 'Not a weapon. Maybe something on the wall.'

Nikki continued. 'My head hurt, and it went quiet. I felt so tired, and I went to the sofa and sat down. I could see him watching me. He told me to stay where I was and close my eyes and be quiet or he'd hurt me again. I couldn't talk anyway. He walked behind me and I heard him open more drawers and empty them. He left the room and I could hear noises but I don't know what he did. I tried to stand but I fell. I lay still. Then he came back.'

Bob Crenner spoke: 'Ask her how long he'd been gone.' Jonah relayed the question.

'A few minutes. He shone the flashlight at me. He asked me if I could hear him. He sounded worried, I don't think he'd realized I was really hurt. He was swearing lots. I wasn't breathing much then. He was scared. He went to leave but he'd forgotten the jewellery box so he came back. He looked at me again. He went to the front door, I think. I heard banging and a smash and then the door opened.'

She stopped. Ten seconds passed.

'Nikki?' Nothing. Jonah waited.

'Is she gone?' asked Crenner, urgency in his voice. 'We need some description of the man. Is she gone?' Jonah shook his head for the camera. She was still there, still strong. She was resting. Jonah knew when to press and when to let a subject recover. He gave her a little longer before continuing.

'What happened then, Nikki?'

'I heard a voice. It was my dad.'

Crenner made another suggestion: 'Ask her where the voice came from.' Jonah understood the implication, and asked Nikki.

'From upstairs above me. I heard their bedroom door, and then I heard the man run outside, slamming the front door behind him. Dad's footsteps came down the stairs, quick, and I was afraid the man would come back and get him too. He was calling, "Is someone there?" and he was angry and scared. He stopped and called out again. I think he wanted to scare whoever it was away, but the man had gone. Dad turned on the lights. My mom asked him what it was. He didn't answer, he was looking at me. He came in, holding Granny Mo's old walking stick in front of him. He saw me, and I wanted to tell him the man had gone, that I was OK, though I didn't really think I *was* OK. He was crying. He shouted to Mom. He told me to hang on, but it went dark again. I think I died then.'

Jonah looked to a camera and gave a firm nod. She was telling the truth, no question, and it was all on camera. Relief flooded him.

'Well done,' said Never over his earpiece.

'Yes, well done,' said Crenner. 'Now let's get anything else we can. Details of the man. Anything she can recall.'

Now that there was enough to shift focus away from the father, Jonah wondered how long Crenner would make him continue questioning. Nikki was still strongly present, but time was against them. He was desperate to allow the girl to speak to her parents, and for them to speak to her.

'Nikki, I've got some more questions, and then you can talk to your parents, OK?' He hoped the explicit reference would focus Crenner's mind on the prospect. Too much questioning, and the detective would be denying this child her last chance to tell her parents she loved them.

'OK.'

Crenner guided the questions. 'Start with clothing. Then voice. Then anything else she remembers,' he said.

'Can you tell me what the man was wearing, Nikki?' asked Jonah.

'I think he had jeans on. A brown jacket. But it was really dark and he had the flashlight. I only saw his legs and feet. I think he had black gloves on. A scarf around his face.'

'Can you describe the scarf or anything about his face?'

'Don't know. I didn't see. He may have had a cap but it was so *dark*. Where's my mom?' Nikki Wood was getting impatient, and scared. Scared that Jonah had lied to her about talking to her mother.

'She's coming now, Nikki. Your dad too.' He looked to a camera and nodded, knowing his action would be understood. He heard Crenner on his radio, contacting Johnson.

'OK, OK. Send them in. But Jonah, we need something. Anything you can get. Voice, maybe?'

'Nikki,' said Jonah, 'some final questions while they're on their way. Can you tell me about the man's voice? An accent? Anything?'

'His voice was deep but not very good.'

Jonah thought for a second before grasping what she meant. 'You mean he sounded like he was disguising his voice?'

'Yes. When he first said something he just sounded normal, but then he went all deep.'

'When he first spoke, did you recognize the voice? Was it familiar?'

'No.' Running out of time.

Crenner spoke up: 'The parents are coming. Ask her if she can remember anything else unusual. Anything at all. Then it's up to you. If you think she has more, we need it. Get it if you can.'

'Last thing, Nikki. Was there anything else, anything you can think of that might help us catch him?'

Nikki was silent for almost twenty seconds. Jonah tensed. He heard the front door open, Nikki's parents and Nala George entering the house, talking with low voices.

'He had a cough,' Nikki said. 'He kept coughing.' She fell silent again. Jonah gave her a moment. He heard Crenner swear, frustrated, and Jonah was frustrated too. But instinct told him there was nothing more she could offer, and he trusted his instinct. That was all they were going to get.

Jonah looked into the camera.

'That's all she knows,' he said, downcast. 'She's still here, but we don't have long.'

Crenner paused, then asked the Woods the formality: 'Are you ready to speak to your daughter?'

Jonah could hear Nikki's father: 'Oh please, God, yes.'

Jonah smiled at Nikki. 'Your mom and dad are here now. Do you want to talk to them?' He too was required to confirm.

'Yes,' said Nikki Wood. 'Thank you.'

*

Once the parents had left, Jonah released the girl. She was content now, and ready: the way Jonah liked them to be at release. Tension slipped off his shoulders as she went. He stood, suddenly shaky and weak – his recent lack of sleep, he thought. He crouched down, focusing on his breathing, but the weakness was joined by nausea. He could feel a headache start up, and hoped it wouldn't turn into a migraine. He stood again and stumbled out to the hall. The parents were by the open front door, speaking to Crenner. Johnson was standing in the dining room behind Never and saw Jonah's pale face. He came out into the hall.

'You look terrible.'

'I need a toilet. Or a bucket.'

'Come on.' Johnson bundled Jonah outside.

The crowd had thinned a little but movement from the house sparked interest. Johnson guided Jonah two doors down, where an elderly couple stood in the doorway.

'Need your bathroom,' he said to them as he approached. Seeing Jonah, they said nothing and stood back.

The toilet bowl triggered Jonah's stomach, and he vomited powerfully, bile and coffee. Johnson stepped outside and closed the door.

Jonah dry-wretched for several more minutes. He took off the single glove he still had on his left hand, shoving it into his pocket, and turned on the cold water faucet, splashing his face.

He looked in the mirror and, for an instant, felt surprise at seeing his own image. Confused, he dismissed the feeling and opened the door, out of breath but with a little colour back in his cheeks.

'I need air,' he said to Johnson, and they went back outside, thanking the owners as they went. Outside by the gate Nala George stood, worry on her face. As he reached her, the strength in his legs failed again and he crouched, breathing with great care.

'Sorry about that,' he said. 'Sometimes it hits you at the end.' *But not this hard,* he thought.

'Forget it. Really,' said Johnson. 'That was amazing.'

'Me throwing up?'

Ray Johnson laughed. 'What you did. You got her back, and the father's clear. Guess I owe everyone an apology.'

'Damn right,' said Nala George, still a trace of anger in her eyes. She looked at Jonah and the anger vanished. 'Thank you.'

Jonah looked up. 'Yeah. We got nothing else, though. A man, taller than Nikki, who coughs and can't do a convincing deep voice. Case closed.' He tried to stand, using the brick gatepost at the edge of the garden for support. 'It could've gone better.'

'You still did well,' Johnson said.

'Not well enough. She seemed like a good kid.' Something felt suddenly strange in his head, something he couldn't pinpoint. He rubbed his face, then moaned a little and slid down until he was sitting on the ground again.

'You want me to get Never?' said Johnson.

'Give me a minute, I'll be OK. And shouldn't you be . . .'

He stopped, as an image of long grass in sand filled his mind. A strong smell of the sea. He recognized it from the surge he'd had bringing Nikki back. The image came again, swamping him: the sea, distant over flat wet sand, the tide out. A voice shouted a name. *Nikki.*

He turned and saw an old woman making her slow way to where he sat in the sand.

Granny Mo, thought Jonah automatically, a deep recognition that puzzled him.

He groaned.

It had been a while since he'd experienced the remnant effect, and this sure as hell felt like it. Dead memories that were unbidden, and unfamiliar. Remnants of the images and sensations he'd been bombarded with during the surge.

My meds need changing, he thought. He heard Nala George again: 'You OK?'

Jonah looked up at her and hid his confusion. 'I'm just tired.' He was suddenly keen to find Never. It was far too soon for remnants to hit. The earliest he'd ever known it to happen was after a day, a distressing but ultimately harmless picture show.

And there was something else, something elusive. He felt distant, somehow. Vague.

It struck again. The same location, the grandmother close now. *'How's your leg, Gran?'*

'Still there, sweetie,' she said. He was struck by the odd familiarity of the sentence. Struck by the way the old woman's voice had filled him with warmth, and by a curious detachment he felt when his eyes opened again.

He felt the headache worsen. *It's just imagery,* he told himself. *Just memory.*

He stood, leaning heavily on the gatepost, angry at the unwelcome complication – knowing the anger would be shared by Sam Deering, and aimed at him and at Never. *Yeah, right, take it easy, have a break.*

Outside their house, Julie and Graham Wood had emerged and the crowd had gathered again. Jonah's need to see Never overwhelmed his dislike of having to pass through the throng. His friend would still be inside, disassembling equipment. He lurched off through a gap in the metal barriers.

'Hey, steady . . . You should rest longer,' said Johnson, keeping pace. Nala George was a few steps behind.

'I need to talk to Never,' Jonah gasped, ducking under the tape. Julie and Graham Wood were on the street, talking to Crenner. They looked better than they had before, the therapeutic value of the revival clear.

Seeing them provoked panic deep inside Jonah, a panic he couldn't understand. He intended to walk past, but Julie Wood intercepted him.

'I wanted to thank you in person,' she said softly.

Jonah nodded. 'Thanks, I have to . . .'

He stepped around her, and there in front of him was her husband, offering his hand.

'I can't shake, I'm sorry,' said Jonah, holding his own hands up.

'I just want you to know,' said Graham Wood, a hitch in his voice. 'I want you to know how grateful we are.'

But Jonah found himself unable to concentrate, desperate to move on, feeling that – somehow – time was short. 'I'm sorry,' he said. 'I have to go inside.'

He took one step, then became aware of something, a noise: he strained to listen. It was important, he thought, but he had no idea why. Julie and Graham stared.

'Where's Never?' Jonah said, his voice fading, eyes looking around but not seeing. He stumbled, stayed crouched for a moment, and stood up again.

Johnson and Nala exchanged a glance.

'I'll get Never,' said Johnson, and hurried off.

'What's wrong with him? Can we help?' asked Julie Wood.

'I don't know,' said Nala.

Jonah was staring around at the people by the barriers. He stepped towards them. Their low chatter subsided as they saw this oddity watching them. Nala George stepped over and touched his arm, that hint of chill making itself known again.

'Jonah, please come inside the tent. You need to sit down. You need to rest.' He shrugged her off. The crowd was silent now, and Jonah could feel the weight of their eyes on him.

He was as baffled as they were. He felt compelled to follow the source of a sound he couldn't hear, and now there was no sound at all save for a distant hum of traffic. The feeling of detachment had grown – a feeling that he was watching himself.

Then he heard it. A clearing of the throat. A *cough*, or what Nikki Wood had meant by it. Familiar now, and close by. He moved to his left and waited. It came again. Closer. The faces before him were deeply uneasy.

He felt another hand on his shoulder. It was Never, fear in his eyes.

'Jonah, come inside,' he said. 'Please, come inside.'

Jonah shook his head. His sense of detachment retreated for a moment, and he leaned towards Never and whispered. 'Something . . . There's something in my head, Never . . .'

The sound came again. Jonah snapped his head around, horribly dizzy for a moment, but then he could see the man, further back, obscured by a group of women with toddlers. Jonah put his hands on the steel barrier; ignoring Never's protests he vaulted it, landing hard on the other side.

The women stared fearfully at him as he moved through them.

He stepped towards the lone man, who watched him warily. Jonah's eyes dropped to the ground. The man was wearing shabby trainers, ancient and tattered. Jonah looked down at them. He had no idea why he was looking. The first two letters of the Reebok logo had come off the side of his left shoe. He remembered Nikki's words in the revival: *I only saw his legs and feet.*

She hadn't described the shoes, but somehow he recognized them.

You, he thought. *You.*

Already Never was at his side, and Jonah turned to him. 'The shoes, Never,' he said. 'It's him. The same *shoes.*'

Jonah turned back and looked at the man, at his eyes. There was fear there, and shock; but there was defiance too, and the instant Jonah saw that defiance he felt anger boil inside himself, an overwhelming rage he had no source for. It terrified him.

Jonah felt giddy, distant. He heard his own voice, quiet and uncertain at first. 'You killed me,' he said to the man. The man's fear visibly grew, and he stepped back. Jonah sensed he was preparing to run. 'You *killed* me,' Jonah said, louder now.

The crowd watched, bemused, eyes turning from the paper-suited reviver to the man he was accusing.

The man turned and ran, but Jonah was faster, diving for him. Jonah became disoriented, feeling like an observer, like his actions weren't his own, hearing himself scream again and again, his hand clasping something, feeling chill hit hard and realizing it was the man's throat he was squeezing.

Arms were pulling at him, shouts of people he recognized – Johnson, Nala George, Never Geary, Crenner.

Graham Wood, Julie Wood. *Dad,* he heard in his own head. *Mom.*

He was dragged back, held standing as the rage subsided. Everything was draining from the world around him. Light, colour and sound faded to nothing. But before it did, he caught the eye of Graham Wood, stunned and inches away.

'I'm sorry,' Jonah heard in his own voice, but certain it wasn't him speaking. 'It was him, Dad. He did it. He killed me.' Then black.

7

'You been to the States before?'

Annabel Harker frowned and cursed to herself. She'd been looking out of the airplane window, watching engineers do their thing and the luggage loaders come and go. The last thing she wanted was conversation.

It was the early flight from London Heathrow, due in to Washington's Dulles International at around 1 p.m.; with the five-hour time difference, her body would make it six in the evening. She had hoped to settle into her flight routine: soak up the peace, try to get a little work done, and avoid dozing. That way, when her dad picked her up at Dulles they would still have plenty of time when they got home before she'd collapse into her old bed, under the fading Leonardo DiCaprio poster.

So far, though, she'd had no peace at all.

She switched her frown to a fixed smile before turning around. The man in the next-but-one seat was in his late forties and not wearing it well. He'd started gabbing the moment he'd taken his aisle seat in Annabel's row. She had the window seat; the middle one was empty.

Each time he'd started talking, Annabel had responded as curtly as she could, hoping he'd get the hint, but if he kept on like this she knew she'd have to be firmer. That was always a problem: she'd inherited a trait for politeness from her mother, one that, as a journalist, she often wanted to rid herself of. She'd also inherited her mother's tall good looks, though, which invited attention from exactly the kind of assholes who would only fuck off when literally told to.

'Born and raised there,' she replied. 'Only left when I was eighteen.'

'How come you don't have an accent? That can't have been long ago!'

Annabel winced at the line. 'Seven years,' she told him.

'See, now that I know, I can hear it in your voice here and there. How long did it take you to lose the accent?'

'Not long,' Annabel said. She faked a yawn and closed her eyes, pretending to be trying to sleep. The man fell silent at last.

Losing her accent had taken about a week, truth told. Annabel had left her parents' home, headed for University College, London, and had soon found herself speaking like her mother. After all, her mother hadn't lost her own gentle English accent, and Annabel had grown up with it. Was it any surprise she'd found herself adopting it so quickly, and so naturally? It had snapped back to her Virginia accent the moment she'd gone home that first time, only to return as soon as she was in England again. Within a year, it was fixed in place, and different enough from her mom's to be her *own*.

Now that she was going back, she knew her voice would become Americanized for a while. She'd get teased about it at work, but she didn't mind. She tried to sound as American as she could with her father, worried that her voice reminded him too much of her mother's, and that every word from her mouth would make him feel the loss that much more. She knew it wasn't just her accent that could be a reminder – though her hair was her father's dark brown rather than her mother's strawberry blonde, facially she resembled her mother most of all.

She was always wary, coming back. She loved him so much, and every year she found it harder to leave him to his grief, but every year he was adamant – he wanted to be left alone to get on with it. Yet the first few days were inevitably uneasy; him coming out of his shell, and her gradually forgiving him for what she saw as selfishness.

It had been twelve days since she had spoken to him directly; ten since she had received an email, replying to her confirmation of flight times. 'Thanks Annie xxx,' he had written, and that was the last she had heard. Even the previous conversation had been short, just enough to establish in Annabel's mind that her father was over the worst of his annual depression and looking forward to her arrival. They'd spoken about his latest novel and the problems he'd been having with it, the discussion vague as he didn't like to reveal much about works in progress. He'd mentioned he had been working on some nonfiction, promising her more details when she came.

That morning, she'd called him nine times throughout the day, before setting off for the airport. She made her last call an hour before the flight, and like the others it was intercepted by the answering machine with its short greeting.

Not taking her calls meant he wasn't as over it as she'd thought; each attempt made her irritation with him grow.

*

When she arrived in Dulles, it was one-fifteen in the afternoon, local time, but the flight had exhausted her.

As she waited for her bags, she took her phone out of her pocket and switched it on, looking to see if it would connect successfully to the local network. It did, and she immediately called her father's cell phone number, getting an automated message telling her his phone was switched off. She tried his home number and got the same message she'd heard so often before: 'Hi, this is Daniel, please leave your message.'

'Hi, it's Annabel, I've landed. Pick up the phone, Dad.' Nothing. 'Come on . . . Dad?' Then, cold: 'You'd better be on your way.' She hung up and sighed.

Bags collected, she took an empty seat in the meeting area in Arrivals, buying a Coke to give herself a jolt of sugar and caffeine.

Over the next half hour, she called her father's number five more times. Five more variations of 'Hi, it's Annabel, I've landed. Pick up.'

She waited thirty more minutes, then made another call, trying to keep the anger out of her voice. 'Dad, I'm getting a car and coming there. I'll see you in a couple of hours.'

Tired and aching, she made herself focus. The moment-to-moment tasks distracted her from her annoyance as she set off to hire a car, but the distractions were short-lived. All too soon, she was familiar with the small left-hand-drive Renault. All too soon, she was on US 29, sure of her route. The journey to her father's home outside Charlottesville would take two hours or so of mundane driving, and she had run out of ways to distract herself.

'Shit, Annie,' she said aloud. In the past seven years, she'd only had to do this once before. Three years back, when she'd been going home full of excitement, having landed a job as a junior writer for *Metro*, the free London daily paper. That time, she'd found him drunk, not expecting her for two more days, embarrassed at losing track of the date; she'd screamed at him, all her frustration and fear coming out like knives. It had taken most of her visit before things had been repaired. The prospect of going through that again didn't appeal.

A truck, pulling into her lane without warning, roused her from her thoughts. She jabbed at the horn, holding it down as she pulled around.

The highway wasn't busy. She kept pace with the faster cars and reached Charlottesville without encountering significant traffic.

The journey was a strange mix of the unknown and the familiar. She always insisted that he pick her up when she visited. It gave them a chance to begin to catch up in the car, and forced him to sober up and get out of the house, probably for longer than he'd managed in total in the previous few months.

'Nearly home,' she said. *Strange*, she thought, *how it's always 'home' when I'm this close to it.*

Her parents had bought the house when her father's book *The First Reviver* gave them more money than they'd ever had before. It was at the south edge of Shenandoah National Park, which her mother loved; she'd found the house and fallen for it instantly. Annabel, fifteen then, loved it too. An old place set on twelve acres of woodland, plenty of character, and one thing in particular that had sold her father on it. Privacy.

The house was isolated, the nearest neighbouring building a farmhouse a half-hour walk away that had been sold four years before; her father had claimed, with a curious pride, that he'd still not met the new owners.

Out of Charlottesville now. Another turning, and the small road was enclosed in an arch of foliage, tree branches and huge bushes shaped by the passage of trucks that she hoped she wouldn't encounter coming the other way. She drove under the arch in the patches of sunlight, resenting her anger more because without it, she knew, she would have loved this drive.

The private lane leading to the house appeared, and she turned the car. As the house became visible between the old oaks that lined the way, her chest tightened, taking her by surprise. For the whole journey, it had been annoyance she had felt, turning to anger. But now, suddenly, there was something else. Something that her anger had masked, too strong now for her to ignore.

Fear.

No, she thought. *Not you. Not now.*

She parked quickly, ran to the door and rang the bell. She waited for a count of ten, then rang again. She called out. She ran to the rear, glancing in windows. Nothing.

The spare key was under a large planter near the back door. She returned to the front and let herself in.

'Dad?' she called. Half-hearted. '*Dad?*' There was no sound. Leaving the front door wide open, she opened the living room door, bracing herself, suddenly aware that among her fears, there was one that was lucid and specific – that she would find him here, motionless and cold and alone. The living room was empty. Kitchen next. Washed dishes and empty wine bottles in the drainer by the sink. She opened the fridge. Some salad leaves in a bowl had turned. The milk was tainted. The smell of sour milk gave her another thought. She had not noticed a smell when she came into the house. The thought – just *having* that thought – made her feel sick.

Move on, she told herself, and went first to the dining room and then the play room with its pool table and the giant television on which she and her father would contest whatever video games she could convince him to play.

Upstairs, then. Her old room, with its comforting barrage of colour and eleven-year-old posters. Two spare bedrooms. Both empty. The bathroom, as with the rooms in use downstairs, was untidy. The whole house could have used a sweeping and vacuuming, layers of dust everywhere she looked.

The door to her parents' bedroom. She steeled herself for it, grabbed the handle and pushed. The bed was unmade. A deep laundry basket in the corner was overflowing. There was nobody here – sleeping or otherwise. 'So where the hell are you?' she said.

The last room upstairs was her father's office. His computer would be inside. Daniel Harker didn't own a laptop, preferring to be chained to an office rather than make everywhere his workplace. Annabel understood the reasoning. For her, leaving the office didn't mean leaving work. Her job was with her wherever she went. It usually struck her as liberating, but she would admit there were times when it was simply oppressive.

Annabel hoped to be able to find all his contacts there, and then she could start calling around, just as soon as she was sure she hadn't missed something obvious – a note, perhaps, pinned up or fallen to the floor. Perhaps his emails would reveal something.

She went into the office and bent under the plain pine desk his monitor and keyboard sat on, finger poised to switch on the machine. She froze, confused for a moment. The computer wasn't there, just unplugged leads and indentations on the carpet.

She noticed the state of the desk, uncharacteristically empty – computer monitor, lamp and a desk tidy. Then she noticed *behind* the desk, where her father had a cork board, normally covered in scraps of paper – notes for his work. Apart from a scattering of map pins, the board was bare.

She checked drawers. Several reams of unopened printer paper in one. The others empty. His desk had been cleared out. The fear in her chest was limbering up and turning toward panic. Something was wrong. Part of her had known it for hours.

Call the police, she told herself, but the thought felt like giving in to the fear. *Call someone else first. Someone he knows. They'll have an idea where he might be.*

She went downstairs and grabbed the phone handset from its cradle. It was flashing: messages. The absurd thought hit her that one might be from her father. She studied the handset to see how to play the messages back, terrified of deleting them, but at last she managed to start them playing.

There were fourteen calls. They were all from her. She paced as she listened to each one, hearing her own voice, first when it was untroubled, then as it changed, getting more and more annoyed, then angry.

There was nothing new here.

She swore and slammed the handset onto the kitchen table, horror-struck as it skittered across and fell off the other side, hitting the floor. It cracked apart and spilled its battery pack. Hand over mouth, she got on her knees and picked it up. It was still functional. Damaged, but functional. She sympathized.

Annabel felt her strength drain. She placed the sorry handset on the table and sat heavily on one of the four wooden chairs. She was light-headed. Allowing herself a moment, she closed her eyes and breathed deeply. She felt in free fall, adrenaline making everything spin and shake – ground, hands, thoughts. She reached for the phone again, then set it back down as if it were hot. Calling the police would crystallize everything, make it *real*.

Where was he?

Another thought struck her: his car. Leaving the phone on the table, she ran out the front door. She had no key for the locked double garage, but around the side was a window, hemmed in by hawthorn and holly bushes. She shimmied along the narrow gap, ignoring the scratches she was suffering, until she reached the window. Inside under a sheet was her mom's one extravagance, a red Porsche Boxster, which her dad had kept even though he didn't drive it. He always opted for Sensible Cars, but there was a space beside the Porsche where her father's Volvo should have been.

Images hit her of the car, tangled and burning. *Come on*, she told herself. She had her mother's strengths, she didn't fall apart. *Wherever you went*, she thought, *whatever made you want to get away. Just be safe. Be safe so I can shout at you, and call you a selfish old bastard, and you can hug me and tell me you're sorry. Be safe so I can forgive you.*

Back inside the house, it took four minutes for her to settle herself. When the threat of tears had gone for the time being, she realized how thirsty she was. She went to the kitchen and took a glass from the pile of clean dishes in the drainer. As she was filling the glass she saw something and froze.

On the window ledge in front of the sink, between a dying pot of basil and a Christmas cactus, was her father's wedding ring. He had taken it off to wash those dishes and hadn't put it back on.

He wouldn't have left without that. He had lost it once, the year after her mother died. Its loss, although brief, had devastated him. It had finally turned up in the money tray of his car. Since then he removed it only when he washed up or showered.

He wouldn't have left it here. Annabel picked it up, her fingers shaking. He wouldn't have left it, no matter where he'd gone.

'Oh Christ. Daddy? *Where are you?*' she said, and then tears overwhelmed her.

8

'Hey,' said a voice. 'Good to see you awake.'

Jonah looked to his right, confused, wondering where he was. The voice was that of a female nurse, who was smiling at him. He looked around – a private hospital room, movement visible between the half-closed slats of the blinds on the room's one large window, past the foot of his bed. He had a strong feeling of déjà vu but couldn't place it. He'd last been in hospital when he'd had his breakdown, but it wasn't that.

The nurse took the chart hanging from his bed and wrote something in it. 'How are you feeling?' she asked, without looking up.

Jonah started to speak, then had to clear his throat. 'I'm not sure.' He groped for some context: any recent memory, anything at all, and the only image that came to mind was of a beach and blue sky. 'What happened? I don't remember why I'm here.'

The nurse gave him a kind look and avoided the question. 'I'll get Dr Connelly to come and speak to you as soon as he can. You hungry?'

Jonah had a flash of himself being sick in a stranger's toilet. 'No,' he said, trying to hold the memory, unpleasant as it was. Hold it, extend it. Work out what had gone on.

The nurse nodded and replaced the chart. 'Well, buzz if you need anything.'

She left, and Jonah tried to sit up. As he did, a tug on his arm made him notice the drip they'd hooked him up to. With a sudden shock, he realized they'd catheterized him as well.

He thought, hard; piecemeal, the Nikki Wood case came back to him. Incomplete, but enough for him to understand he was in trouble. He felt himself shrivel inside when he recalled attacking the man he'd seen. What the hell had made him do that?

Remnants. It had been remnants, leaving him confused. There was something else, something important, but the specifics evaded him.

'Shit,' he said. First, the delusion and hallucinations at Alice Decker's revival. Now, a simple case of remnants and a flash of paranoia had led him to assault a member of the public. Sam would certainly ground him until he could be given an all-clear.

He sighed.

The feeling of déjà vu he'd had on waking hit him again, and he struggled to understand why. Then it came: he'd woken alone in a private hospital room after his mother's death, fourteen years old, traumatized from the accident and utterly disoriented. The first person he'd seen that time had been his stepfather, walking in and bringing it all back, drenching Jonah in horror and panic.

The memory made him shiver. Not good times; not good times at all. For an instant he expected his stepfather to walk through the door again, that cold face torn between duty and revulsion, with the reserved anger that Jonah had spent four subsequent years living with.

The day after he'd woken that time, he had been visited by another man. Jonah had found himself liking him instantly; the first kind face he had seen since he'd woken, the first eyes that had met his without disapproval or fear.

The man introduced himself. 'My name is Dr Sam Deering, Jonah. I'm here to talk to you about what happened.' It seemed to Jonah that Dr Deering was nervous. A long time later, Sam would confess: every other senior researcher in Baseline had dodged the unenviable task of talking to this boy, Sam the only one who had accepted, however uncomfortable it would be.

'I've brought some people with me,' Dr Deering said. 'Is that all right?'

Jonah nodded. Dr Deering motioned with his hand, and in walked a roughly handsome young man whose smile seemed somehow incomplete. Behind him, a young woman, with short auburn hair and eyes he found hard to look away from.

'This is Will Barlow,' said Dr Deering. 'And this is Tess Neil. They're revivers. You've heard of revival, Jonah?'

Jonah gave him a look and raised an eyebrow. Everyone in the *world* had heard of revival, and he had spent the previous twenty-four hours thinking of nothing else. He smiled nervously at the revivers. Tess Neil returned the smile. Will Barlow returned half of it.

'Can I shake your hand?' asked Barlow. Jonah didn't yet understand what chill was, not really – he'd heard of it in articles he'd read on revival, but his impression of it was of a gentle sensation, some kind of tingle. It wouldn't take him long before he understood and grew wary of physical contact, but for now, bemused, Jonah held out his own hand without a pause and shook the hand of Will Barlow. Reviver to reviver, there was no chill, of course. There *was* a sensation, though – a curious sense of recognition.

Will Barlow looked at Dr Deering and nodded. 'Very strong,' he said.

The fourteen-year-old Jonah had looked at Will Barlow and wondered why he didn't like the man. Perhaps it was Barlow's uncertain smile. No, he'd thought: there was arrogance there, in his eyes. More than that: cruelty.

Then Jonah had looked at Tess Neil, still smiling at him, and for the first time since his mother had died, he had felt hope.

*

The door opened and a lanky male doctor came in alone, shutting the door behind him and grabbing Jonah's chart off the foot of the bed.

'Hi, Jonah,' he said. 'Dr Connelly. Glad to have you with us. I've been asked not to discuss your situation in depth, I'm afraid. Dr Deering wants to speak to you directly, he's on his way.' Connelly glanced at the charts, then looked up. 'I think we can have the drip out now.'

Jonah's eyes darted to the doctor's hands – ungloved. The doctor saw the glance. 'Don't worry, Jonah. It didn't take us long to work out who had – uh – chill, isn't it?' Jonah nodded, and Connelly smiled. 'Some things can be done with thicker gloves on, but some,' he said, as he removed the needle, 'need a little more delicacy.'

'And the catheter, please,' Jonah said. 'Before I noticed it, it wasn't a problem. Now it just feels *very* strange.'

The doctor smiled again as he placed a plaster over the needle mark on Jonah's arm. 'I can imagine. I'll send a nurse in when I'm done.'

There was one question Jonah had been desperate to ask since waking. 'How long have I been here, Doctor?' *How long do you have to be unconscious to need a drip and a catheter?*

Dr Connelly's smile faded. 'How do you feel? Rested?'

'To be honest, yes. I ache a little all over, but yes.'

'Good. You've been out for over two days. When you arrived, we thought you might actually be in a coma. Turned out to be exhaustion. Deepest sleeper I've ever seen.' Connelly leaned closer and smiled. 'You were tired.'

Jonah laughed nervously. 'I was tired. Right.' The doctor clearly didn't know the rest; the assault, for one. 'So it's . . . uh . . . Monday?'

'Sunday. Now, I was told you're not hungry, but I'd like it if you ate something. No reason why you shouldn't, and every reason why you should. Any chance I can convince you?' Jonah was about to decline again, when his stomach spoke up; a loud gurgle that broadened the doctor's smile. 'Good. I'll have something brought in. Dr Deering should be here within the hour.' He left Jonah to his thoughts.

*

Those thoughts turned to the time he'd finally been allowed to join Baseline. After meeting Sam, Will and Tess, he'd been invited to visit the facility every few months, but only for counselling. It was a two-hour journey to the ramshackle collection of buildings that Baseline consisted of, a bizarre mixture of decrepit and new buildings, which all had an inescapable greyness. The transcending purpose of this place – the search for what revival was, and for what lay beyond death – was at odds with the bland and grubby surroundings. He'd expected polished steel and glass, not all this worn concrete.

Jonah met none of the other revivers on those trips. It had still been too raw, too difficult. He'd found himself isolated at his school, even though no one there knew anything about what had really happened. But the other kids sensed something different about him. It was the chill, growing in strength; he avoided contact all he could. He became good at it.

Then, the month before he turned seventeen, he was invited to join Baseline as a reviver. That first, accidental revival of his mother was burned so deeply into his mind that he found himself dreading the thought of doing it again. Yet he knew he also wanted to discover more about this curious magic, this necromancy. He wanted to know what he was, and if this was the only way, so be it.

Jonah was introduced to the revivers that morning. He found it overwhelming, so many people shaking his hand, genuinely pleased to meet him. In the middle of this, he started crying openly, covering his face and unable to stop. Someone took charge and guided him out of the room for a little privacy.

He pulled his hands from his face and wiped at the tears,

finding himself in a small kitchen area: kettle, sink and microwave, and a few chairs. A handkerchief was put in his hand, and he blew his streaming nose.

'Come on,' said a woman's voice. 'It's good to let it out.'

Jonah looked up. 'I guess I'm not used to so many people,' he said, stumbling through his words as he recognized her. Tess Neil. He'd not seen her since that day in hospital.

Tess nodded and smiled and Jonah smiled back, realizing how beautiful she looked, and so much older than him, maybe mid-twenties; the thoughts of a sixteen-year-old boy filled his head and threatened to swamp everything else. He tried to ignore them.

'My name's Tess. We met before.' She held out her hand.

Jonah shook it. 'I remember.' There was warmth to the touch, and the same feeling of recognition he had had with Will Barlow, but most of all he felt an electricity. And it was nothing to do with revival.

He found himself staring at her lips.

She chuckled a little – kindly, he hoped – then let go of his hand and sat him in a chair. 'Coffee?'

Jonah nodded, sniffling and wiping the tears away. 'Two sugars,' he said.

'We all know who you are, by the way. Your . . . story.' Jonah's eyes widened, nervous. 'Don't worry, I didn't mean it to sound like a bad thing. You're among friends now. You'll like it here.'

'I hope so.' He blew his nose again.

Tess came over with two mugs and handed one to Jonah. She sat beside him. He could smell her perfume, subtle and glorious.

'Keep the hankie,' Tess said, smiling. Jonah laughed, and felt better for it. 'So, are you sure you're ready for all this?'

'I've been in counselling for long enough,' Jonah said. 'I must be. *Apart* from the crying, I guess . . .' With a nervous grin, he took a sip of his coffee. 'Strange thing is, I pushed for it. Every week, I called or wrote. Now that it's happened I don't know how to feel. I think I wanted to be here so I could *belong*. That's pretty stupid, huh?'

'Not at all.'

He smiled at her again, sheepish. 'How were you, when you started? How did they find you?'

'Most of us were found in sweeps,' she said. 'I knew, myself. Things that Eleanor Preston had said in her book struck me in ways they didn't strike others. I turned up because I knew what I am, and there were all these other people who just wanted the money that the work could bring. One by one they'd be tested, and they'd leave disappointed. Then it was just me.'

Jonah was lost in her. He was staring at her mouth again. He wanted to kiss her. He felt like an idiot. He tried to douse himself, tried to shake it off.

Tess continued. 'They showed me into a room. It was Will doing the first-round tests, the chill tests. He's a nice guy, best reviver here. And he knows it!' She laughed. Jonah tried to ignore the fact she'd called Will Barlow a nice guy. He could still remember that gut feeling he'd had about the man. 'Everyone that morning had had chill. And when I went in, Will just said, "Yeah, you're one of us." Before he even took my hand. Like that, like there was no question. I haven't met anyone since who could tell that easily. Then we shook hands and . . . well. Then I really knew for sure.'

Jonah smiled and nodded. He blew his nose again, acutely aware of the thick, wet sound it made, and of how sodden the hankie was now. 'Were you scared?' he asked.

'It's OK to be scared.'

Jonah said nothing, nodding. He felt tears prick his eyes again.

Tess Neil put her arm around his shoulder and smiled at him. 'You'll be fine, Jonah. We'll look after you.'

And as she had smiled, he had felt the warmth of that smile flood him. It had buoyed him up for the day, and for the week, as he had listened to what he was taught, as he had observed the dead come back to a kind of brief life.

As he had learned what he was.

*

Sam Deering finally arrived as Jonah was finishing the dinner Dr Connelly had sent him.

'Hey,' Sam said, a broad smile that showed genuine relief.

Jonah looked up, his mouth full of dessert. He hurried to swallow. 'Cookie dough ice cream, Sam. Just the thing for a not-quite coma.'

Sam pulled over a chair and sat. 'How are you feeling?'

'I'm sorry. I fucked up.'

Sam frowned. 'Damn right you did. I can't believe you took the case at all after what I'd said. There was no need. Jason could have done it, and nothing came up the rest of the day.'

'You weren't too hard on Never, though? I talked him into it.'

'I was disappointed, Jonah. I'd asked him to watch you, for exactly this reason. I know *you*' – he prodded Jonah's arm – '‘don't know what's good for you.'

Jonah lowered his voice. 'The man I attacked . . . is he, uh, pressing charges or anything?'

Sam looked away as he replied. 'After they pulled you off him, Bob Crenner took the man away for a few words.'

'To talk him out of it?'

'No. To talk to him about Nikki Wood. What do you think happened, Jonah? How much do you remember?'

'I'm still hazy . . . I can remember bits here and there.' He thought about it for a moment – there was more, he knew, just out of reach, but it still wasn't coming. 'I think I had remnants. It just overwhelmed me.'

'It was too soon for remnants, Jonah. You'd only just finished the revival.'

'What, then?'

'You thought you recognized his shoes – that was what you were shouting about. Do you know why?'

'I can't remember. Not for certain. But it felt like remnants, Sam. It was swamping me . . .' He stopped. 'And that doesn't explain the attack.'

'It was like Alice Decker, Jonah. Symptoms of burnout. Hallu-cination, severe fatigue. Anything could have been going on in your head.'

'So the man's not pressing charges?'

Sam shook his head. 'Bob played a hunch. He interviewed the man. They examined his shoes. They found glass particles that matched the glass at the scene.'

Jonah was staring. 'And?'

'The guy confessed. Took Crenner to the jewellery he'd stolen.'

Jonah's mind swirled. 'What does that mean?'

'You probably saw the shoes in the surge, that's all.'

Then something else came to Jonah: 'Nikki hadn't seen his face, hadn't mentioned his shoes during the revival. It must have been a remnant memory, Sam. What else could it have been?' Things kept getting worse.

'It's unheard of, for it to happen so quickly.'

Jonah was looking at a month of leave, then assessment, and eventually another round of tests to improve his medication. 'I recognized the shoes,' he said, more details coming back to him. 'His cough, too, and then his shoes. But it wasn't just recall, Sam, it was more intrusive, like a . . .'

And then he fully remembered what it had been like, how it had felt when he'd attacked the man. Jonah looked Sam in the eye and remembered that strange sensation, of being outside himself, watching; and his certainty that somehow Nikki Wood had stayed with him. Not just memories or images overpowering his thought, the way remnants were supposed to occur. She'd been present, and worse – in control. *She'd forgotten about the shoes*, he thought. *She only remembered when she saw them again.*

'Jonah?' There was a flicker of something on Sam's face, some-thing that worried Jonah. He was already facing weeks away from revivals. If he told Sam the truth, how long would he have to wait?

Would he even be allowed back?

'I think I need to see Jennifer Early again.'

'You need to rest up, come back fresh. Put all this out of your thoughts. I want you to stay in the hospital until tomorrow, then two more weeks away from work. I've arranged for you to see Stephanie Graves on Friday. She's the nearest thing there is to an expert in remnants, and if there's even a chance that's what you had, we have to look into it.'

Stephanie Graves had been the senior Baseline medical doctor. When Baseline shut down, she'd continued in a university research position; very rarely FRS staff would be referred to her.

'Pricey,' said Jonah. He smiled.

'She'll see that you're fine. And you can tell her whatever it is you won't tell me.'

Jonah's cheeks reddened. Sam could read him too well.

Sam continued: 'She'll have to give you the all-clear before you start revivals again. I'm gone in a week and a half, and I don't want Hugo being talked into letting you back for any revivals until Stephanie says so.'

'Sam, I—'

'No *argument*, Jonah. You've shown you can't be trusted to look after yourself. Now, as I said, you have to stay here overnight. I haven't told Never you're awake yet. He would've beaten me here. He can visit tomorrow and help you home.'

'I'll be glad to get out,' Jonah replied, then added: 'Sam?'

'Yes?'

Part of Jonah wanted to tell him the truth. The part that was scared: scared by the knowledge that it hadn't been him that had attacked that man. It had been Nikki Wood, and all Jonah could do was watch.

'Nothing,' he said instead. Sam would explain it away as hallucination or delusion; Jonah knew it was more than that.

After Sam left, Jonah lay back and thought about his other recent delusion: about Alice Decker, and where *that* truth lay.

9

Come morning, he woke with a persistent noise that intruded into his mind before sleep had fully left him. High-pitched tones, short sounds that were familiar. He opened his eyes.

'It's about bloody time you woke up,' said Never from his left. Jonah turned his head to see Never playing on a handheld console, the source of the bleeps. Jabbing at it, Never paused his game, then looked up and grinned when he saw Jonah's bleary face. He reached to one side, picked up a tiny US flag and waggled it. 'Happy Fourth of July. How are we this morning?'

Jonah sat up and gave the question some real thought. 'I think I'm fine. Maybe going insane, but fine. Did Sam tell you anything?'

'He told me Bob and Ray got their man. He said you must have seen something in the surge, enough for you to recognize the guy. The stress of the revival and your chronic overwork led to the attack. Makes sense.'

'I don't . . .' started Jonah. Then he paused, not wanting to put Never in an awkward spot. 'I guess it does. Sam's making me stay off work for two weeks, and off revivals until I get approval from Stephanie Graves.'

At the name, Never raised his eyebrows. 'Right,' he managed.

'It'll be fine,' said Jonah, suddenly uneasy – Never Geary being lost for words was unnerving. The situation was serious, and Never clearly knew. 'I'd rather not talk about it.'

'Whatever you want, mate,' said Never. 'Look, uh . . . Bob Crenner's invited us out for a drink the night after tomorrow if you're up for it. We're meeting halfway, that ex-cop's place in Stafford. He wants to celebrate the result, but only if you can be there too.'

Jonah's face screwed up. 'That's not such a great idea.'

'Oh, go on. You're not forbidden from having a drink. I asked.'

'You *asked*?'

'I wanted to pre-empt excuses. Your doctor said it'd be good for you to get out. You can have one drink. Two at a push. And I'll drive.'

'They'll be talking about the case, Never. I don't want to.'

'I'll take that as a yes. You're allowed home at noon.' He waggled the flag again and handed it over. 'In case you're desperate to get celebrating independence.'

'I want to go home, shut the door and have a shower. You celebrate for me.'

'I'll do my best. Meantime, we've got an hour to kill. Game?' He reached into a bag on the floor and pulled out a second console. Jonah realized it was his.

'You went into my apartment?'

'I did,' said Never. 'Your cat's fine, by the way.'

Jonah swore. He'd forgotten about his cat, Marmite. The animal had been a gift from Sam after he'd recovered from his breakdown two years before. The name had come from Never. When Jonah had seen the cat, he'd refused point blank to accept it, so Never had called it Marmite. 'You hate it now but you'll love it in the end,' he'd said. Jonah had had to Google it.

He had resented the idea that was so clearly behind the gift – to give him a focus and some responsibility, and stop him from trying to do anything similar again. Even so, he had warmed to Marmite the cat. It had crapped in Never's lap that first day, so warming to it hadn't proved hard.

'Your milk was off too,' continued Never. 'And the heat's made the dishes in your sink go rancid. I would've washed them but I had to find a bag and grab you some clothes. Now,' he said, hurling the console at his friend. 'Pick your game.'

*

Jonah had to admit it, he felt good as he walked into the sunshine, a welcome fresh breeze taking the ferocity out of the heat. The rest had been long overdue, and he was full of energy.

He wanted time on his own, though, and Never understood, seeing him into a taxi and making him promise to call later that day and let him know how he was doing.

The taxi to his apartment building passed the FRS office on the way. His apartment was only a ten-minute walk from it, the proximity being one of the reasons he lived where he did – that, and the level of privacy he had there, top floor of a six-floor building, nobody above him and quiet neighbours.

He bounded up the stairs to his front door. Inside, his apartment was suspiciously tidy.

In the kitchen, the dishes were done, a fresh quart of milk in the fridge. 'Sometimes, Never Geary, you surprise me,' he mumbled with a smile.

He dumped his bag on the sofa beside his sleeping cat, then turned on the television, flicking between the coverage of the July Fourth celebrations.

He switched off his brain and let them get on with it.

*

Jonah and Never arrived twenty minutes after the time they'd been told, at the small bar in Stafford that Bob Crenner had chosen for the sole reason – according to Never – that he knew one of the owners, an ex-detective from Philadelphia who had a habit of getting drunk and doling out free drinks to fellow law enforcers. Jonah looked around and approved of the place. It was quiet.

He spotted Bob Crenner and seven others, seeing Nala George at the far corner of the two tables they had pushed together.

Crenner nodded in greeting, and Jonah waved and pointed to the bar.

'I'll get them in,' Never told him. 'You go sit.' The look in his eye made it clear he was kidding. He knew better than anyone where Jonah's comfort zone was.

'I'll wait.'

When they ordered, the barman told them their drinks were on Bob Crenner. They took the spare seats beside Crenner and Ray Johnson at the end of the table nearest the bar.

'Jonah!' said Crenner. 'Glad you could make it.'

'Well, Never said you'd not do it without me.'

A sly smile crept onto Crenner's face. 'It got you here!' He raised his glass and his voice. 'Everyone, to Jonah. A good day's work. Cheers!'

All the others raised their glasses. Jonah could feel his cheeks redden and his smile stalling. He was relieved that conversations started up quickly.

Bob Crenner clinked his glass against Jonah's. 'We were all worried about you,' he said. 'I figured I at least owed you a drink for what you did.'

'No problem, Bob. Strangling bystanders is all part of the service. Lucky he was the right guy.'

Bob smiled. 'No luck in it.' He lowered his voice. 'That kind of thing happen often?'

Jonah met his eyes and grimaced. 'First time for me. But they've taken me off revivals for a while. Overworked.'

'Yeah,' Ray Johnson chipped in. 'Tell me about it.'

'Not quite the same, Ray,' said Bob.

Jonah took a drink. 'I owe you. If you hadn't questioned him . . .'

'We'd have missed him, and you'd be up on aggravated assault and suspended?' Jonah nodded, with a nervous laugh, and Bob laughed back. 'All part of *my* service. But I wasn't psychic. You should've seen his face when we pulled you away from him. He was ready to give it up. The guy was *sweating* guilt. He'd been planning on stealing the jewellery, making it look like a burglar got lucky, messing the place up as quietly as he could.'

Ray Johnson stepped in, eager to tell. 'Nikki was an accident. He hadn't realized she was badly injured until he was leaving. He broke the glass to raise the alarm. Fucking obscene, really, prick like that fucks up and a girl dies.' Ray paused, shaking his head. 'Bob implied the glass particles on his shoes would be enough on its own, but the guy was assuming he'd been named in the revival. We told him we couldn't comment on that. Made the man think it was his last chance to get it off his chest, make it clear it was an accident. He bit.'

Jonah thought of Nikki. The pointlessness of it; her death was a stupid mistake, by a fool who had given himself away by trying to help her, but had left it too late.

'Did he know the family?' asked Never.

'He lived on the street,' said Bob. 'Knew them in passing.'

Jonah waited to see if there was any sign of Nikki Wood in his head, but there was nothing. He looked at Bob. 'What are they charging him with?'

'They could argue felony murder and go for first degree, but I think he'll plea bargain for second.'

The four men were silent, reflecting.

'A result, all the same,' said Bob. 'Cheers.' He lifted his glass.

*

Jonah sipped at his drink, listening to Bob and his colleagues exchange stories of earlier cases they'd been on. They didn't talk any more about the Nikki Wood case, and for that he was grateful.

He returned from a rest-room trip to find Never waiting for him by the bar, Coke in one hand, beer in the other.

'You're driving,' said Jonah.

'This is for you,' said Never, handing over the beer. 'It's good to see a smile on your face. Thought I'd keep it there awhile longer. You're normally such a miserable fucker.'

Jonah smiled, welcoming the drink. 'What would my doctor say?'

'He'd say you're a miserable fucker too. Now, uh, Jonah . . . you notice that the lovely Miss George is here?'

Jonah guessed his meaning. He shook his head. 'No. I could feel the chill when she put a hand on my shoulder last week. Shirt and overalls in the way, so she didn't notice, but I could tell. It'd be pretty strong.'

'Sorry. Uh . . . you OK if I . . . ?'

'If you want a shot, be my guest.'

Grinning, Never slapped his hand on Jonah's back. '*You* are a good, good friend.'

Jonah said nothing in reply. *You too.*

As they sat, Ray Johnson pointed out Never's Coke. 'Designated driver?' Ray asked.

Never laughed, seeing Ray's orange juice. 'Snap. Been driving all day, feels like. Onsite in Elizabeth City. Five-hour round trip and we were there for two hours. Apparent suicide, a well-off old guy found hanged in woodland.'

'Genuine?' asked Ray. About one in eight suicides was revived, a deterrent both to the suicidal and to those thinking about passing off murder as one.

'Oh aye,' said Never, giving him a weary look. 'Deeply fucked off that he'd been brought back, and in no way *helpful*, but definitely a genuine suicide.'

'Jesus,' said Ray. 'You guys must have some tales to tell.'

'Nikki Wood was your second revival, right?' Never said.

Ray nodded. 'Second as detective. Third I ever witnessed. Just over a year before I made detective, I was first on scene at a homicide near Motts Run Reservoir, body dumped in haste. The head had been partially hacked off at the scene, an obvious attempt to prevent revival, but they'd been interrupted. There was blood everywhere. I stayed to help with scene control as the better-paid took over.' He got a groan from the other detectives around the table. 'I ended up chatting with the liaison officer the forensic revivers had sent out to assess the situation. The officer had said it was a long shot, and she was right – it proved *too* long in the end. I watched, and it was pretty grim. All that goddamn *blood*, but no luck. Even so, they had an ID soon enough. The killers had been so worried about taking the victim's *head* off they hadn't searched his pockets thoroughly. His driver's licence was there.' He waited for the laughter to die down. 'It was only four days before I heard they'd found their guys, and in the end it was the mess of blood that had guaranteed conviction. Traces in their car, clothes, everywhere. Even the ones who think they know what to do get it wrong, and thank God for that.'

Across the table, Nala George nodded to Jonah and Never. 'We've been sharing ours, you two must have some. What's the strangest case you've had?'

Jonah and Never shared a look. 'Suggestions?' he asked Never, trying to pass the baton.

'Shit, man. You worked in Baseline. There was some pretty bizarre stuff there.'

The others were suitably impressed by mention of his Baseline past, and Jonah had just enough alcohol in his bloodstream. What to tell? There were plenty of revivals that stuck in Jonah's mind, not least that twisted wreck of a car, when he'd had to bring the unseen subject back by reaching into the wreckage. But that was too raw. Something else. 'OK, OK. Since you mentioned your case, Ray, with the head partially hacked off. Early on, they didn't know much, and things were limited to whatever bodies happened to find their way to us, but once the forensic research kicked off they were trying *everything*. I did a *head* once. Seriously. I mean, now we know that total decapitation rules revival out, whatever you do after. Nobody has any idea why, but nobody really knows what the hell revival is anyway. Back then, they were trying to see where the line was, and they had varying test subjects with different amounts and types of connective tissue still attached between head and body. They thought something interesting might come out of it if they could narrow it down. So one of mine was a head. On its own.' He took a drink and looked around at the grossed-out faces. 'And I sat there and I reached out a hand. I mean, what the hell do you do? Grab an ear? I cupped this corpse's cheek and began. I concentrated.' He lowered his voice, putting on as serious an expression as he could muster. The others stopped smiling, listening in silence. 'There wasn't a sound, everyone just watching, waiting to see if this corpse-head's eyes would flicker open. And five minutes later . . .'

He let them stew for a few seconds.

'What happened?' said Nala.

'I burst out laughing. And it was contagious. Everyone in the room was on the floor. End of revival attempt.'

In the middle of a laugh, Ray caught himself and frowned. 'That's pretty sick.' Then he started laughing again.

'Like Never said, Baseline did some bizarre things.'

'Another!' said Ray.

Jonah finished his beer and held it up. 'A story for a drink,' he said.

'Fair enough,' said Ray.

'I warn you,' said Never. 'He normally says fuck all, but if you get him drinking you can't shut him up.'

While Ray went to the bar, Jonah considered what story he would go with. He settled on the revival of Lyssa Underwood, another case at Baseline where they were trying to push limits. Fresh beer in hand, he began: 'I'd been requested for a project at short notice, no information about its nature, but that wasn't unusual. In Baseline most of the revivers weren't permanently affiliated with a specific project, and things came up at short notice sometimes. But when I went in I didn't recognize any of the project staff, and the unfamiliar faces made me uneasy. Then I saw the subject. A young woman, in her late twenties. Rare in Baseline, the norm was older, terminal patients willing to take part in exchange for improved care in their last weeks, and money for their families. But it was what surrounded her that gave me the creeps.

'Her body was on the usual gurney. On one side was equipment that resembled a dialysis machine, clear liquid with a hint of green and blue running through spinning components and emerging through tubes which fed into the body at multiple entry sites – neck, arms, chest. A soft mechanical whirr came from the machine, but there was another sound too, the thing I found the most unnerving. A regular, driving beat.

'The machine had a pulse.

'They explained that it was all about preservation. Reduction of rigor, improving revival chances. Pump the blood out, switch in a synthetic version. They hadn't had any success, but then they hadn't come to me before.' Jonah grinned and got an uneasy laugh. 'We started, and to begin with it was tough. At last I figured it, and in the end it was easy, like realizing that a door says *push* when you're trying to pull.'

He thought back to the moment he'd sensed Lyssa Underwood. She had still seemed distant, which had struck him as odd. 'They were working with scripted questions, so the researcher would call out a number and I would read out the question. Right from the start she seemed confused, and there was a terrible loneliness. Question 1, they said, and I asked for her name. All she said in reply was: *The cities are burning*. Question 2, and I asked her when her birthday was. She replied: *The shadow is falling*.

'Every question, she said the same kind of thing. "The cities are burning." "The shadow is falling." There was no hint of evasion or lying, but her confusion was considerable. I started to ask her if she understood what was happening, but the researchers ordered me to stick to their questions.

'The final question was the one that I remember most. I thought, *Why the hell would they include something like that?* The question was: Why are you frightened? She said nothing for a while, then she gave her answer. *The cities are burning. The shadow has come. Everything dies.* After that they stopped the revival. They looked as baffled as I was.'

'What the hell had happened?' Nala asked. Jonah looked at her, realizing how unnerved she was.

'Sometimes they come back confused. I'm more used to that now, but like I said, in Baseline the subjects were typically terminal patients, well prepared before they died. This one can't have been prepared at all. Something about the preservation techniques must have exacerbated it, because it was more than simple confusion. The answers she gave made no sense. Whether they kept trying with the project, I don't know, but put it this way: you'll have noticed that we don't *use* those techniques. I can remember how lonely she felt. Isolated and bewildered.'

He looked at the faces around him, seeing the same deep unease he felt himself. He suddenly regretted the story. He'd run with it because it had always been the moment that had creeped him out most of all, but he'd misjudged. It was too solemn, too dour, not the simple campfire creepiness they'd wanted. That wasn't the only reason he regretted bringing it up. It had been a stressful time in Baseline, with upheaval and controversy that he didn't want to think about. Bad choice.

He looked at Never. 'Your turn,' he said. 'Something more fun, I think.'

Ray spoke up. 'First things first, Never. Why the name? Is it Irish?'

Jonah and Never both grinned at that.

'It's how often he's quiet,' said Jonah.

'Shut *up*,' Never said. 'Ignore him. It's how often my equipment fails.' Ray and Nala shared a look, then both started laughing. 'That's not what I meant,' Never said, defensive, looking to Jonah for backup.

Jonah shrugged, smiling. Although Never had a dozen different explanations of how he'd got the name, Jonah knew this one was the truth. Back when the FRS was just starting up, he'd been plain old Rob Geary. The revival recording equipment design team he was part of had been given an acceptable failure rate of one in a thousand revivals. Rob Geary had campaigned so hard for a rate of *never* that he'd ended up being named after it.

'Tell them a story, Never,' Jonah said, and Never reeled off his favourites.

The stories continued, and Never moved seats to be beside Nala, who was obviously fascinated by the topic and wanted to hear more. Jonah listened to the others but kept an eye on his friend, wishing him luck as he kept her laughing and shocked in equal measure.

At ten-thirty, Ray stood. 'Sorry, guys, I have to get going. Early start.'

Groans came from around the table, and those depending on Ray for their ride began gathering their stuff. That included Nala George. Never caught Jonah's eye and shrugged. Jonah raised his eyebrows as a question, but Never gave a small shake of his head. *Didn't get anywhere.*

Nala stood and made her way around the table. She stopped at Jonah and crouched to his level. Jonah tensed.

'I wanted to say thank you,' she said. 'The way you treated the parents . . . It let them get through it.' She nodded towards Never. 'He told me how some of your colleagues would've handled it. Doesn't bear thinking about. Anyway, thank you.'

Jonah assumed Never had been talking about Jason Shepperton, hopefully not by name. He opened his mouth to reply; the distraction of thinking what to say made him fail to see it coming.

Too late, Never saw what was about to happen. 'Don't . . . !' he called, raising a hand.

By then Nala had already moved her head over just a little, to give Jonah a peck on the cheek.

A friendly kiss, a kiss of gratitude. The chill Jonah felt was immediate and intense: an agonizing cold, a strong taint of death. He jerked his head back, then turned. Nala was staring at him, horrified, her eyes wide and wet. She'd not experienced it before, and would have felt it even more acutely than Jonah had.

'Oh Jesus . . .' she said. 'I didn't . . . I didn't know . . .' Then she started rubbing at her lips, fear in her eyes; Jonah's face crumbled, and she stood and backed away, trembling.

She hadn't known. Some people just didn't. Didn't understand it wasn't only contact with a reviver's hand that gave chill. Didn't realize how severe it could be.

Jonah didn't know where to look, and stared down at his drink, aware that the table had fallen silent. He was first to move, heading for the exit, ignoring Never's call.

'Jesus Christ,' Never sighed. He grabbed Ray's arm and nodded to Nala, who had slumped back down into a chair and was staring at the floor, rubbing hard at her lips every few seconds. 'Hang around for another drink, Ray. She needs it.' He turned to Bob Crenner. 'Well, Bob, I gotta go.'

'Will he be OK?' asked Bob, looking at the exit door as it closed behind Jonah.

'He'll be fine,' said Never. 'Occupational hazard.' He hurried through the exit, half expecting Jonah to be wandering off down the street, but he was waiting right outside, so visibly tense he was almost shaking.

They drove back home in silence. When Never pulled the car over by Jonah's apartment building, he put his hand on Jonah's shoulder.

'It's not your fault,' he said. There was no reply. 'It's not your fault,' he repeated.

Jonah looked up slowly. 'I need to get inside.' He wanted to run and hide, to get into his apartment and bolt the door. He was only just managing to hold back.

'Look at me,' said Never. 'Look at me and tell me you'll be OK.'

Jonah heard the worry in his voice. He looked at Never. 'I'll be OK. Please, I'll be OK. I'll give you a call tomorrow.'

'Deal. But call before noon, or I'll be round to check up on you.'

Jonah smiled a broken smile and got out of the car, feeling cold in spite of the hot summer night. He buttoned his jacket and headed for the door to safety.

*

Jonah opened his fridge and reached in for a beer, cursing when he realized there was none. He'd had four already in the bar, but he wasn't in the mood to be sensible. He looked over his options: vodka, Jack Daniel's or a bottle of wine Sam had got him for his birthday.

He grabbed a glass and poured himself a strong JD and Coke, then he went into the living room and found an old Karloff movie to watch.

His mind wasn't so easy to settle, though. He thought back to earlier, and his choice of the Underwood revival.

Jonah had walked in for the Underwood session to see a group of people he didn't recognize, except for one unwelcome presence. Will Barlow was there, smiling his fake smile among the unfamiliar lab staff. At the back of the room was a dark-suited man looking both bored and severe, a man he'd seen around before, but as with the lab staff he had no idea who he was.

Jonah was told he was stepping in as Barlow was on a long tail, and their other designated reviver was down with flu. Jonah read the session notes before signing, but it was sparse. Lyssa Underwood. Twenty-nine. Cardiogenic embolism; an underlying health condition had made her high risk.

'What difficulties have you had?' Jonah asked.

'Something about the process makes it tough to even begin,' Barlow said. 'We get nowhere. We don't know why, and until we do we're at a loss how to proceed. Any help you can give would be useful. We'll want you to describe in as much detail as you can what the problems are, as you see them.'

Jonah began the revival attempt. At once, he could sense difficulty, and he struggled to understand what was happening. Five

SETH PATRICK

minutes in, he noticed a resigned look on the man in black. Barlow's smug face had *I knew he'd fail* written all over it.

But then he understood. He recognized the problem, because he'd been here before.

She feels too fresh, he realized. That's why it had been so hard, why they'd had no success. They'd kept her *too* fresh, and the only person that had ever been able to bring them back so soon was . . .

It wasn't coincidence. That was why he was here, surely. The illness of their other reviver was a ruse. Will Barlow probably wasn't even on a long tail.

They had brought Jonah in because of his mother. *Too fresh.*

Most revivers were unable to get anywhere until an hour after death. The official minimum achieved under verifiable conditions was just shy of fifteen minutes. That terrible day, Jonah had done it within four, judging by eyewitness accounts.

Will Barlow had certainly known all about what had happened, and here they were, trying to get him to repeat it. Hoping that their problems with their preservation system were the same ones that made the time after death so important. Hoping that Jonah could point the way for them to follow.

Part of him had wanted to stop and tell them where they could go. But another part – the part that was riled by the look on Will Barlow's face – had wanted to try.

When it was over, Barlow had wanted a full report; Jonah had explained to them what they were doing wrong.

He tried to work out how long ago the Underwood session had been. Probably eight years, the year before he transitioned from Baseline to the FRS. Eighteen years old. It seemed a lifetime ago.

So much had happened since. He'd found his calling, he'd made the first close friend he'd had since he was eight. The incident with Nala George was an unwelcome underscoring of what *hadn't* been happening, though.

Marmite hopped onto his lap and sprawled; Karloff raised shambling zombies among the bamboo.

Jonah kept on drinking.

It wasn't long before thoughts of that mass of contorted metal came to mind; that revival of a subject he hadn't even been able to *see*. It was the thing he always fixated on when drunk and morose.

An idiot in a fast car had lost control one night, crossed the barrier into oncoming traffic and taken out a family in a station wagon before smashing into the support pillars of an overpass. Father, mother and two kids, six and two years old. Their car had gone up in flames. Witnesses had heard the family screaming for minutes, but the fire was so bad they couldn't get to them.

Dominic Pritchard was the man who came up as the owner of the car that had lost control, and was presumably the driver. Either way, whoever had been driving that mangled wreck was obviously dead, their right arm cut off above the elbow and left on the tarmac. Their open-eyed stare was visible through the contorted metal to the crew at the scene with the help of a flashlight, but it was impossible to identify that blood-soaked face. Pritchard, though, was a serial drunk driver, habitual speeder.

But other witnesses had given inconsistent accounts; one, ahead of Pritchard and looking in his rearview mirror, had suggested that a third car had been involved, possibly shunting Pritchard's. The possibility prompted a revival request of the dead father, and it had fallen to Jonah to make the attempt. It failed. Short of decapitation, fire was the most likely scenario to prevent revival. The man had been the least badly burned in the vehicle, but it was still too much, the heat in his hand enough to cause Jonah pain during the attempt.

The attention moved on to the driver in that twisted wreckage.

The paramedics and fire crew had known to leave the body in the vehicle, just in case. As it was, the severe injuries made revival chances very low, but extricating the corpse could have made it impossible.

It was a curious set-up. One camera took in that open-eyed stare, but that was the only angle that captured any of the subject.

Jonah cautiously positioned himself in among the sharp, raw edges, able to get an arm through to take hold of the corpse's shoulder.

An easier death, Jonah thought. Instantaneous, not the long burning the family had gone through. Getting him back proved easy, and the first task was to confirm the man's identity as Dominic Pritchard. Then Jonah asked if another car had been involved. Pritchard took the bait, claiming he wasn't at fault, that there had indeed been another car. That was all that Jonah needed, because he could tell Pritchard was lying. Jonah told him that he might as well come clean. Pritchard refused. They weren't going to get the details, but it was over. Case closed.

It was what happened next that Jonah couldn't forgive himself for.

The observing officer signed the revival off. Pritchard was still there, angry, goading Jonah, yelling that he was an abomination, a liar. Jonah was about to release him, but he paused. He asked the officer and the tech at the case to give him a moment alone. They had assumed he'd let the subject go, that he'd finished. But Jonah hadn't.

The family's car was thirty feet away. When he turned he could see the faces inside it, charred. He'd seen them close up, and knew those faces would stay with him. So no, he hadn't finished. He had things to say to this man.

His hand still ached from the contact with the father. The cooked flesh had been doused, but had still been hot to the touch. Jonah didn't expect there would be any blistering, but the pain served as a reminder.

A reminder of what the man before him had done.

There was no one within earshot. He had his privacy.

Pritchard was silent now, after the outburst a moment before when Jonah had again declared him a liar and the revival had officially concluded. Coming to terms, Jonah thought. The truth of the situation – the futility – sinking in.

'You're dead, Pritchard,' Jonah said, measured and low. Even if someone had been standing right next to him they would have been hard-pressed to make it out, but he knew Pritchard heard. 'And you took a family with you.'

Nothing in reply, but Jonah could sense a denial of responsibility. He longed to show this man just what he had done, show him in a way that could not be avoided.

Thoughts of his stepfather intruded, another man who had been unwilling to accept any blame, shifting attention instead to what had happened after the accident that had killed Jonah's mother. Anger at the supposed desecration of his wife by her son.

'An accident,' said Pritchard. He was fading now, but it was the misery at his own lot that was taking him away. Not the shame of his actions.

'Had you been drinking, Pritchard?'

'No.' Lying.

'You've done this before.'

'Not this.'

'Do you have kids?'

No reply, but a terrible anguish. Then: 'Haven't seen them in a while. I'm . . . I'm . . .'

Jonah thought of the charred corpses in the backseat of the other car: the six-year-old boy hardly recognizable as human, the two-year-old with half his face still barely touched by the flame, his right arm raised for protection.

He felt Pritchard's mind flinch.

Curious, Jonah thought of the younger child once more, picturing him as intensely as he could. Pritchard reacted more strongly.

'Please . . . no . . .'

Jonah's anger was white-hot. He pictured the family, burning, screaming in their metal cage. He pictured the two children, in unspeakable pain, clawing at the flames around them. And he pictured this man, behind the wheel of his car, veering and laughing and not giving a damn.

Pritchard shrivelled away from it, calling out for mercy; in amongst the fear, Jonah could sense shame. Just a hint. Pritchard was finally beginning to understand.

Jonah's anger was undiminished, and now it had its purpose. He poured his horrors out – the scene replayed, over and over, of the parents and the children dying, mixed with the blackest images, the darkest feelings that Jonah had encountered in the revivals he had performed.

He heard Pritchard scream, his heart cold to the man's cries.

It was only when he felt Pritchard fading again that Jonah realized what he was doing. He recoiled from it at last, in horror.

Jonah had let go, stepped away, and then thrown up beside the car.

That had been two years ago, the real trigger for his breakdown. He'd not told anyone what had happened, not even Never, his breakdown blamed on overwork and burnout. Perhaps that did explain his state of mind at the time. Perhaps he had not been himself.

But that was just trying to wriggle out of the guilt he felt. There were things he could pin it on, yes: stress, exhaustion and the way Pritchard's denial had reminded Jonah of his stepfather.

Yet it had still been him, standing there, reaching through the wreckage to grip Pritchard's shoulder. It had been him, terrorizing the dead man.

Since Jonah's first days as a reviver, he had nurtured his ability to bring something positive to his revivals. It was not for him to act as a judge. He saw how little respect some other revivers gave to their subjects, handling everyone like just another job, treating a victim with the same callousness they'd give a killer.

In a matter of weeks, he would be presenting a talk at the International Forensic Revival Symposium. He was calling it 'Respect for the Dead'. In it, he hoped to demonstrate that revivers who adopted a more aggressive stance during a revival showed results that were worse overall than those who took a more respectful approach.

It was about control as much as anything, Jonah thought. As such, it was very similar to emotive feedback – the emotions of the subject, passed to the reviver, amplified and returned, until the revival came to an abrupt end. Control was everything for a reviver, making careful decisions about the best strategy to coax testimony from a subject.

There was no place for retribution. With Pritchard, he had stumbled; he had let himself down badly. States with the death penalty revived all executed inmates, to obtain full and accurate testimony of the crimes committed and to determine if other crimes may not have been confessed. Of course, it was also a test of guilt itself – over 85 per cent had proved guilty, a figure that some governors had considered impressively high – and in the cases where guilt was established, the revivers involved had needed to maintain their professionalism in spite of uniformly appalling crimes and often unrepentant subjects.

Much of the evidence he would use for his presentation came from death row cases, which showed that even when retribution could be considered justified, it was detrimental to the results.

Jonah himself had not performed a death row revival, but he hoped he would be able to show the same professionalism if the need ever arose.

That professionalism meant a lot to him. Especially now, with Dominic Pritchard's screams still ringing in his ears.

10

It was one-thirty the next day when Never called. Voicemail kicked in after five rings, and Never was starting to leave a message when Jonah picked up and answered, his voice croaking.

'Hello, Never.'

'You said you'd call.'

'You woke me.'

'You OK, though?'

Jonah sat up, too hungover to consider himself OK, but that wasn't what Never was driving at. 'Fine.'

'You don't sound great. You didn't keep drinking when you got home, did you?'

'Half a bottle of bourbon. So I'm not *quite* up yet.'

'That's one way to take things easy, but don't mention it to your doctor.'

'Shit.' Jonah rubbed his eyes with the back of his hand. 'I won't if you won't.' He paused. 'Did you hear anything about Nala? Was she all right?'

'Ray Johnson emailed me. She downed a few and they took her home. She's fine, more or less.'

More or less, Jonah thought. Give her a few more days, and maybe she would be.

'You're off to Baltimore to see Stephanie Graves tomorrow, right?' said Never. 'You want me to go with you? I could drive. I'm sure Sam would give me the time off.'

'Thanks, but I'd rather go alone. I'll be OK by tomorrow. And believe me, I'm doing nothing this evening.'

'Look, are you really OK? I was *worried* last night.'

Jonah thought for a moment. 'Yeah. I'm still spooked by the Decker revival, and whatever the hell happened with Nikki Wood, but I'll get a handle on it. I'll feel better after seeing Graves.'

'So what are your plans for the rest of your enforced vacation?'

'I'll read, watch some movies, play some games. Eat. Drink. Lie in the bath.' *Put like that*, he thought, *it doesn't sound too bad.*

'I get the idea. No talking to the dead, then?'

'I'll leave that to all of you. I'm also planning to restrict talking to the *living* to a minimum.'

'I guess you earned it,' said Never. 'But Tuesday night is Sam's retirement bash, so you have a little more conversation to endure before you become a shut-in.'

'I'll be there,' said Jonah, knowing he'd have to show his face at least. It didn't have to be for long, though. *Shut-in.* It carried a certain appeal.

*

'Just stare at the cross, Jonah. Relax.'

He was encased in four tonnes of metal and plastic, being bombarded with a combination of X-rays and intense, high-frequency oscillating magnetic fields while the rapid loud thumping of the machine was hurting his ears. *Of course I'll relax*, he thought.

He lay flat, on thinly padded metal, his skull held in place with a tight-fitting neck brace. When he'd first seen the slab he'd been asked to lie on, he thought of a mortuary table. As he'd been strapped down and pushed into the cramped heart of the medical imager, he thought of a coffin.

'Keep staring at the middle of the cross, Jonah,' said Dr Stephanie Graves. She was trying to reassure him. Directly above Jonah's face was a small screen, a plus sign filling the projected image. He stared.

When Jonah had first come to Baseline, Stephanie Graves had been one of the people he had seen most of. Then, she had been studying the physiology of revivers, attempting to hunt down common biometric traits, seeking the reasons behind the mental and physical toll of revival. She and Sam had been close friends for a while; Jonah knew it had soured, and there had been rumours of an affair, but nothing he'd believed. When Baseline disbanded five years ago, Stephanie Graves had found a position at Johns Hopkins University. She still specialized in revival research, and her expertise in the longer-term health implications made her the doctor of choice for those private revivers who could afford to pay for the use of the imager.

And so here he was, staring at the cross.

'OK, Jonah, don't be alarmed, but the images will begin to change now. They'll flash. Please keep staring at the middle of the cross. If you begin to feel sick, say so.'

'OK.'

The screen began to cycle through a range of colours, the rate of change accelerating gradually. Then each quadrant of the cross began to change independently. He kept staring and began to feel disoriented. His mind became blank, whatever he tried to think about. The flashing became more rapid, and he felt like he was plummeting. His stomach lurched.

'Feeling sick,' he said, and shut his eyes. The sensation of tumbling was extreme. He ground his teeth until it passed. When he opened his eyes again, the screen above him was blank.

'We're bringing you out, Jonah,' said Graves. A minute later he emerged from the imager, and the strapping was removed. Jonah sat up and tried to catch his breath, grateful that it was all finished. Graves came over and smiled. 'You did well,' she said. 'We'll give you a few minutes before the next run.'

Jonah grimaced.

*

After a further forty minutes of testing, their time with the imager came to an end. Jonah was led to a private room and waited while Graves completed her analysis.

When she came in at last, she smiled. 'You're fine,' she said. 'Or at least, you will be.'

'Did you find anything?'

'Nothing definite.'

'What were you looking for, Stephanie?'

Her smile faltered. 'It's under-researched, but we have some idea. I was looking for remnant markers. Remnants are the result of overwork and half a dozen other exacerbating factors, but almost always they're simple things – images, smells. Recognition of things you hadn't seen personally. One theory holds that you experience them all in the surge, but that's far from proven. The condition can get out of hand, and that's when it becomes more serious.'

'Serious?'

'Yes. The delusional behaviour associated with revival burnout can hook into the remnant sensations, Jonah. It can make you feel detached, make you feel like something else is happening.'

'Make you feel like you're watching it happen? Watching some-one else think?'

Stephanie nodded. 'Exactly. Is that what you experienced? Like you weren't in control of your own body?'

'Yes. I didn't want to tell Sam. I was worried about what it would mean.'

'Sam thought that might have been what happened. That's why he sent you to me. That, and the Decker revival the week before.'

'He told you about that?'

'Of course. Hallucination, a classic example. A minor symptom, nothing you should be concerned about. What happened with Nikki Wood was far more worrying, the dissociative illusion most of all. It's not real, Jonah. But the illusion can be strong. The brain knows these memories are not its own. In a sense, it can reject them, isolate them. The patient can lose . . .' She groped for the word.

'Their mind?' he joked, immediately regretting it. The bravura was a front; what Stephanie was saying scared him, and he was whistling in a graveyard.

Stephanie's face was as solemn as he felt inside. 'They can lose perspective. It can be a trigger for serious conditions.'

'So you believe me? About how it felt, like I was watching Nikki think?'

'Absolutely. But the news is good, Jonah. From the cases I've studied before, I've identified clear indicators, the markers we were looking for. You have none of them now. Whatever the problem was, it was short-lived. It's gone.'

'Do you mean I can get back to work now?'

Stephanie laughed. 'Sam *told* me you'd ask that. No. This has happened because of overwork, and you need the rest. Sam wants you off for another week, and I agree. You'll be fine to revive when you get back, with the longer tail rest periods. And when you do, you'll have to have your revival medications adjusted. I'll recommend you increase your BPV dosage. That always knocks it on the head.'

Jonah frowned. 'A BPV increase?'

Graves tilted her head a little. 'I see perhaps ten cases in a year, Jonah. All of them are private revivers who get scared but can afford to pay for the scanning. Half are just imagining it. The other half are fine with the higher dose of BPV, even to do additional revivals. The FRS just ups the BPV for all remnant cases, however minor. It works. You're the first FRS case I've seen in three years. Sam wanted to be sure. There's usually no point paying for scans if the outcome's the same, although it'd be useful for the research I do. Your records show your current dosage is far higher than average.'

'I had some . . . problems. Two years ago. A meds reappraisal followed, and they bumped up the BPV level.'

'And they let your work rate grow back to what it had been, right?' She shook her head. 'They shouldn't let it happen, and nor should you. Short tail and high skill, they're the people I see most often.'

'I'll try,' he said, even though the work rate was driven as much by himself as anyone.

'I know the forensic side is more pressured, Jonah. One thing I've recommended before is a switch to private work. Even for a year. Easier cases, and you can cut right back and still have the same kind of pay you're on now.'

Jonah smiled and shrugged. 'So I hear. I've thought about it before, but I guess private work isn't for everyone.'

'You can have your BPV upped again, but you have to take care of yourself. Overall you need to reduce your accumulative meds intake and have sufficient breaks from it altogether. That can only come from longer tails. I'm recommending a 50 per cent BPV increase. The higher dose will be fine with the long tails and strict limits on how many revivals you should be doing. We'll review it after six months.'

'And I'll be fine?' He felt uneasy. Given how compelling the effect had been, this 'dissociative illusion' that had left him feeling like an onlooker in his own body, he needed more than simple reassurance.

'You'll be fine. I promise.' Graves watched him, and his uncertainty must have been clear on his face. She sighed. 'All right, Jonah. We're all done, but before you go, come with me. I'll show you what I've been up to.'

She led him to the small control room and sat him beside her in front of a trio of monitors, then took something small out of her pocket.

'This,' she said, holding up a memory stick, 'contains the results of the work I've been doing for the last six years on remnants. I hope to publish later in the year, once I finish writing it up. Most of the interesting stuff has happened in the last three years, when we got this new imager.' She plugged it into the USB port on the PC under the desk. 'Much of what I have comes from functional MRI scans of revivers suffering remnants, but I've been able to look at other areas as well. What I find most exciting is the revival scanning – monitoring the reviver's brain activity during an actual revival. We did that kind of thing at Baseline. You probably saw the result, but the resolution and sensitivity of this imager is vastly superior. Back then, you could resolve activity down to a matter of seconds, and you had to repeat something time and again to tease out the results. The Baseline work didn't find anything surprising. Scanning a reviver actually *performing* a revival is awkward and expensive, so there was little incentive to keep doing it. No one is looking at this these days. Not in academia, at any rate. The kind of equipment available now to private research outstrips what I'm using just as far as this outstrips what we had ten years ago. If they'd kept going they would be far ahead of me by now. Sometimes I wish I'd taken one of the offers of private work from Andreas Biotech and the rest of the companies that participated in Baseline.'

'Why didn't you?'

'I suspected they'd sit on the results of anything I did with them, for as long as they could. Keep it for themselves. And like you said, Jonah, private work isn't for everyone. Now, watch.' Filling a monitor screen in front of him was an imaged cross section of a brain. Every few seconds a pulse of blue flashed from a central position, crossing the scan. 'This was one of the easier things to do. We were looking at chill. Here, a reviver is gripping and releasing the hand of my most chill-sensitive research associate. Look.' Graves pointed towards the middle of the image. 'Left lower amygdala. Chill starts there, flows outward. It correlates well with revival ability, but there are excellent revivers who get it mildly, and lesser ones who get it strong. No idea why. Yet.'

'If we know what it is, can we stop it?'

'The signals can certainly be disrupted. You know that alcohol affects it?'

Jonah nodded, smiling. 'A *lot* of alcohol.'

'Same problem for everything else we've tried. I worked with the Andreas Biotech team who developed BPV at Baseline, Jonah. Disruption is part of what BPV does, both there and in the hippo-campus. It was based on treatments for post-traumatic stress that the company had been developing. We were hoping that the same kind of mechanisms were involved in remnants, and BPV is very effective. But chill is just too strong a signal. Enough drugs to counter it would render the reviver an incapacitated amnesiac.' She smiled. 'Just like with alcohol.'

She brought another sequence up on screen. 'This is a full revival.' Jonah watched, fascinated. 'I've only managed to do four of these. Four in three years. This one has a very strong surge.' An red-orange wave burst out from the same area as in the previous sequence, but it swamped the full scan, staying that way for twenty seconds.

'Christ,' said Jonah.

'Again, although it's much faster, you can just about see that it originates from the amygdala, spreading out and invoking a cas-cade of activity. But watch, immediately before. If we filter out the stronger signals, take them right back . . .'

This time, just before the burst of activity from the centre, he could see something else: a sudden, short-lived flutter of blue around the very edges of the brain, converging on the centre before the surge began.

'It's a *very* weak signal,' said Graves. 'Not even EEG can pick it out from electrical noise. We couldn't know it was there, until now.'

'What does it mean?'

'Maybe nothing. But we saw it consistently for the revivals we did. We called it a GT signal, and just maybe it's something we can follow back, work out what triggers it. Whatever it is, it's something new. With revival research it's been *forever* since there was any-thing genuinely new. At the very least it should be enough to get us better funding, and other groups would pick up the challenge again.'

'What's this one?' Jonah asked. The footage had continued as she spoke, a similar sequence with a red-orange hotspot, then played again with the sensitivity turned up and the strongest signals filtered out.

'You're looking at the questioning phase of a revival. The activity you see in red is consistent with audio processing of the spoken words of the subject. You see the symmetry, the left and right ears, the path of the signal from ear to auditory processing areas. What's interesting here is that this reviver is profoundly deaf in his left ear, but there is absolutely no difference in the origin of activity or in how it gets processed. We know that whether deafness affects a reviver's ability to hear the subject depends on the position and extent of the damage in the auditory pathway. Leads us to think we can track down exactly where it originates, but even this scanner isn't enough. Now, look . . .' The sequence showed faint blue at both sides of the brain, near the ears; thin trails, tracking inwards like slow branching rivers. 'Those GT signals again. Crucially, they happen fractionally before the subject speaks, before any sound has been made. It's like an intentional precursor – the activity in your own brain just before you commit to an action. With this, the delay is a few hundredths of a second. Not enough to be aware of it, but enough for us to reliably measure. The reviver starts to hear the words *before they've even been spoken*. Exactly the same traces are seen in a non-vocal revival. It suggests that everything comes from the reviver, or at least *through* them, then to the subject's body.'

Jonah nodded, and as he did a question occurred to him. 'What does "GT" stand for?'

Graves looked sheepish. 'It was the first name I came up with, so I might change it before I publish. I couldn't resist a little melodrama. I called them ghost traces.'

Jonah felt cold. 'And what was it you were looking for, in my scans?'

She hunted until she found the right clip. 'All the remnant cases that I've been able to run through this imager showed a set of marker signals under standard visual hyperstimulation protocols, like we took you through. The markers are stronger by far, but they mimic the GT signals in duration and pattern. When the remnants are gone, so are those markers. The severity of a case is directly reflected in the strength of the markers. Something about the revival, about the stress the reviver was under, meant that the brain kept producing these signals, triggering these unusual waves of activity. It seems inevitable that such activity causes disruption to normal thought processes.'

'And I had none of the markers?'

'You were all clear, Jonah. And if you follow my orders, you'll stay that way.' She stood. 'Now get home and rest.'

'Sam's retirement party is on Tuesday,' Jonah said. 'Will you be going?'

'Far too busy, Jonah.' He could see regret in her eyes. For the first time, Jonah realized there might have been some truth to those rumours. Stephanie Graves hesitated before adding: 'Wish him all the best from me.'

'I will,' Jonah said.

His footsteps were light as he walked to his car. He trusted Stephanie Graves. If she thought his experience with Alice Decker was just hallucination, then it was; if she said he'd be fine, then he would be. Really *believing* it would take some work, but he was starting to think he'd get there.

His mind brought the phrase *ghost traces* into sharp focus, accompanied by the sudden cold he had felt when first hearing the term. *No,* he thought. *Just words. Nothing to fear.*

It would all be behind him soon enough. The overwork and the complications that had come with it.

Alice Decker would be a thing of the past.

11

Annabel Harker waited in the darkening house, sitting in her father's armchair, staring at the phone that refused to ring.

It had been over a week since she'd arrived, and she was drained. There was only so much fear before numbness took hold.

A bottle of brandy sat on the small table next to her, calling, but she ignored it.

She knew it in her bones, in her blood: that the news, when it came, would not be good.

*

Her call to the police had been surreal, as she gave details of her father and explained the situation. As she spoke, she felt suddenly foolish – that she should have waited, that a benign explanation was staring her in the face.

She answered each question as well as she was able.

'Has anything happened recently, Miss Harker? What does your father do for a living?'

'He's a writer.'

She could hear the double take.

'*The* Daniel Harker?'

'Yes,' she replied, but her mind was elsewhere. *Has anything happened recently?* How would she know? Every year, her father took himself away, cut himself out of her life. Every year, he became a stranger again.

'What was your father's state of mind, Miss Harker? Could he have intended to harm himself?'

She froze.

Her first thought was of a time the year after her mother died, when Daniel's mood was at its darkest. She had stayed with him then from the middle of April to the middle of June, terrified that he would harm himself, be it through drink or a blade to the wrist.

'You should go home,' he had told her one night. 'I'm better. I'm much better.'

'Not yet.'

'What are you waiting for?'

'To be certain that you won't do anything stupid.'

Her father looked at her, sad and proud and sorry. He hugged her. 'I couldn't do that to you, sweetheart.'

They held each other for a time before he added: 'Besides, I wouldn't be able to face your mother if I did.'

It had been a joke, of a sort. Annabel knew her father had no faith in an afterlife, or at least not in one that brought that kind of meaningful reunion. The great irony of the man who had found Eleanor Preston.

'Miss Harker?'

The voice on the phone brought her back from her thoughts.

'I'm sorry . . .'

'I understand this is a difficult question, but it's important. Have you any reason to believe your father intends to harm himself?'

No, she thought. *Of course not.*

'It's possible,' she said. 'He has a history of depression.' She felt her cheeks burn. Saying it aloud felt like betrayal. Bringing the police in *at all* felt like betrayal. She was *making* this happen, by acknowledging it. 'There's something else you should know.'

She explained that her father had received numerous Afterlifer threats. The police had been aware of them, and of the one which had actually been carried out, but they assured her that any connection was unlikely. The assurance was automatic; by their tone, Annabel knew they would treat it as a serious possibility.

The image was strong in her mind of a man screaming outside the house, red from the waist down, one hand raw. Bloody stumps where two fingers were gone.

The Afterlifers had mellowed through time, by necessity – revival had overwhelming public support. But in the early years, they had attracted plenty of followers who were disaffected enough to take extreme positions, dedicated to stopping revival at any cost. Nine years ago, a series of threats were sent to Daniel's home, with instructions on a public denunciation of revival, which Daniel ignored and the police played down. It culminated in a parcel bomb. Annabel had been at home and was first to hear the soft thump outside, then the screams of pain; she had opened the door to see the young courier on the ground, and all she could do was stare at the blood as her father came past, running to help.

The next eight months had been the longest of her life. Her father hired ever-present security until the threat subsided, and even at school she had felt some level of risk each time she opened her locker or walked out of the gates.

Annabel wondered if they had returned at last. Closing her eyes she saw the screaming man again, but this time he had her father's face.

*

She had started to drink the remaining alcohol that night, getting viciously drunk and regretting it in tears the next morning. She was disturbed by the symmetry of finding herself sitting in her father's chair, despairing and intoxicated, as he himself did every year.

The isolation was the worst. She needed to talk, but who to call? Her father was her only family. She had a roster of colleagues, some of whom she thought of as friends, but each time she'd come close to ringing them she'd stopped. None was close enough for this kind of burden, bemused sympathy and well-meaning encouragement all she could expect. *Worse than nothing,* she thought.

Nine weeks before and she would have called her then-boyfriend, a record four-month relationship that had come crashing down so fast it had left her head spinning. Even so, as she'd got increasingly drunk she'd come close to making the mistake of calling him.

As she dried her tears in the morning she thought about her failed relationships, and the way she spent so much time worrying about her father, gearing up each year for another emotional beating and resenting him for it.

There was a curious paradox. She was always relieved when a relationship ended, and it was because her own parents had loved each other so completely. It was that absolute love that had led her father into his absolute despair. Into grief so deep that he was still drowning in it.

Love always turned to grief. Was it any wonder she was relieved whenever she failed to find it?

Hungover, waiting for the police to call and struggling to function; she did nothing that day, her mind always returning to one thought: *I wasn't here. I wasn't here to help him.*

She considered pouring the alcohol away, but opted instead to move the bottles out of sight. After all, she reasoned, she might really need them.

*

Two detectives came to the house the next afternoon. It was still very warm and humid, but everything seemed drained of colour. Both detectives looked tired and harassed.

'Hello, Miss Harker,' said the older-looking of the two, a gray man in a gray suit. The colour was even leeching from the police, Annabel thought. 'Detective Harrington; this is Detective Weathers.' His colleague was a woman, just as colourless save for a hint of lipstick. The woman nodded as her name was spoken.

Annabel stayed at the door, reluctant to invite them in. She'd been told they were coming, by phone call that morning, but letting them inside would cut the final strands of denial. It felt dangerous, like inviting a vampire across the threshold.

'Is there news?' she asked. 'They wouldn't give me much over the phone.'

'Yes. May we . . . ?' said Harrington, and Annabel opened the door wide and led the way into the living room.

'Ah!' said Weathers to Harrington. 'Thank God, cooler in here.' She looked to Annabel. 'Car air con's given up, apologies if we're sweaty.'

Annabel found herself smiling and was glad of it. 'Sweat away,' she said. 'But cut to it.'

The officers sat and shared a glance. Harrington spoke: 'Your father's case has been escalated, Miss Harker.'

'Annabel. Please.'

Harrington nodded. 'Annabel. We found withdrawals from your father's bank account. One was from an ATM at a gas station in Greensboro, North Carolina. This was six days ago, 11.23 p.m. Five hundred dollars. A second in Atlanta two days later. Nothing else, and no credit card usage. Just those cash withdrawals.' Harrington paused, seeming to gather himself. He glanced at his colleague, and Annabel felt cold. 'Security camera footage at the gas station clearly shows your father's car.'

At this, Weathers produced a photograph, CCTV from the station forecourt, two vans and one car, a silver Volvo. Then an enlargement showing the car licence plate, clear enough to make out.

Annabel's voice was trembling: 'So have you found him?'

Weathers produced another photograph, a still from inside the station. She handed the picture to Annabel. 'This man was the only known occupant of the vehicle,' Weathers said.

A tall man, scrawny, plain white tee shirt and jeans. Thinning hair. He could have been anywhere from his twenties to his forties. Wearing sunglasses at night.

'Who is he?' said Annabel.

Weathers didn't flinch, but Harrington's face registered disappointment.

'You don't recognize him?' said Harrington. 'A friend of your father's?'

Annabel looked again. 'I don't know him.' She felt empty. 'What is this? What's happening?'

'Your father's a rich man, Annabel,' said Harrington, and the ground lurched under her.

*

They sent a forensic team before five that evening. Annabel watched every move, aware that they must have been cursing her – cursing the time she'd spent in the house, tainting every part of it. But there had been no signs of struggle when she'd first arrived, nothing to indicate that her father had been assaulted there. *Kidnapped* still seemed so bizarre to her. No motive necessary other than greed.

With no contact and no demands for payment, the police were working on the theory that Daniel was being forced to transfer his own money. There had been no movement in any of her father's ordinary bank accounts. The police spoke of the possibility of offshore funds, and of private accounts with daily transfer limits that would require any kidnapping to extend over time. They seemed too certain, Annabel thought. Neither she nor her father's accountant knew of any such accounts, but the police insisted. Then she realized that it was the only scenario they had with a positive outcome. Of course that was what they would tell her.

She was left alone again by ten that night. It would be better to keep the story quiet, they told her, while investigations proceeded. She would be informed of progress.

Whatever the reason he had been taken, and wherever he was, her father would be frightened and alone. Even if he was returned safe, he would be forever changed.

She sought out the alcohol she'd hidden the day before and retreated, surrounded by the ghosts of her family. The days passed, and she took her cue from her father, calling nobody. When the phone rang, it was always the police, to inform her that nothing had changed.

But things *had* changed. She knew it, because she had no more hope left. Each day that passed made the outlook more bleak. She told the police not to call again until they had something to tell her.

And so eight nights after leaving England, Annabel sat in the darkening house, staring at a phone that refused to ring.

She knew that it would ring soon enough.

12

It was late afternoon on Sam Deering's last day at the FRS, and Never was sitting at his desk writing up the first of three in-house revival reports he had to complete before the day's end. The prospect of Sam's retirement party that evening was buoying him.

Sam had been buzzing around the office constantly, increasingly agitated, desperate to tie up loose ends. He headed Never's way.

'You got a minute?' asked Sam.

'Yep.'

'I'm going to sign off on that hardware request you gave me last month.'

'The one you said stood zero chance?'

'The same. It's a going-away present. You want?'

'You kidding?' said Never. 'I want.' Sam nodded and smiled, but Never could see how tired he looked. 'You OK?'

'I've got, what . . .' He checked his watch. 'Less than two hours. Then Hugo's in charge, and I'm retired. Nothing to do.'

'You'll be fine, Sam. You have the symposium in a few weeks, and I'll bet that's not all you're down for.'

Sam smiled. 'Yes . . . but the occasional conference is hardly the same. And Helen won't approve when she finds out. She's expecting her husband to be a man of leisure from now on.'

A moment of silence. The air between them had been frosty

since Jonah had taken on the Wood case, but not today. Time running out, Never thought.

'Look, Sam,' he ventured, but Sam was ahead of him.

'I'm sorry too, Never. I was feeling guilty, and I took it out on you. We've both done it, pandered to the boy.' Sam frowned. 'Shit, listen to me. Boy. Jonah's a man now, and there's my problem. I still treat him like a kid. I let him have his own way too often, and so do you.'

'Yeah . . . we do.'

'Look out for him, Never.'

'I'll do my best. But for the record?'

Sam raised an eyebrow. 'What?'

'I'm glad Jonah handled the Wood case rather than Jason Shepperton.' He shrugged. 'Can't help it.'

Sam leaned over and lowered his voice. 'You know what, Never? I am too.'

As Sam went back to his office, Never heard someone call his name from the office entrance. He looked over to see J. J. walking towards him.

J. J. had returned from Seattle the night before, after a two-week stint helping train new technicians at the West Coast offices. The timing of the trip had meant Never hadn't seen him since the Decker revival, for which J. J. had been the technician. That morning, things had been rushed, and there had barely been time for J. J. to give Never a summary of how his Seattle trip had gone before he'd had to go out for an onsite revival.

'Hi, J. J.,' said Never. 'How did the onsite go?'

J. J. shrugged. 'By the numbers. Nothing interesting.' He paused. 'Hey, Never, maybe this can wait until later, but . . .'

'Go ahead.'

'When I got back in I went through my emails. I got to the one from you, about the Decker revival.'

'Oh, that. I was just thinking we should make it standard practice to leave the recording going until we take the equipment down.

We can set it up so the police copy can be taken without stopping everything. I wasn't criticizing, just thinking it'd be sensible.'

J. J. nodded. 'Thing is, your message reminded me. There was an outage after the revival. I should've told you about it before I left, but things were hectic. Sorry.'

'Outage?' The suggestion made Never's pride bristle – it was his system, designed with enough redundancy to cover most eventualities short of a nearby nuclear explosion.

'Yeah. And I didn't even see it until I went to pack up the gear. There was no notification.'

'The power to a camera died? And it didn't warn you?'

J. J. shook his head. 'Not one. All three.'

For a moment Never thought he'd misheard. That kind of thing simply didn't happen. 'Did you see them go?'

'No. I was chatting to the guys and ripping their copy. Didn't notice it. You know how it is, the revival was over, recording had stopped.'

'It should have chimed a warning.'

'I know, but it didn't.'

'So all the backup batteries failed *and* the warning system's broken?' Hardware failure happened often enough, Never knew, but for it all to go at once . . . Then, suddenly, he made a connection and felt ice in his veins.

'That's the thing. When I went in to take them down, I noticed the power was out on the main-shot camera. Then I saw the other two were gone as well. I went to power-cycle the wide-shot camera, but before I touched it, all three came back up on their own. I checked it out when I got back and I couldn't find anything wrong, not with *any* of it. Couldn't work it out.'

Silent, Never realized that his skin was goosebumping.

J. J. spoke again: 'While I was away, I was thinking – there was plenty of static from the carpets in that office. I noticed when I was setting up.' He leaned in, whispering, 'I think we may have a static problem. We need to do some testing.'

'Right, yes. Static.' He suppressed a shiver. 'Look, J. J., do me a favour and don't say anything about this. Not until we know. I mean, we've not had trouble before, but some of the kit configuration is only a few months old.' They'd switched to a different brand for the backup power units six months before. *Maybe that's it*, he thought, unconvinced.

'I wasn't going to. I'll write up a test plan.'

'Thanks, J. J. Good work. We'll get the testing done next week, OK?'

When J. J. left, Never found himself thinking of static and the camera power dropping. He thought of Alice Decker's face in the footage he'd watched. He thought of Jonah, looking up after the revival had ended, seeing that face rise, malign and leering. This time, the shiver came.

*

By the time the day's work ended, Sam was nowhere to be seen. Without a victim to impose a grand emotional farewell on – which Never presumed was exactly why Sam had disappeared – the office dispersed, everyone heading off to get ready for the evening's event in the venue room of a nearby sports bar. The farewell would wait until then.

Rather than have to go all the way home and then all the way back again, Never had worn what he considered his best clothes to work. Nobody had noticed the difference.

He walked to Jonah's apartment. Since getting the good news from Stephanie Graves, Jonah had seemed upbeat enough to stop Never worrying as much as he had been, but not completely.

'Thought I'd pop in,' he said as Jonah opened the door. 'Then we can go together. Share a cab.'

Jonah smiled. 'So you could make sure I didn't decide to stay home?'

'Oh, I know you wouldn't have stayed home,' said Never, sitting on the sofa beside a snoozing Marmite. He tickled the cat's neck.

'You'd have turned up as late as you thought you could get away with.'

'What can I say. My cat would miss me.'

'So this is what you spend your time off doing, huh? Pampering your cat?'

'Yep. That and thinking.'

'Sounds ominous,' said Never. 'What about?'

'My life.'

'That *is* ominous. Come to any conclusions yet?'

'Graves told me it was all in my head, Never. And I want to believe it. I want to, more than anything. But I started to wonder if that was because it's all I can do, you know? This job is all I am. If I can't think Decker was in my head, where does that leave me? If I believe what I saw, it would mean something's *out* there.'

Jonah's head fell. Thinking of what J. J. had said, Never was relieved that Jonah wasn't looking at him; his eyes might have given away the unease he felt. He scolded himself for being so stupid – this was the kind of superstitious idiocy he derided in others. Letting Jonah see he had any doubt was the worst thing he could do for his friend.

'Come on, Jonah. Graves was right, and you *know* it. This is what you want to do, because you're *good* at it. Christ, think about Nikki Wood – you've handled dozens of cases like that. You make a real difference.'

Jonah looked up at him. 'Maybe that's the problem. If I can't walk away, not even from one case, when I know it's for my own good . . . I'll let the workload grow again. Graves suggested I go private. Maybe then I'd be able to let go of it. Lose the urgency. It'd let me recover. I said no, but I'm starting to think leaving the FRS might be the only way. I'll be back at work next week. I guess I'll find out how I feel then.'

In the silence that followed, Never watched him, sizing up how much Jonah meant what he said, and not liking what he saw. 'Shit, mate,' he said at last, trying to shake the moment off. 'Maybe. If it's what you decide. But that's for another time, OK? If we try hard, I think we may still have fun tonight. If that's fine by the moggie.'

'OK,' said Jonah, defeated. 'Give me a minute to change.'

*

They were on to their second drink of the evening by the time Hugo Adler called for quiet. Sam was in torment, standing at the front as uncomfortable as Never Geary could recall seeing him; his face was reddening with every moment, as more and more people drew close and aimed their attention his way.

It got redder still as Hugo gave him his send-off speech, which ended with heartfelt applause. As it grew, Sam's eyes started watering. Then came the farewell gifts.

First, a small selection of impressive wines. Nothing ridiculous, just half a dozen that were expensive enough to put Sam off removing the cork.

'We asked Helen,' said Hugo, as Sam looked at each bottle in turn. 'She told us you were always saying you'd start a wine cellar, if only you could resist drinking what you buy. So we got you some bottles you'll think it's a shame to open.'

'I'm not sure that isn't a form of torture,' Never whispered to Jonah, but judging from Sam's smile the gift seemed a good one.

Second, a more personal memento: a framed photograph of the original FRS team moving in to the Richmond offices: Sam looking trim and Never grinning out of the middle row; Jonah there too, joining them as the expansion began, scarily young.

Sam took a moment to look closely. Calls for a speech made him wince, but he nodded, wet-eyed. 'There's not much I can say that you don't already know. It's been a privilege. I'm proud of you, and I'll miss you. And now, I have one last order as your boss. Enjoy yourselves!'

*

Every conversation that night seemed to turn to FRS nostalgia, leading back to Sam, in the end. It was no wonder, Jonah thought. Sam had founded it, tended it; the FRS was his child in many ways, and Sam had been a father figure to many of his staff over the years. None more so than Jonah, orphaned by his mother's death and befriended by this principled man, a man who was fighting for honour and justice. A man who Jonah wanted to make proud.

Sam was sitting at a table on the far end of the room, with his wife, Helen, on one side, and Robert Thorne, the Chicago-based FRS director, on the other. In theory, Robert Thorne had shown Sam significant respect by coming, but he was a humourless bureaucrat and Sam's expression spoke volumes.

'Thorne has him trapped,' said Jonah.

'Probably making him feel guilty about the cost of the evening,' Never said. 'Look at Sam's face. Every time Thorne speaks, you can see a flinch . . .'

They watched as Sam spoke to Helen and shook hands with someone who'd approached his table. Then Thorne spoke up. The flinch was visible, even at a distance.

'Let's give him some respite,' said Jonah.

'Good idea,' said Never. 'He's nearer the bar too.'

They lifted their drinks and walked over.

'Excuse me,' said Never. 'Sorry, Mr Thorne – Sam, could we have a word?'

Sam smiled at them, then looked to Thorne. 'Do you mind, Robert?' Thorne's cold expression showed that he did, but he pulled out a practised smile and shook his head.

'Not at all, Sam, this is your night. I shouldn't be taking your time up with work.' Thorne laughed, a sound so artificial it made Jonah's skin crawl. Cecily Hunter, the North East FRS head, was sitting to Thorne's left. She watched Sam go with a hint of despair as Thorne started talking to her instead.

'Did you really want anything or was that a rescue?' Sam asked when they were out of Thorne's earshot.

'Rescue,' said Jonah.

'And we're taking you to the bar,' said Never. 'Urgent require-
ment to get you drunk, Sam.'

'I could do with another after fifteen minutes of budget trivia. I
wasn't sure if he was punishing me for leaving or trying to make me
glad to be gone. No more of him, thank God.'

'He'll probably pester you at home,' said Jonah.

Sam laughed. 'Helen and I are heading to the Florida Keys for
the next week and do you know what? I've got a terrible feeling I
haven't left my contact details. Hugo will have to take that bullet for
me.'

As Never approached the bar, Sam held Jonah back. 'I didn't
get a chance to talk earlier, Jonah. Are you feeling any better?'

Jonah smiled, surprised that it didn't feel artificial. He knew a
big part of it was the thought of leaving the FRS. Even the possibility gave him room to breathe, whatever he decided in the end. But
there was no need to tell Sam. 'I'm getting there.'

'I was starting to blame myself for the whole thing. It was my
fault we let you get so overworked. Stephanie Graves emailed me,
and she wasn't kind about how we've been treating you.'

'Don't worry about me, Sam. How are *you* coping?'

'If I'm honest, I've been dreading today. But right now . . . I'm
pretty happy about it. I'm amazed how many old faces are showing
up. Real blasts from the past. So now I just have to fend off Thorne
for the rest of the evening, and try not to think how much all this is
costing.'

As Sam and Jonah reached the bar, they became aware that
Never was watching something behind them, mouth gaping. Jonah
stared at him, bemused.

Sam glanced behind. 'Hell,' he said, a laugh in his voice. 'What
was I saying about old faces?'

Jonah turned and he saw her, walking into the middle of the
room, drawing all male eyes from around her and many female too.

Tall, perfect curves, shoulder-length auburn hair, she was wearing a light dress that gave her an ethereal quality as she walked.

Waving at her, Sam smiled. The woman waved back and headed towards them.

'You know her?' said Never, seeing the recognition on Jonah's face. Then his eyes narrowed. 'Is that who I think it is?'

'Oh yeah, that's her,' replied Jonah. More than once he'd told Never about his old crush in Baseline. She waved and smiled again. He couldn't help but smile back, a smile that broadened relentlessly until he felt he must look like an idiot. He could tell Never was entertained, but he didn't care.

Tess Neil. As a teenager, his yearning for her had been overwhelming, easily enough to overlook her faults. It had culminated in that single brief kiss the last time he'd seen her seven years before, when he was nineteen. She had been twenty-five then. If anything, she looked better than ever. He wanted to kiss her before she spoke, before she broke the spell.

He stepped towards her as she approached. They smiled at each other, five feet apart. Eventually, she stepped closer. In the growing noise of the venue room, she came near enough to be heard even though her voice was low, confidential.

'Hi, Jonah,' she said, her words like fingers stroking his brow. He felt exposed and vulnerable and he didn't mind the feeling.

'Hi, Tess,' he said.

13

Tess Neil's skill as a reviver was almost as high as Jonah Miller's, ranked as a K4 to Jonah's K3. Nine years ago, spending one week in six at the Baseline facility, he had dreamed of her, had lusted for her. He'd just turned seventeen, after all, and Tess was beautiful. He'd been doomed from the start.

Yet he had had to be content with friendly hugs and teasing banter. To the research teams, Tess included, he was a little brother, a mascot.

And Tess was spoken for. She was seeing Will Barlow, charming, intelligent and manipulative. The latter seemed to be a minority opinion held by Jonah – one that others he confided in blamed on Barlow's hold on Tess Neil's affections.

She made time for Jonah, all the same. They had formed a friendship that first day, when Jonah had found himself crying and unable to stop, and Tess had taken charge. Whenever he was at Baseline, she played pool with him every lunchtime in the Baseline rec room. Jonah talked, confided in her. Tess listened. He couldn't read her, though. She was a different person when he saw her in the company of others, Barlow in particular – aloof and cynical, she would hardly acknowledge Jonah's presence. When, in their time together, he managed to get her to speak of her own life, she was typically brief.

She was an enigma, then, but to a young man with an impossible crush, none of that mattered. And in those rare times when she did open up to him, he found himself believing that this was the real Tess; that she could come to feel about him the way he did about her.

As the number of revivers and the breadth of research increased, Baseline grew busy and Jonah saw less and less of her. He spent most of his time on Sam's projects, forensic work under the FBI banner. Tess worked mainly for the large Baseline sponsors like Andreas Biotech.

Then came the allegations.

The researchers at Baseline were at fate's mercy; whatever subjects became available were issued to the most appropriate team. This led to some lines of research stalling through lack of useful subjects. There was frustration.

One of the first things that Sam Deering had done on joining Baseline was to improve the procedures for what were called 'subject acquisitions'. The temptation to use alternative sources had been resisted thus far, but Sam could see the problems on the horizon.

Use of unidentified corpses. The homeless. The unwanted. Sourcing from countries where the poor were at even greater risk of exploitation. The money involved in the current voluntary system could be considerable – 'outsourcing' would, Sam knew, lead to widespread abuse, perhaps even murder. A return to the nineteenth-century resurrectionists.

The system to prevent this was called Subject Tracking. A detailed history, traceable at every stage, for all subjects; random reviews to ensure procedures were adhered to.

But no system is infallible.

Rumours began that at least one Baseline research team had been working outside the system, forging documentation. This was around the time of the Lyssa Underwood revival, and the rumour prompted Jonah to go to Sam. The uneasiness he had felt during that bizarre session had been in part due to the fractured confusion of the subject, something Jonah hadn't experienced in any previous work. All the subjects at Baseline had been through a process of preparation before their deaths. All those Jonah had brought back had understood they were being revived.

All except Lyssa Underwood.

Perhaps it had been Jonah's dislike of Will Barlow that had made him go to Sam after that session, but the confusion in Lyssa Underwood's mind had been too worrying for him to ignore.

'I can't talk about it in detail, Jonah,' Sam had said. 'They used you under the standard Baseline rules, nothing wrong with that. I've heard the rumours going around, but this is the first time I've been given something specific to look into. Leave it with me.'

The rumours stayed internal. Nobody in Baseline wanted to drag the project's dirty linen into public view, not based solely on speculation.

Eventually, an admission was made to minor documentation irregularities. A week later, the project team left Baseline, their departure put down to a reassessment of research priority, officially unconnected to the documentation problems.

Will Barlow left too, supposedly to work as a private reviver. It was obvious to everyone that the research work the team had been doing – whatever it was, and whoever it was for – had simply relocated.

Tess had been angry, and naturally people thought she knew more than she was saying, but she waved away questions. The few times Jonah asked her about Will, she seemed genuinely hurt by the whole situation. She started seeing one of the technicians, a stormy coupling that continued, on and off, for the rest of her time at Baseline.

It hadn't been long after Barlow left Baseline that Sam also moved on, starting his prototype FRS in Quantico. Jonah had stayed behind, in part because of Tess. The month after his nine-teenth birthday, Tess told him she was leaving that day for private work in Canada. She wished him luck and kissed him once, deeply. Then she walked away with a single backward glance, smiling at the teenager.

Jonah secured his place in the FRS nine weeks later, just as they expanded into the office in Richmond.

*

He had not seen her in seven years, and now there she was, standing in front of him. He had no idea what she'd been doing since then, yet she had known he'd gone to the FRS. She had the advantage. She always did.

'Surprise,' she said and took his hand. Jonah was unprepared for the effect her touch had on him. He felt giddy, unable to speak.

Sam smiled at her. 'My God,' he said. 'It's good to see you, Tess.'

'Hi, Sam,' she said.

'I lost track of you after you left Baseline,' said Sam. 'I still had hopes I could convince you to join the FRS. How have things been?'

'Good.'

'Did you ever see Will again?'

Tess shook her head. 'No. You ever hear from him?'

'Not a word,' said Sam. 'So what have you been doing?'

'Private work,' she said. 'Not much of a challenge, but it pays well.'

Sam looked at her, appraising. Jonah did too, noticing the quality of everything she wore. Delicate white gloves. A necklace that was understated but clearly expensive. Her clothes simple but oozing quality.

'I can see,' said Sam. 'You look well.'

'You too,' Tess told him, then turned her eyes on Jonah. 'And you.'

Jonah went red.

At that, Sam's attention was caught. 'Ah, Helen's waving me over. Great to see you again, Tess. We'll chat more later, see if I can't convince you to give up all the riches for public service.'

Tess smiled. 'Your work's cut out there, Sam, but good luck trying.'

Sam nodded and crossed the room back to Helen.

Jonah indicated Never. 'Tess Neil, this is Never Geary. He's a revival technician.'

'I've heard a lot about you, Tess,' said Never, holding his hand out.

Tess shook his hand with a wary eye. 'Not all bad, I hope.'

'No,' said Never. 'There was good stuff too.' It earned him a scowl from Jonah, but the usual grin broke out on Never's face and Tess smiled back.

'Can I steal Jonah for a while?' she said. 'We have some catching up to do.'

'You two go ahead,' said Never. 'I'll catch you later.'

*

Jonah and Tess took a corner table well away from the crowd. Tess took off her gloves and set them on the table. He sat opposite.

She raised an eyebrow. 'So far away?'

'I want to get a good look at you,' he replied, knowing he was blushing again. 'I want to know what you've been up to. And what the occasion is.'

Tess took a sip of her drink, her lower lip sticking for just an instant as it left the glass. Jonah was aware he was staring at her mouth but couldn't help himself.

'I'm here for Sam's retirement,' she said.

Jonah shook his head. 'Out of the blue? How did you hear about it?'

'Through the grapevine. But I admit I had another motive. I wanted to see you.' Tess spoke more quietly. 'I've wanted to see you for seven years, Jonah.'

The answer floored him. 'You could have got in touch any time.'

Tess shrugged. 'Maybe.'

He looked at her for a moment, suspicious. 'So what have you been doing?' he asked.

'You first.'

'FRS.'

'Seven years, and that's it?'

'Yep.'

'And what about your life, Jonah? Conquests? Great loves? Adventure?'

He shook his head. 'I'm quietly content with murder and tragedy.'

Tess tipped her head, mock-sadly. 'Shame. Are you happy?'

The question caught him off guard. 'Happy? Sometimes.'

'You know, I really thought you'd bloom. I thought you'd make your life good.'

'It's not bad.'

'You're lonely.'

The observation cut close. He thought of Nala George's horrified face staring at him. He looked down. 'Sometimes,' he said and sipped his drink. 'But what about you? Did you really not hear from Will again?' *Good God,* he thought. *She's blushing.* He couldn't recall ever seeing her blush before.

'OK, I admit I heard from him a few years back.'

'You ever find out what he was doing? What that project he'd been on was for?'

She thought about this, then shook her head. 'No. He wouldn't even tell me what he'd gone on to do next. He seemed happy enough, whatever it was.'

'Christ, I remember how angry you were when the shit hit the fan.'

Tess looked to the ceiling and sighed. 'All in the past now, but yes. I was raging. I was a little impetuous in those days.'

Jonah raised an eyebrow. 'You mean you're not now?'

She laughed. 'I've changed, Jonah. You wouldn't believe how much. I think . . . I think you'd be proud of me.'

It was Jonah's turn to laugh. 'So you'll be at the FRS soon, then?' He meant it as a joke, but he thought he could see hurt in her eyes.

'That's not something I'll ever be cut out for, Jonah. Private revivals, US and abroad, for one of the more exclusive providers. Good money. Good lifestyle. There aren't many people who can guarantee a revival, given the right conditions. You should consider it.'

'So people keep telling me.'

'Is it something you'd want to do?'

'A week ago I would've said no, but work's been hard. I've been doing too much. Don't say anything to anyone, but I'm giving it some thought.'

Jonah wasn't certain, but she seemed surprised, almost disappointed. 'Well, if you're going to sell out, have you considered one of the more *exclusive* companies? Make some *real* money for a change.'

'If I gave up forensics, it wouldn't be for the money. There are plenty of ordinary people who pay their insurance and get lousy revival success rates in return. I'd be happy bringing the rates up.'

She chuckled. 'One of the reasons I came here was to see how you turned out.'

'And your conclusion?'

'You've not changed much.'

'Is that a good thing or a bad thing?'

'Oh, good.' She smiled softly, a warm, genuine smile, not Tess's well-practised public face. This, at last, was the girl he'd had such a crush on. 'I wish you'd got more of a life going, but I'm glad you're still a sweetheart. All your honour still intact. Very heartening.' She dipped the volume of her voice and leaned across the table. Her right hand slipped off her glass and rested on his knee. The touch was bliss. 'Very attractive,' she whispered, all mischief. 'You were always an idealist. Now, why so far?'

'What?'

'Sit beside me.'

Jonah felt uneasy. He took a drink and glanced around. The corner they were in was secluded, darker than the rest of the room. He couldn't see Never.

'I will,' he said. 'If you answer a question.'

'Shoot.'

'Why did you kiss me on that last day?'

Tess looked away for a moment. 'I wanted to.'

'You had to know how I felt about you. You had to know that it was going to drive me crazy.'

'I was leaving. It was a last chance. It's not like you were a kid, Jonah.'

He shook his head. 'That's exactly what I was, Tess. I was a kid you came to, for what? A bit of light relief? Someone you could wrap around your finger like Will did with you?'

Her face fell. 'Don't say that. That wasn't what it was.'

'Then *what*?'

'I was a better person around you.' She paused, struggling for the words. 'Without all the shit, I was better. And I *wanted* to be better. You made me want to be.'

'Then why didn't you get in touch? Seven years gives you plenty of chances.'

Tess took a deep breath. 'Jonah, you and I both know we're too different. It would end badly. You'd get hurt and I'd be a bitch. I couldn't let that happen. Hell, Jonah, just because I *wanted* to be better didn't mean I would be.'

He felt himself deflate. He knew she was right – always had – but it was hard to hear her say it. 'So why are you here now?'

'Because I'm leaving the country, and I'm not coming back again. It really is a last chance.'

'Why?'

Tess shook her head. 'No details.' She patted the seat to her left. 'Sit beside me.'

Jonah did, wary of her. No details. An enigma to the end. As he sat, it struck him what she'd said. 'A last chance for what, Tess?'

She moved over, her face an inch away from his. He took in her eyes, her skin, that playful smile, all burned deep in his memory. Whatever warning bells sounded, he was already lost in her.

'I want another kiss,' she said softly, the air from her mouth hot against his lips, the smell of tequila and lime mingling with her perfume. He was caught in her headlights. She brushed her lips against his. They felt impossibly good, full and alive, and he wanted to kiss her so badly that he had no choice but to draw away. He felt like he'd been drowning.

The disappointment in her eyes was matched with concern. 'Jonah?' she asked.

He looked away, then picked up his drink and downed the last third. He spoke fast, trying to talk away what had just happened. 'This is a little intense,' he said. 'I need another one. Same again?'

Tess Neil nodded, crestfallen. 'I'm sorry, Jonah, I . . .' she started, but Jonah held up his hand.

'Don't be. And don't move.' He smiled. 'I'm coming back.'

*

The bar was busy. He was glad of the time it would take, time enough to work out if doing what he was about to do was a disastrous idea or not. A hand fell on his shoulder.

'How's it going?' asked Never.

'I'm not sure. You?'

'I'm making friends.' He indicated a group sitting near the bar. 'A bunch of people came down from Chicago with Thorne, and some of the North East crowd have shown up. Seems like a good bunch.' His volume dropped. 'I think that brunette's taken a liking to me.' He grinned.

Jonah took a look. As he did, the girl flashed a smile their way. 'She's cute. Try not to get too drunk, huh?'

'Tell *them* that. They're halfway through the cocktail menu already. Now, come on, tell me. How's it going?'

'Bewildering,' Jonah said, as Never looked him over with a diagnostic eye.

'She's after your body,' Never pronounced. Jonah smiled, nodding, and Never grinned.

'I'm a little shaken,' Jonah said. He found Never's grin hard to talk to. 'Please, be serious. I'm confused. I haven't seen her for seven years and then she shows up like this? I don't know if it's a good idea.'

'So why did she show up?'

'She's here to say good-bye. She's leaving the country and not coming back.'

'Ah! That explains everything. She wants a farewell fuck!'

Jonah glared. 'Please. I'm struggling here.'

'Sorry.' He shrugged. 'She wants to say good-bye. With sex.'

'I guess so.'

'And you're wary because . . .'

'I don't know how I feel about that.'

'Listen, this girl's been in your head since you were effectively a kid, yeah?' He waited for Jonah to nod. 'You want a girl out of your head, best thing you can do is shag her.'

'And exactly *how* does that make sense?'

'Trust me. If you don't shag a girl you fancy you can't move on. It makes it easier to be honest with yourself about her. And in the meantime – *you've had a shag.* See?'

'No.'

'The day after, they're either out of your system or burrowing in deep. Unless . . . shit. Unless you're not sure which of those it'd be. Are you?'

Jonah looked down. 'I don't want it to be a mistake, that's all.'

Putting his arm around Jonah's shoulder, Never heaved a sigh. 'I can't tell you what to do, mate. If you don't know how you'll feel after, you need to be careful. But if she's telling the truth, she'll be gone. This opportunity won't come round again. And if you're going to make a mistake, you may as well make it a big one.'

Jonah looked at him for ten full seconds, baffled. At last he gave up. 'OK. Your logic's impeccable.'

'It is. You're here for a drink?'

'I am.'

'Well, let's see what we can do.' He leaned across the bar and called out, 'Ivan!' repeating the name six more times until the bartender came over.

'*You're* a persistent son of a bitch,' said the bartender, somewhere between amused and pissed off.

'I know, Ivan,' Never grinned, 'but my friend here has a beautiful woman waiting who needs an urgent drink.'

Ivan frowned at Never for a moment, then the frown fell away. He turned to Jonah and smiled. 'So it's an *emergency*,' he said. 'What'll it be?'

*

A drink in each hand, Jonah returned by an indirect path that allowed him to watch Tess unseen for a moment. Her hands were clasped on the table; she was gazing at them, pensive. As he drew nearer, her eyes closed. There was a melancholy in her expression that worried him.

'Hey,' he said, sitting and placing her drink on the table.

She smiled, but there was still an edge of anxiety in her eyes.

'What's wrong?' he asked. 'Are you in trouble, Tess? Is that why you're leaving?'

'It's not like that, Jonah. The reason I'm going is probably the best thing that's ever happened to me. I was just getting nostalgic about what I'm leaving behind. I meant what I said. You always made me want to be better than I am. You're important to me, and I wanted you to know.'

She took his hand in hers, her eyes looking right into his with an intensity that swallowed him.

He opened his mouth to speak. It felt dry. 'Tess . . .' he said, caution brewing in his mind again. 'What are we doing?'

'Unfinished business, Jonah.'

He opened his mouth again, but she put her finger against his lips, then she kissed him, deep and slow. He kissed back hard.

Then they watched each other in silence for almost a minute,

Tess smiling at him with that openness he loved in her, not her usual guarded amusement.

Jonah's mind was made up. He lifted his drink and downed it. 'Let's go,' he said.

Standing at the bar, Never Geary saw his friend leave and raised his glass. 'Good luck,' he whispered.

*

Jonah and Tess sat in silence in the back of the cab on the way to Jonah's apartment, Tess resting her head on his chest.

After the twenty-minute drive, Jonah marched on, dragging a laughing Tess behind him, moving as quickly as walking would allow, up the stairwell to his door. He raised his key to the lock, but before he opened the door he turned to her.

'You know how long I've wanted to do this?' he asked. In answer, Tess grabbed him and kissed him.

Jonah turned the key. They stumbled inside together and began to undress before the door had swung closed, grinning and giggling as they went. Both down to their underwear, Tess stopped Jonah's hand in the act of removing his boxer shorts and shook her head.

'Not until we're in bed,' she said. Jonah laughed explosively, at once embarrassed by the guffaw, but Tess's smile was warm. 'Let's make this last,' she added. Jonah agreed, and turned to the bedroom. Tess was behind, but she stopped when she heard a sound from the kitchen. It was Marmite, mewing. Tess was enraptured.

'You have a cat?'

He nodded, bemused that Tess could be distracted so easily. Marmite was sitting just inside the kitchen door, peeking out at them. The cat mewed again, and she went over, bent down and picked him up.

'What's she called?'

'He,' Jonah corrected. 'Marmite. His claws are in need of a trim and he's a bit frisky, so watch out.' She started to baby-talk the animal as she stroked him. Jonah sighed and went to the fridge, amused and annoyed in equal measure. On the other hand, he thought, things had been heating so quickly it would have been over in an instant. A break was, in theory, welcome. 'You want anything to eat? Or drink?'

Tess looked up. 'Glass of wine or something would be . . .' Guilt ran across her face. 'Oops. Kinda got sidetracked there.'

'A little too easily,' he said. Tess laughed and shook her head.

'Sorry. Soft spot for cats. I had a black kitten when I was five. Kept peeing on the carpet. About a month after I got him he disappeared. My dad told me he'd run away.'

Jonah knew about Tess's dad. Abusive, emotionally if not physically, and a source of real pain for her.

'Turned out he'd sold it to someone else,' she said. 'I only found that out after Dad died.' She ruffled Marmite's head. 'I can't even remember what I called my kitten. That's terrible. Is there any food I can give him?'

Jonah reached out to the box of dry food but had second thoughts. He emptied a tin of tuna into a bowl and handed it to her. Marmite reached up on Tess's bare leg, eager for her to set it down. She did, then watched the cat tuck in with gusto.

'He eats like you,' she said. 'Only slower.'

Jonah smiled. 'You think I'm bad, you should see Never eat.'

She shook her head. 'I won't be around.'

Jonah saw genuine sorrow in her face. 'You're really going,' he said. 'And I really won't see you again.' She nodded, silent. 'And no explanation.'

Tess shook her head and turned to look at Marmite again. In the bright kitchen light, Jonah noticed a straight three-inch scar visible under her hair, just above her left ear. She saw him look, her hand coming up instinctively to hide it. He reached out and caressed the scar. 'Surgery?' he said, worry in his voice. 'Is that what this is about?'

'A minor tumour. Benign. I don't want to talk about it, but it wasn't as serious as it sounds. And it's not why I'm leaving, although I guess things changed then. Made me think about what I really want.' She looked at him in shared silence for a few seconds, smiling mischief. 'Or *who* I want . . .' She reached out and took his hand. 'Bedroom. Now.'

He led her in, thankful his sheets were less than a week old and the room was generally tidy. 'Hang on,' he told her, remembering the packet of condoms he'd got from the bar toilet vending machine on their way out, still in his jacket. When he returned, she was naked, on the bed. He watched her, overwhelmed. She smiled at him quizzically.

'What's wrong?' she asked.

I don't know why you're here, he thought. *I don't know if this is a mistake.*

'Nothing at all,' he said, and closed the door.

*

When he woke, he knew she was gone. He could smell her on the pillow beside him. The night had been long and perfect. They had played, and fucked, and cuddled and caressed, without fear of intimacy, without self-consciousness. He shut his eyes. Images of her skin filled him, the soft curves and the feel of himself against her and inside her, contact from head to foot and every square inch of it a delight. He thought of her mouth, as he kissed it and licked it, as it wrapped around him and explored his neck.

He opened his eyes again. For an instant, he thought she might still be in the apartment, perhaps in the kitchen. He rose and went there but found only Marmite, drinking from his water bowl. Next to the sink was a second opened can of tuna. She'd stayed long enough to feed the cat.

Beside the tin, a folded note, written on a sheet from a pad he kept for shopping lists. He left it where it was and went to the living room, finding his underwear and jeans. He put them on and sat on the couch for a few minutes. He'd wanted to say good-bye, at least. At least that.

He saw the time – eleven-fifteen. He'd slept well and long. She'd probably been gone for hours.

Feeling ready, he returned to the kitchen and read the note.

Jonah, she'd written. *I had to go. Didn't want to wake you. You looked peaceful, and no one should disturb that. Be happy. Tess.*

Deflated, Jonah sat heavily by the kitchen table. Marmite brushed against his leg and he looked down.

'Well, she said good-bye to *you*.' The cat meowed and narrowed his eyes at him. 'That's something, I guess.' Then he started to cry.

He showered and thought about Tess. The water washed the tears from his face, tears that had been long in coming. He felt purged by them.

He thought about why she had come to see him. Unfinished business. Closure.

You're important to me, and I wanted you to know. Had she really meant that?

He couldn't pin it down, but something had been different about Tess. She had always seemed lost, somehow. Rudderless. The night before she had been . . . what?

He rolled it around in his mind until it came. *Focused. Certain.* That was it. He wondered about the surgery that had resulted in the scar above her ear; she'd denied it was serious, but he didn't believe that. He had no idea why she was leaving the country, but whatever the reason, that must be where her new focus came from.

She wasn't lost any more, and he wished her well.

Tess Neil had been a huge part of his life during the difficult years that had followed his mother's death and the discovery of his ability. The chance that he could get in touch with Tess had been an open door ever since. An open door, and in some ways an open wound.

That door was closed now. With luck, the wound could heal.

14

That night, Jonah dreamed of his mother.

It began as it always did. He was looking up at the sky, lost in the clouds. His sanctuary.

'Jonah?' His mother's voice from the front passenger seat snapped him back. He wondered how many times she had called his name before he'd noticed.

'Your mother was wondering if you wanted to go out this evening.' Stephen, his stepfather, always spoke with a flat voice when he talked to his stepson. They tolerated each other, for Claire's sake, but there was an inevitable coldness to their dialogue. Jonah didn't doubt his mother was aware of the strain.

Jonah's father, David Miller, had been an architect. He had died four years ago, electrocuted on a construction site. The out-of-court settlement had been enough to ensure financial security for a decade.

Jonah was ten at the time and had grieved quietly. He cut off from friends and grew insular, far from the carefree child he had been. He spent as much time as he could with his mother, fearful when she was out of sight. Terrified of losing her.

Stephen Brinley was the financial adviser Claire Miller had hired following the settlement with David's firm. He was charming, handsome and earned enough that Claire's own finances were unimportant. Jonah had the wisdom to understand that he would dislike anyone posturing to replace his father, but Stephen's attitude to the boy had made the dislike rapidly degenerate into hate.

To Stephen, Jonah was an irritation, his presence unfortunate. During the courtship of his mother, there were few occasions when the three of them went anywhere as a group, despite Claire's assurances to her son that his approval of the relationship was crucial.

Jonah could see how much happier his mother had become, even as his own happiness dissipated. He felt trapped. His disapproval was open at first, but gradually there was a change in his mother's outlook. She hardened as she came to depend on Stephen, and came to see a future without him as unacceptable.

Jonah realized that he had already lost part of her and risked losing her entirely. He couldn't allow that to happen, and there was only one way to avoid it. He behaved in the manner that Stephen expected, keeping out of the way, speaking rarely, trying his best to appear happy. It worked too well. On Christmas Day, his mother and Stephen announced that they would marry.

He kept to himself more and more, and in her happiness his mother failed to notice he had withdrawn. There was little need for a mask, once the difficult wedding day had passed and life had settled into a routine. Jonah's low-impact presence at home, and his apparent success at school – he got into no trouble, and achieved exactly as much as was expected of him – meant that Stephen felt no threat.

*

Jonah found himself happy only on those rare times that Stephen was gone long enough for his mother to become herself again, to stop reflecting the opinions and personality of her new husband.

And now Jonah was in the car, with one of those times to look forward to. They were off to the airport, his stepfather going on a two-week business trip in Europe. His mother had been adamant that Jonah come along for the send-off. She was morbidly keen on pretending their family unit was a great success, and so a suitably emotional farewell was called for. The emotions had started early, Stephen misplacing his passport and casting blame on everyone but himself. Unexpectedly high traffic made Stephen grow even more tense, running lights and pushing up his speed in an effort to make up time.

'I said, your mother was wondering if you wanted to go out this evening,' Stephen said, his tone impatient. Jonah kept his own voice gentle. He spoke directly to his mother.

'I hoped we'd maybe go see a movie?'

'That'd be nice,' she replied.

'Remember I get in around nine your time,' said Stephen. 'I want you to be home when I call.'

'No,' Claire corrected, innocently. 'It'll be more like eleven. We'll make sure we're back by then.'

Stephen had been pressing close to the car ahead during this discussion, feet away at sixty miles an hour. He accelerated and overtook the car, oncoming traffic far too close for comfort.

'Slow down, sweetheart,' Jonah's mother said. 'We'll make it.'

'We're fifteen minutes away,' Stephen replied witheringly. 'I'm supposed to be checked in within twenty. Unless you can travel through time, just let me get on with driving?'

As he said it, he overtook the truck ahead of them, ignoring the bend they were on, not seeing the oncoming bus.

Jonah's mother called out. Stephen pulled on the steering wheel, tried to get back into the lane, but they weren't past the truck yet. There was nowhere to go. He slammed on the brakes. The car swerved, starting to spin, but the bus was already on them.

'No,' said Claire, her voice vanishingly small as the huge vehicle hit the passenger side.

There were flashes of pain, a terrible wrenching sensation, falling and tumbling and overwhelming noise. Then dark.

In the black, Jonah was aware of a smell of gas and hot metal. He knew he'd lost consciousness for a moment. The world wasn't moving anymore, but his mind spun. He opened his eyes carefully, unable to make sense of his surroundings. He moved his hands, holding them in front of his face and staring until they came into focus, spattered with blood. He looked around him. His mother was in the front seat, her head turned to the empty driver's side.

'Mom?' he said, a dry croak. 'Mom?' There was no response. He unfastened his seat belt, feeling a hot stripe of pain where the belt had bitten into him. His legs felt distant. He moved them with care and leaned forward. There was a stabbing pain in his chest, which he tried to ignore.

Her eyes were closed. 'Mom?' He wondered where his step-father was. The shattered web of the windshield blocked the view ahead. He had to get out of the car. The rear door on the passenger side failed to open. He eased himself along the seat to the other door. It opened easily. He stepped out, reeling from nausea as he stood. The car had come to rest in a muddy field, down a sheer thirty-foot drop after gouging through a line of saplings at the road-side. There were people at the top looking down, shouting to him and pointing. He looked along the field. It sloped up. Three men and a woman had run along the road and found a safe way down.

Stephen was stumbling over the uneven ground forty feet away, waving to them. Jonah moved around the car to his mother's door. He wrenched it open, feeling ill at the sight of her. The side of her head was a mess. He knelt by her, taking her hand. It was warm.

'Mom?' He turned to the helpers coming. *'Please!'* he yelled. *'Please hurry.'* He was crying now. They were having difficulty, the mud sucking them down and slowing them.

Jonah laid his head on his mother's lap and sobbed. 'It'll be OK. It'll be OK. Help's coming, Mom. Hold on. Hold on.' He held her tightly. He couldn't lose her. His voice shrank. He felt three years old. 'Please, don't leave me. Please, don't leave me.'

An image flashed in his mind: his real father, switching on Christmas tree lights and smiling.

'Please, don't leave me . . .' he said, his voice almost gone. There was a brief torrent of light and noise that he didn't understand.

He sensed something. Three seconds later his mother spoke.

'Jonah?' The voice was odd: distant and vague and lost. He froze, stunned, still not looking at her. Part of him knew, even then. Eleanor Preston's story had come to light six months before, a curio he had read with fascination, unaware of the significance. His mother's hand in his, part of him grasped what this was. The rest was overwhelmed with the belief that his mother was alive. 'Mom?' He raised his head, his smile faltering. There was no life in her eyes. No expression on her face. Something was terribly wrong. Yet his need for her to live overrode all doubt. 'Mom?'

He could hear the voices of the people approaching, coming to help.

His mother spoke again. 'Please. Please, let me go.'

He stared at her.

'Jonah. Please, let me go.'

Understanding rushed in, hitting him hard. 'I don't know how,' he said.

The people reached the car. 'Let me help,' said a woman. 'I'm a doctor. Let me . . .' She stopped, staring.

'Please, let me go,' his mother said. Jonah heard a sound from behind him, a man swearing, the word filled with disbelief. The doctor turned her stare to Jonah, unable to speak. Jonah spoke instead, hiding from the truth of it.

'She's going to be OK,' he said. 'She's . . .'

'My God. What are you doing?'

Jonah turned his head. Stephen was leaning on another man, holding his head with one hand, watching with shocked anger. *'What the hell are you doing?'* he said.

'She's going to be OK,' said Jonah, through tears and a smile that was forced and breaking. Stephen stared with horror as the body of his wife spoke.

'Please. Jonah. Let me go.'

His mother's words broke Stephen's inaction. He lunged, throwing Jonah back into the mud, Jonah's hand letting go of his mother's, the contact lost. He felt her leave, relieved by it and devastated even so. Stephen held his wife and sobbed. The others were all staring at Jonah, fear and confusion and horror in their eyes.

Jonah Miller looked up at the sky, trying to lose himself in the clouds. There was no sanctuary.

The only person he loved – and the only person who loved him – was dead. He was alone.

*

Jonah woke before dawn, with the sense of loss as raw as it had been twelve years before. He went to the bottom drawer in his bedroom cupboard and took out a small ring box he had found three months after her death, in a container of keepsakes in the basement that his mother had sometimes shown him and that Stephen Brinley had no interest in. Jonah had gone through the keepsakes, mourning his parents, when he had seen the ring box and taken it, not willing to risk its discovery by Stephen.

He opened it now and took out his mother's original wedding ring, which she had only stopped wearing the day she told Jonah she was to marry again. He took out another item from the box. His father's wedding ring. She had kept them together. There was one other thing the box contained, a note Jonah had held and read so often it was as fragile as smoke. A note to his father, in his mother's hand. He didn't take the note out now, too wary of damaging it.

I miss you, it read.

Jonah replaced the rings and closed the box.

15

Four days later Annabel Harker woke at eleven in the morning to a knock at the front door. She had slept on her own bed, still dressed. She cursed as she remembered: she'd put in a grocery order late in the night. The thought of venturing out to a store repelled her, and she needed the food. She had used her laptop for the first time since her arrival, her father's Wi-Fi settings unchanged since her visit last year.

A week's worth of microwave meals, milk and cereal. She took the bags inside with gruff thanks and closed the door.

Once she had unpacked it all, she made herself have a bowl of cornflakes. Standing at the kitchen work surface, she managed to splash milk out of the bowl as she poured. She grabbed a paper towel and wiped it up, her eye drawn to the clean line she'd made through the growing layer of dust. She stared at it, vacant and lost. She wiped again, extending the clean patch. Then something gave way inside her. She wiped every surface she could see, taking away the dust and feeling better for it.

Without a pause, she hunted down her father's vacuum cleaner and moved her way around the house room by room, a mixture of agitation and elation growing as she went. There was an element of panic in what she was doing, and she knew it.

She reached her own bedroom and took the sheets off the bed, gathering the small heap of clothes she'd been wearing.

Her father's room, then, her breathing fast, her desperation shooting up. She managed to remove the bedsheets before she fell to her knees, distraught and sobbing, days of suppressed emotion coming out at last.

When she gathered herself, she saw it.

Under her father's mattress, it had dislodged as she'd pulled out the sheet. A notebook. The notebook her father had always kept to hand, under the bed to keep away the prying eyes of his wife and daughter, even when those prying eyes were long dead and far away.

Annabel grasped it and flipped through the pages. Notes for his new novel. She recognized the name of a private detective character he'd used in a previous book. She kept flipping. There must have been forty pages of notes, before the final few entries.

And they were different. Two pages, the first a jumble of abbreviations and scrawled phrases, question marks, arrowed lines and heavy underscores that made no sense to her, and in the middle of the scrawl, a date. Three weeks before her father had disappeared, written beside the initials T.Y. Next to that, circled, was the word *UNITY*.

The second page had another date, three days before the disappearance, and the words: *T.Y. NO SHOW*.

Her father had mentioned to her that he'd been looking into something nonfiction. Here it was.

She'd assumed he'd meant something simple, innocuous. The dates being so close to his disappearance could change everything. Thoughts intruded in her mind, of how this could lead to a benign reason for his absence, but she couldn't allow herself to think like that. False hope would only torment her.

No. She would unravel the scrawled text, and if it was relevant she would contact the police.

The capitalized words and abbreviations were the least illegible, and she listed them: *TY, UNITY, BL, AB, BPV, AL*.

She went to her laptop. *BPV* was the first to succumb, the name of a drug used in revival. A line connected it to *TY*, and beside the line was the number fifteen. *BL* seemed likely to be 'Baseline'. She found no clear match for *TY* or *UNITY*.

AB seemed to suggest Andreas Biotech, the biggest sponsor of the Baseline project. *MA* could have been Michael Andreas, the company founder; a thick arrow ran from it to *BPV*.

She read up on Michael Andreas. His face was familiar, and his profile had been high when Baseline had first formed, his company contributing significant money and expertise. Some of the coverage from the time was vaguely suspicious of the man, still under forty, crazily young to have amassed so much wealth. Five years before Baseline, a very public declaration of his personal aims had prompted ridicule: Andreas had stated that death would be eradicated within a century.

He was known to have invested in cryogenics, buying out a whole-body cryogenic storage facility in Nevada, rich clients hoping to avoid the inconvenient permanence of the grave.

When he got involved with Baseline, some commentators derided what they saw as an obsession with death, but as she read through various articles Annabel wondered why they would be surprised: the biggest contribution to the investigation into revival had come from a man fascinated by mortality. It was a fascination some articles traced back to the death of his first love, nine years before revival came to light. How they portrayed the loss depended on the tone of the article, ranging from heartbreaking romance to unhealthy fixation.

Baseline would have suffered without his involvement. Revival was faced with public, political and corporate unease; companies didn't want to be too closely associated with it, and the same went for international funding. Even the United States government was careful to distance itself once the initial rush of public fascination subsided.

Andreas had done the opposite, drawing plaudits at first from the press, but in time cynicism won out. Why was he investing so much of his own money? What was his angle? They attacked him for his morbid obsession, they accused him of profiteering. When Baseline had finally closed down, many wondered if Andreas had had enough. He had withdrawn from the public eye by then, averse to being in the spotlight, behaviour the press interpreted as pique.

Annabel looked at her father's notes. Andreas had been key in developing the drug BPV, which apparently inhibited post-traumatic stress in revivers. Why her father should highlight that link, Annabel had no idea.

She kept the abbreviation *AL* to the end, thinking she knew what it was and wanting to put it off. The only relevant hit was 'Afterlifers', as she'd expected. In the notebook, there were words dotted around *AL* that she couldn't make out, but she finally deciphered one arrowed connection to *TY*. *Abscom if know*, it read. Another Web search took her to an old article about Afterlifer extremism.

'Abscom' had been how some of the most extreme groups within the Afterlifers referred to themselves. Absolute commitment. The word had also been used as a verb, a euphemism for doing what needed to be done, without question. It was a threat to those showing weakness or passing information to the authorities. Anyone who wavered was open to beatings, or worse.

TY must be a person, she reasoned. Someone her father had met and arranged to meet again, who then hadn't appeared; someone with enough old Afterlifer connections to be under threat for speaking to a journalist.

Someone the police could identify.

'What the hell were you getting into, Dad?' Annabel said.

She picked up the phone and called Detective Harrington. She explained what she'd found, barely pausing for breath, not noticing the total silence at the other end until she had finished.

'Miss Harker,' said the detective in a slow, purposeful way that Annabel suddenly found terrifying. 'Annabel. The case isn't with us any more. There have been developments, but . . .'

'Tell me,' said Annabel. She could sense the unease on the other end of the phone.

'Annabel, give me a few seconds.' The line went silent, and she could almost see him scrabbling for information from those around him. Thirty seconds went by. She gripped the handset tighter. Then the line clicked and Harrington was back, cautious and awkward. 'Annabel. I understand there's someone coming to you now. They'll arrive within . . .'

'Tell me. *Please.*'

A long pause as Harrington made his choice.

'They found a body four hours ago,' the detective told her. 'They think it's your father.'

16

Detective Ray Johnson was cold. He was standing in the pathology room in the Richmond FRS building, watching someone hunt for maggots.

Daniel Harker's body had been found in a rented house in Warrenton, Virginia. The rent had been paid two months in advance. The owner had been phoning for days to arrange access to take down an old tree at the back of the property. Unable to raise the tenants, he had gone there in person to find an abandoned house and a smell coming from the cellar.

The wallet in Harker's back pocket had provided an initial ID. With a big story looming, the choice of who would lead the investigation rose higher than normal procedure required: the city, the district, the *state*. A badly managed investigation would be a conspicuous failure, and nobody wanted to be accused of overseeing a shambles in their territory.

The Woods case had been a media favourite for a few days, and Crenner's name was pushed hard by those who wanted to cash in on the good will.

That morning, Johnson had followed Crenner and the pathologist at the scene, Peter Rierson, into the stench and gloom of the cellar, wearing a white respiration mask at Rierson's advice. It was empty, save for the police photographer and the corpse. A single bare light hung from the roof.

In the middle of the concrete floor was a chair, fallen on its side. And in that chair, a figure. Hands tied at the rear. The skin purple and blackened, the appalling smell brought into extreme focus. Johnson noticed movement. There was a maggot on the corpse's cheek.

'Christ,' he said, trying not to retch.

Rierson nodded. 'I've already spent ten minutes gathering the little bastards. I've probably only got half of them. I like my corpses to stay still.' He crouched down and pulled a plastic container and tweezers from his pockets, gathering larvae one by one.

'Shit,' said Crenner. 'I can't even tell if it's him.'

Staring at the swollen and distorted face of the hunched shape in the chair, Johnson knew what he meant.

'How long's he been dead?' asked Crenner.

'We'll need a better idea how warm it gets down here by after-noon,' Rierson said. 'We'd expect a place like this to stay quite cool, but with so many warm nights and hot days recently it plays havoc with the guesswork. These maggots have been feeding for a few days now, probably hatched within two to four days of laying, species and temperature depending. Relatively few larvae, perhaps a single insect in the cellar with him when he died or one got lucky getting inside later. Must be well sealed or we'd be overrun by now. That'd give us maybe five days as a minimum, but by the look of the body I'd say longer. It might not be a species that lays on fresh cadavers. Some wait until they get a little more mushy, and then lay on pre-existing wounds. They're mostly in this area of the neck, so maybe they were laid around an injury. Deep scratches would have been enough of an invite. We'll have a better idea later when an entomologist's had a look.'

'Five days minimum, what's your maximum?'

'Hell, look at the state of him. Could be ten days, even two weeks. He's pretty ripe. I assume you've no intention of trying a revival?' Rierson's expression showed he didn't expect there to be a chance of it.

'Pathology liaison from FRS North East should be here soon,' said Crenner. 'We'll see what they say.'

What they said wasn't encouraging. Onsite was impractical. With the right facilities they gave a 5 per cent chance, even for the best revivers in the country. While it was North East's jurisdiction, all of their highest-ranking staff were on tails. Crenner would have to beg elsewhere if he wanted it done that day, and he knew exactly what his first call would be.

The decision made, Harker's body was removed, covered in polythene sheeting while still tied to the chair. It was transported to the Richmond FRS preparation room, where the corpse was finally untied, the clothing removed and dispatched for examination.

The blackening of the skin was worst around the head and throat, the rest of the corpse lighter, green veins tracking the paths of decay. There was a simple Celtic tattoo design at the top of the left arm. That sealed the identification – dental results and DNA would take days, but the tattoo was visible in a photograph Harker's daughter had supplied. Crenner called it in, and set off to bring the news to Annabel Harker in person, unaware that the news had already reached her.

That left Ray Johnson, watching Peter Rierson continue his examination for an hour, before spotting a few maggots he had missed earlier.

'How long do we think until we're good to go?' Johnson asked.

Rierson looked up. 'Once I'm sure I've got the last of these guys it'll take me another twenty minutes, say, to get the rest of the pre-liminary samples, help us get a better handle on cause of death.'

'What's the working hypothesis?'

'Not pleasant. Severely dehydrated, probably hadn't had food or water in days, but we need to get inside him for that. It looks like he was tied up and left.'

Johnson shook his head. 'Fuck. How long would it have taken?'

'Depending how cool that cellar stays, maybe three or four days before he lost consciousness, another day or two before death. He was securely tied. There were clear signs of him struggling to free himself.'

'Jesus.' His cell phone rang and he answered. It was Bob Crenner. Johnson listened for a moment, then told Crenner they'd be ready in another half hour. He hung up and wandered back to the corpse, watching it for a moment in silence before he spoke. 'Harker's daughter is on her way here. She wants to be present for the revival.'

Rierson raised his eyebrows. 'We haven't exactly done a mortician's job,' he said, his fingers in the flesh of Harker's neck. 'Free of larvae, best we can do.'

They both fell silent as Rierson finished up. Johnson stood back, then noticed something on the corpse's skin. The blackening increased down the lower part of the leg, becoming severe around the foot, but there was a definite mark just above the ankle. He stepped over and looked.

'What do you think that is?' he asked, indicating the mark, less than a centimetre across.

'Tattoo,' Rierson said without looking up. 'Noticed it earlier. Hadn't been mentioned by the daughter, but she may not have been aware of it.'

'What is it?' said Johnson. 'I can't make it out.' The black lines of the tattoo were difficult to see against the blackened and sloughing skin.

'I couldn't either, but we already had the shoulder tattoo so it was just a quick look.'

Johnson peered at the mark. At last, he could see what it was. A tiny tattoo of a robin.

*

By the time Bob Crenner arrived back at the FRS with Annabel Harker, a local victim liaison officer had been arranged and was waiting. Crenner left Annabel in the officer's care, sitting in the observation room with the curtains drawn. He went into the pathology room to brief those involved.

'Boss,' said Ray Johnson, with a nod.

Peter Rierson was at the side, labelling the samples he had taken. Also present were the FRS contingent: Hugo Adler, Never Geary and Pru Dryden. Dryden would be the reviver, something that had disappointed Crenner when he'd first called, but he trusted these people.

'Here's what we know,' Crenner said. 'Daniel Harker was reported missing sixteen days ago. The last verified contact was ten days earlier. Initially it was thought that money was the most likely motive, but there was always a chance that he had been taken by an Afterlifer or similar group. The detectives involved played this down with the daughter and kept the story quiet. Daniel was found this morning, possibly abandoned. He may have died of thirst.

'His car was caught on security camera in Greensboro, North Carolina, an unknown male using his card to withdraw money. Same card was used a few days later in Atlanta. His car has not been found yet, but it now seems likely that the withdrawals were intended to mislead us. They wanted us to think they'd gone halfway across the country. Instead, Daniel Harker was only a two-hour drive from his home. It's possible the kidnapping was over money, but if it was we're looking at incompetents. If it was idealism, then his death must be a statement. But neither feels right.' Crenner started to walk around the corpse, taking slow steps as he spoke. 'If they wanted him revived, maybe to deliver a memorized message, then the length of time before Harker was found makes no sense. Maybe they fucked up. This morning, his daughter found evidence that Daniel had been working on a story involving Afterlifers. He disappeared days after his contact failed to show at an agreed meeting. If this is relevant – if they took him because of something he had been told – then why did they let him die this way? If he'd known something, why did they risk him being revived, and not kill him and decapitate the body? So far, we have nothing from the house where he was found. Remains of several fires in the backyard. Plenty of fingerprints, but nothing matched so far. Description of one man the owner met, with not a single unusual feature. No information on any vehicles. We have ten detectives working on this and getting nowhere, and time running out before the story leaks. We need the revival. If it works, our priority is to get the circumstances of his kidnapping, descriptions of his kidnappers and to fill in the blanks on what Harker had found, if anything. Hugo?'

Hugo Adler raised an eyebrow. 'Detective. Pru will get him back, if it can be done.' He looked Pru's way and got a scared smile in return, then he addressed her. 'Pru, Detectives Crenner and Johnson will be sitting with me and Never in the tech room. Annabel Harker is anxious to speak with her father. The chances are slim, but you should talk to her now while we bring Harker into the revival room and finish prep.'

Pru Dryden nodded. Bob Crenner watched her leave, then found himself looking at the corpse. Dryden was preparing for the challenge of reviving this body. Crenner was scared for her.

*

Pru collapsed eighty-six minutes after starting the revival. From the technician's room, Never had been watching closely. Daniel Harker's naked body on the padded table in the revival room, black and green and distorted; Pru's face, eyes closed most of the time, brow creased, brief flickerings of emotion.

He had been worried since the beginning. Pru had looked far too wary for his liking, the combination of pressure of the high-profile case and the innate difficulty of the revival facing her. He had used one camera to get a tight shot of Pru and could see the effort build, her discomfort growing. He was the first in the room when it went wrong, moving for the door a moment before anyone else had even seen it happening, Daniel Harker's hand slipping out of Pru's. She slouched over in her chair, falling to the floor just before Never reached her, blood from a cut lip leaving a smear on the white tiling when he turned her over.

Hugo was close on his heels. They helped her through to one of the overnight beds in the bunk room down the hall.

Crenner came with them. 'She OK?' he asked.

'She'll be fine,' said Hugo. 'Call upstairs, Never. See who can sit with her.'

Pru sat up as Never picked up the phone. 'Shit. Sorry. The pull was tough, couldn't handle it.'

'You did well to get that close,' said Hugo.

'Stacy's coming down,' said Never.

Crenner looked worried. 'What about Harker? Can she try again?'

Hugo looked at Pru. She shook her head, and he nodded. 'You stay here until Stacy says you're fine, Pru. Then get yourself home and rest.'

When Stacy arrived, Never, Hugo and Crenner headed down the corridor, back into the technician's room.

'We knew it would be difficult,' said Hugo.

Crenner swore. 'We need the revival. You told me that you—'

'I know what I *said*.' Hugo turned away from Crenner's gaze. He looked down at the floor. 'Give us a moment, Detective.'

Crenner nodded, then stepped out into the corridor.

Hugo turned to Never. 'I didn't think it would come down to this,' he said. 'I thought Pru would do it, or get nowhere. But she got *close*. That means it can be done, and we're running out of time.'

'What did you tell Crenner?' asked Never, his eyes narrowing.

Hugo sighed. 'When he called, he asked about Jonah first. I told him Jonah was our backup, that with Stacy and Jason both on tails until tomorrow, it left us with Pru and Jonah as the only ones capable of Harker's revival. I told him I didn't want Jonah doing it, unless . . .'

'Unless we had no option,' Never said.

Hugo nodded. 'The clock's ticking. We have to start the second attempt within ninety minutes. Jonah was due back at work tomorrow. He was given the all-clear.'

'I doubt this was the kind of case they had in mind for his return, Hugo.'

'But what do you think?'

'I think . . .' said Never, then he gave it some serious thought. 'I think if Sam was here, he wouldn't ask Jonah to do it.' Hugo said nothing, but in his eyes Never could see he thought so too. 'I also think, if we don't tell Jonah about it, he'll not forgive us.'

*

When Jonah's phone rang he was in the kitchen, wearing his overnight boxers and tee shirt, making a cup of coffee while he ate a slice of toast. He let the answering machine take the call, but picked up when he heard Never's voice.

'Hey, Never.' He could hear voices in the background. 'Are you at work?'

'Yes, I'm at work,' said Never, with a reluctance that Jonah noticed at once.

'What is it?'

'You've heard of Daniel Harker?'

'Of course.'

'He went missing a few weeks ago.'

'I hadn't heard.'

'It was kept quiet.'

Although Never seemed unwilling to get to the point, Jonah knew the punchline. He knew the question Never had called to ask. The minimum time Stephanie Graves had insisted on before he could work again had passed, but he knew they'd only be coming to him if they had no other option. And that meant a hard case.

Jonah took a deep breath. 'How long's he been dead?'

'Quite a while. He's in a bad way. Even Pru didn't get there. But she wasn't far off.'

'She OK?'

'Shaken up. Worst I've seen her.'

Jonah was silent. He didn't relish facing what she'd faced. 'Why do we need a revival, Never? What does this look like?'

'Looks like murder.'

Jonah thought for a moment. 'Let's see what he has to say.'

He hung up the phone and started to dress.

*

Jonah arrived thirty minutes later. The prospect of reviving a severely decayed subject would normally leave him sick with fear, but the moment Never had called to say he was needed, things had crystallized in his mind. Whatever his doubts about his future, here was something he couldn't say no to. Harker had been crucial in revival becoming acceptable. Every reviver owed the man a debt.

He took the stairs down the two flights to the revival floor, heading straight to the technician's room to see Never. The door to the observation room lay open at the end of the hall. Inside, he could see Hugo Adler in discussion with several others. A few feet from them sat a young woman. She looked exhausted.

He walked into the tech room.

'Hi, mate,' said Never. 'Am I in your bad books?'

Jonah smiled at him. 'No. None of us has a choice here. How's Pru?'

'She's getting her head down in the bunk room.'

Jonah nodded. 'I'll take my meds and get briefed. We can start in ten. Everything's still set, right?'

'We dropped the room temperature after Pru's try. I'll warm it a little. Apart from that, all set.'

Jonah nodded to the feed from the observation room. 'Who'll be watching?'

As he named them, Never pointed them out on the screen: 'Bob Crenner and Ray Johnson. Can't seem to get rid of 'em. They'll be sitting in with me during the revival. That's Peter Rierson, the pathologist. And *that* is Daniel Harker's daughter.'

Jonah shook his head. 'Hell of a sight for her to deal with. Is she here to . . .?'

'Yes.'

Jonah looked at her. Even if he'd been in doubt before, he wasn't now. She looked shattered, and wanted to speak to her father one last time. Perhaps when his work was faceless, anonymous, then Jonah could pretend to himself that he had a real choice, that his fear of the process was enough to drive him from it. But when it was tied to real people, he couldn't conceive of walking away. Tess had been right to say he was idealistic. For all the good it did him.

*

Jonah knocked on the door to the bunk room, and Stacy opened it.

'She awake?' he asked. Stacy nodded. Jonah followed her inside, shocked to see how grey Pru Dryden's face looked. It had really hit hard. Pru was small, but Jonah knew she could take care of herself. She'd had a daughter with a long-term boyfriend who had started to knock Pru around. She'd given as good as she got, ousting the boyfriend, which left her on her own with a two-year-old to raise and a full-time job. Right now, though, she looked impossibly fragile.

'Any tips?' he asked.

'Thought you were off work,' Pru said.

'I am.'

'This is a bad choice of vacation.' The smile she'd been attempting faded. 'The pull was strong and fast. Caught me by surprise. If that helps.'

He nodded. She'd nearly made it, but the ride got too rough. 'Thanks.'

Jonah grabbed a drink from the water cooler in the corner. He'd already been up to his desk to grab his medication. It was bespoke, formulated individually for each reviver; replacement supplies at his new dosage would arrive within a few more days, but as Graves had increased his BPV by 50 per cent, all he had to do was take an extra half pill.

Stacy and Pru wished him luck. He tried to ignore the worry he could see in their eyes.

*

Jonah walked to the observation room, with one last task before the revival could begin. He crossed to Annabel Harker and crouched down.

'Miss Harker . . .'

'Annabel, please.'

'My name is Jonah Miller. I'm going to be making the second attempt at reviving your father. I take it the other reviver discussed the attendance situation with you?'

'She did. Is she all right?'

'She will be. Can I confirm that you want to talk with your father?'

'I do.'

'You have to realize that the chances are slim. Even if I get him back, it's not guaranteed that you'll have any time with him. If I give the go-ahead, you'll be escorted to the revival room. You can tell me what to say. It'll be a non-vocal revival; during questioning you'll see your father's replies on that screen, as I type them. If you get to talk to him, though, I'll simply repeat what he says. Do you understand?'

'I do.'

Jonah nodded and started to get up. Annabel put her hand out, on his wrist. He flinched, just a little, but there was no chill. 'Jonah,' said Annabel. 'Please. Try.'

'I will. If it looks like there won't be time, I'll give him a message from you. If you want.'

Tears fell from Annabel Harker's eyes. 'Tell him I'm sorry.'

*

'It's freezing,' complained Ray Johnson, folding his arms.

'The temperature's kept right down while we're not active,' said Never. 'We raise it a little for revival, but that'll take a few minutes.'

'I guess it keeps the meat fresher.'

Jonah glanced up at the lights on the wall opposite indicating the active audio feeds. There was a red light for the observation room, and he relaxed. 'Just so you know,' he said. 'That red light means the subject's daughter didn't hear your comment.'

Johnson raised his hands. 'Sorry.'

'If we can get started?' said Jonah. The others turned to him. 'OK, I've read the preliminary report. We just need the formal nod to get under way and I can get briefed. No objections to starting? Dr Rierson?'

'No.'

'Detective Crenner?'

'Let's get on with it. Good luck.'

'I'll do my best. With a second attempt at revival it's hard to know the chances, but Pru got close. If it does happen, someone this far gone can be hard to judge. They can go in a flash. Now, take your seats and get comfortable. This may take some time.'

*

Alone, Jonah sat in the chair and adjusted it until it felt right. The curtain on the observation room window had been drawn back, but the audio feed was still off. He limbered up his left hand, his fingers stiff in the cold air, and set them on the keypad. His shorthand was solid. All the revivers who handled non-vocal cases had regular training to keep up their skills – repeating aloud everything that was said was a clumsy way to go about an interview. He typed a few phrases to make sure the pad was in working order, the words being displayed in full on a screen above. An earpiece rested by the keypad, and he put it in place.

'Testing, testing,' said Never's voice.

Jonah raised his thumb. 'All fine. I'm ready.'

He suddenly didn't *feel* ready. He looked again at Harker, the enormity of the task ahead of him impossible to ignore. It was written in the state of the corpse: in the distortion and swelling; in the black veins and the shedding skin. Could he *ever* feel ready for something like this?

He reached out. Daniel Harker's hand felt deeply cold in his own, the flesh rubbery. Unlike the rest of the body, the hand had been cleaned for optimal contact. Jonah ran his eyes down the length of the rotting corpse before him. He looked up, and checked that the Obs feed light was still red. Only Never could hear him. 'I met him once,' he said.

'Yes?' said Never.

'He interviewed me a few months after I joined Baseline. Asked me about the crash, when my mom died. I hadn't spoken to anyone else about it in so much detail. It was cathartic. The next day I called him and asked him not to use it. He agreed without a grumble. Seemed like a decent guy.' He took a deep breath. The cold air kept the smell of decay to a minimum. 'Start recording.'

The bank of lights on the far wall turned to green one at a time.

'Revival of subject Daniel Harker, nonvocal,' he said. 'J. P. Miller, duty reviver.'

17

Daniel Harker's hand rested in Jonah's, the skin of the dead fingers shedding, just as it was all over the blackened and bloating torso. The abdomen greenish, thickly veined. The face puffy and distorted, the eyes swollen.

Jonah closed his own eyes and allowed his mind to flow over the corpse, touching the sheets of loose skin, tasting the rank salt of the wounds around Daniel's wrist and the pitted gouges in his neck where the maggots had fed, feeling the gelatinous rubber of his abdominal flesh.

Minutes passed this way, until he felt it was time to sink deeper, losing himself to the darkness within Harker's corpse. He felt his own flesh degrade as he went. Slowly, his intestines began to dissolve in a rich bacterial sea. His eyeballs started to contract as they lost moisture. He sensed his hair begin to lose grip and shed. Rigor mortis built in his limbs, peaked and faded as the muscle proteins broke down.

In the dark, in the silence, time passed. Jonah felt more dead than he could ever be. His mouth – God, so dry, *so dry* – began to moisten once more with the products of decomposition.

And then his flesh twitched, stirred around his neck as maggots hatched and began to embed themselves, burrowing deep and feeding, forming a writhing mass, growing, drowning him –

It was too much. Jonah came round on the floor, the link with Harker broken. He was sobbing, and Never was there, telling him it would be OK. Jonah gathered himself. He sat up and looked at the clock. Seventy-two minutes since he'd started. It felt longer.

Hugo entered the revival room. 'Enough,' he said. 'I shouldn't have asked you to try this.' He stepped towards the corpse, reaching to the dangling arm, ready to replace it by Harker's side.

'Don't touch him!'

Hugo turned to Jonah, taken aback by the raised voice, by the defiance in Jonah's eyes, even though he looked shattered.

'Don't touch him,' Jonah repeated, quieter now, regaining composure. 'I'm close.' He stood, wiping the cold sweat from his face with his left hand. Given how near he'd been, as long as Jonah started again soon, the chances would hardly be affected. 'I need a minute before I get back to it, but I'm almost there.'

Hugo shook his head, but in resignation rather than refusal. 'Five minutes. See how you feel.'

Jonah spent the first two of those five dry heaving in the toilet along the corridor, while Never stood fretting outside the cubicle. Jonah emerged, rinsed his mouth and began rubbing at his neck to rid himself of the sensation of movement that was still beneath his skin, the intense larval itch that he knew would take days to leave him completely. He drank straight from the tap, gulping down mouthful after mouthful of cold water.

He rose, grabbed a paper towel and dried the water dripping from his chin. 'Thirsty,' he said, out of breath. It was little wonder, given that Harker had probably died of dehydration.

Jonah returned to the revival room and took his position again. He waited until his stomach had settled, until his skin was no longer moving. Recording resumed. He took Daniel's hand, and soon he was back, the maggots ascendant.

Better prepared now, he held on for the long minutes until the maggots fell away, and the degradation of his own body began to reverse, flesh re-forming and regenerating.

Slowly, his eyes filled out, his liquefied innards regrouped. Putrefaction left him. He was Daniel Harker then, intact and pristine, and he called to Harker's essence – whatever that might be, wherever that might be – and he waited, steeling himself for the surge.

An answer came. Jonah felt like he was in free-fall, tumbling uncontrolled as images filled his mind, but he'd not come this far to lose it now. He held on. Moments later, Harker was there.

Jonah opened his eyes. He was sitting as he had started, holding the hand of a ravaged corpse. But now the corpse had become more; he sensed the consciousness within, the thoughts forming. He looked at the clock again. It was forty minutes since he had resumed the revival. It had taken almost two hours in all.

He was exhausted. At last, the work could begin.

*

'Daniel? My name is Jonah Miller. Do you understand what's happening?'

The whorl of thought within Harker clarified. It was slow, the wait for a reply agonizing.

'Yes. I died.'

With his left hand on the keypad, Jonah recorded the words fluidly. He was well practised. In the observation and tech rooms, they would be watching the screens to follow Harker's side of the conversation.

'I'm a reviver with the FRS. I want to ask you some questions about what happened to you.'

'Jonah. I remember your name. You're the boy who brought back his mother. Where am I? And who is here?' Harker's answer had been immediate that time; he felt less vague now, his presence stronger. A sign that they might have minutes left to them, rather than seconds.

'You're in a revival room in the FRS office in Richmond. Detective Bob Crenner is the police representative.'

'Is Annie here? My daughter?' There was heartache in the words that Jonah couldn't transcribe, and a sudden distance that worried him. He would have to get off the topic of his daughter as soon as he could.

'She wanted to be present,' said Jonah. 'When we're finished, you can talk to Annie. I'll make sure there's time. I promise.' A pause. Harker felt even weaker. Jonah wondered if keeping that promise would be possible.

'Thank you, Jonah. Now ask me what you want to ask me. We may not have long.'

'Tell us what happened on the day you went missing. Describe people in as much detail as you can.'

Another delay. Jonah hoped it was just Harker gathering his thoughts, and when Harker did finally speak it was with purpose; he knew time was against them. 'Wednesday afternoon, around one-thirty. There was a knock at the door. I answered, and there was a man, mid-thirties. Short black hair, long face, extremely thin with a sharp nose and cold eyes. Small round-framed glasses, quite thick lenses. Voice was much deeper than I expected, much more confident. Well spoken. I thought he was a fan. He seemed to be there for a reason, seemed to recognize me, know who I was.

'He said a name. The moment he said it I knew I was in trouble. The name of a man I'd met who had told me things he believed people would kill him for. The door chain wasn't on and I was cursing myself, whatever good it would have done. I moved to shut the door but his foot was already in the way.

'He pushed hard enough to send me backwards. I turned to the phone but he was faster and took it. Another man followed him in. Shorter, cropped ginger hair. Hard-faced, a bulldog of a man, nervous eyes, young. Mid-twenties. I was frozen.

'The first man spoke, said he had respect for me, that they'd just leave once I agreed to say nothing about what I'd been told. He put out a hand, said, "No hard feelings". Bewildered, I took it. His grip became firm, then painful. No empathy in his eyes. He grabbed my arm as the shorter man came behind, reached around and held me fast. The dark-haired man put his other hand in a pocket and came out with a syringe. He injected something into my arm, a rough sharp stab that made me understand just how bad this was. I blacked out.'

Harker stopped. Jonah gave him a few moments, hoping he was gathering his thoughts again. In his earpiece, Bob Crenner was asking for the name of Harker's contact.

Keep the flow going, Jonah thought, ignoring the request for now. It would be better coming in Harker's own good time.

'What happened next?' Jonah asked.

'I came round in that fucking chair is what happened next. My whole body was cramping. I was gagged tight. The ginger guy was there, and another guy – fat but tall, brown hair. Ginger called to Fats that I'd woken. They asked me for the code of my ATM card. I stared at them so hard. I hated them. I was *outraged* by them. I knew Annie was coming. I knew how worried she would be. I gave them the code.

'Ginger and Fats took turns watching me. I didn't see the first man again, the gaunt one with the cold eyes. They didn't try to give me food until the evening, gag removed but I was still tied. I started to scream the instant the gag came off. I didn't expect we were in earshot of anywhere, but it just came out. Ginger punched my stomach, and he hit hard. The gag went back on, and he talked to me like I was a child. They left me alone overnight, and tried again next morning. I was hungry, by then. Ginger spooned some god-awful stew into my mouth. He gave me a drink of flat cola.'

Harker stopped. Jonah sensed it with total clarity: it was the memory of the drink that had made Harker pause. Given what had followed, the thought of that drink was a thought of heaven.

After twenty seconds of silence, Crenner's impatience got the better of him. 'Is he still there?' he asked.

Jonah typed his response, for the tech room only: 'Yes.' He didn't think he dared risk rushing Harker yet, but after another ten seconds, he was getting worried himself. 'Daniel?' he said.

'I'm sorry,' replied Daniel, slow and sounding worryingly vague. 'What was I saying?'

Jonah wondered just how much time was left, and if his daughter would get any of it. He phrased his response with care, not wanting to mention the drink again. 'They'd fed you. What happened next?'

Again, a pause. Running out of time, Jonah thought. 'They gagged me again, tied my feet to a short chain that was fixed to the wall, and untied me from the chair. My hands were still tied at the front, my feet at the ankles. They left me alone much of the time, checking in on me every hour or two. I had a bucket as a toilet but needed their help to use it. I tried to make as big a mess of it as I could, hoping they'd untie my hands, at least for a while. I only saw Ginger and Fats, but I heard maybe two others in the house. Some days I heard some of them go outside and a vehicle leave. It would be gone for a few hours at most. When they all went out, they tied me up in the chair again. They only fed me once a day. When they did, I tried to talk to them, but they said very little.

'They'd leave the light on in the cellar. I could only tell how many days were passing by the birdsong in the mornings. I'd counted five days when they started bringing boxes down. Ginger told me the old air conditioning in the house had failed. The cellar was the only cool room. They'd come regularly, fetch something from one of the boxes. I'd hear them in the yard, curious sounds like a failed firework. When I got the chance to talk, I asked them what they were doing. They just smiled. But there was something, something Ginger said . . .'

He stopped. Jonah tensed, sensing that Harker had remembered something crucial, something he was struggling with. Jonah could feel Harker's intense effort to grasp the memory, but it was failing; as the effort grew, the memory receded. Unchecked, it could easily end Harker's coherence. *Something Ginger said.* Whatever the memory was, he had to make Harker abandon it, try again later if there was time.

'Daniel. Who was your contact?'

Nothing. Only the tight desperation in Harker as he tried to remember whatever it was that was sucking him down. Jonah had to try something more emotive.

'*Daniel.* Why did they leave you to die?'

It was like a slap to the face. The tempest of Harker's thoughts froze, crystallized into that one question.

'*Why did they leave me to die?*'

A deep pain in his words, and a horror, but Harker was focused once more. Jonah took a long breath, regretting the cruelty but knowing it had to be done.

'Tell me what happened.'

'Early. Ginger and Fats came down and told me they'd all be leaving for a few hours, that they'd return soon. They tied me into the chair. And they didn't come back. I spent that day in cramped discomfort that was turning to pain, thirst increasing. It was eternity there. When the next morning came, I really started to fear. By that night, I was hallucinating. I saw Robin, my dead wife, and talked to her. I talked to Annie. When I was rational again, I started to understand I would die. I tried to free myself, and became so angry I struggled and threw all I had into it. The chair toppled and I lost consciousness for a while. When I came round, panic took over. I struggled until I was too exhausted to struggle, too exhausted to notice anything. It was a mercy. I suppose I died, eventually. I can't remember it.'

Harker stopped. After a moment, Bob Crenner spoke: 'We need information about his contact, Jonah. What did he know?'

'Daniel. Who was your contact?'

'His name was Tobias Yarrow. He sent me a letter, asking to meet. Something had been going on at Baseline, he said, something secret and dark. He'd got involved with people who wanted to stop it. I was intrigued. I'd heard that kind of thing before. Conspiracy theorists had had plenty of fun with Baseline, like they had with everything else. It always fascinated me, how they could take such little pieces of rumour and speculation and create their bizarre world views. I had a brush with the Afterlifers a while back, but it was the fringes that interested me most. Total belief in the most ludicrous things. And Yarrow clearly fit that bill.

'I've wondered more than once if I could get an article out of things like that, maybe a book, and now I saw a chance. The thought interested me enough to get me out of the house, and if you knew me you'd know just how big a deal that was. We arranged a meeting, and he told me fragments. Yarrow had known someone he called "Fifteen", who'd given him information about the development of BPV. I asked if they had worked at Andreas Biotech, but Yarrow either didn't know or wouldn't say. That information led Yarrow and his friends to stumble on what he called Unity. He didn't tell me what it was, only that his friends wanted to put an end to it, and they had got out of control. He thought there was another way and that I could help him. That was all he told me then. He would tell me the rest at our next meeting, and I agreed. He told me his associates would kill him if they found out. The way he phrased it made me think Yarrow had been an Afterlifer. He didn't show up for our next meeting. I was disappointed but not surprised. I thought I'd hear from him soon enough. I thought I knew what kind of man he was, the kind that thrived on melodrama. I thought what he'd said about his friends was pure exaggeration. I was wrong.'

Jonah waited a few seconds until he was sure Harker had finished. 'Thank you, Daniel,' he said. Deep exhaustion was creeping up on Jonah, a sign that Harker was weakening fast. In his earpiece, he could hear Crenner and Johnson whisper about the information they now had.

He knew there was more, if he could get Harker to remember. And if he did, it would likely use up what little time was left. Break his promise to Harker – and to his daughter.

'What's happening?' asked Crenner. 'Do you think that's all we'll get?'

Jonah typed a message to the tech room: 'No.'

He wasn't certain how strongly Harker was present. 'Focus, Daniel.' Weak, but still there. 'There was something Ginger said. You remember.'

Silence.

'I can't . . .'

'Please, Daniel. Talk to me. You remember.'

Jonah tried to calm his own nerves and get a better grip on Harker. The memory was close; he could feel Harker strive for it again. Then, sudden and bewildering, an image flashed in Jonah's mind, a box upended on the cellar floor. The shock of it caught him by surprise. This wasn't something that had ever happened to him in the middle of a revival.

Harker spoke, 'The box had fallen.'

Jonah focused and pushed hard. It took everything he had, but Harker came back, a rush of words that Jonah could barely keep up with:

'One night the others had gone out and Ginger was alone, drunk. He came down and told me the boxes were going. He took them upstairs one by one. The last box, he stumbled. Fell down the steps. The box fell in front of me. Containers inside, but he was quick. He took the box again, looked at its contents, then looked at me. Mournful eyes. He said that before they let me go, they would tell me everything, and I would write about it. It would be up to me to explain their actions to the world. He told me he wasn't proud. He told me it was just the way things were. Sometimes, he said, sometimes people have to die.'

In the tech room, Crenner cursed.

'What did he mean, Daniel?' Jonah asked. 'What was in the box?' He could sense the moment approach. Whatever it was that had stalled Daniel Harker before, it was coming, and Harker was receding with every second.

'I didn't see what was in the containers, Jonah. I'm sorry. But I saw the shipping label. I think the company was called Alpha

Chemicals or something similar. And I saw the date. I saw it and everything stopped. It was the day she died, Jonah. It was the date Robin died.'

That was all it had been. The date on the box. The anniversary of his wife's death. Jonah felt the despair Harker had felt, as the smallest of details had mocked him. The memory of it was enough to submerge Harker in that despair once more, his presence draining away again, fading too fast now.

Maybe the thought of his daughter would be enough. 'Daniel? Please. Your daughter's here. Annie's here.' Even as he said it, Jonah knew it was a forlorn hope.

Harker's voice was well below a whisper now. *'Will I see Robin? Will I see her again?'*

'Please, Daniel.' Jonah focused. *'Annie's here.'*

But Daniel Harker was gone.

*

The cold of the room had finally got to Jonah as he signed off the revival. He needed to get somewhere warm. The recording lights went out, and he stood, eyes rooted to the floor, as a moment of dizziness came and went. He moved through into the corridor, glancing up as the observation room door opened. It was Annabel Harker. She was looking right at him, angry and lost. Her mouth opened to speak, but nothing came out.

He looked away and continued past.

I'll make sure there's time. I promise. He was shivering now as he moved up the hall to the rest room. Mouth to tap, he gulped water down until he felt nauseous. He lurched to the nearest cubicle, vomiting water and bile until his stomach was as empty as the rest of him felt.

He went to a sink and scrubbed at his hands and at the itching in his neck. A quarter of an hour later, the door opened.

It was Never. 'You've been a while, mate. You OK?' He was always good at giving Jonah the space he needed after a revival, but from the worry in his eyes Jonah could tell it must have been a struggle to leave him even this long.

'Been better.' He grabbed a fistful of paper towels and dried his neck, harder than he needed to. He caught his expression in the mirror. Anger. Disappointment.

'Steady, Jonah. You did well. Bob Crenner left happy enough, although I think he'll have a busy few hours.'

Jonah didn't reply.

'You can't always do it,' said Never, giving him a long, hard look. 'You can't always let them say good-bye. That's not your job. The most important thing is to get what you can.'

Jonah nodded. His friend knew him better than anyone, yet part of him was thinking that saying good-bye was *exactly* the most important thing. Right now, he wanted to get home. 'Is his daughter still there?' He couldn't bear the thought of seeing Annabel Harker's expression again.

'She stayed in the obs room for a while, but she's gone now.'

'Then I'm going to wait a few minutes and go home, Never. Get to bed.'

'You sure you don't want to kip here?'

Jonah shook his head, and Never nodded slowly and left him to deal with it his way.

'Why did they leave me?' Jonah said to his reflection. He hit the wall with an open hand and swore.

*

Back in his flat, Jonah wanted to get straight to bed, but he made himself eat. He knew that underneath the exhaustion, he was hungry. He'd sleep better with something in his stomach, so he threw a spaghetti meal in the microwave. As it heated he cracked open a beer.

He gulped it down, but it just seemed to make him more thirsty. He filled a mug with water and started to drink that too. Then he stopped.

'Shit,' he said. The thirst was overwhelming, left over from Harker's revival, and nothing that water could quench. He sat down and controlled his breathing, trying to relax until the sensation subsided.

The microwave pinged and made him jump.

He wolfed down his meal, pausing only to feed Marmite when the cat came to pester him. He tried not to think about his day's work. It was a skill he'd cultivated well in his years as a reviver. *Don't think about it. Zone out.*

But it all came back, and he could see Annabel Harker's face, and hear his broken promise. And the question that still had no answer.

Why did they leave me to die?

Through the kitchen door, in the main room of his apartment, he could see a shadow on the wall that made no sense to his eyes. A patch of darkness, but nothing causing it. He felt a sudden cold. Absently he itched at his neck.

He closed his eyes, took another deep breath and opened them again. There was nothing there.

18

Detective Ray Johnson sat in an uncomfortable built-in plastic chair in the cramped rear of a command van, Bob Crenner to his left. It was almost three in the morning after one of the longest days of his life, and he needed some coffee. In a second van parked in front of them, an armed anti-terrorist unit was preparing to raid a house two hundred yards away, the house that he, Crenner and the other detectives on the case had managed to locate after Daniel Harker's revival.

In front of him, an array of screens showed streamed images from the helmet cameras the armed officers were wearing. They looked sullen, waiting to be given the go. The moment approval had come through for a rapid armed response had probably been the most exciting point of his police career, but that had been six hours ago.

One thing he'd not expected of a rapid response was how damn slow it had turned out to be; he'd spent the best part of three hours sitting by the roadside a five-minute drive away from the target, before waiting another hour for the reconnaissance officer to report the last light in the house had gone out, then another two hours before closing in. That level of tension for so long just didn't sit well with him.

Harker's revival had given them plenty. The name Tobias Yarrow was linked to Afterlifer protests five years previously, minor felonies during demonstrations.

The shipping label Harker described had sounded like a bull's-eye, but five US companies had names that were considered close enough to 'Alpha Chemicals', and between them there were almost two hundred dispatched items on the relevant date.

Given what else Harker had said, about the 'failed firework', Bob Crenner made some calls to get a list of possible red-flag ingredients, freely available chemicals that could be turned into weapons.

It took good old-fashioned hard work to narrow the field as quickly as they had, and in the end they found it.

Alper Chemicals, and a consignment of six boxes of aluminium powder to a new customer, ordered online. The same credit card had been used to order a selection of different chemicals from other companies over a two-month period. All of them chemicals on Crenner's list, used to make explosives and incendiary devices. All to the same address: the house they were about to raid.

It had been time to call in the specialists, and Anti-terrorism wanted to move fast before news of Harker's discovery got around. Rapid-response unit, full force, Bob and Ray getting to tag along and observe. After all, there was still a murder to clear up.

The rear door of the van opened and the unit captain stepped inside.

'They're go in five,' he said.

Ray's tension level ratcheted up another notch. The time crawled.

At last, the response team van pulled away. Ray watched the camera footage as the van reached the house and the officers streamed out in silence. One officer carried a door ram, and with two strikes the front door gave way. The team was inside, the lead heading upstairs, when a single gunshot sounded. Ray heard a woman's yell. A rattle of return fire. The officers took positions under cover.

'Talk to me, West,' the captain said.

'Swan's down, sir,' said a man's voice over the radio. 'I'm getting her out.' Ray watched the feed from West's camera as he grabbed the arm of the downed officer and pulled.

'Where's the shooter?' said the captain.

Then a muffled shout. Heads turned to the top of the stairs and the shout came again: 'I'm coming down.'

'Hands on your head,' yelled a man's voice. 'Come down slowly. *Slowly.*'

One step at a time in the dark; beams of light from the officers' gun-mounted flashlights trained on the man as he descended.

'He has something,' came another voice.

Ray saw it. The man brought his hands away from his head. In one he was holding a small plastic tub. The other was a closed fist.

'Stay where you are,' an officer shouted.

The man stopped, then opened his fist so they could see what he held. Some kind of remote.

'Pull back outside,' the captain ordered. '*Now!*'

Standoff, Ray thought, but the man had other ideas. Before the squad had evacuated, the plastic tub he had been holding burst into light. Some kind of incendiary gel erupted from it, engulfing him.

'Drive!' the captain shouted to the front of the command van. Ray held on.

Shouts over the radio: 'Some of it's on me. It's eating through my fucking *shoe*!'

Thumps came, explosions.

The command van stopped. The captain picked up an assault rifle and got out.

'Stay inside,' he told them.

Ray looked past him and saw the house across the road, already an inferno.

It was going to be a long night.

*

Jonah shaded his eyes from the morning sun as he got out of the car, staring at the devastated house. 'It didn't go so well, then,' he said.

The suburban street consisted of homes that were widely spaced, with large, long-established lawns, the foliage giving plenty of privacy. Now, both ends of the street were sealed off, residents evacuated. A news helicopter buzzed overhead.

Hugo Adler came around to his side. He screwed up his face. 'Christ, that stinks.'

Jonah nodded. Underlying the harsh smell of smoke was a strong petrochemical taint, but it was the reek of burnt flesh that hit the hardest.

Jonah's night had been an unpleasant mix of exhaustion and fear. The least of it was the continuing episodes of thirst and the itching at his neck. Far worse was the blending of old nightmares with new. He had dreamed of past revivals, of his mother and of Lyssa Underwood; in each case the subject had twisted into Alice Decker, leaving him staring into her devastated face and the terrible *life* in her dead eyes.

He'd gone to the office early. After the revival the day before, he would have been given time off if he'd asked, but it was his first official day back following his enforced leave. He had plenty to get on with. Besides, the night had left him uneasy about being on his own.

At nine-thirty that morning, a call came in from Bob Crenner requesting a pathology liaison to assess a corpse that had turned up in a home in a well-to-do Gaithersburg neighbourhood. The situation was already on the national news but details were scarce. No information on casualties or arrests; confusion and contradiction from the local residents interviewed. Even before the call came, Never had connected the situation to Harker's revival when he spotted Bob Crenner's face on the news.

FRS North East had ruled themselves out again; none of their best people would be back off tails for another twelve hours. Crenner had gone to Hugo, giving fair warning: it was probably a waste of time, but there was interest from his superiors, and pressure to attempt a revival would be strong.

With Stacy and Jason both now available, Hugo had agreed to consider it, as long as a preliminary assessment was made by one of the four Richmond liaisons. He would send Beth Sheridan, and as he was unwilling to put his staff into that situation unsupported, Hugo would go with her.

Jonah's reaction was to go straight into Hugo's office and include himself in the trip, one more observer to back up Beth's decision.

'When did you get proactive?' Never asked him as he was about to set off, and Jonah gave him a rambling answer that didn't even convince himself. The simple truth was, he wanted to see it with his own eyes.

Once they arrived in Gaithersburg, Jonah, Hugo and Beth ducked under the police tape around the border of the charred house. Jonah saw Detectives Crenner and Johnson, and caught Bob Crenner's eye. He waved and the two detectives headed towards them. *Looks like they slept less than I did*, thought Jonah, which was saying something.

'Morning,' said Bob. 'If you can bring this one back, Jonah, you must be Jesus.'

'If we go ahead I'm not doing the revival, Detective. I'm just here to advise.'

'And by the sound of it I'm here on a technicality,' said Beth.

Bob nodded and looked at Hugo, smiling. 'So why are *you* here?'

'Moral support,' said Hugo. 'Thanks for the heads-up, Bob.'

Bob shrugged. 'My pleasure. Long way to bring you out for a rubber stamp job, but the stakes are high. I'd ruled it out the second I saw him, but what do I know? Take a look. The one we're querying is under the white plastic sheeting around the side. Be discreet.' He nodded to the news team prowling the edge of the exclusion area.

'So what happened?' Jonah asked as they walked, and Bob filled them in.

'The fireworks were *spectacular*,' Bob said when he'd described the raid. 'Christ knows what it was, but the whole place was an inferno in seconds. A few small explosions too. It took six hours to get the fire out. The only thing even resembling a body is under that tarpaulin.' He yawned. 'Long night.'

They reached the plastic sheeting.

'How many were there?' asked Beth.

'Five,' said Ray Johnson. 'This one managed to jump from an upper floor window, covered in the incendiary substance they'd been manufacturing, but my God, he was conscious every second. The fall didn't even knock him out. He was lying there, screaming for help, but the heat from the house meant we couldn't get close. He'd gone quiet by the time the fire trucks got here.'

Beth bent down and grasped the tarp. 'Here we go,' she said, and raised the plastic sheeting just enough to give them a clear view.

From the chest down there was nothing but charcoal, blackened bone visible at the bottom of the rib cage; from there to the neck, it was clothing melted onto skin. Much of the face was intact, shielded somehow. That was probably the only reason they'd thought a revival was possible. The rest of the head was roasted and charred, the hair gone.

'Shit,' said Beth. 'Definitely not talkative. Jonah?'

Jonah was staring at the corpse. 'It's the one Harker called Ginger,' he said.

'Are you sure?' asked Bob. 'I'm not sure Ginger would have recognized *himself*.'

'I'm sure.' He found it troubling, and caught Hugo's concerned glance, but there was no denying it: that face made him angry, just as it had made Harker angry. He wasn't recognizing it from Harker's description. This was far more deep rooted.

'So definitely no chance?' said Bob.

'No way,' said Beth. 'Just too cooked.'

'I wasn't expecting anything else.'

'So what next?' asked Hugo.

'We need to work out the target for their little venture. We have a preliminary ID for three of them but confirmation could take time. We'll go public with Harker's death soon, and then we have to track down anyone else involved. Everyone we've got an ID for had Afterlifer involvement, so I'm guessing FRS offices will have to up their security until we know.'

Beth laid the plastic back down, and Jonah found himself thinking that if there had even been the remotest chance of reviving that devastated flesh, he would have championed it. Without that, Harker's last question would always remain unanswered.

*

Beth, Hugo and Jonah walked to the car.

As Jonah went to get in the back, something caught his eye. On the far side of the road, he saw someone standing in the shade of a tree, facing his way. With the sun high and behind them, it was too dark to make out much: a hunched figure, arms by the sides, long coat. Jonah looked harder and felt the hairs on his arms prickle, cold air on his neck. The shape was watching him, unmoving. He could feel its eyes, staring, and thought of Alice Decker's twisted face. But this wasn't Alice.

'Come on,' Beth said from inside the car.

Jonah glanced at her, then back. The shape had gone.

*

Jonah spent the next morning taking some trainees through footage from six revivals. Only one of them had been his, from four years before: an armed robber, shot dead by police and mishandled at first by Jonah. The atmosphere had been tainted, the dead man's colleagues having escaped and severely wounded a civilian and an officer in the process. Anger and retribution had surrounded the revival, and Jonah's approach to it had been too aggressive.

He winced as the footage played, watching his own errors, his younger self missing the signs that his tactics were failing. It was hard to watch, but as it was one of the cases he intended to use for his talk at the symposium at the end of the following week, he would have to get used to seeing it.

He paused the footage to allow the class to comment. They got the general idea, and when at last they saw the approach shift, they seemed genuinely impressed as Jonah's gentle coaxing became a conversation, establishing trust and a mood of confession, turning it around as precious seconds passed. The dead man gave away enough for the police to find his colleagues.

At lunchtime, Jonah ate at his desk, letting his mind go blank as he stared out the window.

Across the road, deep shadows were being cast by the afternoon sun. Under the awning of the bakery where he'd bought his sandwiches that morning, in the deepest of the shade, a figure stood. It was little more than a variation of the dark, and he had to look for a few moments to be sure there was anything at all.

But then he felt the hairs rise on his arms and neck. He knew it was there. He knew it was the same figure he'd seen the day before. He leaned further towards the window, straining to see it, feeling ridiculous for the thought that crossed his mind, the thought that said, *Don't let it see you.*

The figure looked up. Jonah snatched himself back from the window, far enough to be out of its line of sight.

A hand fell onto his shoulder and he jumped. '*Christ!*'

'Whoa!' said Never. 'What's up with you?'

'Nothing,' he muttered, moving back toward the window and stealing a glance. The darkness in the shadow was gone.

'O-*kay* . . . Just wondered how it went this morning? The training?'

'Went fine,' said Jonah, his eyes and his mind still bolted to the place the figure had been. He shook it off and looked around. 'When do you get to babysit?'

'I'm due to take three of the trainees onsite later, if anything comes up.'

'Well, they seem capable enough, they'll behave.'

'Yeah, it'll be fine . . . So, uh, Beth mentioned the house? Yesterday? Pretty extreme. News is still vague about it, and there's no mention of Harker yet.'

'I hope it won't be long before they go public with it. The curiosity's killing me.'

'So do they know who those guys were targeting?'

'There's speculation that it's an Afterlifer campaign. Maybe involving arson. Hugo's looking into temporary additional security here. And when . . .' He had a sudden urge to look at the bakery again. He glanced and froze. The figure was back. 'Look out there. Please.'

'Where?'

'The baker's. Can you see someone in the shadows? Standing outside?'

Shading his eyes, Never looked to where Jonah was pointing. As he did, the figure looked up, and Jonah could feel its gaze. He wanted to pull away from the window again, but this time he stayed where he was.

'*Do you see it, Never?*' It was clearer now, hunched shoulders, long coat. He wasn't imagining it.

'Nobody there, mate.'

Jonah continued to stare.

'You look exhausted, Jonah. Are you OK?'

Jonah took a deep breath and looked Never in the eye. 'I'm not sure I am. I think . . .' He looked back to the street, to the shadow where – now – there was nothing. 'I think the Harker revival's catching up with me.'

'Then you should get home. You're all done here, right?'

'I've got some odds and ends to get through.'

'Come on, that shit can wait. Go home. Maybe take a few more days off. I'll let Hugo know.'

'But what about the trainees?'

'We can cover it, Jonah. Go.'

When he left the FRS building, Jonah crossed to the bakery and stood in the shadows he had been watching, feeling nothing at first. Then he looked up to the window by his office desk.

The figure was there, looking out at him.

*

As he walked home he sensed eyes at every corner, and caught glimpses of the figure in patches of darkness along the route. He lowered his head, his pulse quickening and cold sweat dripping from him by the time he reached the door of his apartment. He entered, and his cat padded toward him, unworried and purring.

Eager for calm, Jonah spent the rest of the afternoon reading the paperback of *David Copperfield* that Sam had bought him for Christmas, and which hadn't been picked up in three months. He tended to read books in occasional bursts; it was only when work was quiet that he found himself in that frame of mind, and work was rarely quiet for long. Given how tricky Harker had been, he thought it would be at least a couple of weeks before Hugo allowed him to do another revival. He suspected he'd get more reading done, if nothing else.

After three hours, hunger took him into the kitchen. He microwaved a chicken curry, grabbed a can of Coke and sat in front of his PC, browsing the latest news. He sat up when he saw the police had gone public at last with Daniel Harker's death, although they still hadn't revealed the link with the raid on the house.

He found the most recent report.

It opened with shots of the FRS building, the road to Harker's home, and the house he'd been found in, while the voice-over summarized the little information that had been made public: 'Daniel Harker's body was found in the cellar of a rented house. Despite the condition of the body, a revival was attempted two days ago here at the Forensic Revival Service. Police announced that the revival was successful but gave no other details. Another police statement is due tomorrow.

'Mr Harker's daughter, who had flown from her home in England following her father's disappearance, is believed to have been present at the revival but was not prepared to comment.'

The picture cut to a shot of Harker's daughter driving up the lane to the Harker home, reporters barking questions at her. The camera closed on her grim face as she drove by.

The report continued: 'The revival is a tragic and ironic end to the life of Daniel Harker, the man who made his career by breaking the story of Eleanor Preston, the first known reviver, twelve years ago.'

The report cut to archive material, an overview of Daniel's life. Jonah was familiar enough with the details, but he watched all the same. Little things annoyed him, liberties taken for the sake of easy journalism. But the thing that grated most was the way they presented Harker as an opportunist and his career as a fluke: he happened to be in the right place and milked it for what he could. They gave him no credit for how he paved the way for revival to become accepted.

His novels didn't even rate a mention. Jonah knew the first three had been modest successes, but Harker's fourth had taken flight onto bestseller lists around the world. His alias had been an open secret. Not even to get a mention was disappointing . . .

He thought of the next book he'd been planning, existing only in handwritten notes in his home, ideas that were just beginning to come together into . . .

Jonah swore, knocking over his Coke.

Just as with Nikki Wood, his thoughts had not been his own.

He understood the figure in the darkness. He knew who had been lurking there, following him since the burnt-out house.

It was Daniel Harker.

19

The next morning Jonah called Stephanie Graves. By noon, he was back under the scanner, Graves waving away his protestations about how awkward a situation he was putting her in.

She took him to her office afterwards. 'There is evidence of remnants,' she said. 'Strong evidence. You should have been fine with the revival, even though it was such a difficult one. I don't understand why the BPV increase didn't take care of it.'

Jonah felt his cheeks burn. 'Sorry. I just grabbed my old medication and took an extra half pill.'

Graves frowned. She opened her mouth to speak, then paused and shook her head. 'Not the smartest thing to do, Jonah. But it was the right dose. It should've been fine. Maybe I should have insisted on a longer break, or only let you take on easier cases. Whatever the reason, right now rest is what you need, more than anything. The remnant effect you experienced with the girl was short-lived. Hopefully the same will be true for Daniel Harker. I'll give you a three-day course of a cocktail that will clear this. It'll leave you feeling odd, so be careful. It's a powerful memory disruptive and it may make you extremely drowsy. Take it each night before you go to bed. You'll experience some disorientation and further drowsiness in the mornings, but that's normal. It'll soon wear off. Your symptoms should stop. Let me know at once if they don't. I'll brief your office counsellor. You need weekly assessments, then come back for another scan in a month. I want to be sure this time. Once you're clear, simple revivals only until we see how you're getting on.'

'You said the remnant was strong. How strong?' Graves squirmed a little. There was hesitance there, reluctance. 'Please?'

'It was particularly strong, Jonah. I've seen stronger, but not often.'

'How bad can this get? It scared me. The feeling of being watched. Seeing something follow me . . .'

'Your mind's way of interpreting these stray thoughts. Unsettling, but it'll pass.'

'And then when Harker's thoughts began . . . I felt like I was watching someone else think. Like I wasn't in charge. Like I was a spectator. How can that happen?'

'Jonah, most researchers in the field dismiss remnants as unwanted memories, like post-traumatic flashback. You and I know they're more than that. There's a theory that the normal way we understand other people is by actually carrying a model of them within us, like a simplified simulation. The brain's ability to do that is what drove the explosion in the complexity of human social interaction. The better we know someone, the more detailed the simulation of them becomes. We're starting to be able to view the workings of the brain with a resolution fine enough that we might expect to *see* these simulations, but so far there is nothing to distinguish them from our own thoughts. It makes sense that the brain simply creates them using the mechanisms that drive our own consciousness. Jonah, I think that in the most extreme form of remnants, the mind deals with the unusual waves of activity, and the corresponding triggering of unfamiliar memories, by separating that activity, *quarantining* it, so that it acts as a fast track to forming one of these internal representations. If you have ever imagined how another person would feel in any given situation, or what they would say, then what you've been experiencing is just a more extreme version of that. The delusional feeling that your thoughts are not your own happens because you have a well-established internal model for someone who is essentially a stranger. At heart, though, it's based on a perfectly ordinary mental process. It's not something you need to be afraid of. The medication I've given you will fragment those memories enough to let them dissipate naturally.'

'But how bad can it get, Dr Graves?'

She sighed. 'Do as I've said: get plenty of rest, and you'll be fine. We've caught it before it went too far.'

Too far, Jonah thought, wondering what exactly that meant. 'Have you ever had a case where it did?'

Graves paused, looking past Jonah for a moment. Then she nodded. 'Once, six or seven years ago. A high-rated private reviver. He did a stint as a forensic reviver in Toronto, but he had problems and returned to private work south of the border. The private revival firm he worked for referred him to me after he'd been following the wife of one of his subjects. She'd reported it, and he'd been arrested, drunk. He insisted he *was* her husband. The tests showed he had four clear remnants at that point, all strong. And one strong enough to leave him so confused that he believed he was somebody else, for a time. That's the worst I've ever seen. The delusion was compelling. Recovery took months.'

Jonah nodded. He couldn't help pressing for something more. 'What happened to him? Did he ever work as a reviver again?'

'I advised him not to.' Graves went to a cupboard and returned. She handed him a small clear pill bottle. Inside were three yellow tablets that looked like they'd take some swallowing. 'Here. They work like a charm. The second-worst case I ever saw was a forensic reviver. With these pills and one month of rest that person had a complete recovery and went back to work, with no further episodes. You'll be fine. Remember, take one just before you sleep. When you've finished the course, Daniel Harker won't trouble you again.'

*

Back in his flat, Jonah started writing an email to Hugo Adler to let him know what had happened. As he wrote it, he wondered if he should tell Never the details. He decided it would be better to leave him out of it and save him the worry.

He thought about Stephanie Graves, and how keen she had been to spend that expensive scanner time on him – and then promise more later. Perhaps she had seen an opportunity for a case study, like the other case, six years before.

Then it occurred to him: six years ago, Graves had still been part of Baseline, and the case had pertained to forensic revival. The close ties between the FRS and Baseline meant there was a good chance that the prior case she had mentioned would be somewhere in the FRS archive. Whether Jonah would have clearance to view such documents was another question, especially with remote access, but he thought it was worth a try.

With the email to his boss unfinished, he logged onto the FRS system, brought up the archive and tried searching for relevant terms. In the list of hits he saw a document by Stephanie Graves entitled 'A summary of factors affecting BPV remnant suppression'. There was an additional reference number beside it. He clicked on it.

A window popped up, warning him that the content was sensitive and contained personal medical information. 'Please ensure you view this document in a private environment,' the window advised. Jonah glanced behind him. Marmite was settling down on the couch for a nap.

'I hope you can keep a secret,' Jonah said to the cat. Then he clicked 'OK'.

An error message appeared. 'You do not have permission to view this material.'

Jonah swore under his breath, and then jumped as his phone handset rang loud and *close*.

It was Never. 'Hey, Jonah! Saw you'd logged in, thought I'd see how you were.'

Jonah kept his voice low, a harsh whisper. 'You were keeping tabs on me?' He realized how angry he sounded, an overreaction to being caught.

There was a pause before Never replied. 'Uh . . . OK. I'll leave you in peace. Just thought I'd say I'd cleared it with Hugo for you to be off until this time next week, and you should actually *take* the break. Working from home doesn't count.'

Jonah bowed his head. 'Shit, man. Look, I'm sorry. I'm tired. How's *your* day been?'

'I'll let you off, mate. This morning was a juicy one. Young newly separated wife, strangled. Boyfriend in the next room, beaten to death with what may have been a crowbar.'

'Nasty.'

'And messy. Double onsite, we had Stacy and Terry reviving, with me and J. J.'

'Was it the ex-husband?'

'That was the theory, and he *had* gone AWOL. Turned out to be more complicated. The boyfriend had started on her, she'd managed to phone her ex for help. He got there to find her dead, so he killed the boyfriend. Then vanished. He sounds as big a nightmare as the boyfriend, though. That girl could pick 'em. Anyway, how are you? Better after yesterday? Still, uh, seeing things?'

'I just need to rest, Never.'

'You'd tell me if there was something up, right?'

Jonah knew exactly where this concern was coming from, and he knew Never could read him; it wasn't fair to his friend just to play dumb.

'There's something I'm looking into. It's probably nothing, and I promise I'll tell you soon, but I need you to do me a favour and let me deal with it.'

'OK,' Never said, sounding wary. 'But I'm holding you to that, and I'll be checking up on you. If there's anything I can do to help . . .'

A thought occurred to Jonah. 'Well . . . There's a case I want to look at. It's in the FRS system, but I don't have permission to view it. You're an admin, right? Is there any way . . .'

'You sly dog. Make yourself a coffee. By the time you're done, you'll have access. Just don't tell anyone, OK?'

*

Jonah did exactly as instructed. Coffee in hand, he sat back down and searched for the same key words as before, then clicked on the link.

This time, the case report appeared on screen.

The reviver's name was Victor Eldridge. As Graves had said, the reviver had been brought in after approaching the wife of a subject he had revived a week before. The wife had not felt directly threatened, and had not pressed charges against him, but the company he'd been working for had contacted Graves. Eldridge had been one of their best revivers. They wanted him looked after.

'At this time,' the report read, 'the remnant effect is assumed to be a mild presentation of memory and emotion originating from the surge phase of a revival. Yet this patient had periods of lucid interaction during which he seemed to think he actually *was* the subject. Under interview, these periods were observed five times, the longest episode lasting twenty-seven minutes. The patient's responses were consistent and detailed, and information specific to the revival subject seemed accurate. After each episode, the patient was asked how aware he had been, and confirmed that he had been conscious at the time yet somehow observing these thoughts arise without direct control. This suggests that if sufficiently extreme, the remnant effect could amount to a kind of parasitic intelligence, with the survival of patterns of thought and behaviour from the revived subject dominating the mind of the host. How long-lived these effects might be if untreated is currently unknown. In this case an extended course of high-dose novadafinil and propanolol was effective.'

Jonah took a deep breath. It was just as he'd experienced it. Yet the words Dr Graves had used in this report were very different from how she had presented it to him, as an ordinary mental process being misinterpreted by a mind under stress.

She had been trying to put his mind at ease. Delusion. Nothing to be afraid of.

In practice it was much more. Graves had called it 'parasitic intelligence'.

It was a form of possession.

He noticed a reference beside the paragraph he had read, and when he followed it he came to a list of dated files, each titled 'Interview excerpt' with a reference number. Wondering how many laws he was breaking, he opened the first.

A single camera, pointing at a man he presumed was Eldridge: wide-eyed and nervous.

'Were you aware you'd been talking?' asked a voice – muffled; it sounded like Graves.

'Yes,' said Eldridge. He had an earnestness, an openness, a smile that suggested damage. He seemed horribly fragile. 'I could hear every word. I could hear the thoughts that *led* to the words. And none of them were mine. That's the way it always is. I can't influence them. I'm trapped in my own head and all I can do is watch.' The broken smile remained as he spoke, but his voice was despairing. The clip stopped. Jonah went back to the report. There didn't seem to be much else, beyond what Graves had already told him. Eldridge was a mess, and although there was only one remnant strong enough to intrude into his waking actions, testing had revealed evidence of others.

Jonah thought of the term Graves had used: 'ghost traces'. It seemed horribly appropriate now.

He switched between report and interview footage for half an hour, getting increasingly agitated by both the content and his guilt at the illicit access. Yet it was Eldridge's expression that had the greatest impact. The man seemed to have given up hope.

He read the section on the drug treatments being used.

'The patient has been experiencing episodes of profound para-noia,' it read, 'making references to an external force he believes to be following him.' Jonah thought at once of Harker's lurking pres-ence. There was a reference again, which he followed.

Eldridge's weary face appeared once more. It looked like the same interview location.

The voice off screen: 'What are you afraid of, Victor?'

'There's something watching me. Something *with* me.'

'You feel it now?'

'Yes. Scratching at the back of my mind. I heard it whisper once. Sometimes I think I still hear it.'

'When did this begin?'

'Ever since the Ruby Fleming case. Something else was *there*.' Eldridge said it in an urgent whisper, glancing around as if he may be overheard.

Jonah felt very cold. It wasn't Harker's remnant presence he was reminded of, not now.

It was Alice Decker.

He went back to the report text: 'Prior case was during patient's employment with Toronto Forensic Revival Department. Case was considered by Eldridge's superiors to have been a result of his own state of mind affecting that of the subject, leading to subject's panic and contact loss.'

There was another link, which he presumed would be to the review of this prior case. Instead, there was footage from the revival itself.

Canadian procedures closely followed those the FRS used. The footage had three separate image feeds, the long shot giving context to the other two.

A narrow street, an alleyway with an open door leading into a lit corridor, black bags of garbage mounted high by the wall. At the extremes of the image, Jonah noted tape sealing off the scene. On the ground by the door, a woman lay, her dead eyes open. There was no obvious sign of trauma.

Eldridge ducked under the tape and entered the picture. Jonah was startled by how healthy the man looked, his frame full to the point of being overweight. A confident man, unrecognizable given the shell he was to become.

Eldridge stated his name and the case details as he took the corpse's hand.

Not aware he was doing it, Jonah's left hand gripped the desk, needing to hold on to something firm. He wanted to stop watching, but he couldn't. There was silence for several minutes as Eldridge began the process. Jonah sped up the footage, until he saw the corpse shift. He wound back slightly and played it through.

The woman's chest was rising and falling in the slow, exaggerated movements the dead had when breathing.

'Ruby,' said Eldridge. 'Can you hear me? My name is Victor.'

Jonah watched the revival proceed, his grip on the table tightening, along with every other muscle in his body.

He was good, Eldridge. Very good indeed. The subject had been revived with reasonable speed, perhaps a little slow, but his subsequent handling of her was exceptional.

Ruby co-operated fully, describing the attack on her, describing the man she had seen, linking him explicitly with a man she had served at the bar she worked in. Eldridge told her that the man had been caught on camera. That the testimony she had given would be crucial in finding him and securing a conviction. That she had done well.

'Thank you,' said Ruby. And then the tone changed. A subtle change he couldn't pin down, but Jonah felt as if the temperature around him had plunged. He shivered.

Ruby spoke again. 'There's something here,' she said. 'Something in the alley. I can feel it. It's dark, too dark to see. *There's something here.*'

Eldridge was taken aback by this. He glanced at the camera and shrugged. A voice came from off screen – the officer overseeing the revival. 'She's losing it, Victor,' the voice said. 'We nearly have what we need, get her back to the man.'

'Ruby, is there anything else you can tell me about the man who attacked you?'

Ruby breathed in, slow and deep. 'It glistens in the dark. It stinks. It's just out of sight. I can't see it. Please. Let me go.'

The officer spoke up: 'Come on, Victor, either get her back on track or wind it up.'

'Ruby, I want to talk about the man.'

'The *smell*. It's strong now. So *strong*. Like bad meat.'

'Please. The man who attacked you. You said he was talking as he choked you. Can you remember anything else he said?'

'I . . . it's *here*. Please, let me go!'

'Ruby? Don't be alarmed, there's nothing here. There's nothing here.'

'But it's *here*! Please! Help me! I can't see it! I can't see it! It's *coming*.'

'Ruby, listen to my voice. Try and be calm.'

'*Please, it's coming closer. I CAN FEEL IT, IT'S RIGHT BELOW ME, I –* '

Ruby's body froze. Gradually the chest sank.

'Ruby? Ruby, can you hear me?' Eldridge looked to the camera, talking directly to it and those observing. 'I don't know what happened. I think she's gone. Ruby?'

'You mean you lost her? Contact lost?'

Eldridge held up his right hand, Ruby's hand still grasped in it. 'Contact wasn't broken. And she didn't slip away. She's just gone. She just stopped being there.' He let go of her hand and stood back, looking at the camera. 'Nothing there. Nothing.' He looked lost, shaking his head.

The footage ended. Jonah stared at the frozen final image, Eldridge's face looking into the camera with the beginning of that helpless bewilderment that would later consume him. Jonah kept staring until a pain in his hand roused him, his grip on the table so tight that his hand had cramped.

I can't see it, he thought. *It's coming.* It was too close to the words Alice Decker had used. Far too close.

*

He spent the rest of the evening trying not to think about it. He saw movement in every corner, and jumped at the slightest noise. He told himself there was nothing to fear. Nothing.

But he knew what it meant. Alice Decker had not been mere hallucination. Whatever had spoken to him had stalked the dead before. With Eldridge, it had been dismissed as the subject panicking. He wondered how often something similar had occurred through the years since revival began, to be just as easily ignored.

Eldridge had claimed this thing whispered to him. Jonah wondered what it had said.

He found his neck itching, thirst growing – outward signs that the Harker remnant was still with him. It was time to take the medication Stephanie Graves had given him, he thought. Time to put an end to Harker's lingering presence.

The pills were still with his keys, on the shelf by the door where he'd left them on arriving home. He decided to take them now and get straight to his bed. No need to wait.

He went to the kitchen to fill a glass of water. As he reached out to the faucet, he felt a sudden cold and stopped. He turned, staring out through the kitchen door into the rest of his apartment.

It was dark. Everywhere but the kitchen, the lights were out. A moment before, they had been on. Now, his apartment was a patchwork of black shadow.

He rubbed his neck and tried to ignore the thought that there was still movement under his skin.

His borrowed thirst was stronger. He was aware of something

else, something that for a moment he could not pin down. His stomach fell away from him when he identified the feeling.

There was something in the room. There was something in the room, and it was watching him.

He moved to the kitchen door, slowly, his own shadow moving ahead of him. In the corner, in the deep black, was a shape. Someone was standing there, against the wall.

'Hello?' he said. He took a step forward. 'Hello?'

He stared, trying to make it out. So little light, yet there – hands, clasped. There – a darker recess, the eyes. There – a whiteness that could only be teeth.

The shape breathed.

'*Daniel?*' he said, almost pleading with it. *Not Alice*, he hoped. *Dear God, not her.* He reached up to where he thought the light switch should be, his eyes not moving from the corner, letting his fingers seek it out.

The shape moved, almost imperceptibly.

'*What do you want?*' he asked, fear surging. He turned on the light.

The corner was empty.

He strode to the door and took the pill bottle, then returned to the kitchen.

Just hallucinations, he told himself as he filled his glass. *I'll sit and calm down to whatever crap's on television. No point going to bed in this kind of a state, and . . .*

Ice filled him. He straightened, the water still running. The glass fell from his hand, smashing on the floor. Behind him. He sensed it behind him. He turned, slowly, to face it.

The rank and bloated corpse of Daniel Harker stood at arm's length, head bowed, wearing the same long coat it had worn since the first time Jonah had seen it. Jonah's legs would not move. The corpse shuffled closer, the dead face rising up as it came, without expression, eyes closed. Its mouth sagged open, and it exhaled, fetid air escaping with a sigh that was almost a hiss. The lights began to dim as the corpse's arms lifted, settling on Jonah's shoulders, the skin seeming to flow somehow, Harker's body dissolving into gore and noise that spread darkness where it touched.

Jonah tried to scream, but it was too late.

20

Flashes of awareness came, memory and dream combined.

The moment he let go of his mother's hand.

In his car, driving along a road he had not seen before but that was utterly familiar.

The family Dominic Pritchard had killed.

A door opening, a young woman's confused face.

The baffling answers Lyssa Underwood had given to the questions he'd been told to ask her.

And then, cold and real: he was Daniel Harker, tied to a chair in a dim-lit cellar. In front of him was the face Jonah had seen scorched and twisted under a white plastic tarpaulin two days before; alive now, but grim, his eyes wide with fear and alcohol.

'We're the only ones who know,' said Ginger. A bottle of vodka in hand. He swigged. 'We're the only ones who can stop it. Something came from the dark. It came from the dark and *talked* to them.'

*

Jonah opened his eyes, pain in his head and the larval itch still present. His mouth tasted terrible. He rubbed furiously at his neck, the dreams fresh and unwelcome in his mind. He sat up, looking around him, confused and cold and drowsy, feeling like he hadn't slept at all.

Then he realized that he had no idea where he was.

The room was both familiar and alien – a jumble of old trinkets on every surface, a large-screen television in one corner, book-loaded shelves covering the walls. He stood from the couch he had been laying on, wary. His jacket was draped across an armchair, his car keys on top. As he went to pick them up, he saw a framed photograph on one shelf. Daniel Harker, his wife and daughter. Beside it, a picture he had seen before. The one Harker had used for the jacket photo in his revival books, of him standing alone on windswept shingle, the sea behind him. Wearing a long coat.

The pieces began to slot together in his mind. The image came of Harker's corpse, advancing towards him. He shivered. Harker had brought him here. The same thing that had happened to Victor Eldridge had happened to him. The remnant had taken control.

With one difference. Eldridge had been fully aware while powerless, but Jonah had no idea what Harker had done after taking over. The shards of dream and memory from the night before were all the clues he had, and they were already slipping from him. Vague images of Harker's daughter were all that came now.

'Something came from the dark,' he said aloud, wondering where he had heard those words. Then he remembered Harker's kidnapper, fearful eyes and terror in his voice.

Remembered? Could he call it that? It was Harker's memory, not his own: *It came from the dark and talked to them.*

A noise from another room startled him – a clink of glass, sharp in the silence. He went to the hall, turned and saw Annabel Harker asleep, slumped with her head on the kitchen table, a bottle of whisky and an overturned glass in front of her.

He wanted out of there. He went back and got his jacket and keys. He wanted to get home and take those damn pills before it could happen again. At the thought of the pill bottle, he hunted through his pockets.

Gone. Of course. Probably the first thing Harker did. Get rid of them before they got rid of *him*. Jonah knew what that meant. *Harker wants to come back again,* he thought.

He went to the front door but stopped. However much he wanted to leave, the urge to know what had gone on in his absence was overpowering. He turned and went to the kitchen.

'Miss Harker . . .'

She stirred.

'Miss Harker?'

One eye opened. She winced, then sat. 'You're awake. You're you.' She eyed him. There was hostility in her expression.

He realized he was trembling. 'Please, what happened here?'

'Sit.' She looked exhausted. Drained of emotion.

Jonah sat opposite her. She delved into a pocket and produced the missing bottle of pills. He held it up, surprised to see the yellow diamonds within. But only two. One had gone. *He doesn't want me to have them all*, Jonah thought.

'There's one missing,' he said.

Annabel Harker looked him in the eye for a full ten seconds, clearly not approving of what she saw. 'Here.' She pushed a cell phone across the table towards him. He picked it up. The video playback app was on the screen, paused. He looked at the image. Himself, sitting exactly where he was now. Glass of whisky in his hand. That bottle of pills in front of him.

'Play it,' said Annabel. She stood and walked out, back into the living room.

Jonah looked at the face in the image. He took a long, deep breath before he pressed the screen. The footage played.

'Good morning,' his image said, taking a deep drink of the whisky. *That's why my head feels this way*, Jonah thought. 'Hell of a night. I didn't mean this to happen. Believe me. I had no idea what I was doing. No idea *how* I was doing it. Wait, that's no place to start. Introductions first. I'm Daniel. You already knew that. My daughter, though, took some time to convince.' Daniel Harker sighed. 'We have things to discuss, Jonah Miller. But before we do, I owe you an apology. I'm sorry. Jesus, I'm sorry. What did I do?' Harker looked at his own (*Jonah's* own) hands in disbelief. 'If you could make this last, it'd be a hell of a way to cheat death, don't you think? I was watching, you see. Watching as you went to Stephanie Graves. Watching when Graves gave you *these* . . .' He picked up the pills and rolled the bottle between his fingers. 'And I was thinking, I have to say good-bye to my daughter. You didn't give me the chance. I was angry, and then . . . Christ. Here I am. But there's more. You see, I want to know. And my daughter wants to know. What the people who killed me were trying to stop. Yarrow had called it Unity. I'd thought he was just a crank. But then they took me. *We're the only ones who know,* they said. *The only ones who can stop it.* I saw the fear in their eyes. I want to know what they thought Unity was, and if there was any truth in it. I want to know how they planned to stop it. And most of all . . . I want to know why they left me to *die.'*

Harker punctuated the last word by slamming the pill bottle on the table, then took a slow breath before he went on. 'Help my daughter. I'm not there to watch her back, so you'll have to do it instead. You owe us, Jonah. Do this for me. Do this for Annabel. And in exchange, she'll find what you want.'

Harker paused for another gulp of whisky.

'What do I want?' Jonah asked the screen.

His own stolen face smiled back. 'Eldridge. You want to talk to Victor Eldridge. You want to know why what happened to him has happened to *you*. And most of all, you want to know how he ended up, so you don't have to be so damn scared about how *you* might end up. So, please. Help her.' Harker lifted the pill bottle up, looking at it. Jonah could see the fear in his eyes. Those were the pills that Stephanie Graves had promised would be the end of Daniel Harker.

Jonah felt cold as he watched Harker open the bottle and take out one pill. A second death. Harker held it in silence, turning it over in his fingers, watching it. Then he looked at the camera again. 'What am I, do you think? Graves made it sound like I'm a patchwork, a ragbag of memories. I'm a figment of your imagination. I'm a *dream.* Let me tell you, that's not how it feels.' His gaze drifted away from the camera. 'The greatest mystery of revival. Even with all we saw, we still didn't know what it meant. What it meant for *after*. I'm not a religious man, Jonah. About as far from it as you can get, if I'm honest. Not that I ever said as much, not publicly. Who would credit that the man who found Eleanor Preston was an atheist? My wife knew. She asked me how I still could be, now that we'd found out there was an afterlife. I told her we don't even know *that*. Revival could just be an encore. A tease. A joke. The sum total of everything we've been and done, all our memories, dreaming of being real.' He looked back to the camera and smiled. Gentle, bemused. 'Some would say that's all we ever were.'

He put the pill in his mouth and washed it down with more whisky. 'Good night, Jonah Miller,' he said, reaching out to the camera to stop the recording. The video ended.

*

Jonah sat for five full minutes before he plucked up enough courage to walk to the living room. Annabel Harker was sitting on the couch, staring ahead, eyes wet with tears.

'Miss Harker, there's something I should tell you. The men who took your father were found. The connection hasn't been made public yet, and I don't know their identities, but . . .'

She looked at him. The hostility of before had faded; now it was all just exhaustion. 'I know.'

'How?'

'I found out who I needed to pay, and I paid them well. Don't be surprised. My dad was pretty wealthy. I'm a journalist, and I suddenly find myself with funds. Dangerous combination.' She smiled at him, and he was surprised to find himself smiling back, despite how drained he felt. Drained and battered and desperate for sleep. It hadn't just been the alcohol Daniel Harker had been drinking that had left Jonah so drowsy, he realized. It was the medication too, just as Graves had warned him. He sat at the other end of the couch and closed his eyes.

'I don't think I've seen you smile before,' said Annabel. 'Suits you.'

Jonah opened his eyes and looked at her, remembering the exhaustion on her face before her father's revival; and after, when the exhaustion was coloured with anger. No, he hadn't seen her smile before either. And even though the smile she wore now was so fragile, it was preferable by far. 'You too.'

'Not much to smile about.' Her smile flickered and disappeared. A tear fell. 'But I got to say good-bye.'

Jonah looked down. 'I'm sorry. It wasn't . . .'

'No. *I'm* sorry. It had seemed like such a small thing to ask, such a little mercy, and then it was taken away. But you did what you had to do. You were there to help find out what happened, and that's what you did.'

'I still let you down.'

She smiled at him through tears and moved to take his hand. He flinched at the sudden contact, pulling his hand back a few inches even though there had been no chill. Her smile faltered for a moment, but she persevered and took his hand anyway. 'You have to do your job day after day, and you still care. That can't be easy. It must cost you. And then someone like me gives you a look like *all of it* was your fault . . .' She shook her head. 'I take it back. If that's OK.'

'That's OK,' he said, feeling impossibly weary. He lowered his head to the cushion beside him.

*

His eyes snapped open again. He knew he'd been asleep but had no idea how long. Judging by how he ached, it had been hours. Annabel's head was on his lap. She was asleep and still holding his hand. He watched her, wary of the contact, uncomfortable because he knew it was Jonah's curious link with her father that had stopped her letting go.

After a few minutes he moved, carefully positioning a cushion and lowering her head onto it. He went to the kitchen and made two cups of coffee, bringing them in on a tray with a jug of milk and a bowl of sugar.

She woke as he came in. She sat up, looking startled, a hint of red appearing in her cheeks.

'I didn't know how you took your coffee,' he said.

'Black, one sugar.' She looked over to something behind Jonah. 'My *God*. Did we hibernate?'

Jonah followed her gaze to a clock on the wall. It was half past two. 'Shit,' he said, and hunted for his phone. It had been switched off, so he turned it back on and waited. As he'd thought, Never had been calling him.

'Ten missed calls,' he mumbled. *I'll be checking up on you,* Never had said. Jonah stepped out to the hall and called him.

'Where the fuck have you been?' said Never.

'Long story. I'm fine. Don't fret.'

'Easy for you to say. I've been ringing since before noon.'

'Honestly, I'm fine. I'll explain later.'

It took a few more reassurances before Never sounded appeased. Jonah ended the call.

'Who was that?' asked Annabel. 'Your wife?'

Jonah smiled and shook his head. 'Friend of mine. He gets worried about me.'

Annabel sipped her coffee. 'What, does he think he's your mother?' It was just a flippant remark, but after a moment's delay her face fell. 'Shit, Jonah, I didn't mean to . . .'

It took a few seconds for him to understand. 'How did you know about my mom?'

She glanced down. 'My dad told me about you, years ago. When he interviewed you. He told me about the accident, and what happened with your mother.'

'Sixteen when he talked to me. Fourteen when she died.'

'I couldn't believe how hard it must have been. You'd lost both your parents, and . . .'

Jonah said nothing, letting Annabel finish the thought. She closed her eyes for a moment. 'Shit,' she said at last. 'So, do we get any special discounts as orphans?'

Jonah laughed, loud and hard. '*That* is in really bad taste.'

Annabel shrugged. 'There's a phrase for it. Incongruity of effect. It means when things get really fucked up, you grow an equally twisted sense of humour.'

'Then we're in *deep* trouble.'

She smiled and nodded, and they fell into silence, drinking their coffee.

Annabel set down her cup. 'So why does your friend worry about you?'

Jonah looked at her, baffled by how comfortable he felt at the prospect of talking about it. 'He found me. Two years ago, I'd been working too hard, under pressure. Something happened, and things spiralled. I took time off and withdrew, and he made sure to keep in contact with me day to day. I resented it, but I hadn't understood that he'd seen something in me that nobody else had. A week later I wasn't answering my phone. He broke into my apartment. I was unconscious on the floor of my bathroom, soaked in vomited alcohol that was peppered with every medication I'd been able to find. And now he worries about me.'

'Does he have reason to worry?'

Jonah looked down. 'Not anymore. I've been OK.'

He was waiting to see if she would ask the obvious question. Wondering if he would answer.

She took a deep breath before she spoke. 'What had happened? What had happened that made things get so bad?'

He said nothing, eyes to the floor. He wondered what it meant, that he had been comfortable talking of his suicide attempt yet couldn't tell her about Dominic Pritchard.

'I shouldn't have asked,' she said. 'I'm sorry.'

They sat in silence. After a few moments, Jonah got up. 'I should go,' he said.

'If you want to,' said Annabel. 'Or you could stay and do what my dad asked. Help me.'

'I'm a reviver. That's all I can do. I've no idea what use I can be.'

'You can make more coffee,' she said, and smiled.

He found his dark mood lifting just enough to allow him to smile back. *Why not*, he thought. If he had penance to do, he may as well get on with it. 'I'll help. Where do we start?'

Annabel leaned over the side of the couch and came back with a thick folder of paper. She let it drop onto the coffee table with a heavy thud. 'We start here,' she said.

21

When Annabel opened the folder, Jonah stared at the picture on the top sheet.

It was the man who had been at Daniel Harker's front door that day. The face in the picture was much fuller, though, not nearly as gaunt as he remembered. The eyes were just as cold, however. 'Did you show any of this to, uh, your father?'

Annabel nodded. 'He recognized him too,' she said. 'On the page underneath you'll see a man called Peter Welsh. They believe he was the one my father called Ginger. Look a few pages down, you'll see the scene photographs from the house where they were found. You can tell that corpse is Peter Welsh. There's enough of his face left. For the others, matching the names to their remains will take longer.'

'I saw Welsh's body. I was there.'

Annabel's eyes widened. 'Was there a revival attempt?'

'On Welsh? They'd hoped so, but no chance.' Other pictures, then: things he hadn't seen that day, images taken inside the house, close-up shots of charred masses, the white of the skulls visible where the incinerated flesh had come away from bone. Jonah flicked back to the first few pages. The picture of the cold-eyed man, the information below it identifying him as Felix Hannerman. Then a smiling image of the man Daniel had called Fats, identified as Brad Grimmet.

'You recognize him as well,' Annabel said.

It hadn't been a question. Jonah's expression made it clear that he did. 'So the police know who they were.'

'They'll keep that information quiet for now. Six bodies. Not all of the house was destroyed, and they found enough items left intact to identify the men. All of them were associated with Afterlifer protests. Hannerman had been in prison twice over it. But it was minor stuff. Nothing they had done suggested they'd be capable of anything like this.'

'And what about Tobias Yarrow?'

'There was almost nothing on Yarrow. Forty-eight years old, only trouble he'd ever been in was a fight in a bar ten years back. Alcoholic, and at the time he'd just separated from his wife of ten years over the drinking. He was one of the six bodies they found in the house. It was easy to match his corpse to the name, because his face was in perfect condition.'

Jonah sat up, astonished. 'What? They said nothing about a body in good condition.'

'The police didn't find him until thirty hours after the raid, when the house was considered safe enough – and cool enough – for a thorough search. He was in a freezer, presumably for weeks. Shot in the head and decapitated. They'd made sure he wouldn't be talking to anyone.'

'Did they find anything on what they were planning?'

'They were prepared to kill, and prepared to die in a way that would stop them from being revived. They'd built dozens of incendiary devices. The thinking is that they were planning a widespread firebomb campaign.'

'Hannerman and his friends were scared of something specific. Unity. *That* has to have been their target.'

'I agree, but the authorities are going down the same path my dad took. To them, these people are cranks. *Why* they're doing this is almost irrelevant, it's expected to be a mishmash of paranoid drivel. The priority is to find anyone else involved, and so far they're confident there was nobody. Each of these men seems to have cut off contact with friends and family at least a year ago. Hannerman was wealthy enough to fund the entire thing. The only person we know of who might have answers is the one Yarrow called Fifteen, someone who knew about the development of BPV.'

'Do the police have anything on that?'

'The police are out of it. The murder investigation is effectively over. Now, everything is with an FBI domestic terrorism unit. They'll be trying to identify someone with the nickname "Fifteen", but . . . My dad talked about this last night. He didn't think they'd find anyone.'

'Why?'

'Dad told me how Yarrow had brought up the name. *"Let's call him Fifteen."* Looking pleased with himself. Dad thought the nickname was Yarrow's own invention. His little private joke. If we want to find out, we need to identify Fifteen ourselves.'

*

Jonah got back to his apartment before 6 p.m. He shut the door behind him with an overwhelming sense of relief at being home.

Marmite scampered out from a corner and looked him over with suspicion. Jonah knelt down and reached out, tensing as the cat gave his hand a wary sniff. At last, Marmite meowed and started to rub against his legs, purring.

Jonah relaxed. He headed to the kitchen, cat in tow, and swore when he saw the remains of the glass that had shattered there the night before, the one he had dropped when Daniel Harker had come for him. It was hard to believe that so little time had passed.

He set the folder Annabel had given him on the kitchen table, cleaned up the glass and put down some cat food. Marmite had been his excuse to leave, one Annabel had been amused by, but the truth was that the situation had become too much for him. He had needed to get to familiar territory.

With Alice Decker, he'd thought at times that he was losing his mind. With Daniel, that was *exactly* what had happened. And however ashamed Daniel had professed to be, Jonah was angry. Anger and guilt, not a healthy mixture.

He sat down at the kitchen table with a beer and opened the folder. Annabel still had the digital originals saved on her laptop; Jonah had promised to read through the file by the next evening, and then they would compare notes and see what their next move could be.

A thought struck him, and he pulled the pill bottle from his pocket. He set them on the table, looking at them with the same wary eye Daniel Harker had the night before. Later, he thought. When he'd done all he could for the night.

Before he had left, Annabel had told him what else she'd obtained. Given the connection between BPV and Andreas Biotech, which her father had already noted, she had hunted out a wide selection of articles about Michael Andreas and the companies he owned. She had also included old payroll records.

'Christ,' Jonah had said. 'Police information, and now this? It must be seven shades of illegal.'

'I know a guy in London.' She'd thrown him a coy smile.

'London?'

'The information age, Jonah. You can break laws in every country without having to leave your bedroom.'

He had shaken his head, and while the illegality of it was way outside his comfort zone, something else had left him more unnerved. The way she'd said, *I know a guy in London,* and the way he'd found himself feeling about it.

Jealous.

That had been the point when he realized he had to get out of there.

*

Jonah read through the notes. For a few moments he looked at the image of Felix Hannerman, thinking of the gaunt face and cold eyes of the man who had come for Daniel Harker. Hannerman's profile was more extensive than those of the others, perhaps not surprising as he'd been the one with previous convictions. He came across as a spoilt rich kid who had grown into a confused, angry man, his dislike of revivers put down to a botched job when his mother died, and the effect that had had on his family. His father had taken his own life when Felix was twenty, leaving Hannerman and his sister Julia alone in the world with no other close relatives. Julia had dealt with it by relocating regularly, travelling country to country and staying for no more than a year or two, having little contact with her brother. She was currently thought to be in New Zealand, but they had yet to track her down to give her the news of her brother's death.

Jonah thought about what it would be like for her, her life interrupted by the news of her brother. He'd seen it firsthand – relatives of those who had died after committing terrible crimes. Trying to come to terms, overwhelmed by an awful shame, a terrible guilt. As if daring to grieve at all made them somehow complicit. It struck him as one of the worst kinds of grief.

He read on, going through the articles on Michael Andreas and the companies he had founded or bought. It was all vaguely familiar, Andreas having been such a big contributor to Baseline. The part he really remembered, though, was the press focus on the morbid interests Andreas had, and the suggestion that he wanted to outrun death. In particular, his dabbling with cryogenics, something that had crossed Jonah's mind after the Lyssa Underwood case, given the nature of the body preservation systems being used.

Outrun death. The thought brought to mind what Daniel had said to him on camera, speaking with Jonah's own lips: *If you could make this last, it'd be a hell of a way to cheat death, don't you think?*

By midnight, he had gone through two beers and was working on another. He'd moved over to the couch to be more comfortable and had read through everything but the payroll information. Looking it over, he knew it was pointless. No salaries, no job descriptions, no dates. Forty dense pages of unsorted names, with payroll and social security numbers and a variety of abbreviations.

They could prove useful as potential contacts, people Annabel could get in touch with and see what they knew. But she wanted Jonah to look through the names and check if there were any he recognized from Baseline who might open up more to Jonah than they would to a journalist calling them out of the blue. Until she'd said that, it hadn't occurred to him that Jonah's past in Baseline was the reason Daniel Harker had thought he might be useful.

Jonah assumed that the abbreviations beside each name identified which of Andreas's companies the employee had worked for, as they seemed to match the information Annabel had included about those companies: Andreas Biotech, Reese-Farthing Medical, Sankley OptiSen, MLA Research. The smallest was MLA Research, with over eighty staff. Given how many names were listed on the sheets he held, Jonah wondered if it actually covered everyone who had ever worked for these companies. He marvelled again at how the hell anyone could get hold of this kind of information.

He skimmed the names. Halfway through, he got thirsty and swigged his beer, but the thirst was stubborn. He continued skimming, then stopped suddenly and set his drink down. Anxious, he went to fetch the bottle of pills from the kitchen table.

It hadn't been ordinary thirst.

He went back to the couch, pills in his pocket. Thirst was one thing, but if anything *really* out of the ordinary happened, he wouldn't take any chances. He'd take a pill at once and get to bed.

By the time he'd reached the end of the names, it was two in the morning. He yawned, exhausted.

'I'm done,' he said. 'More tomorrow.' He took the pill bottle from his pocket and went to open it.

He stopped and set the bottle down. A hunch. He told himself it was stupid. Even so, he took up the payroll names once more, going back to the middle third, the part when he'd felt the thirst hit. He read.

Again he felt it, thirst growing so slowly that it was impossible to really pin down when it had begun, even to a specific page. But the implication was clear.

Harker's remnant was still present, enough to see something Jonah had missed.

'What is it, Daniel?' he said.

He took the six pages he had got through before the thirst had hit and went through the first three again. Nothing, even after waiting to the count of sixty. He was narrowing it down. He went one page at a time with the rest, waiting a minute after each. Thirst for the third page.

He started to read the names on that page aloud, and as he did he noticed something. Dotted throughout were French names, possibly French Canadian, flagged as staff in MLA Research. Armand Dion. Isabeau Poulin. Lafayette Girard. Xavier Vernet. Delphine Lavoie. It tallied with the company information he'd read before. MLA Research was Canadian. It had started up in Montreal, then a decade ago it had moved to Toronto.

Victor Eldridge had worked for the Toronto Forensic Revival Department. Could he have been doing other things, on the side? Sure, his name hadn't been in the list, but what if . . .

He shook his head. *Coincidence,* he thought. *Nothing more.*

But could it be what Harker was drawing his attention to?

He read out only those names again, a sixty-second pause between each.

Armand Dion.

Isabeau Poulin.

Lafayette Girard.

Xavier Vernet.

Thirst.

He stared at it. Repeated it aloud. *Xavier Vernet.* That was what Harker was showing him, but he couldn't see why. Was it a name he should recognize from Baseline? Perhaps it was a name familiar to Daniel but not to Jonah?

He said it again: Xavier Vernet.

Then he got it. Jonah swore and took a pen. He circled the name and in the margin wrote the man's initials, pressing hard on the page, drawing over the lines repeatedly to thicken them.

He laughed.

'Shit, Daniel. And I thought the Eldridge thing was a stretch. All these names. The chances of us finding *someone* who fits can't be that low . . .'

But he knew this was what Daniel had been trying to tell him. And he knew there might be something there.

Jonah took out the pill bottle again and looked at it. Then he stood, walked over to the apartment door and set it on the shelf beside his keys. *It can wait*, he thought. *Right now, we need all the help we can get.*

It was almost three in the morning, and his exhaustion was catching up with him fast. He took the page with Xavier Vernet's name into his bedroom and left it on the bed while he got ready. As he slid under the covers, he looked at it again and smiled. He knew that, however much of a red herring it turned out to be, Annabel would appreciate what he'd found. And that felt good.

Xavier Vernet.

XV.

Fifteen.

22

Jonah woke eager to tell Annabel what he'd found and called her before ten. He said nothing of the continued presence of Daniel, claiming to have simply noticed Vernet's name. She sounded intrigued but sceptical; two hours later she called him back with a single instruction. Be at the airport by 1 p.m. She hung up, and none of his subsequent calls were answered.

With no option, he headed for Richmond International Airport without any idea what he was about to do. When he arrived he called her again. This time she took the call, and told him which check-in desk to get to.

As he approached, she smiled at him. He smiled back, trying not to notice how good she looked. He pushed inappropriate thoughts out of his head.

'So,' he said. 'What's going on?'

'It checked out, Jonah. Vernet worked on BPV. I called MLA Research and told them I was with human resources in a big pharma company out East. I had that company's website up just in case they gave me anything awkward. Told them Vernet had applied for a position and had given them as a reference. I asked them to confirm various things.'

Jonah nodded, impressed. 'Sly. By *confirm*, do you mean tell you stuff you didn't actually know?'

'Absolutely. He's from southern France, joined MLA after

three years in a biotech outfit in Paris. He left MLA five years ago and had indeed worked on aspects of BPV, although they couldn't say more.'

'OK, Annabel. But why are we here?'

She shrugged. 'Oh, I tracked down his number and called him. He's in Chicago. We're booked on the next flight.'

He looked at her and blinked. She was serious.

*

On the flight, they settled into easy conversation. Little more than pleasantries, but the kind of thing that Jonah would normally find hard work.

Annabel gave him a selection of books about Baseline, including those her father had written.

'I need to brush up,' she said. 'Anything you think would be useful, tell me.'

'Does he know who we are?'

'I thought it'd be less complicated if he didn't. As far as he's concerned, I'm Sarah Townes. You're John Sullivan. We're journalists, doing an article on the early days of revival from perspectives that haven't been covered. An unsung-heroes thing.'

'That's all it took?'

'Enough for him to agree to meet. Although today is the only time he could manage in the next two weeks, hence the rush. Let me do the talking; you listen out for anything unusual he says. Yarrow's death hasn't been made public yet, so I'll try and drop his name in. We'll see what reaction we get.'

Xavier Vernet had agreed to meet them in the north of the city; outside O'Hare, Annabel gave the address of the coffee shop he'd specified to their taxi driver and they reached it with ten minutes to spare, ensconced in a corner with a pair of cappuccinos. It was the kind of trip Jonah would have spent a week planning, and Annabel had done it on a whim.

They waited, watching each new customer. At last, in came a

lanky man in his forties, whose eyes darted around the shop until they settled on Annabel. She smiled at him as he came over.

'Sarah Townes?' said Vernet, his French origins still very clear in his accent. 'I'm Xavier.'

'Good to meet you. John? Get Xavier a coffee.'

'Double espresso, please,' said Vernet.

Jonah went to order, choosing to wait for the coffee and give Annabel a chance to put the man at ease. While he was waiting, his phone rang. He glanced at it and answered.

'Hello, Never.'

'Your cat was hungry.'

'You're at my apartment? Are you stalking me?'

'I thought I'd drop by and say hello, and you're not even here. Where are you?'

'A coffee shop.'

'Can I come there? You're worrying me.'

'It's, uh, in Chicago.'

Silence for a moment. 'You're in Chicago?'

The double espresso arrived. 'Look, Never, I've got to go. I promise I'll explain in a few days. OK?'

Silence again. 'You already promised to explain. I'll give you two more days, and then I'll guilt-trip you so badly even your *shit* will be apologizing.' He hung up.

Jonah sighed, then turned off the phone in case Never decided to pursue things. He grabbed the coffee and returned to the table to find Annabel and Vernet laughing like old friends. *She has a knack,* he thought.

Vernet took the coffee and thanked him.

'Xavier was telling me he actually *worked* on BPV,' Annabel said. 'Isn't that something, John?'

Jonah nodded, wanting to avoid speaking if he could, in case he called her Annabel rather than Sarah.

'Not the original development,' Vernet said. 'This was one year on, some work on BPV variants. Improvements. Everyone who writes about this gives the impression that after the drug was developed that was it, you know? But BPV was a blanket term for a related family of compounds. Efficacy doubled, thanks to us.'

Annabel smiled. 'Exactly the kind of thing we want to cover, Xavier. The man who gave us your name thought you'd be perfect for that kind of insight.'

Jonah almost flinched at the gambit; Annabel clearly didn't want to tiptoe around things.

'May I ask,' said Vernet. 'Who told you of me?'

'Someone a colleague of mine knows,' she said, her eyes fixed on Vernet's. 'Tobias Yarrow.'

Vernet said nothing for a moment, his eyebrows raising in surprise. 'Tobias Yarrow?'

'Yes. You remember him, surely? It wasn't *that* long ago.'

Vernet thought. 'Three years.'

'Ah. I haven't met him, I've heard things secondhand through my colleague. Apologies if I've got things wrong, but it seems you had plenty of things to tell *him*, and he certainly remembers you.'

Vernet still looked a little mystified. 'So, he told you where we met . . . ?'

Annabel simply nodded. Jonah was impressed by how authoritative that nod was, considering she had no idea.

Vernet nodded back, frowning. 'Then you know more about me than makes me comfortable.'

'None of it goes in the story, Xavier,' she said.

Vernet lowered his voice. 'I met Tobias Yarrow at an AA meeting. We went for a coffee after. Did the same the next week, and after that I didn't see him again.'

'But you remember him, so he left some kind of impression?'

'He was very intense. I remember I told him some of the stories, and he lapped it up. A little too much, I think.'

Jonah leaned forward. 'What stories?'

'You know, the usual thing people want to hear about the early days of revival. I started my career working on Alzheimer's and

memory, then I found myself in revival work, rumours flying everywhere, knowing it was happening in the building we were in.
People forget what it was like, you know? They forget how creepy it
was. Time does that. We get used to it. We get used to dead people
talking. I was drinking pretty bad at times – still do, now and again
– but those first few years of revival work were the worst. Now
some people, God . . . they love to hear about it. They *love* all that
creepy shit. Yarrow, he seemed to get a kick out of it, so I told him
things.'

Annabel nodded. 'What did you tell him?'

'I started telling him about the BPV manufacture problems.
This is what I was telling you before, about how we improved the
drug. Eight, maybe nine years back. We had three licensees, and
the efficacy was variable. Not by that much, but enough to warrant
suspicion. Quality control was the first candidate, but they seemed
to be identical. Turned out it was enantiomers. Impurities with
the same chemical structure, but mirrored. The manufacturing
processes varied a little, and the proportions varied too, from one
to four per cent of the mirrored version. A few months after identifying the problem, we were tasked to examine the properties of this
taint. We started by increasing the proportion, see what it did to the
effectiveness.'

'Effectiveness?' said Jonah. Annabel sat back a little to let him
know he could take over.

'Sure. BPV was a family of variants of a drug used for post-
traumatic stress disorder. Messes with the memory systems
that PTSD is caused by. Its main purpose is to disrupt the laying
down of deep memory during a crisis, or in revival what the brain
treats like a crisis. In short, it suppressed remnants. So to see what
the mirrored drug did, we tried going the other way. Boost the
levels . . .'

'And?'

'People we tried it with, hell . . . Hit them hard.'

'Volunteer revivers?'

Vernet smiled. 'They got paid well enough. Thing was, it *boosted* revival ability. Normal BPV does that a little, but the mirror was far more powerful. Now, the users of BPV, the revivers, they can have the drugs tailored, the proportions finely controlled. You want as much of the boost as you can get, without incurring the side effects. And there are other things that you can put in the mix to offset the downsides. We tried extremes, huge doses of the mirror with huge doses of countering drugs. It didn't improve performance any more than the lower doses. But then we were told to try certain other BPV variants, slight chemical modifications. Some of these were just as effective but didn't form the mirrored version *at all* in manufacturing. Much cheaper to make pure. But we were asked to see what properties the *mirrored* versions of these might have. Forcing the mirrored forms wasn't easy, but one of them gave a *massive* boost to performance. There were just a few problems. Hardly anyone could even tolerate it, and there were severe side effects that made it useless. We stopped testing it.'

Jonah tensed as he spoke. 'What kind of side effects?'

'Hallucinations. Remnant problems. Psychological disturbance. That kind of thing. Some of our test subjects still wanted it, though, when they knew we were going to just destroy it. Performance enhancer like that could get them some good money, they thought. None of them were high-rated revivers, and they figured it'd take them up a level, even though the side effects were eventually crippling. Crazy.'

Jonah stayed quiet and Annabel shifted forward again. 'Is that all you told Yarrow?' she asked.

Vernet looked at them warily. 'What is this?'

Annabel put her hand on his. 'It's important, Xavier. Please.'

Vernet shook his head. 'Well, for what it's worth. After that, MLA Research did no more BPV work. We were studying some chronic degenerative diseases, a few broad-base approaches that looked promising. We had a little success with some. I was glad to get back to the areas I'd been trained for. My drinking stopped, mostly. Anyway, a few years after the BPV work finished I moved on, ended up in a great place here in Chicago. Not long after I started, I was at a conference where I ran into some people I used to work with who'd moved on too. That night we drank, you know? Like I said, I still do sometimes. The conversation took a turn where we'd try and outdo each other with the stories we'd picked up. One of them told how he'd heard something about that old forced mirror drug variant. Said it had been used since. Said it had boosted things so much that something went wrong in a revival. They'd brought the subject back, but when it started talking it wasn't them. He said it was something long dead, something not human. Said they wanted to bring it back and make it stay.'

Vernet's face was intently serious as he said it. He was looking right at Jonah, and Jonah could feel the colour draining from his face. Vernet broke into a smile and he laughed. 'Hey, I'm sorry. This is just talk. You shouldn't take these things seriously.'

'Did Tobias Yarrow take it seriously, Xavier?' asked Annabel.

'Yes. Even when I told him it was nonsense. He didn't find it funny. I told him to relax, but he didn't seem the kind who *could* relax.'

'Was that all you knew?' Annabel asked, and got a nod in reply. 'So did you tell him who it was that had told you?'

'It was another couple years before I saw Yarrow. I was drunk the night I heard the story. I can't remember who was *there*, let alone who said it. Pretty sure they'd heard it secondhand anyway.'

'Have you ever heard of Unity?'

Vernet said he had not. Annabel and Jonah spent another twenty minutes with him but got nothing else. Annabel left him a card with her number, bearing the name Sarah Townes, just in case he remembered any more.

In the taxi to the airport, Jonah found his mind churning, unable to make the pieces fit.

'Yarrow spoke to Vernet three years ago, Annabel. Why so long? Why so long before he did anything?'

Annabel shook her head. 'Maybe not before he did *anything*, Jonah. Whatever Vernet says, he must have given Yarrow enough to go on. Yarrow could have tracked the story down and found the man who'd told Vernet in the first place. If that's true, unless Vernet remembers what else he told Yarrow, we don't stand a chance. And if Yarrow's story to my dad left out something crucial, we're equally screwed. Shit. I can't believe we found Vernet and this is all we get. A campfire ghost story.'

She settled into grim silence for the journey to the airport, scribbling notes and looking more and more frustrated. Her terse mood kept up during the flight home; at Richmond International they went their separate ways, with Jonah strangely distressed by how distant she suddenly seemed.

'I'll hear from you?' he said as they parted. 'About Eldridge?'

She mumbled something non-committal and headed off to where her car was parked, leaving Jonah struggling to deal with how he was feeling.

In his apartment, he heated up some chilli in the microwave and ate it on the couch, flicking around the channels without settling anywhere, with Marmite huddled up and insisting on some attention. The meeting with Vernet had seemed immune to failure on the trip out. He understood how tired Annabel must be, and how disappointed that her best lead, while proving interesting, had really led nowhere. Jonah knew that if it had been him in her position, he would have shut the door and nursed his wounds for a while. Maybe that was all this was. Perhaps it would be for the best, he thought, if she stopped looking. Perhaps it would be for the best not to find Victor Eldridge too.

Jonah couldn't help but think about what Vernet had said: *Something long dead. Something not human. They wanted to bring it back and make it stay.*

Wondering what kind of answers might come for him, and for Annabel, Jonah suddenly felt cold.

23

Annabel got home from the trip feeling uneasy, and not just about what Vernet had said.

The disappointment of reaching a dead end had been made worse when she'd noticed something in the way Jonah was looking at her. It was a look she'd seen many times before, and one she knew she may have to dampen down.

There was a reason her relationships all failed. She had an unofficial rule: don't get involved with a guy you actually like. That way, distance was easier to maintain, and the inevitable breakup less painful.

She liked Jonah. She always had, she confessed to herself – ever since her father had told her about the boy who'd revived his mother yet still wanted to do whatever good he could with what most people would have called a curse. She'd been fifteen at the time. Things like that leave an impression.

When she'd recognized his name on the day of her father's revival, it had seemed fitting that he be the one to do it. But actually seeing him had left her unsettled, and at the time she'd not given much thought to why.

It had been the morning after her father had made his appearance in Jonah's stolen body when she'd understood what had unnerved her, finding it hard not to look at Jonah's grey-blue eyes. Complications like that were to be avoided at all costs, especially now. She wondered what her father would have said about the situation, if he hadn't taken that pill and left her alone.

She would have to dowse any interest Jonah had in her, and make sure that he knew she had no interest in him. Tackling it directly might not prove easy, but if things worked out the way she'd planned, it wouldn't be a problem.

*

Jonah wasn't entirely surprised when Annabel called him at nine the next morning. She said little, only asked him to come to her father's house to discuss their next move, but her tone was upbeat again, her enthusiasm clear. He wondered where she got it from, those mental resources to fall back on. He knew he could do with some.

She greeted him at her door and brought him through to the kitchen.

'I'm sorry for yesterday, Jonah. My hopes had been too high. This morning, though, I did a little planning.'

'About what we do next?

'Way I see it, either we wait for Vernet to tell us something he forgot, or we stumble into whatever else Yarrow found out. Neither of those appeals to me. So . . .'

'Uh oh.' Jonah smiled, but only on the outside. There was a look in Annabel's eyes that he was starting to recognize. One that he wasn't keen on.

'I figure we have to find someone else who knew what was going on. Someone else who'll be able to fill in the blanks.'

'Who?'

'Michael Andreas.'

Jonah laughed.

'I mean it. He's notoriously hands-on. He'll know something.'

'Good luck seeing him. I tell you what else he's notorious for: being hard to *meet*. Even if you do, what makes you think he'll tell you anything?'

'Jonah, what's the one thing a reviver needs a subject to do during a revival?'

Jonah shrugged. 'Talk.'

'Exactly. If they talk, you can tell when they're lying. You can tell when they're evasive. I'm a journalist. What you do with the dead, I do with the living. I get the man to talk, and I'll know. And as for getting to see him? I'm going to be the grieving daughter wanting to write a piece about my dad and his contribution to revival. Andreas was such a big part of Baseline, he's a natural element of that. I've put out some feelers. If we get a bite, it'll hopefully be soon.' She smiled at him.

Jonah shook his head and smiled back. 'I love the way impossible odds don't faze you. But you could've just told me all that on the phone. Why did you insist I come out here?'

'Partly because I wanted to apologize face to face. But there's also something I owe you. You helped me find Vernet, and now it's my turn.' Near the sink was a folder, a handful of sheets of paper inside. She took it and handed it to Jonah.

'Eldridge,' he said, glancing at the first sheet. 'Your guy in London again?'

She nodded. 'Eldridge isn't exactly in good condition. He spent the last four years in and out of a psychiatric hospital in North Carolina. Eight months ago he was diagnosed with prostate cancer. It's run on and on, but he got a place in a hospice in south Baltimore that specializes in psychiatric patients. He's been there four months now. He doesn't have long left.'

'What are the chances he'll even agree to see us?' Jonah asked. Annabel smiled and raised her eyebrows; Jonah felt his stomach knot as he saw that look in her eye again and realized what it meant. 'Christ, Annabel. You don't waste any time. When?'

'We're going there this evening, although I don't know if Eldridge is aware of it yet. And this time we may as well go as ourselves. With Vernet, I didn't want to scare him off, in case he had more of a connection to Yarrow that we thought. Here, though, we'll play it like we'll do with Andreas. Grieving daughter doing a piece on revival and her father's legacy. Getting the views of various revivers, and surely those of a *dying* reviver are even more poignant? In the end, though, there's one big advantage Annabel Harker has over Sarah Townes, and that's what's really getting our foot in the door.'

'I don't follow.'

'The hospice he's in makes a specialty of handling psychiatric patients free of charge if they can. Catching the people who fall through the cracks, and the cracks are pretty big. But they struggle to keep that going.'

Jonah looked blank.

'I'm going to *donate*. We leave in an hour and a half. First, I need to eat. I'm fixing some pasta. You want some?'

'I guess I could do with eating something.'

'Good.' She showed him to the living room and pointed out a door in the far wall. 'I won't be long. There's a rec room through there, try and relax.'

'Thanks,' said Jonah as she left, managing not to add: *I know*.

He walked through to the rec room and stood by the pool table, taking in the room and feeling a strong sense of *home*. He glanced around, finding with ease the remote for the huge-screen TV on the wall, and flipped on the power for the main audio unit. He ran through a dozen channels before settling on music. He wanted to be active, but mindlessly so, and playing pool seemed a good choice, a little music in the background to take the edge off the oddness he was feeling.

He racked the balls and showed off his ineptitude for ten minutes as his mind began to wander. In the corner of the room was a small bar. On top, there were several framed family photographs.

He picked one of them up. It showed Daniel with his wife.

'Robin,' he said. Robin Harker. Jonah winced at the agony of it, the ongoing, relentless agony. He set the picture down quickly, his hand drawing back as if the photo were dangerous. He turned, intending to play more pool, but another memory surfaced.

Annabel standing in the doorway, eyes red with tears.

'Didn't you think I'd be upset, Dad?' she said. She was younger; her accent far less English than the one Jonah knew. 'I *needed* you there. *Mom* needed you there.'

'I couldn't do it,' said Daniel, his back to her. 'I couldn't.'

'She didn't understand, Dad.'

'I'm sorry.' Daniel turned around. Jonah groped for the context; then it hit him, and it hit hard. Robin was dead. Daniel couldn't deal with it. He'd refused to attend the revival.

'It was your last chance to say good-bye, Dad. It was *her* last chance. Don't you realize how much that hurts? She *missed* you, Dad. Jesus. She missed you.'

Annabel looked at Daniel with such disappointment, it was unbearable; he looked away from her.

'Christ, Dad. Don't you even give a *damn* how hard it was for me?'

Daniel said nothing, until his daughter turned and walked off. He started to cry. 'Annie, I'm sorry. Please.' She strode to the door and didn't look back. Daniel went after her. 'Please, Annie! I'm sorry. *I'm sorry.*'

His daughter went out into the night, not shutting the front door, leaving a black gaping hole. His wife was dead. His daughter hated him. Daniel Harker fell to his knees, crippled by it all.

Jonah was suddenly aware of the present. He felt the heat of panic, disorientation. He felt thirsty.

'Jesus,' he said. He felt his pocket. He was still carrying the bottle of pills Stephanie Graves had given him. Just in case.

Maybe it was to be expected. Familiar surroundings. Old, bad memories. Someone *else's* old, bad memories. Remnants of the kind he was more used to.

Annabel came through with two bowls of penne. 'You OK?' she said. 'I thought I heard something.' Jonah shook his head and reached for his bowl. As she passed it over, her hand brushed his.

Reflex kicked in. He pulled his hand away; the bowl thudded to the ground, intact but contents spilled. She looked at him, puzzled.

Angry with himself, Jonah looked at the mess, then back at Annabel. 'Sorry. It's habit. People get chill really badly from me.'

'You know I don't get chill.'

'I know, but contact makes me . . . jumpy. Hard habit to break. You must have met revivers before. I can't be the *most* fucked up person you know.' He smiled but bent down the moment he'd finished speaking, just in case he saw the answer in her eyes and didn't like it. He started gathering the spillage back into the bowl.

'I met a few,' said Annabel. 'When I was a kid. While Dad was writing the second book, we'd have them over. Some people have a real fear of revivers. Not me. Maybe because I didn't get chill. Mom and Dad didn't get it either.'

'I'm sorry,' he said, handing the bowl back to her. 'I'll get a cloth, and—'

'It can wait. Jonah, you have to promise me something.' She looked at him until he nodded. 'Don't ever apologize for things that aren't your fault. And don't ever be ashamed of what you are.'

She watched him, waiting. 'OK,' he managed.

'Good. Now, follow me.' She tapped his bowl. 'There's more in the kitchen.'

They ate in silence at the kitchen table, hunger taking over.

Finished, Jonah looked at the clock on the wall. It wouldn't be long before they left to see Eldridge, and there was something Jonah had to ask her.

'What did your dad tell you, Annabel? About why I wanted to track Eldridge down?'

'You shared the remnant problem. Eldridge had the same thing, a revived subject taking control.'

'That was all he said?'

She nodded.

'There was something else, before my remnant problems started. Something happened in a revival. It was dismissed as hallucination, written off as overwork. Eldridge had a similar revival experience, just before *his* remnant troubles boiled over. They wrote his off as overwork too. There's a connection here, and I want to understand it.'

'What happened?'

'The revival subject in both cases panicked. They thought something was *coming*, something dark and terrifying, something *predatory*. Eldridge's subject just stopped being there. Mine, I let go before that could happen. And then . . . Then it *spoke* to me. Nobody else witnessed it. But it spoke.' His voice fell to a whisper. 'Something long dead. Something not human.'

She looked at him, pale. 'So what Vernet said . . . It didn't strike you as just talk.'

'No. Whatever it was, there was one overriding sense I had of it. *Evil*. I want it to be explained away. I want it to have been all in my mind. But I don't think it was.'

*

They arrived at the Walter Hodges Hospice just after 5 p.m. Much of the front of the main building was enclosed in scaffolding; at the base of the scaffold was a placard, a cartoon of a smiling circle with a single giant hand, thumb up, 'Thanks for your donations!' printed below. The hospice was adjacent to a larger and more modern medical centre that looked in much better health than its ailing sibling. They parked in the shared lot at the rear of the building complex; Annabel had taken her mother's red Porsche Boxster, insisting Jonah ride with her rather than take his own car. He'd spent the journey going over the information Annabel's hacker had unearthed.

They walked around to the front entrance. Directly across the road was a billboard ad for the Afterlifers. Jonah stopped and frowned at it, finding the irony unpleasant. This was what the

Afterlifers meant to most people now: benign, well-funded campaigners.

Inside, the reception area was busy. Annabel introduced herself, and after a ten-minute wait an athletic, greying man emerged to greet them, his face so chiselled that Jonah could only think of the 'before' picture in a male hair-dye commercial.

'Dr Edward Buckle,' the man said to Annabel. 'My condolences, Miss Harker.'

'Thank you. This is Jonah Miller, co-writer for the piece.'

Buckle smiled. 'Annabel, Jonah, you're both very welcome. Anything I can do to help you, I'll try my best. Your generosity is going to make a difference. Hospice funding is often overlooked, let alone hospice care for psychiatric patients.' His gaze went to the main window, the view of the billboard opposite. 'You saw the repair work we're doing at the front. This whole building is riddled with similar problems. Yet I see that damn billboard every morning when I get to work, and I think of the money people give to them. So damn righteous, all that concern about the dead. But the living are the ones who need the help the most.' As he spoke, he led them along a short corridor and into his office. 'I read that the kind of people who donate to the Afterlifers are more likely to give to dying animals than dying people. You know what charities they give to least? Hospices and the mentally ill. You can guess where that puts us.'

Annabel nodded. 'I know exactly what you mean. The Afterlifers have managed to create this intense media focus on death, but it's all from the wrong direction.'

'Precisely!' said Buckle. He sat behind his desk and gestured for Annabel and Jonah to sit too. 'All from the wrong direction. Death is an expensive business. Insurance companies have improved since I started here, I admit, but once they find a way to disown a patient, it's not pretty. We offer as many free and partly funded places as we can, but it's a struggle. So many people fail to get the care they need at the end of their lives, but worries about revival are what make headlines. Perhaps it's something that would make a story in its own right, Miss Harker.'

'It's something I'll give serious thought to, Doctor. Now, though, the matter at hand . . .'

'Victor Eldridge,' said Buckle, folding his hands together. 'Victor has many problems. Confidentiality prevents me from saying any more, but he's perfectly competent, perfectly able to make his own decisions.'

'Did he agree to talk to me?'

'You said that your donation was not contingent on his agreement. That's still the case, yes?'

'Yes,' said Annabel. Jonah felt like swearing, but if Annabel felt the same she gave no hint of it.

'As long as that's clear. Yes, Victor's very happy to talk to you. He's permitted to receive visitors whenever he wishes, but . . . well, he doesn't get many. I have things to attend to, but I'll send someone to take you to him.'

*

They waited in Buckle's office, uneasy and impatient. Annabel switched her phone off to avoid interruption; Jonah's was in his pocket, already switched off. He'd not had it back on since he'd last spoken to Never.

After ten minutes, a young male orderly arrived to take them to Eldridge. As the orderly led the way, Jonah turned to Annabel and whispered, 'He's working in a place like this, but he looks about twelve.'

'And?'

'And I'm kinda worried for him.'

Annabel shrugged. 'You know, I'm sure my dad thought the same about you working in Baseline.' She caught up with the orderly and checked his name badge. 'So, Greg, you worked here long?'

'Six months.'

'College, right?'

'Uh huh. Majoring in psychology.'

'Pay well here?'

Greg grimaced. 'It's OK. Gets me by, just about.'

'What can you tell us about Mr Eldridge?'

'I'm supposed to take you to him and wait for you outside.'

'He's OK on his own with us?'

'Victor's fine. He gets a little uptight, but he's pretty quiet these days. He'll pull the cord or call if he needs me.'

'So, uh, what exactly is wrong with him?'

Greg stopped, looking so thrown Jonah wanted to pat him on the back and tell him he'd be fine, but by the determined look on Annabel's face, he thought that'd be a lie. Greg lowered his voice to explain. 'I . . . I really can't discuss a patient's details, Miss. It'll be up to Victor, what gets disclosed.'

'It's just . . . well, you said he's pretty quiet *these days*. Implies he used to *not* be quiet, that's all. And if you knew why, it'd be really useful.' Annabel put her hand into Greg's pen pocket and left behind a hundred-dollar bill. Greg took it out and stared at it in silence. 'That's a freebie,' said Annabel. 'But I'll top it up to five hundred if you tell me.'

Greg said nothing and walked on. Annabel seemed unworried. *Journalist with money*, thought Jonah. *Like she said: dangerous combination.*

*

They walked in silence, the innards of the building showing the lack of investment that Buckle had referred to. At last Greg opened a door that led outside. They stepped out into the open air, and the main building door swung shut. There was nobody else around.

They'd come all the way through, and beyond the eight-foot-high wire fencing they could see the parking lot they'd left forty minutes before.

'Victor Eldridge is in number eleven,' said Greg. 'We have

twelve of these units. Self-contained, bedroom, bathroom, small living area. We don't typically use them for our psychiatric patients. With Victor, well . . . He's behaving, and the doctors chose to give him a little dignity. A place of his own, first time in years.'

Annabel looked hard at Greg. 'You want to elaborate?'

Greg nodded but was clearly uncomfortable. 'Hell. OK. Here's all I know. Before Victor Eldridge came here he had a suite of symptoms, including auditory hallucinations, extreme panic attacks. He was prone to fits. He was terrified of everything and everyone. He was unpredictable. He attacked staff from time to time and was often confined to secure units. When he was diagnosed terminal, it changed.'

'Because of the diagnosis?'

Greg lowered his voice, glancing around. 'More than that. He'd always had calm periods, and during one of those, they let him join in with some group recreation. One day the group wanted to play bingo. They all had their cards and those little short pencils. The story goes that one of the other inmates saw him do it. Push the pencil into his ear. Calm as anything, the inmate said, until a little stub was sticking out, maybe an inch and a half. One of the staff there at the time told me all this when Victor was transferred here. She reckoned the pencil would've already been through the eardrum by then. The pain must've been appalling, but like I said, Eldridge was calm. He stood, walked to a wall and hit the side of his head as hard as he could against it, driving the pencil in. He collapsed, blood pouring out, but he survived.'

'What was the damage?'

'Surgery got the thing out. Fucked up his hearing in that ear, and the pencil made it an inch into his brain. Victor was a changed man. From that day, he was no trouble.'

Annabel looked at Jonah with a hint of disappointment. Jonah raised an eyebrow; they were both thinking the same thing – was there much left of Victor Eldridge that was worth speaking to?

'No trouble?' said Annabel. 'You mean . . . ?'

Greg shook his head. 'What, is he a vegetable? Shit no. The guy's about as ordinary as you get. Polite, a little quiet. He'll try and talk anyone he can into a game of chess.'

'So what had changed?'

'He said it had stopped the voices. Said they'd only been in that ear, said that once he'd found out he was dying, he decided he wanted some peace and quiet.'

'But if the voices were in his head anyway . . . ?'

Greg shrugged. 'That's all I know.'

'Thanks,' Annabel said, handing him four more bills. Greg said nothing and led the way.

The apartments had a prefab look, like the shoebox offices Jonah recalled from Baseline. Arranged in four clusters of three, with well-tended grass and flowerbeds between, there was a wide pathway connecting them to each other and to the main building.

At the end of the path to each cluster, a panel showed the names of the residents on small handwritten cards tucked into transparent covers.

And there, at the last cluster, was the name: 'V Eldridge, Apt. 11'. Greg knocked.

The door was opened by a nurse, a woman in her late thirties, her name, 'Jan', announced on a badge.

'Hi, Greg,' she said.

'Hey, Jan. Couple of people here to see Victor.'

'So I heard. I'm all done here.' She looked at Annabel. 'Limit it to a half hour at most, please. He's tired today, but he's a stubborn one.'

Jonah looked past the woman and saw an open door leading into a bedroom: bulky monitoring equipment, cylinders of oxygen and a drip stand were visible. To the left, Jonah could see a kitchen area. An old man was shuffling around in it.

'Victor?' called the nurse.

The old man turned, and Jonah was taken by surprise. He wasn't so old. Slow, and extremely thin – almost cadaverous – but

245

no more than fifty. The man walked out of the kitchen, each step taken with care, each marked by a slight wince on his face. It took Jonah a moment to accept that this was the same man he'd seen in the video footage.

'Is it those people, Jan?' Eldridge was smiling, with effort. He approached, reaching for glasses that hung from a chain around his neck.

'The people Dr Buckle mentioned, Victor, yes.'

Annabel stepped forward. 'My name's Annabel Harker, Mr Eldridge. This is Jonah Miller.'

Eldridge's smile became warmer. 'Good to meet you, Annabel.' His eyes drifted to Jonah; he popped his glasses on and looked at Jonah for a moment, uncertain, his smile fading.

The nurse was concerned. 'Victor?'

Eldridge forced his smile back, but it didn't quite reach his eyes. 'I'm OK, just dizzy for a moment. Jan, you can go, I'll be fine.'

'You're sure?'

Eldridge smiled at her, then turned to Annabel. 'Bless the woman, but she's hard to get rid of sometimes.'

The nurse laughed and turned to leave, but then thought of something. 'Actually, before I go . . . we're doing a little fund-raising. I wonder if you'd care to donate? Anything you can give would be appreciated.'

Jonah caught Annabel's eye. 'Allow me,' he said, then took out his wallet and gave the nurse a single twenty. He wondered how much Annabel's donation had been.

The nurse looked pleased and put the money into a fanny pack she was wearing, taking something from the same pack. She handed it to Jonah – a small button badge, the same cartoon smile with a thumbs-up he'd seen on the scaffolding by the main entrance. He looked at it in silence for a moment, and the nurse must have taken his reaction as dislike. 'We have some key rings and fridge magnets for the larger donations, if you'd like,' she said.

'No, no, this is fine.'

'Now, promise me you won't make him overdo it.'

Jonah nodded.

'I'll wait by the main building,' said Greg. 'When you two are done, I'll take you back in.' He and Jan walked off, chatting as they went.

As the door shut, Victor Eldridge's smile vanished. 'Thank God she's gone,' he said. 'I meant it about her being hard to get rid of. She *talks* . . .' He raised his eyes to the ceiling. 'Come over here, I need to sit down.'

They sat, Eldridge in a reclining chair with a tray attached to the armrest. He took a glass of orange juice from the tray and sipped. He looked around the room, appreciating it. 'Nice little place to spend some time.' There was no bitterness in his voice, not even resignation. Simply matter-of-fact. 'So, you're Daniel Harker's daughter. The good doctor told me what you're writing, but I have to say I'm not clear why you want to talk to *me*.'

'You were a talented reviver, Victor,' Annabel said.

Eldridge smiled, but there was an edge to it. 'Oh, please. You're here because I'm dying and you thought there was irony in that. That's all I see in the press these days. Irony and cynicism.'

Annabel opened her mouth but nothing came out. Eldridge had left her speechless.

'That's not why we're here,' said Jonah.

Eldridge set down his drink and sat upright. His face hardened. 'Then why?'

'My name is Jonah Miller.'

'I heard.'

'I'm a reviver.'

Eldridge paused for a moment, then he nodded. 'I thought there was something familiar about the name. What do you want?'

'Do you remember Ruby Fleming, Mr Eldridge?'

Eldridge was clearly uncomfortable. His hand went to his right ear, and he rubbed hard with the heel of his palm. 'I don't know anyone called that.'

'You remember her,' said Jonah.

Eldridge stared, his eyes wide, almost pleading. He shook his head. 'Please . . .'

'You remember Ruby. And you know what? Almost the same thing happened to me. They told me it was overwork, that it was just in my head. And then my revival subjects started to . . . well. You know, don't you?'

Eldridge looked dazed. 'They stayed with me. I was lost inside them.'

Jonah nodded. 'I was treated by the same doctor who treated you. Stephanie Graves.'

'She was too late. I couldn't work anymore. But they didn't believe what I told them. I told them there was something out there, and they didn't pay any attention. But I could still hear it. Yes, I remember Ruby Fleming. I remember her screaming out to me for help. Something was coming for her. Something was coming and I did *nothing*.'

Eldridge's hand went to his ear again. 'The voices have gone now, Victor,' Annabel said. 'But what did they say to you?' She took his other hand. 'Victor?'

Eldridge's eyes grew distant and frightened. 'I heard the whispers after Ruby. It was trying to talk to me, but I wasn't . . . I wasn't strong enough to hear. Thank God. But it was always there. I could hear it trying to get through to me. Just before I found out I was dying, it started to get louder. It was getting clearer. *Stronger*. I knew that if I heard what it was saying it would be the end of me . . .' Panic in his eyes, he turned to Jonah and reached out, seizing his hand. As he made contact with Jonah's skin, chill flooded them both. Eldridge released at once and snapped his hand back, rubbing it, shock in his eyes.

'Well, would you look at that,' said Eldridge, dazed. 'A reviver getting chill from a reviver. I guess I've lost the skill. Maybe because I'm close to death now.'

'Tell me more about the whispering, Victor,' said Jonah.

'I had to stop it. It's hard to kill yourself in places where they're used to people trying. I'm dying anyway, but I had to stop it before I *heard*. So I took the pencil. I thought if I went deep it might stop. I hoped it would kill me. It didn't.'

'But it put an end to the whispers.'

Eldridge nodded.

'Do you know why it happened to you, Victor?' Jonah asked. 'Have you heard of others?'

Eldridge's eyes widened. 'Only me. Maybe there were others, but none I knew of.'

'I know a few things about you, Victor,' he said. 'There's something I don't understand.' Annabel caught his eye and gave him a questioning look. He hadn't said anything to her, but he'd spotted something in Eldridge's notes, something that had nagged at him. Details of his original revival registration in Canada, and then his later registration in the US.

'You were at the top of your game, Victor. Private work, forensics. You were a great loss to both. But it doesn't add up.'

Eldridge looked nervous. 'What do you mean?'

'Your rating was too low. I saw how you did revivals. You were good at it. Nobody with such a low rating is that good. Nobody with such a low rating gets forensic work.'

'I was re-rated. Better training. It happens.'

It did happen, Jonah knew. Revivers improved with practice. But the timing and location were too close to be just coincidental. 'You came out of nowhere. Making a living in revival, sure, but you were low rated. Bottom of the heap. Suddenly your ability rockets. Later, you start to suffer from remnants, worse than any reviver before you.'

Eldridge said nothing.

'Have you ever heard of MLA Research?' said Jonah, looking Eldridge in the eye. After a moment, Eldridge looked down.

Annabel looked at Jonah, then Eldridge. She leaned forward. 'You were part of their trial?'

Eldridge still refused to look up. Annabel put her hand on his. 'Victor, please.'

Eldridge shook his head, but he looked up at last. 'I was a poor excuse for a reviver, low rated. Doing insurance jobs in Toronto, not much money. Getting back one in three subjects, weak and brief. I was a joke. But there was a drug they were testing, and for a few it made us *better*. And I stole some. I was one of the few who could take it. Maybe the *only* one who could stand it for long. I stole some and used it. For two *years* I used it. Put the improvement down to better training. It wasn't unheard of. Got myself higher rated, got a job in forensics. Less money than I could've got, but I knew I was a fraud, you see? I wanted to make up for that. I wanted to make a difference. But the drug had a cost. Of everyone I'd had the least problems, and I thought I'd gotten used to it, built up a tolerance. Wishful thinking. It all caught up. The remnants you know about, but I think there was more. It made me able to reach further. What if I reached too far? Because there *is* something out there, out in the dark. And I think I know what it must be. I could hear it. And it's getting *stronger*.'

Eldridge stopped himself for a moment, overwhelmed. 'I'm glad to be dying. I'm close, now. *Close*. But sometimes the thought terrifies me. Lost in the dark, alone with the shadows . . . I think of Ruby Fleming. I think of when the Devil came to take her.'

24

They left Eldridge soon after; the dying man was badly shaken, but feigned a smile when Greg the orderly jogged over to the doorway to check on him.

'Well?' Annabel asked as they got into her mother's car. 'Did you get what you came here for?'

Jonah shook his head. 'I don't know. He's damaged, in ways that fit the pattern of burnout. Overworked. Repeated breakdowns. He was taking a drug that magnified all the downsides of revival for years. I had the same result from pushing myself too hard. Maybe that *is* all that links us.'

Annabel glanced over at him. 'But you don't believe that.'

'He thought he reached too far. What I *want* to believe is that we both caused the same kind of panic in revival subjects, but maybe we were *both* reaching too far. Getting too close.' He shook his head. 'I don't know.'

Annabel took out her phone and switched it back on. Jonah left his off, wondering how long he could avoid talking to Never. Not much longer.

'Well, well,' said Annabel.

'What?'

She showed him. An email from the office of Michael Andreas.

*

Andreas had agreed to be interviewed for the article Annabel was pretending to write, the meeting to take place the next day in Sankley OptiSen, a facility west of Philadelphia.

Jonah stayed over at Annabel's, getting to sleep after a quick meal, ready for the early start the next morning. He took the couch. The idea of sleeping in Daniel's bed wasn't raised by either of them.

The Sankley OptiSen building was exactly how Jonah, twelve years before, had expected Baseline to be. Every surface seemed honed; even the greenery looked crafted rather than grown.

At precisely 2 p.m. they were taken up to the top floor.

Michael Andreas opened the door to his office. He was a handsome man. Stunningly so. He exuded comfort, reassurance, capability. 'Miss Harker,' he said, taking her hand. 'There's little I can say. The loss of your father was a terrible thing.' A genuine sorrow, considerable sincerity.

Jonah was suddenly finding him easy to dislike.

Andreas invited them through. Jonah found himself gawping at the sheer scale of the room.

'Sit, please,' said Andreas. He took up position behind a vast oak desk. Annabel and Jonah took their seats.

'I'm glad you contacted me,' Andreas said. 'You father deserves far more respect than he's been granted. It would be an honour to help redress that.'

'Thank you. Can you remember first meeting my father?'

'Sam Deering introduced us. The man who launched forensic revival.' He looked at Jonah for a moment, leaving him uneasy. 'I understand he retired recently. This was before any of that had begun. Back then Sam was the FBI representative within Baseline. In the early days, they had representatives from so many religious denominations that it sometimes seemed like the scientists were in the minority. Daniel, though, was a scientifically minded man. I liked him at once.' Andreas took a drink from a small glass of water on the desk in front of him. 'He interviewed me twice, both brief occasions that focused on the research, not the person. He was certainly well respected. Would you like me to elaborate?'

Annabel gave a slow nod. 'Maybe later. First, I was wondering if you knew anything about the work MLA Research did on dangerous BPV variants eight years ago.'

Andreas looked at her as if she'd gone crazy.

Jonah did the same.

Andreas folded his hands together and watched her in silence. He sighed. 'Why are you here, Annabel?'

'The men who kidnapped and murdered my father believed that something terrible was about to happen. They believed it involved a drug your company created. I'd like to hear what you know about it. Did you mean what you said, about redressing the respect my father deserves? Because right now, nobody seems to give a damn about what really motivated the people who killed him.'

Andreas stood and walked to a window. 'I did mean it.' After a few moments he returned to his seat, and his expression softened into a wary smile. 'It seems you've been busy since your father died, Annabel. I admit, I was expecting something unusual in your visit, if you bring along the man who revived your father.'

'Thought it might intrigue you,' she said.

'It did indeed.'

Jonah looked from Andreas to Annabel, feeling out of his depth. Of *course* Andreas would check out the background of those coming to see him. He'd been used as bait.

'So, do you tell us?' she said to Andreas.

Andreas gave it a moment of thought, then nodded. 'Yes. They did work on a BPV variant that happened to increase remnants. They refined it.'

'Under your orders?' said Annabel.

'I was aware of it. We had a range of phenomena that were poorly understood, and it was a promising line of research. But the more powerful drugs were discontinued. The side effects made them too dangerous to be useful.'

Jonah took over. 'Were you aware that some of it was stolen?'

'No.'

'Were you aware of rumours that the drug was used to contact something long dead? Something not human?'

'Jonah, what you're telling me is a ghost story.'

'A story that Daniel Harker's killers had believed. A story others had heard.'

'Oh, I didn't say I haven't heard it. But it is a ghost story. A tale told to chill the blood. An invention. A distraction.'

'So you *have* heard of it?'

'Sometimes there's something you want to hide but it's already out there. People know some of it. All you can do is muddy the water, put out some distractions. It's an old tactic. It put the aliens into Area 51. With revival, they told ghost stories.'

'What do you mean?'

Andreas shook his head. 'I'm not prepared to say.'

'They killed my father,' said Annabel. 'All I want to know is what they thought was going on, and why.'

'I'm sorry, but . . .'

'They killed all the family I had *left*, and you don't give a damn. You don't give a damn because you don't know what it's like.'

Jonah saw the anger in Andreas's eyes. Annabel was provoking him, hoping to make him careless, but they could just as easily end up back out on the street.

Andreas closed his eyes for a moment. When he opened them, he looked calm again. 'I almost had a family, Annabel. I fell in love at twenty, still at Harvard. At twenty-four I developed a novel technique for DNA insertion that I managed to patent. Based on that, I got the funding to set up Andreas Biotech. Huge money was floating around, and I managed to get a share of it. We were financially secure, doing what we both loved. When we were close to hitting our thirties, we decided to have kids. She was eight months pregnant when she died. Eclampsia. Our son died too. We hadn't married.' Andreas looked down and paused. 'The irony haunts me, that I was at the forefront of the most advanced medical knowledge in human history, and my *family* had died in one of the oldest ways there is.

'When revival came along, I wanted to know what it meant. The government wanted research partners, but there was so much hesitancy, they were having trouble. Everyone wanted the answers, but no companies wanted to be so clearly associated with something everybody felt so uneasy about. They'd give a little here, a little there. But I went for it. I committed. The press liked me at first, pushed me out there as a hero of sorts, but they were always just as uneasy about revival. Then Baseline started to falter. They started to question my motivation. They stopped calling me an altruist, starting calling me a profiteer.

'There was a time when I cared about profit, Annabel. But only to keep my companies strong, not to boost the wealth of shareholders or fill my own pockets. I'm a rich man. All the rich people I've met have fallen into two categories. Some get addicted to collecting wealth, and it consumes them. Some understand what that money could really achieve, and it changes them in an entirely different way.

'I could stand the press's cynicism, but then they brought her death into it. One story suggested I'd invested in cryogenics to preserve her, and then in revival so I could . . .' Andreas looked up to the ceiling and paused. 'One called me the "Modern Orpheus". Hell, it made me angry. But maybe I was angry because they weren't far from the truth. I bought the cryogenics firm two years after she died, but it wasn't about closing the stable door. I wanted it to stop, I wanted the *pain* to stop. It hurts to lose people so close to you. You know that as well as anyone. I wanted to put an end to grief itself.

'Baseline was already crumbling, with no clear direction. I was planning to move more of the work out into my own companies. Then there was something that would've been a scandal if they hadn't managed to keep it internal. Sam Deering told me all about it. He knew I would have found out soon enough, and that I'd pull out immediately if there had been any attempt to keep it from me. You know what I'm referring to, Jonah. I know you were there. You remember Lyssa Underwood.'

Jonah nodded. 'The body sourcing problems,' he said. He turned to Annabel. 'There were questionable revivals done; the subjects hadn't gone through the system properly.'

'It was more than body sourcing,' said Andreas. 'The question was *why* would they source outside the system? What were they doing? But I know they kept going when they left Baseline.'

'And *did* you know what they were doing?' Annabel said.

'I knew very little, but they managed to keep a lid on it. It's not up to me to let it loose now. But I told you your ghost story was something I'd heard. I also heard, Jonah, that the same people you did Underwood for put that story out. It was their cover. It sounded crazy enough that even the parts that were true got dismissed.'

'Please, Michael,' said Annabel. 'I need to know.'

'I sympathize, but I have my own concerns. I trust you not to say a word of this before it's announced, but things have happened to make me reassess my priorities. I'm pulling out of the company. I'll be having surgery in the next few days, and things won't ever be the same again.'

'I'm sorry to hear that.'

'Thank you. But please, our time is over.' Andreas stood and walked them to the door.

As the door was closing on her, Annabel put out her hand and stopped it. 'Won't you reconsider? It's not much to ask, is it? To know why my father died?'

Andreas bowed his head. When at last he looked up, his eyes looked wet. 'Then ask Sam Deering,' he said. 'Ask him about Kendrick.'

As they left the building, Jonah turned to Annabel.

'I was bait,' he said.

'Don't sulk,' she said, sounding irritated. 'You wanted to be useful, right? And I got to see Andreas. Job done.'

For a moment he just looked at her. The fact she'd used him that way without telling him was bad enough, but she didn't seem to give a damn how he felt. Whatever he'd thought had been there the previous day, it was wishful thinking and nothing else. He just had to deal with it.

'OK,' he said. 'Let's go see Sam.'

25

Sam opened the door wearing a baggy tee shirt, the sunburned skin on his face peeling. 'Jonah!' he said. 'You should have called. We only got home yesterday. Helen's already back at work, so I'm a house husband, and that makes it a *very* disorganized house. What's the occasion?'

Uneasy, Jonah glanced across to his car in the driveway. He'd asked Annabel to stay in the car and keep her head down until he'd had a chance to talk to Sam, and decide if her presence would make Sam more likely to tell them what he knew or less. 'Just wanted to catch up. Good trip?'

Sam beamed. 'Wonderful. I think retirement will suit me when it's one long vacation with Helen. I got to catch up on some grandparenting and spend time with little Jess. She's six now, hard to believe. But after a morning on my own, I'm already at a loose end. I think I might start going crazy.'

'How's the speech?'

Sam had the opening speech at the symposium to prepare for the end of the week. He gave a non-committal shrug. 'Pretty much done. I guess it'll keep me busy for the next few days, but I need to work on getting Helen to retire too. So, come in, I can do with the company. Are you just here to check up on me?'

Jonah stayed where he was. 'Not quite. I wanted to talk about something. I did another revival, Sam. My first since Nikki Wood.'

'How did it go? You didn't have any problems?'

'It was Daniel Harker.'

Sam's face darkened. 'The Harker revival. I saw the news of Daniel's death. I called Hugo to see how the revival had gone. He managed to avoid saying *you* were the reviver.'

'He didn't plan it that way. There wasn't a choice. But something happened, and I need your help. *We* need your help.'

'We?'

Jonah waved over to Annabel. He still wasn't sure if her presence would be better or worse, but he wanted to be honest.

'Who's she?' asked Sam, watching Annabel get out of the car and walk towards them.

'Annabel Harker. Daniel's daughter. If you'd rather just talk to me, that's OK, but if there's anything you can tell her . . .'

Sam nodded. Annabel reached them, and Sam took her hand. 'I'm sorry about your father. Now come inside, and tell me how I can help.'

*

'Are you here as a journalist, Miss Harker?' Sam asked. They were sitting in Sam's living room. Sam had fixed himself a stiff drink, which Jonah and Annabel had declined.

'Right now, I just want to find out why my father was killed.' She looked at Jonah, prompting him to start.

'The people who kidnapped Daniel Harker were found with a stack of incendiary devices,' said Jonah. 'They triggered them when discovered. They all died, and none of them were fit for revival. All this is still being kept quiet. They were planning some kind of campaign, and the police think it was targeting revival somehow, because all the people involved had Afterlifer connections. We think Daniel was taken because one of them had contacted him, telling him about something called Unity. The contact was killed, and possibly Daniel was held to keep him quiet. The authorities thought it was conspiracy-theorist paranoia and paid little attention to it, but we want to know what they thought Unity was.'

'Unity? It means nothing to me.'

Jonah looked at Annabel. She nodded. *Go ahead*.

'The kidnappers were scared of something,' Jonah said. 'They'd picked up on an old rumour. The rumour had it that a revival subject had been brought back, but when it started talking it wasn't the subject. It was something long dead, something not human. Something they wanted to bring back, whoever *they* were. We think the kidnappers wanted to stop this from happening.'

Sam's faced became stone, his smile frozen. 'What bearing did this have in the case?'

'You mean, what do the authorities think about it?'

'Yes.'

'They didn't know that part. We tracked down the source ourselves. The rumours seemed to originate with work done on BPV. This was confirmed.'

'Confirmed how?'

Annabel spoke. 'Michael Andreas.' She waited, watching Sam's face.

Sam was visibly anxious. 'You spoke to Andreas?'

Annabel nodded. 'He told us that the rumours were a cover. He told us we should ask you about it. And about someone called Kendrick.'

'And about Lyssa Underwood, Sam,' Jonah said. 'Andreas claimed Underwood was part of it. Whatever "Unity" is, it stems from the same project as Underwood. Something that the people who killed Daniel Harker were terrified of. Please, Sam. If you know anything about it, tell us.'

Sam took a deep breath. 'It's classified.'

'Dr Deering,' said Annabel, 'I want to know what motivated these people. They were directly responsible for my father's death, but Unity is the real cause.'

Sam looked at her. 'Miss Harker, I owe your father. Baseline owes him. Every *reviver* owes him. I'll tell you what I know. All I ask is that you don't reveal me as a source.'

Annabel nodded. 'Guaranteed.'

Sam took a drink. 'Miss Harker, would you be surprised if military intelligence organizations used revivers?'

'I'd be surprised if they didn't.'

Sam smiled grimly. 'The legal position was vague then. The dead have rights now, of a kind, but then there was *nothing*. We knew there would be cases where nobody gave a damn how the subject was treated. A victim dies, and you want to treat them with respect. But a killer? We knew how easily a subject became unhelpful, even if they had every reason to co-operate. How do you deal with a hostile? That's what the Kendrick project was for. Aggressive interrogation of the dead.'

Jonah could only stare. Sam looked away, refusing to meet his eyes.

'It was started in collaboration with military intelligence advisers. Kendrick was an expert in what they call *enhanced* interrogation. He was present at the Lyssa Underwood session. Cold man, not an ounce of empathy to him. Always in a black suit.'

Jonah thought back to the heartbeat sound of the cryogenic pump, the unnerving expression on the face of the man in black. 'I remember him.'

'Kendrick was obviously well funded, and he poached the best people. Dr John Gideon was Andreas Biotech's best. He'd led the team that developed all the key revival medications, including BPV. And as you know, Will Barlow was one of their revivers. What little I saw gave away what Kendrick had in mind. They'd moved on to countermeasures, training people to resist, to be quiet, under any pressure. Even after death. And then, anti-countermeasures. How do you break that training? They were weaponizing revival.'

Jonah thought about Lyssa Underwood, about the list of questions he had read from and the curious answers she had given. 'They told me Underwood was about preservation technology. About keeping them fresh to improve revival chances. But something about her felt wrong; she seemed disoriented and her answers made no sense.'

'Jonah, she must have been trained, a well-paid volunteer with a terminal illness, her answers part of her training. I don't know exactly how her revival fitted into Kendrick's work, but I know what the goal was. Kendrick developed interrogation methods for revivals that I'd guess are in use by US intelligence agencies, and probably also by their allies. Even what I'd been *allowed* to know about went further than I'd thought moral or possible. But it was classified, and it was fiercely protected. After the basic results on hostile questioning, I found out very little more.'

Sam downed his drink and stood. His face became thoughtful, then resolved. Decision made. 'I have something to show you.'

He stood, walked to the corner of the room and knelt by a small cupboard. Inside was a personal safe. He entered a code and opened it, pulling out a large thick envelope.

'Every project in Baseline followed rigid guidelines for subject sourcing. We didn't want to be accused of a modern form of grave robbing. Those documents were classified. But Kendrick's team was cheating. When you came to me, Jonah, you thought maybe Underwood hadn't gone through the system. Turned out you were right. I forced their hand, and there was no documentation for her. None at all. They said it had been misplaced, but it was obvious they just hadn't got around to *faking* it yet. I think they had their own supply of terminal patients, trained and ready, people whose names they wouldn't want on anybody's system. Kendrick's team left in a hurry, before I could pin anything more serious on them. If I had, I'd have been able to get access to all their reports before they took them away. But before they'd gone, I took a risk. I gained entry to Kendrick's office and took a handful of documents. Most of it was so caged in euphemism and double-speak that you'd be hard-pressed to tell the difference between that and an order for stationery, but one was more explicit.'

He opened the envelope and handed the contents to Jonah.

The top page was headed 'Session Assessment'.

Jonah read aloud: 'Aggressive imagery techniques were blocked effectively by countermeasures. Emotion bombardment (stage 2) and pain transferral approaches still proved effective in this case. Subject revealed extensive pseudo-confidential knowledge.

'Recommendations: examination of aggressive imagery blocking to determine strength of conditioning. Focus on stage 2 emotion bombardment, although intensive pain transferral is by far the most effective technique. Note that all attempts at passing false information were detected. No valid information was flagged as suspect.'

Jonah handed it to Annabel, and realized he was shaking. He couldn't help thinking of Pritchard and all the anger Jonah had let loose at the man. 'Aggressive imagery? Emotion bombardment? *Pain transferral?* For Christ's sake, Sam. This isn't talking about interrogation. It's talking about *torture.*'

Sam nodded. 'With a living subject, information you get under torture is so unreliable it's typically worthless. Even so, they still do it. But with a revival, you force it out of them, and you *know* if they tell the truth. Revival is the *only* way to know for certain. Suddenly it's their best option. Kill to interrogate.'

'You really think they would kill people just to be able to question them?'

Sam sighed. 'Of course they would, Jonah. Kill, revive and torture. Kendrick's team wanted the best way to do all of it to maximize the chance of success. They wanted the full military toolkit for revival. How to do it and how to stop others from using it against you. I got them to leave Baseline, but I know damn well they kept going. And sometimes I think they'd already started doing it, right under our noses.'

Sam poured himself another drink. 'There are ten other documents there that I found. None of them is a smoking gun, but keep them. For what it's worth. Maybe you can make something of it.'

Jonah felt exhausted. His own passion for respecting the dead seemed worthless with this kind of abuse happening, and he'd been one of those who had helped bring it about. Hell, he'd been a *pioneer*, helping them understand how to get their overly fresh subjects back.

'Dr Deering,' said Annabel, 'do you think any base of operations could be in the area?'

'Maybe,' said Sam. 'Langley's not far. Plenty of CIA and NSA satellite locations.'

Annabel turned to Jonah. 'Maybe the locations the kidnappers were targeting match up with this abuse of revival . . . Jonah?'

But Jonah wasn't listening. He was reading through the rest of the documents Sam had found, feeling sick at what was there. Yes, the phrasing was verbose and vague, designed to make a benign interpretation plausible, but in it he could recognize enough to understand some of what they had achieved.

The problem of emotive feedback, one of the first things a reviver learns to deal with, had been turned on its head. Preventing the disorientation and panic of a revival subject from infecting you, cascading to dissolution and the end of the revival; reversing that, just as happened in revivers with burnout, the reviver's own state of mind affecting that of the subject. The mental turmoil of a reviver creating panic and paranoia in the person they revived.

A sentence caught his eye. 'Generating an artifice of controlled unequivocal hostility allows self-actualized emotive extremes to be targeted effectively.' He could see through the words, because they were familiar. They were familiar, because that was how it had felt with Pritchard.

Vindictive, spiteful. But disciplined, not the wild emotive feedback of the untrained. Extreme emotions, sharpened into a blade.

He looked up when Annabel called his name again. He was horrified. How close they'd come, he thought, to a world where this kind of revival was the norm, where terrorizing the dead in their last interaction with the living world was considered acceptable. It would begin with the clear-cut, the unrepentant killers scoured until they showed their remorse, but in time any amount of wrong-doing could be used as justification. How close they'd come, and how close they still were.

There were enough people like Sam, he thought, to have established a high standard of moral duty and an environment where such casual barbarity couldn't thrive. But would it take much for standards to slip? If it became common knowledge, wouldn't it be inevitable?

Jonah looked at Sam. 'How could you let Kendrick start this? As soon as you found out, why the hell didn't you see where it was going and shut it down?'

Sam looked away for a moment. When he looked back, Jonah saw shame in his eyes. 'It wasn't Kendrick who started it,' Sam said. 'It was me.'

Jonah stared at him. 'No.'

'We were only beginning to understand the potential of forensic revival. We *had* to investigate how to deal with hostile subjects. Some of it fed back into current FRS training. *Your* training. If I'd thought for a moment that it would go so far . . .'

Jonah looked at Sam, then back at the documents in his hand, wondering what he was feeling, then understanding it: *betrayal*. 'Not you, Sam. God, not you.' He stood.

Sam stood too, and put his hand out to Jonah's arm. 'Please, Jonah . . .'

Jonah flinched from the touch as he would from chill. Unable to speak, all he could do was shake his head. Then he walked out.

*

Annabel stood, wanting to go after Jonah but resisting. She turned to Sam. 'Are you sure about using the documents, Dr Deering? You could take the brunt of this, whatever we do.'

Sam shook his head. He looked exhausted. 'I deserve my share. It's taken me a long time to do what was right, Annabel. I hope he understands, one day.'

Annabel left, finding Jonah in his car with the engine running. When he saw her, he angrily folded Sam's documents and put them in his pocket. She got in the passenger seat, still holding the first page Sam had given them.

'Jonah,' she said. 'When we go public with this—'

Jonah snatched the page from her hand, leaving her open-mouthed. He crunched it up and put it in his pocket with the rest of the pages. 'We can't use those documents, Annabel. If we make it public, it'll drag revival down with it.'

They drove in uneasy silence back to Jonah's apartment block. He got out and went around to open her door, solemn-faced and avoiding eye contact. 'Your car's just up there,' he said, pointing to where Annabel had left it earlier.

'Jonah,' she said, getting out, 'this is evidence of something that has to be brought into the open. Something that has to be stopped. What are you going to do with the documents?'

He walked over to the entry door to his apartment block and put his key in the door, not looking at her. 'Burn them. There are things in there people can't be allowed to know.'

'You *can't*,' she said. 'This isn't something we can just let slide, this is *important*.'

'If people started using this kind of technique as part of normal procedure . . .'

'Christ, Jonah. *Nobody* would allow that to happen.'

He looked at her. 'Annabel, ten months ago I revived a woman who'd been raped and murdered, her body set alight, burned almost to the point where revival would have been impossible. We handled it at the scene, non-vocal. I got her back, but she was just screaming in my head, terrified. Nothing I did would have calmed her. The investigating officer wanted me to continue, until either I got her to talk or we ran out of time. But I let her go. I faced an official complaint as a result. It wasn't upheld, but one member of the complaint panel found against me. They thought it was my duty to get testimony whatever the cost to the woman. *Whatever* the cost.

That kind of thing has happened before, and it'll happen again. I don't want what's in those documents to be an option for people like that. I don't want it to be part of what I do.' He turned back and opened the door.

'You have to believe people are better than that, Jonah.'

He paused. 'I want to, Annabel,' he said, still facing the open doorway. 'But I don't think they are.' He went inside and closed the door behind him.

After a minute, Annabel went to the door and stood, wondering if she should try to talk to Jonah now. Make him see sense before he did anything rash. It was important to the story.

She reached out to his apartment buzzer but pulled her hand back before she pressed it. The story wasn't the only thing making her want to speak to him, she realized. He was upset, and she wanted to change that, to clear the air between them.

You have to believe people are better than that, Jonah.

I want to, Annabel. But I don't think they are. She wondered if his response had been partly aimed at her, if the plan to keep Jonah at arm's length had worked too well. She thought of the look in his eyes when she'd boasted of using him to see Andreas. The memory made her stomach knot.

That was the problem. The plan may have worked on Jonah, but it didn't seem to have worked on *her*.

She walked to her car and left.

26

He told Never everything. Almost.

When he'd called Never the day after seeing Sam, Never had clearly been anxious to know what had been going on. He arrived at Jonah's apartment so soon it was like he'd teleported there, eager for the explanations Jonah had promised.

Those explanations left out the awkward detail of Daniel Harker's remnant, of course. If Never knew about that, Jonah feared it would be impossible to stop him from telling Graves or Hugo; at the very least he would put pressure on Jonah to do so. Instead, Jonah said that Annabel had sought his help, hoping Never wouldn't question the lie.

Jonah gave him Annabel's original folder of documents, Never wincing as he went through the photographs from the scene of the inferno.

'Shit,' Never said. 'Did they ever unpick which lump of charcoal was which?'

'I don't know. Yarrow and Peter Welsh – the one Harker called Ginger – were the only two I know they had for sure. They still haven't gone public, even now, so maybe they haven't sorted it out yet. I can't help but think of their friends and family. Hannerman had a sister. He was her only living relative, and he died like that. In agony. In disgrace.'

Jonah told him about Vernet and about Eldridge; abridged versions, glossing over the deep fear that had nestled in the pit of

Jonah's stomach at the time. *Something long dead. Something not human.*

Finally, he reached Andreas and Sam, seeing Never's face fall as Jonah told him the truth that the ghost story was intended to distract from.

'I need a drink,' said Never, and beer was duly provided.

'What do you think?' Jonah asked.

'I can't believe it's been kept quiet so long.'

'That's it?'

'You want me to say how outraged I am? Well, damn yes. Of course I am. But face it – are you surprised the military would do shit like this? That they'd plumb every depth possible, in the blink of an eye? There's a saying that for good people to do evil things, it takes religion. But I reckon national security does the job just as well.'

'Not just the military, Never. If this idea was out there, don't you think the FRS would be under pressure to use it?'

'You don't really think that's possible, though? Do you?'

'From what I read, it didn't even sound difficult. I think most revivers could do it. And there's bound to be someone who thinks it's a great idea.'

'Jonah, there'll always be fuckwits with terrible plans, but I can't believe it'd be tolerated.'

They sat and drank their beers in silence for several minutes, Never finally breaking it.

'You know what else I can't believe? Annabel Harker. I mean, Annabel *Harker*?' He paused, looking at Jonah.

Jonah stared back, thinking his lie – about Annabel having come to him – had failed to convince; that he would have no option but to reveal the truth about Daniel's remnant. 'What about her?'

'Is that even legal?'

Jonah closed his eyes and shook his head. 'Jesus Christ, Never. It's not like that.'

'A little out of your comfort zone, but that's not a bad thing.' He lowered his voice. 'She likes you. I can tell, because she spoke to you more than once. Well, that's the rule I've always gone by.' He grinned, then dropped it when he saw Jonah's expression. 'OK, sorry. Just trying to lighten the mood.'

'But what about *Sam*, Never? Aren't you angry with him?'

'Sam's a good man,' Never said, soft but serious. Jonah tilted his head, about to interrupt, but Never held up his hand. 'Hear me out. Sam's a good man. You know it. Things were different back then. Some of what he did was for good reasons. And the rest? He's ashamed of it. You can't ask any more of him, Jonah.'

Jonah hung his head. What good were heroes if you couldn't look up to them?

*

With Friday's symposium only a few days away. Jonah struggled more and more with the talk he was due to present, unsure if he could go ahead with it. Respect for the dead. He was going to stand before an audience and tell them that for a reviver, respecting the subject was paramount. Whatever your feelings for the subject, and for what they may have done, the subject had to have the benefit of the doubt. Those who claimed that an aggressive revival worked were just *wrong*. He had collected figures that helped demonstrate his point.

Aggression. Disdain. These made revivals less successful.

Honesty. Respect. These made revivals more successful.

Jonah hadn't found any cases where aggressive revival had led to a result he thought couldn't have been achieved or exceeded with a respectful approach.

Aggressive revival didn't work. That was what he would stand up and say.

What a joke.

No, he told himself. The figures were genuine. It was a worthy hope that people like Shepperton would see the numbers and change their methods. Aggression was inferior.

If aggression was as far as it went.

But take it further, like Kendrick, and you discover that there comes a point where respectful questioning cannot compete. That you can rip the truth from the heart of your subject, regardless of the morality. But it takes more than aggression. It takes terror.

Respect on one side. Terror on the other. And he had used them both.

So, he chipped away at the task at hand, improving the speech without enthusiasm.

Jonah's interim appraisals by Jennifer Early had come and gone. It wouldn't be until after his next session with Stephanie Graves that he could be given any idea of when he'd be allowed to revive again, and that session was over a week away. There had been no hint of intrusion from Daniel Harker since he had helped spot Xavier Vernet's name, and Jonah was still putting off taking the rest of the pills Graves had given him. He was beginning to think Harker was gone for good, and that there would be no need to take them at all.

He still carried them with him, just in case.

*

By the time Friday arrived, Jonah woke with the level of confidence he'd been expecting; he felt sick with anxiety. He got ready, the nausea persisting, then stood on the street outside his apartment building waiting for Never to give him a ride, holding the folder that contained the notes for his talk.

'All set?' Never asked as Jonah shut the car door.

'All set,' said Jonah, and that was the full extent of their conversation until they arrived at the conference venue, Jonah reading over his notes and trying to decide if he was really able to do this.

They parked, then headed around to the main entrance, through the security checks and into the hotel foyer. It was early, another forty minutes before the opening address, but the foyer was already filling up and a dozen or so huddles of people had formed. Jonah looked around. Revivers abounded in the hotel, many he recognized, some he knew. Almost all were forensic revivers, but there were a handful of renowned private revivers as well. His mind went back to Tess, oozing money and amused by Jonah's indifference to it. He wondered where she was now, then tried to push thoughts of her out of his head, still unsure how he felt about the way things had gone.

'Do you people have permission to be here?' said a stern voice. Jonah looked to his right to see Ray Johnson smiling at them.

'Detective Johnson,' said Never, grinning. 'Business or pleasure?'

'Here to sit and listen, then eat the buffet lunch. Bob was asked to send a representative, and he picked me. I think they want us to give a talk next year and Bob's wanting me to do it rather than him. There's an officer from NYC doing one today. I'm going to pick her brains and see if she's as cute as I've heard.'

'The perils of making the news, I guess,' said Never. 'For a moment I thought they'd drafted you in as extra security.'

Johnson looked around and shrugged. 'Happy to be a civilian for the day. Besides, they have enough without me. Not just hired staff, either. Plenty of officers on duty, if you look. But I'll see you guys later. I have a cop to charm.'

As Ray Johnson left them to it, Jonah looked around. The thick-necked private security guards were all he could see, but he took Johnson's word for it.

A few people waved to him; Jonah nodded back as he and Never joined the short line at the registration desk.

While Never finished signing in, Jonah read over the schedule for the day. The various talks were split across three function rooms; the smallest of the three was upstairs, his own talk scheduled there for 11 a.m. Seeing it in ink flooded him with anxiety.

'You OK?' asked Never.

'No.'

'Once it's over I'll buy you a drink.'

He couldn't suppress the thought of beer slopping around in his stomach. 'Not helping.'

'Sorry. But I do plan on getting you royally drunk this evening, one way or another.'

A shout of 'Geary!' from across the foyer caught their attention. It was J. J. Metah and the rest of the FRS team who were attending – Pru Dryden and Jason Shepperton the reviver contingent, J. J. being the other tech representative. Jonah and Never headed over.

'Good luck with the presentation, Jonah,' Pru said. 'It was my turn last year.'

'You lot up for drinks later?' asked Never.

'Can't,' said Pru. 'My mom's babysitting Elsa, I promised I'd get back. But I'd put money on these two being up for it.'

Shepperton laughed. 'Face it, listening to talks the whole day will make us *all* want a drink.'

'Uh, actually,' said Jonah, 'can everyone just skip mine? I'm really nervous, it'd be a big help.' *And I couldn't do it if Jason was in the audience.*

As they all promised to steer clear, Jonah heard a voice behind him.

'Morning,' said Sam.

Jonah turned, unable to keep the discomfort he still felt off his face.

'Jonah,' Sam said. 'I wondered if you and I could –'

Jonah turned away from Sam and spoke to the others. 'I'm going to go and read over my notes,' he said, striding off without looking back.

*

Jonah stood alone outside the main hall doors as the time for Sam's opening address approached. He snatched glimpses of Sam preparing at the lectern and chatting to Never and the others, who'd all taken seats at the front. The thought of doing his own presentation was nothing compared with how he felt watching Sam now, wondering if things between them would ever be repaired. With the address about to start, the hall doors were closed. Jonah stood where he was for a few minutes, before setting off upstairs on his own.

As he climbed the stairs, he found himself scanning faces in the still-busy foyer below. It felt like he was looking for something specific, and the feeling baffled him. The security guards were a constant presence, low-key but unmistakable, their practised eyes looking everywhere without seeming to. Checking for trouble, Jonah acknowledged. Maybe that was what he'd been doing too.

The hall upstairs was a third of the size of the main hall. Jonah sat through the talk before his own, to get used to the room. He paid little attention to what was being said, looking over his own notes and trying to focus.

All too soon, the talk finished, most of the audience filing out. He took his place at the lectern up front, arranged his notes, and was taken through some sound checks. Then all he could do was wait.

With five minutes to go, and the audience growing, Never appeared at the door and walked over to him.

'I know it's against orders,' said Never, 'but I wanted to wish you luck.'

Jonah smiled. 'Thanks. You still have to get out of here, though.'

The grin that appeared on Never's face was wide and welcome, the only thing so far that had made Jonah feel in any way better about the prospect. 'Fucking off now,' said Never. 'Come find me when you're done, right?'

Jonah nodded. One of the organizers prompted him that it was almost time. He shooed Never towards the exit, grin and all, and as the door shut behind his friend the lights dimmed. Jonah took a sip from the glass of water left out for him, his mouth suddenly dry with fear.

Too late to back out.

*

'My name is Jonah Miller,' he said. Uneasy; halting. Hell, he'd been *reading* that, reading his own name, and still his voice was cracking. The hall was half full, the audience spread out across the seats with the front row empty. He knew that if he'd been in that audience, right now he'd have started to feel uncomfortable on behalf of the poor bastard choking in front of them all. He took another drink and leaned closer to the mike. 'When I . . .' Too close. Too loud. Feedback howled. He took another drink and a long breath. He cleared his throat. He felt a wave of nausea. Worse than before a revival, he thought. 'When I started in forensic revival seven years ago, I knew I'd found something that I was good at. Something that made a difference. I saw the effect a well-handled, respectful revival had on the family of the subject; I saw the results it had for the investigation.' He paused again, another breath, another drink. His eyes locked onto his notes and stayed there, not wanting to look up. 'Respect should always be a priority. For the private reviver, that's what their job *is*. For the rest of us, it's what we should aspire to.'

He turned a page and reached for his glass, surprised to find it empty. He refilled the glass from the jug next to it, eyes locked on the task, avoiding seeing past to the restless audience. His hand was shaky enough to spill some water over his notes. He wiped it off. 'But there are those who take a different approach and say it works. Sometimes we all feel that way. Many of us have revived a subject suspected of terrible things. A father in a murder-suicide. A drunk driver wiping out a family.' Another drink. He coughed, regretting the reference to Pritchard. He couldn't stop the image of the two-year-old boy with half a face from coming to him; the sound of Pritchard screaming in his mind.

He took another drink and realized he'd finished the glass again.

Realized how thirsty he felt.

Why was he so desperate not to look up? His heart was loud in his ear; adrenaline was magnifying the nausea. He breathed slowly and made himself look.

At the back of the bright hall was an incongruous patch of deep shadow. Daniel Harker was standing in it.

Jonah snapped his eyes down and tried to find his place again. 'Many of us have . . . and . . .' *Where is it?* 'And . . . and we've treated them with contempt. It may have felt *just*, but we all need to recognize something . . .'

He looked up again. The shadow had moved across the back of the hall towards the doors. As he watched, Harker raised one arm, pointing to the exit.

Jonah coughed. He went to refill the glass again, but his hands were trembling too much.

'We need to recognize . . .' Jonah closed his eyes, wanting to be anywhere but there. He looked up. Harker was at the door now.

'I'm sorry,' he said to the audience. He stepped down from the lectern and strode to the back of the hall, murmurs from the audience growing as he went, his face reddening. He felt the beginnings of panic but managed to hold on. Ahead, Harker had gone.

He burst through the hall exit into the corridor outside and walked to the balcony overlooking the busy foyer. A cool breeze hit him. He stopped, leaning on the metal railing, watching the crowd below.

Jonah closed his eyes, the fresh air just what he needed. He breathed deep, waiting for the panic to subside.

And as it did, and Jonah found himself able to think again, one question struck him.

What did Harker want?

He opened his eyes and found himself scanning faces once more, not knowing why he was doing it. Then he saw, in shadow at the far corner, Daniel Harker standing with his head bowed.

Harker's arm raised slowly. The hand was bloated, skin sloughed away. He was pointing into the drifting mass of people in the foyer.

Jonah stared at Harker and followed the line of the arm. He couldn't see. 'What, Daniel?'

And then:

A face. Short beard, gaunt. Glasses. Hair extremely short. Black shirt and black jeans. Press pass pinned to the shirt. The man was unrecognizable, at least from the photographs the police had used, even though Harker's description during the revival had made it clear how much thinner the man had become. Jonah, though, knew that gaunt face. Knew it from Daniel Harker's memories.

Felix Hannerman. Alive. Here.

How he was alive was a question for later. Why he was here, that was far more important. *They suspected this was a target,* he thought. *It still is.*

His mind whirled with adrenaline. Should he follow? He had good sight of him now. If Hannerman moved, he might lose him as he descended the stairs. He took his phone and dialled. No signal.

Jonah watched Hannerman, whose eyes were scanning the crowd with a hungry expectation. A desperation, almost. *He's planning something.*

Then Hannerman stopped looking around and started moving with purpose, Jonah unable to tell what it was Hannerman had seen.

Jonah hesitated, then knew he had to follow. Down through an enclosed stairwell, emerging into the crowded foyer, trying to look calm, trying to spot Hannerman again. He couldn't see him.

'Shit.' He looked around, then jumped as Harker was there again at the far wall, pointing from shadows. Jonah walked in the direction Harker was indicating. He moved faster with each step, knowing he couldn't risk breaking into a run.

Round past the reception. A glass corridor leading to a walled garden area at the back of the hotel, a scattering of people walking along it. Hannerman was just entering. Ahead of Hannerman, Jonah saw Sam with Jason Shepperton and Pru Dryden, strolling in the same direction halfway down the corridor.

Who was Hannerman following? Not them, surely?

To risk coming here himself had to mean Hannerman was

working alone, all that was left; the desperation on his face a sign he was making it up as he went. Maybe Hannerman just wanted to hit at revivers any way he could. Jason and Pru were among the best revivers in the country.

Or Sam, he thought. Sam, who had initiated the project that had kick-started Hannerman's whole venture.

God, no, Jonah thought. He tried Never's number again. It rang.

'Jonah?' whispered Never. 'Thought you were in your talk?'

'Where are you?'

'Tech presentation, Hall 2. J. J.'s here with me.'

'Felix Hannerman isn't dead.'

'*What?*'

'Hannerman's *here*, Never. In the foyer, heading to the garden. He's planning something. I think he's following Sam. I don't want to spook him. Tell security.'

A moment of silence as Never digested what Jonah was telling him. It was fair enough, Jonah thought. A few seconds to decide if his friend had gone crazy. 'On it,' said Never.

Sam and the others were nearing the end of the corridor. *He's not following them*, Jonah told himself.

A slip of paper fell from the speech notes Sam was carrying. He stopped walking and picked it up, then continued.

Hannerman stopped too, matching their steps.

Sam was in danger.

Jonah increased his pace, wondering what Hannerman intended. Wondering what the hell he could do about it.

Sam and the others reached the end of the corridor, rounding a corner into the walled garden area. As Hannerman approached the corner, Jonah could see he was closing on them.

Hannerman slipped one hand into a pocket and pulled something out, keeping it hidden in his fingers. The sun glinted off it for an instant. A blade? He may not have risked bringing anything through security, but getting some kind of knife in a hotel wouldn't be hard.

Hannerman was speeding up. Jonah did the same, the indecision painful now. He started to run, started to gain ground. Hannerman looked back, his eyes meeting Jonah's, a sudden fiery realization on his face; he turned back again and ran on, long strides that Jonah couldn't match.

No, thought Jonah. *NO.*

'*Sam!*' he yelled. '*Run!*' He heard a shout from behind him and caught a quick look as he reached the turn: two security guards, not yet at the far end of the corridor. Ahead, he saw Sam, looking past Hannerman at Jonah, not noticing Hannerman bearing down on them all. Jonah thought his shout had made things worse, but Jason Shepperton had seen, moving towards Hannerman as the blade raised and descended.

Jonah was there in five strides.

Hannerman's hand shot out again and again, Shepperton's arms flailing in the way of the blade, blood flying. Sam and Pru were hitting out at the attacker. Jonah let his momentum do the work, lunging into Hannerman's side, grabbing tight and taking him down, the fall heavy, Jonah on top. Hannerman was splattered in Jason Shepperton's blood, and Jonah could feel it soak through his own shirt.

The grip on the blood-covered knife was lost; it skittered out of reach, just a small paring knife that Hannerman could have stolen from the hotel kitchen.

Hannerman was winded, but there was more: severe chill where bare skin contact was made. Jonah used it, putting his hands fully over Hannerman's face. The shock in the man's eyes was clear, but it didn't last. He brought his knee up, hitting Jonah hard in the thigh, pushing him off with ease. The man looked thin but he was strong, up and running before any other help reached them, bystanders getting out of the way as he ran to a closed doorway in the wall around the garden. He kicked it open and ran through.

Jason Shepperton was lying on the ground, blood everywhere, arms covered in wounds, one pouring blood even as Jason tried to clamp his other hand over it. A rush of people started helping; Sam and Pru crouched by Jason's side, both covered in blood, Sam's face grey.

The man he'd taken as a security guard now had a gun drawn, a detective's badge hanging over the breast pocket of his jacket. He was on his radio, giving rapid orders, looking around for Hannerman. 'Where?' he yelled.

Jonah took a breath. 'This way,' he said, and ran.

*

Jonah led the way out the door Hannerman had broken through, into a staff and hotel vehicle lot, passing service entrances to the hotel before catching a glimpse of Hannerman rounding a corner in the distance. By the time they reached it to find themselves at the front of the hotel, there was no sign of him. The detective was waving to other officers and security guards while Jonah tried to find anyone who'd seen Hannerman run past, but they all were just staring at him. He looked down, realizing how much blood was showing on his white shirt. Hannerman, all in black, had been less conspicuous.

A car passed along the hotel driveway ahead of him. From the driver's seat, Hannerman's eyes met his, and the car sped away.

'There!' he shouted to the detective, running after it, stopping when it was clear the chase was pointless.

But Hannerman had pushed it too hard. Two hundred yards down, at the tight bend joining the main street, the car skidded, the rear hitting a concrete fencepost hard. Hannerman gunned it repeatedly, tyres screeching and digging up gravel, but the wire fence had snarled the car; it wasn't going anywhere.

'Get everyone back,' the detective instructed, eyes fixed on the car. 'Inside the hotel. *Now.*'

Hannerman got out and went to the rear of the car, disappearing from view as he worked at the tangled fencing.

Jonah felt rage grow inside him. He had little time for Jason

Shepperton, but he was a colleague. The injuries had looked serious and would leave their mark. Sam, though: that was the real source of his anger. Sam was family.

The rage sent him running towards the car. A shout came from behind him, but the anger was all he knew. He ran, full stride, as hard as he'd run in his life. Then he froze.

Hannerman had seen him. He stood slowly from behind the car's rear, eyes wide. A gun in his hand.

Another shout came from behind Jonah, but his mind had blanked, his legs unable to move. He suddenly understood where the rage had really come from. Daniel Harker, woken long enough to want to charge down the man who'd killed him.

The gun came up.

At once Jonah sensed something coming fast at him from his right; the gun fired; Jonah was shunted from the side; he heard the bullet whip past. The force of impact took him to the ground, over a low wall that ran alongside the road, into struggling greenery and rag-tag bushes.

He felt shaky with panic and started to stand. Another shot came, stone chipping from the wall, alarmingly close. He felt hands grab him and pull him down. He looked beside him.

It was Never Geary, panting, red-faced and *annoyed.* 'For fuck's sake, *stay down.*'

Jonah said nothing. In his mind he could see the gunman running towards the wall, see him standing over them both with a wide bloody grin, shooting until their faces were pulp and gristle. Fear and adrenaline were making him shiver. He heard a car door open and shut. The sounds of distant sirens. Shouts coming closer. More shots fired. Tyres squealing.

Then Never slowly raised his head and looked over the wall.

'You OK?' came a man's voice.

Holding up a hand, Never nodded, then thought to make sure about Jonah. '*Are* you?' he asked. 'You've got blood all over you. Check it's not your own.'

Jonah ran a trembling hand over himself. 'OK. I think.'

'What the fuck was that?' asked Never. 'You went all Bruce Willis on me.' He stood and gave his hand to Jonah, helping him up.

'I don't know. I just lost it. I didn't know he had a gun. If I'd known . . .' Even as he said it, he wondered if it would've made a difference to how he'd reacted. How *Daniel* had reacted. 'Christ, Never, if you hadn't come after me . . .'

'You're welcome. For the record, though, first I knew about the gun was when the fucker fired it.' He smiled at Jonah, a pained smile. Jonah smiled back in relief. Then, in unison, their smiles failed, their thoughts synchronized. Jason. Pru. Sam.

*

Grim, they ran back to the rear of the hotel.

The area was filling as the hotel emptied, people desperate to see what had happened, both police and security struggling to marshal them back inside.

'Jonah!' It was Ray Johnson. 'What the hell happened?'

'Hannerman,' Jonah said.

'Hannerman's dead,' said Johnson. 'I heard they'd identified his body.'

Jonah thought about the charred remains he'd seen after the catastrophic raid on the house, remembering Bob Crenner's words that day: *The only thing even resembling a body is under that tarpaulin.* 'They were *wrong*. I don't know who made the mistake, Detective, but they were *wrong*.'

The flow of people was moving against them now, as those around the back were being corralled to the main entrance.

'You can't go that way,' called one of the security team, but Johnson showed his badge and they hurried past them all, emerging and seeing blood-soaked towels in a pile beside a small group. A man and a woman were kneeling beside Jason Shepperton, the name badges they wore identifying them as symposium attendees.

Pru was standing six feet away. The sirens were growing louder. Help was on its way.

Jonah saw Sam sitting on a bench, alone, looking pale and distant, wrapped in a blanket that one of the staff must have given him, drying blood spattered across his face and on his sleeves. Jonah hurried over to him, while the others went to Pru and Jason.

'Sam?' Sam's eyes looked towards him, lost. Something about the expression on his face scared Jonah. 'Sam?' Jonah turned his head, catching Never's eye and calling him over.

'Jason's stable,' said Never. 'He's badly cut, but they've managed to stem the blood flow, so they don't think it's life-threatening.' He saw the look in Jonah's eye. 'What?'

'Something's wrong with Sam.'

Crouching beside Jonah, Never put his hand on Sam's arm. 'Sam? Talk to me.' Sam's eyes were glazed. 'I think he's in shock.'

Jonah took Sam's hand, startled by how cold it felt, then pulled one side of the blanket away from his lap. He moaned at the sight. From Sam's hip down to his knee, his jeans were drenched in fresh blood.

Looking close, Jonah spotted the small cut in the cloth of Sam's jeans where the knife had entered, just above the hip. He looked up and saw two paramedics hurrying around the corner heading for Jason, but Never was already shouting to them for help.

*

Jonah and Never sat, restless and silent in the hospital general waiting area. The blood on Jonah's clothes was long dried and starting to brown; two police officers were on guard by the entrance, another waiting by the operating theatre where they were working on Sam. Hannerman had not been found yet, the police presence a precaution. But Hannerman seemed a life away, almost an irrelevance, as Sam fought to survive.

Jason and Sam had been taken at once in the ambulance; Jonah and Never had followed after giving hurried statements to the detectives at the scene, Jonah keeping it simple, telling them that handling Daniel Harker's revival had allowed him to recognize Hannerman.

It had fallen to Jonah to call Helen Deering, pain in his voice as he told Sam's wife what had happened. Helen was in the surgery waiting room now, insisting on being left alone in spite of Jonah's pleas.

Jason, meanwhile, was stable and awake upstairs. Jonah and Never had been to see him, police guard at the door, his girlfriend by the bed; he was as eager as the rest of them for news of Sam. His arms were bandaged, a total of eighty-seven stitches, without an artery nicked or a tendon severed, while Sam was close to death from a single wound. Jonah and Never had returned to the general waiting area and had been there ever since.

'I'm going to go see Helen,' said Never. 'See if there's any news.'

Alone, Jonah found himself thinking about standing frozen while a gun raised towards him; thinking about Sam, and how the last words they'd exchanged had been words of anger.

He had reached no conclusions by the time Never returned.

'Nothing yet,' said Never. 'They'll tell us as soon as they have anything.'

It was three hours before news came, and when it did it was Helen they saw approach, dismay on her face, bursting into tears as she reached them and embraced Jonah. He held her as her sobs shook them both. After a time, she managed to speak.

'He's out of surgery, but critical. They don't know. They don't know if he'll pull through.' It was all she could get out before the sobs took hold again.

*

Jonah was focused on the clock in the Emergency reception area. Six o'clock came and went and he watched each and every tick, the rate of time impossibly slow. Helen was beside him, head in hands, staring at the floor, taking a few moments before she went to the post-op area, where Sam was due to be taken shortly. Robert, their son, was on his way from Florida, and was expected to land before seven. Jonah would be glad when he got there, someone to provide the real support that he was failing to give.

It was just the two of them, Never having gone to get a round of coffee.

Helen sniffed gently, staring up at the clock Jonah was watching. 'We do have it, you know.'

Jonah turned, puzzled. 'What?'

'If it came to the worst.' Not moving her eyes from the clock. Her voice one-tone, curiously detached.

'I don't know what—'

'Revival insurance.'

Jonah felt ice fill his soul.

'He was always telling me not to expect too much,' she said. 'Premiums rise as you age, you see. Inevitably you can't afford the best. And he had all his own people to compare against. He's so proud of you all. Maybe a little biased.' She looked at Jonah and chuckled, the jarring sound loaded with despair. 'Eighty-three per cent. That's the figure. Eighty-three per cent chance of successful revival. That's their best-case scenario too. Like rolling a dice and hoping you don't get a one. And they don't try again if it fails, not with the insurance we have. You only get one chance at it.' She looked at Jonah and tried to smile. 'Sam often talked about the way you handled things, Jonah. About the care you'd take with a family and the effect that had on them.'

Jonah's heart was pounding. Suddenly the room was airless.

Helen went on. 'I know it's not fair. I *know*. And I know he wouldn't admit to it. But deep down Sam wouldn't want anyone except you doing it.'

Jonah's mind reeled. Helen's tear-filled eyes were glued to his, the request clear enough. Jonah said all he could have said: 'He'll pull through, Helen. He's strong.'

Helen Deering nodded without conviction. 'I don't have any

right to ask, Jonah, but I can't bear it. I can't. Please. Promise me. If it comes to it. Let us say good-bye.'

With nowhere to hide, Jonah found himself nodding.

When Never returned with the coffee, Jonah excused himself and found a toilet, retching hard until his stomach was empty and he was spitting nothing but bile.

27

Ray Johnson's day wasn't going the way he'd hoped. When he'd tracked her down first thing that morning, the New York cop giving a presentation had turned out to be very cute indeed, but very married. Then all hell had broken loose. Thoughts of that buffet lunch were long gone.

Once Sam Deering had been taken to hospital, the conference was cleared; more officers were brought in to take witness statements, but with so many people there it was mostly a case of logging contact details and sending them home.

This wasn't any of Ray's business, not officially, but his connection to the case was obviously relevant and he felt a level of blame he couldn't shake. He hadn't been the one who'd signed Hannerman off as a corpse, but he'd seen Hannerman's picture enough times and imagined it with the thin features Daniel Harker had described during his revival. With Hannerman presumed dead there was a chance those pictures hadn't even made it to the briefings for the conference security teams, and even if they had, they'd have been considered peripheral.

Ray was one of a handful of people who could have recognized the man, and he hadn't spotted him.

He made himself known to the detective in charge at the scene, one Earl Pellman, a weathered cop who looked old enough to be a grandfather but tough enough to one-punch most men to the floor. Ray told him he'd been on the Harker case; Pellman was already up to speed on that and what had followed. The assumption was that Hannerman had simply not been present at the police raid that had led to the inferno and had been working alone since, attempting one desperate, final act.

Whether the conference had been an intended target originally was unclear. If so, this was certainly not the well-planned attack that Harker's kidnappers would have had in mind. If anything, it looked like Hannerman had been making it up as he went along.

'Frankly,' said Pellman, 'I doubt he expected to escape.'

'If there's any way I can help, sir,' said Ray. 'I reckon I know Hannerman's face better than anyone else here. And I know Miller and Geary. Makes it personal.'

Pellman looked at him for a moment. 'Miller, huh? The reviver who tackled Hannerman, the one who identified him? I read his statement. Tell me, are all revivers that crazy?'

'Not as far as I know, but I'd say they earn the right.'

'Amen to that. Well, I tell you what. If you really want to help, I'd be a fool to say no. This is a situation we need to turn around before we all look like we couldn't yank our own dicks unassisted, so I'm sending some of my people out to see if we can narrow down which way Hannerman went. We don't even know if he drove out of Richmond or went to ground in the city. CCTV or eyeballs, *something* saw which way, and the sooner we know, the better. Tag along with one of them. If you know the man's face so well, there might be some footage you can rule in or out.'

Ray thanked him, unsure if Pellman thought he could really be of any use, or just understood how Ray was feeling.

Eight detectives, four cars; Ray chose the one that was heading out north towards DC, partly because it was closer to home territory, and partly because the kidnappers had originally put down a false trail to the south of Harker's home, all the way to Atlanta. When people put down false trails, they'd want it as far from themselves as possible. The opposite direction was sometimes the best place to start.

So north it was, Detective Ellen Pierce driving, her partner Dom Lloyd beside her, and Ray in back.

It was with darkness falling that a Fredericksburg Police cruiser spotted a car matching the description that had been put out; the plates differed, but those reported from the scene had proved to be false anyway, registered to a red Nissan. Hannerman may have changed them.

The officers had thought they'd seen apparent bullet holes, one in the driver's door, perhaps two or more in the rear, not obvious against the black metalwork. They had called it in and followed at a distance until the vehicle had pulled into a 7-Eleven gas station on Lafayette Boulevard. The officers had driven past without slowing, turning out of sight up ahead and stopping where they could observe unseen.

When the call had come in, Pierce and Lloyd were closest and the first of the police officers to be notified; by the time Hannerman had pulled into the 7-Eleven, they were less than ten minutes away. They were instructed to pass by and confirm ID if possible, then join the cruiser and await backup.

As they passed the gas station, Ray saw a man come out and immediately light a cigarette. It was definitely Hannerman. That was why he'd stopped, Ray supposed. Just to buy cigarettes. Well, why not? He'd had a stressful day.

The gas station had no other customers, and the road wasn't busy.

Let it stay like that, Ray thought. 'That's him.'

'You sure?' said Detective Lloyd.

Ray understood his doubt. Lloyd was going from the fuller-faced police photograph. 'I'm sure.'

They pulled up by the police cruiser and waited, keeping an eye on things. Unarmed and unofficial, Ray would be out of the take-down, of course, but he'd still get satisfaction from the night's work.

Hannerman stood for a few minutes, taking deep drags until

the cigarette was finished. Then he stood on the butt. *Have another*, thought Ray. Backup would be with them very soon.

But Hannerman got back in his car.

'Damn,' said Ellen Pierce. She started the engine, ready to follow.

The black car began to move, but it simply manoeuvred from the space at the edge of the parking lot to beside a pump. Hannerman got out and lifted the fuel nozzle. Inside the gas station, Ray could just about see the attendant glance up, then away again. A car passed their position – a station wagon, mom and dad up front, sleeping kids in the back. As they passed, Ray saw the mother motion to something ahead, and he had a sinking feeling.

'Shit,' he said. 'Tell me they're not stopping.'

The car slowed and pulled in to the other pump. The mother got out and started to fill up. Hannerman opened the rear door of his car. He took the fuel nozzle out of his tank, then into the car through the open door.

Ray's eyes widened as he saw gas splashing from the interior onto the surface of the parking lot.

'Jesus,' he said.

'He's going to burn the evidence,' said Dom Lloyd.

'He'll burn the goddamn *street*,' said Ellen Pierce.

Indecision, weighing up the knowledge of the man's gun and the expectation that backup would appear at any time. But the attendant had seen it now, and the woman from the other vehicle shrieked and jumped back in her car, the husband driving off before her door had even shut again. Along the street the shouts were heard by a group of youths, drawing them closer.

'Hell with it,' said Ellen. 'We have to.'

They drove fast and stopped well back from the parking lot, then Pierce and Lloyd got out, guns drawn, using their car doors for cover.

Ray stepped out too, waving to the onlookers. 'For Christ's sake, back off!' he yelled at them. '*Police! Get back!*' Those at the front had been able to see what had happened, and they were willing enough to step away. '*Get back NOW!*'

Still holding the nozzle, fuel pouring around his feet, Hannerman pulled the gun from his pocket. Ray stared as the gun came up. He froze for an instant, realizing he was more exposed than Pierce and Lloyd and wondering what Hannerman had in mind. But the gun kept rising, until it was straight up in the air. Hannerman fired twice, then the gun clicked empty. The onlookers ran back down the street to a safer viewpoint. In the 7-Eleven station, Ray saw the attendant dash for a back exit.

Hannerman raised the gas nozzle to his chest, dowsing himself, then dropped it on the pavement. He walked to the driver-side door. Ray saw the fuel splash under Hannerman's shoes, a dark pool spreading out from the vehicle. Hannerman tossed his gun to the ground, almost with disdain. He opened the car door, sat down in the driver's seat and pulled the door shut.

'What the hell is he doing?' said Dom Lloyd, but it was clear enough. It wasn't about destroying evidence.

'Wherever he planned on going, he's reconsidered,' said Ray. 'The man's reached his end.'

Dom Lloyd turned to his rear and saw another group of onlookers straining to see. '*Get back!*' he shouted. Pierce turned to look as well. By the time they turned back again, Ray was already halfway across to the other car, hands high to show he was unarmed.

'*Johnson! What the hell?*' barked Pierce.

Ray was wondering the same thing. When it came down to it, he wanted Hannerman to talk. He wanted to know why Harker had died. 'Call in, buy me time,' he yelled over his shoulder. 'I'd rather flashing lights didn't show and spook this guy.'

Ray approached the car. The driver-side window was open, and he saw Hannerman raise an unlit cigarette to his lips.

'Give yourself up,' Ray said, gentle and calm. 'There's no need for this.'

Hannerman looked at him. Ray had known Hannerman's

picture so well, had thought he could take that full face and imagine the thin version that Daniel Harker had described, but up this close the difference was shocking. It wasn't just thin – the man looked like he had wasted away. Hannerman brought the back of one hand to his mouth and coughed, leaving a smear of fresh blood, and Ray made the connection. The bullet hole in the driver's door. Hannerman had been hit, and it had taken him this long to accept that he was going nowhere.

'There's a need,' Hannerman said. 'Too many questions. And I don't feel like talking.'

Ray was finding the gas fumes unbearable. He noticed the passenger seat. On it were half a dozen plastic boxes, semi-transparent, contents obscure but wiring visible through the plastic. Maybe Hannerman's plans for the conference had been more elaborate after all. 'Don't do this.'

Hannerman paused, then let out a sigh that gave Ray the creeps. As much as anything, it sounded like a death rattle. He raised a cigarette lighter and placed his thumb on the spark wheel, looking Ray in the eye. Ray saw cold commitment there, and a horrible sense of purpose.

Then he felt a hand grab his shoulder and drag him away. He heard air rushing, and a man screaming behind him. He ran, glancing back as he reached the road, the car an inferno, a burning arm flailing through the fire. Ray kept running. Halfway across the road, there was a sudden change in the sound behind him, an undertone, high-pitched and rising.

Something punched him in the back, and he felt great hands close around his ears and take away all the noise. He tumbled, uncontrolled, his sight filled with glass and flame and road.

28

It rained during the funeral, a persistent, soaking rain that made a change from the run of hot sunshine. Jonah welcomed it. With his face already wet, the tears that came were hidden in plain sight.

As Daniel Harker's body was finally put beneath the ground, Jonah sensed that some of the tears he was crying were Harker's own: tears for his daughter, tears for Harker himself. Tears for such a vicious end.

Most, though, were Jonah's. Tears for Sam. He had been left in an induced coma after the surgery. Nine days now, and there was still real uncertainty whether he would pull through. Even if he did, there were complications arising from internal bleeding that would make a full recovery slow.

Jonah had allowed himself to visit just once. Robert, Sam's son, had by then brought his wife and child up to Richmond for the vigil. Seeing the close family bond was difficult for Jonah. It reminded him of what he didn't have. He may have thought of Sam as a father, but it was sentiment and nothing more.

Jason Shepperton, meanwhile, had made good progress, released after only two days. His right arm had taken the brunt of the attack and movement was restricted and painful, but his hands were almost uninjured. Jonah hadn't seen him since he'd been released, but Never had, reporting that Shepperton had been anxious to get out of the hospital. He had been due to leave on vacation in the next few days, and he still intended to take it. Given what had happened, wanting to do nothing but lie in the sun and be pampered by his girlfriend was understandable.

Now at Daniel's funeral, the rain began to subside. Jonah stood at the back, as out of the way as he felt he could get without becoming conspicuous. He felt out of place, but Annabel hadn't allowed him to bow out of attending.

She had emailed him the night before, the only way they'd communicated since Sam's revelations; she'd called him after the attack at the symposium, but Jonah had let it go to voicemail, emailing her back instead to tell her what had happened. He'd kept Sam's documents intact for now, but it wasn't a subject he wanted raised. Annabel seemed to understand enough to give him space.

She stood at the head of the grave and asked if anyone wished to speak about her father. Once they had finished, she took her turn, talking of her love for him and of her memories of the man they were burying. She kept it short, visibly struggling to hold herself together as she thanked everyone around her. She nodded to Jonah, then began to walk from the grave where both her parents now lay.

Unlike the other mourners, Jonah didn't follow. He'd already made it clear that if he came, it would be to the funeral only, not the wake. One of the black suits broke from the stream and approached.

'Jonah,' said Bob Crenner, taking a position beside him, facing Harker's grave. He was silent for an awkward few seconds. 'I was sorry to hear about Sam.'

Jonah nodded. 'How's Ray?'

'He was lucky. Cuts and bruises. Claims there's not an inch of him doesn't hurt like hell, and he's half deaf. Will be for a few weeks yet. Worst part for him is being off work. I hear you're the same.'

Jonah smiled at him. 'Insufferable.' He'd been to see Stephanie Graves only the day before. She had found no remnant traces, although Jonah didn't believe that Daniel had completely left him yet. Even so, he was officially in the clear. Graves had given him a tweaked meds regimen to trial for ten days. He had to take small doses five times a day to assess whether the combination suited him. It meant carrying his meds around wherever he went, and he was lousy at remembering to take each dose, but if the new regimen did suit him, he'd be back on revival duties within three weeks.

'Keep in touch,' said Crenner, tagging onto the tail end of the few remaining mourners.

Jonah watched them all leave, then stood alone in the fading rain, hunting in his mind for signs of Daniel Harker. Just as he was about to go, the thirst came. Weak, but unmistakable. He turned his head. In the shadow of a great rhododendron fifty feet from where he stood, he saw a figure watching him. Grey shade on black, hints of form like the strokes of an oil painting magnified; a smear *here* suggesting a smile, and *there* suggesting an arm raised, perhaps in farewell. As the form merged back into deep shadow, it occurred to him that Annabel, speaking of her father by the graveside, had not stirred the borrowed memories that had been with him for what seemed like years, yet had only been weeks.

Maybe he had gone now. The answers that had come, the only answers they could ever get, gave Jonah no satisfaction, no sense of justice. He didn't imagine Harker felt any different.

'I'm sorry, Daniel,' Jonah said, before walking from the grave.

*

Jonah reached the FRS office by two o'clock, having changed out of his sodden suit in his apartment.

'Hey,' greeted Never as Jonah passed his desk. 'Have fun?'

Jonah frowned with his eyes, but Never's words earned a slow smile. 'Great, thanks. Saw Bob Crenner. He says Ray Johnson's doing OK.'

'And Annabel Harker?'

'Not my place. I left her to it. You been to the hospital today?'

'Yeah. Everyone's looking shattered and there's no change, but as I understand it, that's the best we can expect. They're going to let

Sam come out of the induced coma in five days, and that'll be the critical time. Robert said he'll keep us informed.'

The weekend came and went, the rain hanging on. Jonah stayed in his apartment, reading.

Annabel emailed him, to thank him for being at the funeral and to let him know she was sending him a package, copies of more documents she thought he'd be interested in.

On Monday morning, Never waved as soon as Jonah came in through the office door. 'Mail for you.'

It was the package from Annabel, a small padded envelope. There was nothing inside except a memory stick – the contents too large or too sensitive for email, he presumed. He put it in his pocket. It took a moment before he realized Never was still watching him. Jonah looked up. 'What?'

'I saw who it was from, Jonah. It had her return address. Aren't you going to look at what's on it?'

'It'll keep until I get home,' said Jonah, Never's disappointment palpable.

'Back to yours later for a beer, then?'

Jonah sighed. He wasn't sure if Never was simply interested or if he'd switched into baby-sitting mode. Either way, the option of keeping him out of it was long gone.

*

Once Never arrived that evening, Jonah sent him on to feed Marmite and grab some beers as he booted his PC and started to look through the files Annabel had sent. From his desk he could see through to the kitchen, Never in the act of pouring dry cat food in the vague area of Marmite's bowl, then running to the fridge and grabbing two cans.

Breathless, Never sat beside him, hungry eyes watching the monitor. 'Come on then.'

They read.

Most of it was about Felix Hannerman, details from the police investigation into the attack on Jason and Sam. Annabel's documents showed how well Hannerman had accomplished his own death, making sure there was no possibility of a revival. That was part of Hannerman's style, not leaving anything to chance. Multiple redundancy.

His car had contained five incendiary devices. An inferno had been guaranteed. The explosion that followed made doubly sure – its cause was still under investigation. Whether Hannerman had brought the devices solely for that purpose, or if he'd hoped to somehow use them at the symposium, was impossible to know. Certainly, the increased security would have stopped him from getting any weapon into the building, hence the improvised knife.

The biggest issue was the premature declaration of Hannerman's death three weeks earlier, the reasons for which had not yet been made clear. With everyone involved believed dead, the investigation had lost most of its urgency. If the investigators had known Hannerman was still alive, things could have been very different.

And there it was, in one of the last files Annabel had sent. Jonah swore as he read.

Only four of the remains had been identified with certainty; Yarrow and Ginger had been the easy ones, but DNA samples from relatives had been used to establish two others. An FBI statement to be released soon would clarify that in the absence of suitable DNA for comparison, personal effects were used for the final two. Confidence in the identifications had been overstated, and they would apologize. The body they had thought was Hannerman was still an unknown.

Personal effects.

Annabel's source revealed that they had managed to identify and trace a cell phone, found with one of the corpses, to Hannerman. It was almost destroyed, but the SIM had been intact.

When Never read this, he looked up at Jonah. 'So they said Hannerman was dead, and the only thing they really knew had died was his fucking phone? What a mess.'

Jonah nodded. He felt suddenly weary. He'd brought home some documents from work, intending to read over them that night but doubting he'd be up to it. A court appearance was waiting for him in a few weeks; it struck him that it was a miracle how Hugo had managed to keep the prospect of court testimony at bay while Jonah was recovering. Then he realized how short a time that had really been.

'So, um,' said Never. 'Will you get in touch with her again, or is this it? Her sending out what she finds?'

For an instant Jonah reeled at the thought. They had done all they needed to do. This could indeed be all the contact he would have with her. Jonah pulled himself together but saw the look in Never's eyes. He'd seen Jonah's reaction.

'Oh. My. God. You and her . . . Something *did* happen.'

'Nothing happened.'

'I said *something,* not *everything.* With you, *something* is rare. You like her.' He said it without a trace of mockery.

Jonah nodded. 'For what good it'll do me.'

'I don't see a problem.' He paused, then grimaced. 'Well, I'd suggest you, uh, wait a little longer after the funeral. Timing's not *brilliant* . . .'

And as long as her dad's actually gone from my head, thought Jonah. 'All pretty academic,' he said, clicking through the remainder of Annabel's documents. 'Early on, I thought there was something. It was just my imagination, Never, or maybe it was down to everything she's been going through. I can understand.'

'Or you could – and I mean this with all due respect – you *could,* maybe, just this once, actually show some fucking nerve and call her in a couple of weeks? Jonah?'

But Jonah wasn't really listening anymore. He was staring at the monitor, thirsty as hell, eyes scanning the last page of the file, realizing that the thirst meant there was something to be seen. Daniel Harker was still around, still watching. Still interfering.

'There's something here, Never,' he said. 'There's something important on this page.'

There were two images from a report on the apartment the police had tracked down after Hannerman's attack. Hannerman had been renting it for over a year under a false name, using it occasionally, his presence noted far more often since the time his colleagues had died.

The first image was a close-up on what seemed like a holiday snapshot of Hannerman with a woman of similar age: blond hair, striking features – almost beautiful, but her eyes were set too close together, her nose too long and thin. Hannerman looked much younger than in his police photograph but also much thinner, his face far closer to the one Daniel had known. Jonah could see Hannerman's resemblance to the woman, and intuition told him who she was: Hannerman's sister, Julia. Given the pieces of paper overlapping its edges, it was clear that this snapshot had been stuck to another surface when it had been photographed.

The second image revealed what that surface had been: a picture of the kitchen in Hannerman's apartment, as it had been found by the police. In the far corner was a fridge. On its door, Jonah could make out the position of the snapshot of Julia and Felix, surrounded by other assorted scraps.

Then he saw.

Another sheet of paper was stuck to the centre of the fridge door with something yellow. Something that was small and indistinct. A fridge magnet. Jonah stared at it, looking close, the shape of it clear.

'Jonah, what is it?'

Jonah kept staring. Maybe he was wrong. He magnified the image. The resolution had been high, and he could see it clearly. There was no doubt now.

'Jonah!'

The image showed a yellow magnet, a cartoon of a smiling circle with a single giant hand, thumb up. 'Thanks!' it said.

He still had the badge he'd been given at Eldridge's hospice in his jacket. He went and got it, and held it up for Never to see. They were identical. Like the badge, the fridge magnet was generic. Nothing to identify where it had come from. Whoever had searched the flat had ignored it because they couldn't have known what it might mean, but Jonah did.

Hannerman had been to the hospice.

'What is it?' said Never.

'Answers,' said Jonah. He felt suddenly cold. 'If we want them enough.'

29

Victor Eldridge opened the door to a grinning man.

'Mr Eldridge?' asked the man.

Irish accent, Eldridge noted, squinting at the silhouette before him, the setting sun low and right in his eyes. He nodded.

'Detective O'Donnell. The staff inside sent me through, said it'd be OK. I'd like a moment of your time.' The man took something from his pocket and held it up. ID of some form, dark with the sun behind it, and gone too fast to mean much to Eldridge's tired eyes. He assumed it was genuine.

Eldridge frowned. 'What about, Detective?'

'May I . . .' said the man, and Eldridge moved back to let him inside. The man stepped around him, and there was something in his manner that gave Eldridge concern, made him wish he'd looked harder at the ID, but there was no time: as Eldridge put his hand to the door to close it, the door opened hard against his fingers. He yelped and backed away. A figure walked in, shut the door and stepped towards him. Eldridge saw his face for the first time.

'You,' he said to the reviver, contempt in his voice and eyes.

'Hello, Victor,' said Jonah Miller, Eldridge seeing the contempt coming right back at him. 'I have some questions.'

*

Jonah watched Never, aware how uneasy his friend had been from the moment Jonah had come out of the hardware store carrying a bag and a pair of wire cutters. His agitation had peaked as Jonah cut through the fence at the rear of the Walter Hodges Hospice. The security was poor – a single camera for the area, which had a vast blind spot.

Jonah shared the unease but was overwhelmed by a righteous fury and a resolve fuelled by the rage. Jonah didn't doubt that Hannerman had been here, that somehow Eldridge had known him. Known, and stayed silent.

His silence could have cost Sam his life.

Eldridge looked more papery than he had two weeks before. He was glaring at Jonah. 'One shout from me,' he said, 'and you'll both be in jail within the hour.'

'I don't think so, Victor. I think you know damn well why we're here, and police involvement is the last thing you want. Now, sit.'

They put him in his chair. Jonah took a roll of tape from his pocket and began to work on Eldridge's forearms, securing them to the armrests, then taping his legs to those of the chair. Behind him stood Never, his discomfort clear on his face.

'I'm dying,' said Eldridge. 'I've nothing to fear from the police.'

'This is how they left Daniel Harker,' said Jonah, watching Eldridge's wide eyes. 'Strapped to a chair and abandoned. Left to die. I don't want to hurt you but I will if you don't help me.' He was counting on Eldridge not seeing through the bluff, but the anger in his voice was unmistakably genuine. He had brought the police picture of Hannerman and held it up. 'Do you recognize him? He'd have been *much* thinner, so think hard.'

Eldridge shook his head, but Jonah saw the lie in his eyes.

'Think very carefully, Mr Eldridge. Do you recognize him?'

Again he shook his head, then he looked away. Jonah thrust the photograph back into his line of sight. 'The man in this picture was responsible for the kidnap and murder of Daniel Harker. Then one of my friends – someone I *love* – was almost killed when this man stabbed him. He's unconscious and could still die.' Eldridge's body sagged. He was staring into space. 'You can appreciate how we happen to be quite so *fucking angry.*' Eldridge started at Jonah's suddenly raised voice. Holding up the photograph, Jonah asked again: 'Do you recognize him?'

Eldridge said nothing.

'You can't protect him, Victor. I know that's what you think you're doing. You can't protect him because he's dead.' He looked for the reaction and saw it, Eldridge's face slackening at the words. 'He killed himself after the attack. Incinerated before anyone could ask him *why.* Just like all the rest of them.'

'All dead . . .' said Eldridge.

'Even Tobias Yarrow,' said Jonah, seeing the recognition in Eldridge's eyes. 'Did Hannerman tell you he'd killed Yarrow? Was it you who told Vernet the story?'

Eldridge shook his head, eyes closed, and Jonah thought he was going to keep on denying everything. But when Eldridge opened his eyes again, Jonah could see there was no fight left in him now.

'I don't know a Vernet, but I know Tobias. *Knew.* Hannerman told me Tobias had lost his nerve and run. He didn't mention he was dead. Tobias Yarrow had heard a rumour and spent years tracking it down. By the time he did, the man he'd been looking for was dead. But he found me, and I told him.'

'And he believed you.'

'It was the truth.'

'No, Victor. It was a ghost story to *hide* the truth, that a military intelligence goon had turned revival into just another weapon. Foolproof interrogations, murdering people to find out what they knew. It was . . .'

Jonah trailed off. Eldridge had his head down, and he started to jerk softly, in a way that made Jonah assume he was sobbing.

When the man looked up, Jonah realized he'd misread it. Eldridge was laughing, and the laugh became a series of coughs.

'What's so funny, Victor?'

Eldridge glared at him. 'What makes you think they can't both be true? You come here trying to find some answers. What are you going to do when you know? Hannerman had the courage to face it, and he risked everything. You think you're the good guys? You're just bystanders. *They* were the good guys. Now they're all dead. There's nobody left to stop it.'

'Stop what? *Tell me.*'

'He wanted to expose Unity.'

Jonah stared.

Victor Eldridge looked into Jonah's eyes. 'Cut me free. Then I'll tell you everything.'

Jonah watched him, thinking it over. Then he fetched a knife and cut through the tape.

*

'I had a friend,' Eldridge began. 'When I was a kid in Vancouver. Robert Durmey. Good with cars. Left for a girl in Boston at nineteen, lost the girl but found a job. We kept in touch, on and off. Two years after revival appeared, he showed up in Vancouver again. Hadn't seen him in a while. I was thirty-four and in a rut, doing odd jobs to get by, then Rob appeared and he had this news. He was a reviver now. Getting well paid. Then he told me I had the talent too, said he could tell when he'd shaken my hand. He was much better than I was, even ended up working in Baseline while I did shitty insurance jobs for people I disappointed half the time. But he did right by me over the years. I saw him now and again. It was him got me the gig at MLA Research, paid a damn sight better than what I'd been getting.

'This was about eight years back. After that, I didn't hear from him again until a little over two years ago. By then, I was spending half my life in psychiatric care. They'd let me out, but I couldn't cope for long. Not when I could hear it whispering, knowing that something is out there, *waiting* for us. Back when Ruby Fleming happened, back when I first heard the whispers, I'd told Rob all about it. He listened better than most, but like everyone else he told me it was just in my mind.

'When he came back, though, he was frightened. Told me it all. He'd come to me because he believed me now. He'd come because he wanted to see if I knew what it really was.

'It was Rob Durmey that Tobias had been looking for all that time, but when he managed to track him down, Rob had died. Hit by a car, four months after he'd come to me. Accident or not, I still can't decide. I was at his funeral, and so was Yarrow, asking questions.'

Eldridge stopped and pointed to a glass of water that was sitting on a table next to Jonah.

Jonah handed it to him and waited for Eldridge to take a drink. 'So what was it that Rob Durmey knew?'

'He'd been working with a man called Kendrick. The goon you mentioned. Secret things. Interrogation techniques for use in revival. They had it down, countermeasures, anti-countermeasures. There was a reviver called Barlow working with Kendrick that Rob didn't like. Didn't trust. Kept coming up with odd ideas that the team would work on. The BPV variant research at MLA, that'd also been on a hunch from Barlow. But there was one idea. A crazy idea. Kendrick liked it. Hell, he thought it was positively *humanitarian*.

'Think about it: a revival interrogation is the only way to be sure someone's telling the truth. The *only* way. Normal interrogation can be beaten. Lie detectors are easy to fool, whatever they tell you. And torturing the living? Unreliable. Desperate people are *very* inventive. Revival is the only cast-iron way. Problem is, you have to have a corpse. The need to kill limits how useful the technique is. It draws more heat, and you only get one shot.'

Eldridge paused and took another drink. 'They were still at Baseline, doing all this. It wouldn't be long before suspicions were raised and they had to leave. But you already know about that, yes? I know who you are, Jonah Miller.'

Jonah stared back. 'What does this have to do with me?'

'When you said your name, I couldn't believe it. Yarrow was

always going on about destiny. It worried me about him. Hannerman was the same. But when you came here . . . Tell me, do you remember a subject called Underwood?'

Jonah felt his skin turn to ice. 'Yes.'

'Rob Durmey told me all about it. Kendrick's little plan was failing. Barlow's crazy idea wasn't working out, and they brought you in. You made a big fuss afterward. An internal investigation found the paperwork for the corpse was fake, and Kendrick got booted out of Baseline. All because you thought there was something *wrong* with Underwood.'

'Yes,' Jonah said. 'There was something unusual, something different.'

'You were right. The paperwork was fake because there *was* no corpse.' He reached out and gripped Jonah's arm tight enough to hurt, ignoring the chill they could both feel. The man's face became urgent, desperate. Jonah wanted to pull away, but he couldn't take his eyes off Eldridge's own. 'She wasn't dead, Miller. *She wasn't dead.*'

Silence. Jonah stepped away, staring at Eldridge. 'What?' he said at last, barely audible. He looked at Never, but his friend was pale, and was staring at Eldridge as well.

'Please,' Eldridge said to Never, 'could you pass me those pills? Behind you?' Eldridge took two, closing his eyes for a few seconds, his breathing ragged.

Jonah waited for his own shock to settle before speaking. 'What *exactly* was Kendrick doing?'

'How dead is dead? That was Barlow's question, the one that started it all. The human body can be shut down, cooled until lifeless. People have survived drowning in frozen waters, pulled out after an hour or longer. Surgery using body-cooling techniques has been routine for years. You can stop somebody's heart, do what you need to do and start it up again. In that state, it's effectively a corpse. So, how dead is dead? How dead does someone have to be before you can bring in a reviver?'

'They have to be *dead*,' said Jonah.

'Easy to say, Miller, and I felt the same when Rob Durmey told me. But it seems Barlow was very persuasive. Everyone had a reason to want it to work. Kendrick hoped it'd allow an interrogation to go ahead without the need to kill. Not that he was squeamish; it would just have made everything less *complicated*. Their lead researcher was called Gideon, one of Andreas Biotech's best, and Gideon found the idea fascinating, hoping he could pinpoint the precise moment when revival became possible. Michael Andreas's interest in cryogenics had led to some of the technologies used in low-body-temperature surgery. They took the equipment and tried it with living subjects. It didn't work, but Barlow thought it was close. They kept failing, until they realized what the problem was.'

Jonah knew where Eldridge was going. 'They felt too fresh.'

'If anyone was going to be able to do it, you were their best chance. You were the only reviver who'd ever brought anyone back so fast. The only case. You were unique.'

'My mother.'

Eldridge nodded. 'They said she'd been dead less than ten minutes, possibly as little as three. So in you came. And you started it all.'

'This is bullshit,' said Never, bewildered and dismissive. 'What the hell does it mean to *revive* someone who's alive? How can that *work*?'

Eldridge sighed. 'Oh, it didn't work.'

Jonah glared at him. 'But you said Underwood –'

'It didn't *work*. Think about the answers you got to your questions, Miller. They didn't make sense. Think about what she said.'

The cities are burning. The shadow has come. 'What are you telling me?'

'It wasn't *her*. It was something else. Revival opens a door, and on the other side of that door you find the soul of the person you revived. But *this* . . . You open that door when the soul is still in the body. The door's open, but there's nothing to come through it. *It's an invitation.'*

'For what?'

Eldridge's eyes were manic and frightened. His breathing was growing ragged again. 'Something long dead. Waiting for a way out. After you stirred up trouble, Kendrick's team went elsewhere. Rob went with him. They gave up on live revivals soon enough. The results were useless. Kendrick thought it was simply not working, that the words that came were nonsense, end of story. Gideon and Barlow left. Rob spent the following years being very well paid to do things he didn't want to tell me about. Shameful things he didn't have the decency to be ashamed *of.'*

'And then, two years ago, Rob heard that right after parting company with Kendrick, Gideon and Barlow had gone to Michael Andreas for funding. They'd been working on it ever since and were ready to do it. Bring something ancient and evil into the world. They'd worked it out. They called the act *Unity.* It was something very few revivers could have pulled off, something that needed the BPV variant researched so long before. That had struck a chord with Rob. He'd told people about it, then sought me out. For so long I'd known there was something out there, and finally someone believed me.

'I don't know if Rob's death was to silence him. Kendrick may not have believed any of this, but Rob was talking out of turn and he knew what Kendrick had been doing all these years.

'I told Yarrow everything Rob had told me. I didn't hear any more until Hannerman came to see me. He said they'd managed to stop them, for a while; Andreas had found only one reviver capable of creating Unity, and Hannerman's people killed her. Andreas had problems finding a replacement. Hannerman had been trying to discover who the replacement was.'

'Do you know why Hannerman's group was planning some kind of bombing campaign?'

'He didn't tell me the details, but I know they wanted to cover every eventuality. He came to me after his friends died. He was alone, and needed to be sure he was doing the right thing. I told him he had to stop them, whatever it took.'

'Whatever it took? They killed an innocent man, seriously wounded another.'

'I meant what I said. Because I felt it. For *years*, I felt what was out there. It had managed to use me to prey on Ruby Fleming, but I could tell it was trapped somehow. The whispers I heard were eager but distant. When you came to see me before, you talked of Ruby. You said the same thing happened to you.'

'It did. A woman called Alice Decker.'

'Did you . . . did you hear the whispers?'

'It didn't whisper, Victor. It spoke. It spoke to me through Alice.'

Eldridge closed his eyes, shaking his head. 'Dear God. Does that mean it's closer now?' He opened his eyes and met Jonah's. 'God help us if they succeed. Whatever Andreas wants to bring into our world, there's no one to stop him anymore.'

*

They drove in silence in Never's car. Twenty minutes of putting distance between themselves and the hospice, before Never finally spoke.

'You believe him?'

'Yes. I saw it too, Never. I saw what was out there. And everyone told me it was in my mind.'

'What the hell can he even mean, Jonah? What can be out there?'

'I don't know. Problem is, what do we do? Who the hell do we try and convince?'

They were silent for a minute before Never spoke again. 'Hang on. You heard what Eldridge said. Andreas needed a replacement reviver. Maybe Hannerman had discovered who it was. And Hannerman attacked Jason Shepperton.'

'Eager to get out of the hospital. Getting ready for a long holiday. You think he's taking Andreas's money?'

'Not after we talk to him.'

Jonah took out his phone and dialled Annabel's cell number.

'Jonah,' she said, sounding surprised but pleased.

'We found something, Annabel. I saw Eldridge again. He told me what Unity is. Andreas is behind it. Where are you?'

'At home.'

'Me and Never are on our way there. They needed to hire a reviver. We know who they got.'

*

It was close to midnight when they arrived at Annabel's. Her Porsche was in the drive, the garage doors closed, outside light off.

'Nice car,' Never said, hanging around the Porsche.

'Come in when you finish drooling,' said Jonah, going on ahead to Annabel's door. It was open, just a crack. He put his hand on it, a warning sounding in his head.

'Annabel?' He pushed the door open and stepped into the unlit hallway. The closed door to the living room was on his left, light coming through the gap at its base. He opened it. 'Annab—'

There was barely enough time to register Annabel, wide-eyed and gagged, sitting in her father's favourite chair with her hands bound. On either side of her were two huge men, dark jackets and black jeans, sunglasses and stony faces. Annabel jerked her head and he was suddenly aware of movement behind him. He was grabbed as he turned, but outside he could see Never, still by the Porsche as he saw what had happened and froze.

'Jonah! What the—'

The man holding Jonah called to the others, 'There's another one outside. Get him.'

Jonah yelled, 'Run, Never!'

As Never started to move, the man to Annabel's right strode

past Jonah to the front door, reaching in to his pocket. Jonah saw the weapon and swore.

In one smooth movement, the man's arm came up to aim at Never.

And then, without warning, he fired.

30

They were searched – hurried and rough, their phones taken – then bundled into the windowless rear of a black unmarked van.

'We're not going to hurt you,' they were told as the van doors slid shut. Jonah was unconvinced.

They drove for hours. Jonah brought Annabel up to speed on exactly what had happened with Eldridge. Their requests for a break were shouted down from the front. There was a dim light above them, and Never's complaints were growing louder by the minute. Being hit by a Taser was bad enough, but it had made him empty his bladder. Every time he moved, he squelched.

'I can't believe they fucking *shot* me,' he said, trying to rub the impact site of the Taser, low on his back. 'I didn't realize how much those things hurt.'

'Not as much as a bullet,' said Annabel.

'I can't believe I pissed myself,' he said, sounding defeated and scared. 'I can't believe we're even here at all. What are they going to do with us?'

'Depends who they are,' said Annabel. 'Maybe they're going to warn us off and let us go.' Jonah looked at her, then away. She didn't really believe it would be that easy, he thought. She'd said it for Never's sake. He figured they were either from Andreas or from Kendrick. Whichever it was, engineering an accident would have been the simple way to get rid of them; they wanted to talk, at least, and find out what they knew. He hoped that was all.

'Jonah,' Annabel said. 'What do you honestly believe? Do you think Eldridge *isn't* crazy?'

'He's crazy, all right. But not wrong. Since Alice Decker I've been trying to convince myself it was all in my head, but Eldridge can't have been far off the mark. He said reviving a living subject was like opening a door. How can we possibly know what's out there?'

When they finally stopped, they had to wait for a long time before the van door was opened. They were in a large basement garage. Six security guards hustled them through a door and a tangle of corridors before leaving them in a small office, which seemed to be a general dumping ground for unused furniture. Along the far wall were three desks, each with a second desk inverted on top, half a dozen office chairs in front. To their left were five empty bookshelves. A clock on the wall showed just shy of six in the morning. Two sides of the office had large windows, the blinds on them closed. Jonah opened one set up, just as one of the guards appeared on the other side and held what looked like a large piece of cardboard over it. Another guard ripped tape off a roll in his hand and fixed the cardboard in place.

Jonah closed the blind again, the sound of ripping tape continuing as the rest of the windows were sealed. Only the small window in the office door was left uncovered, presumably to make it easier for the guards outside to check on them.

'Hasty measures,' said Annabel. 'They did this on short notice.' She looked at Jonah, and he thought he knew what was on her mind. They'd been grabbed by people unprepared for it. Just as her father had been.

'Do you know where we might be?' he asked her.

Annabel walked to the desks and began to methodically open drawers. At last, she found a single crumpled Post-it. She unfolded it and looked, then held it up. It was printed with a company name and a logo that seemed like a stylized DNA double helix.

'Reese-Farthing Medical. One of Andreas's companies. A

biotech firm that deals with virus and gene therapy work. That puts us a little outside Pittsburgh. For what it's worth.'

Ten minutes later the office door opened again. Two of the men who'd been at Annabel's entered and took position on either side of the door. Then Jonah's mouth fell open as Will Barlow walked in.

'Shit,' Jonah said.

'Now, Jonah . . I didn't expect a cheer, but things like that can hurt a guy's feelings.' Barlow's smile looked about as genuine as it always did.

'You know him?' Never asked.

'We go way back. This is Will Barlow.'

Then Michael Andreas entered as well. He was wearing a cap with the Andreas Biotech logo; Jonah could see that part of his scalp had been shaved. The cap covered most of it, the white edge of surgical dressing just visible near his left temple.

'Mr Andreas,' Jonah said, deadpan. 'How's the health?'

'It's excellent, Jonah,' Andreas said. 'I admit I overstated my condition, but it's good of you to ask.' He was wearing the impossibly sincere smile he'd had on his face when Jonah and Annabel had last seen him. 'My apologies to you all. Jonah, Annabel. And especially to you, Mr Geary.' He looked Never up and down. 'The rough-housing was uncalled for.'

'Fuck off,' said Never. He scowled. Like his grin, it took up most of his face. 'Any chance of a change of fucking trousers? It seems I pissed myself when your apes electrocuted me.' He glared at the apes, but they didn't twitch.

Andreas's smile didn't waver. He looked at Will Barlow. 'Will? Please, arrange for Mr Geary to shower and organize a change of clothing.' Barlow acknowledged the request and left.

'What is this, Michael?' Annabel asked.

'Please, believe me, Annabel. We're not going to hurt you.' He turned to the guards. 'Wait outside,' he said. The guards went without a word. Andreas closed the door and took a seat, indicating for Annabel to join him. She did; Jonah and Never both remained standing. 'We've been taking an interest in your activities. I'm afraid that's included tapping your phone, but it's lucky for us we did. The moment it became clear that you were too close to our interests, I decided it was time to intervene. Our plans have been delayed for too long already. We couldn't risk more disruptions, and we didn't know how much you knew. It was safer to have you here, as my guests. You'll be allowed to leave when we're finished.'

'I don't think you quite get the meaning of *guest*,' Annabel sniped.

Andreas was unfazed. 'When you came to see me before, you already knew so much that I decided to throw you a bone and hope it would keep you occupied. The bone I threw you may only have been part of the truth, but it *was* true. Did you speak to Sam Deering, Annabel?'

'I did.'

'I surmise he told you what our authorities have done in the national interest?'

'He did.'

'Torturing the dead. An inquisition of souls. In your phone conversation, Jonah, you said you spoke with Victor Eldridge, that he told you what Unity is, and that I was behind it. I knew of Eldridge, knew that he had spoken for years about other *things* being out there, whispering to him. When his psychiatric problems first began, he'd contacted staff in MLA Research to admit to misusing the BPV variant you asked me about. Indeed, Andreas Biotech paid for his care for a time, although he abruptly stopped accepting our generosity a few years ago. I had no idea he knew anything about Unity, but believe me, whatever he told you was wrong. So, you tell me what you *do* know, and I'll tell you the rest.'

Jonah laughed. 'Why the hell would you tell us?'

'Because you can't stop this. We'll keep you here until we're finished, and then we'll be gone. I would have preferred not to have involved you so directly, but now that our hand has been forced your presence seems fitting. I came to the conclusion that I'd rather you know the truth, not a Halloween camp-fire tale. Your father died tragically, Annabel, and you deserve some answers, at least. And Jonah . . . You may not realize it, but without you none of this would have been possible.'

Jonah stepped aggressively towards him. 'Then I'll tell you what I know. I know that your people were working on *live* revivals. I know they *used* me to make it work, but there's something else out there, something that could use the live subject as a host. I know you plan to bring something ancient back and make it stay.' He moved forward and leaned until he was inches from Andreas, his voice a harsh whisper. 'And I've *seen* this thing. I *felt* it, felt the evil of it, just like Eldridge did. I don't know why you want to do this, but I will do *anything* I can to stop you.'

Andreas nodded. 'I heard about your experiences, Jonah. Your hallucination, your suspension from revival duties, and—'

'You heard? You seem to know a hell of a lot.'

'You confronted me in my own office, Jonah. *Interrogated* me. Of course I was going to make inquiries.'

'Did you know about Hannerman?' said Annabel. 'Did you know before they took my *father*?'

Andreas frowned. 'For God's sake, Annabel, what do you think we are? We didn't know about Hannerman until your father was found. We realized the kidnapping was connected to us, garbled and inaccurate as Hannerman's information must have been. We changed our plans. We relocated here and delayed until the threat passed.'

'But your plans are either crazy or dangerous,' said Annabel. 'Can't you see that?'

'There's little I can say to convince you. But I want to *try* and show you that we are not the fools you believe us to be. And that we are not crazy.' Annabel watched him with impassive eyes.

Jonah scowled. 'Andreas, what I felt was something to be *feared* . . .'

'Your experience was overwork.'

'Please. Don't do this.'

'The world won't end, Jonah. This isn't Armageddon.'

'How do you know?'

'What we encountered was more than intelligent, Jonah. It was *wise*. Unity is a beautiful thing.'

'Unity,' Jonah said with a sneer.

'The term we use both for the process and for our group. Permanent unity with these beings. We've been working towards that goal for seven years.'

'What you're talking about amounts to demonic possession.'

'Oh, please, Jonah. Don't be childish. Not *demons*. Not some great *threat*. As I said, this isn't Armageddon.'

'How do you know?' pleaded Jonah. 'How do you *know*, the moment you succeed, these *creatures* won't show their true nature?'

Andreas's smile softened. 'Because we've already done it.'

Jonah paused. He turned to look at his friends, their eyes wide. He turned back, his voice shaky. 'What do you mean?'

'We've done it before. The first successful Unity was sixteen months ago.' He allowed himself a gentle laugh. 'No monsters.'

'You're lying,' said Jonah. Fear crept over him, hot and alive.

'Perhaps you'd like to meet the first?'

Jonah's eyes widened.

Andreas shook his head. 'There's no need to be afraid, Jonah. No need at all. You've met her before.'

And at that, Jonah felt sick, felt faint, even before Andreas opened the door, even before she came into the room. The moment Andreas said 'her', he knew who it would be.

'Hello, Jonah,' she said.

'Hello, Tess,' he replied.

31

Jonah stared at her.

'Who the hell is she?' Annabel whispered to Never.

'Tess Neil,' said Never. 'Kind of, uh, Jonah's ex. *Recent* ex.'

'Oh,' said Annabel, going quiet.

Jonah was still staring. He took a deep breath. The moment he'd seen Tess, he'd felt a dizzying panic. Its after-effects still left him edgy. So many questions were churning in his mind, but there was one he needed to know first. 'What are you going to do with us?'

She looked at him with genuine surprise, hurt by the implication. 'You're *safe*, Jonah. We're going to keep you here until we're done, and then you'll hear no more from us. We'll let you go. Two days at most. I'm sorry you had to go through this, and I'm sorry Never got hurt.'

'Maybe you didn't hear about Sam. He nearly *died*, Tess. He still might.'

'I heard.'

They locked eyes, and Tess was the first to look away. He could see real pain, real regret. She was sorry, but he was so angry he wanted to scream at her.

Michael Andreas spoke: 'Soon after Will Barlow and John Gideon broke away from Kendrick, they came to me. Their story was astonishing, and hard to believe. They said that they'd found some lost souls, trapped and needing help. Lost for so long they'd even forgotten their own names. They told me these beings had *answers*. They showed me what they'd encountered, and I felt honoured. Privileged to be one of the few to see this and be in a position to help. It's not easy. An ordinary revival couldn't possibly bring these beings through. The process needs a living subject to be cooled, their heart stopped, to—'

'I know what the process is.' Jonah could picture Tess, hooked up like Lyssa Underwood with artificial blood pumping through her.

'Of course. When those who experienced it came to, they would feel the presence of these beings within them, now part of them. Memories came, vague and confused, with impossible images. We hoped, given enough time, that we could help them find out who they were. And we knew how important a discovery that would be.'

'So what are they, Andreas?' asked Annabel.

Andreas smiled. 'An ancient race. Older than humanity. Much older. We spoke many times to the being you first brought forth in Lyssa Underwood. It was disorientated, confused, but it spoke again and again of a great cataclysm. Their own world was destroyed. It spoke of knowledge preserved, of warnings for those who would listen. Of the Thirteen, chosen from the last of their kind, who volunteered for a sacred duty. The rest we learned is open to interpretation, but I'll tell you what I believe. They preserved all that they know from destruction in a living vault. The Thirteen were charged with passing on their knowledge, and we will be the first to hear it.'

'Always an angle, Andreas,' she said, and Andreas looked angry.

'Don't mock, Annabel. This is not for me. This is for us *all*. We've spent years trying to understand how to help these beings remember what they are. They have been alone, trapped in the darkness, for an unknowable time. Hundreds of thousands of years, millions. Perhaps much longer. They've forgotten everything they once were. Try to imagine, the long silence they've endured. It was Will who realized that we could bring them out of the dark.

After each revival, the beings would still be present in the minds of the woken revival subject, but the effect always faded. It would last for a few hours, no longer. Yet when we spoke to the beings again, *they* had memories of that time also. It had been a true joining, a true Unity. It wasn't a simple remnant effect. They were part of us, for those brief hours.

'The pieces fell into place one by one. The BPV variant we spoke of was crucial. It focused the effect considerably, and without it we would have progressed no further.

'We were able to slow down the degradation of the effect, and make it last days rather than hours, but it wasn't enough. We hunted for a more permanent solution, using imaging, live scans of the brains of our subjects. After identifying areas of the brain that contributed to the degradation, we speculated that small lesions could be created in a handful of sites, and brought in a neurosurgeon to—'

'A neurosurgeon?' said Jonah. The word jumped out at him. He thought of the scar he'd seen in Tess's hair that night, and her explanation. *Surgery. A minor tumour. Benign.* She'd been unwilling to say more, and he'd respected that, assuming it was difficult for her to talk about. But no: it had been difficult for her to *lie* about. Suddenly he understood the operation Andreas himself had gone through, the shaved area on his head. Jonah felt shaky. 'Christ, Tess. You let them hack at your fucking *brain*?'

'The surgery went off without a problem,' Tess said. 'We proceeded with the revival ten days later, and Unity was achieved. It had worked.'

Jonah looked at her, astonished. He had always thought of Tess as self-confident, independent, intelligent. Here she was admitting to being a train wreck, so desperate to find meaning in her life she was willing to let someone take a knife inside her skull. *We're all a little lost,* he thought. *Some just hide it better.*

'Yes,' said Andreas. 'It had worked. But it would take time for these beings to recover their identities, their memories. And as we brought them back in turn, the next was revealed. They had formed a series of protective shells, with the last, the Thirteenth, at its heart. Each was weaker, more difficult to bring out than the one before it. We persevered until only the last remained. Then our best reviver died in a car crash. A French woman called Grace Ferloux, the strongest reviver I'd ever met. We'd thought it was an accident, then. Now . . . I'm not so sure. We needed her for the final revival. The weakest of all these beings, yet their leader. The most respected. An Elder, if you like.'

'And let me guess, Andreas,' said Annabel. 'By the look of the work you've had done to your own head, you're the one the Elder will have Unity with? Since it's your money paying for it all, makes sense you get the pick of the seats.'

Andreas looked at her with irritation, ignoring the comment. 'Only a very strong reviver stood any chance at success. Grace was the only one who could do it. We needed a replacement and drew up a shortlist. But the process needs the reviver to use the extreme variant of BPV, and few can tolerate it. To find a reviver strong enough who suffered no ill effects required, well . . . lateral thinking. I own the company that supplies medication to revivers worldwide. The strongest revivers have their doses precisely tailored, their medication individualized. We added the variant in small amounts, then we waited to see who we could rule in or out.'

Jonah was glaring at him. 'The side effects . . .'

'With such a small dosage, for most it would be a slight reduction in revival success, a slight increase in how long it took to bring a subject back. Any detected reduction in performance, information that is routinely passed back to us as part of their medication assessment.'

'But for some . . . hallucinations. And remnants.'

Andreas said nothing in reply, just nodded.

Jonah put his head in his hands. The medication that Eldridge first tested. The medication that had caused Eldridge's remnants. Here it was, at last. The link between Eldridge and Jonah. And before Daniel Harker's revival, Jonah had taken a double dose of his old, tainted BPV – triggering the worst case of remnants he'd ever had. 'I was on the list. You doctored my medication. That's why you're so sure what I saw with Alice Decker was in my mind.'

Andreas nodded again. 'You had a particularly strong reaction. For most, it was barely noticeable. When we had a dozen possible candidates, Will Barlow put them in order, and we approached them one by one.'

'How did Will know?'

'He had a feel for it. He'd been the one who found Grace. He said it was instinct, but whatever it was it worked. Then one of us would meet with them, and rule them in or out.'

Jonah turned to Tess. 'Was that why you came to see me?'

Tess smiled. 'You'd already reacted to the medication, Jonah. Even if you hadn't, I knew you wouldn't take the offer. I knew the money wouldn't sway you. No. I came because I wanted to see you before I left.'

'So how much were you offering?'

'Five million.'

Jonah paused. He hadn't expected anything like that. 'Christ.'

'One by one,' said Andreas, 'we crossed people off until we found our reviver. And this will be the last. When we're done, we're going where we can't be found. We achieve our final Unity today, and then we'll be gone for good.'

Jonah looked at Tess again. 'You weren't lying, then. About it being good-bye.'

'No, Jonah,' she said. 'We'll be gone. If you hadn't come here, you wouldn't have seen me again.'

Jonah looked right at her. 'And why did you . . . ?'

She smiled. 'Now, *that* was all for Tess. I hope it's not something you regret, because I don't.'

He looked at her, then down to the floor, suddenly aware of Annabel watching him. 'You'll be trying to work out who you all are? *What* you all are?'

'Yes. We don't know how long that'll take.'

He couldn't shake the sense of dread. Even though he now had an explanation for what he'd seen in the Decker revival. All in his mind, as he'd always been told, as he'd *tried* to believe. Hallucinations from tainted medication. But he hadn't been able to believe it then, and he didn't believe it now.

'Tess, there's something else out there. I've seen it.'

She shook her head. 'Please, Jonah. We've done this twelve times before. Don't you think we would know? If there'd been evil trying to come through, wouldn't it have happened by now?'

Jonah looked her in the eye, knowing he wouldn't be able to convince her to call this off. He had a sudden sense of vertigo, then, realizing how much she had invested in this. If she wasn't deluded, she had allowed herself to be bonded with something unknown. If the ultimate purpose truly was to summon evil, what did that mean for her?

'But what do you think *now*, Tess? What *are* these things? You don't seem different to me.'

'It's within me, Jonah. Dormant most of the time, but not always. I feel it, trying to remember. Sometimes memories come, overwhelming and strange. Soon I'll start to understand. When I had my first encounter, there was a warmth, a *hope*, a feeling of such protection and honour and trust . . . When I left my parents' home for the last time, Jonah, I stole two things from them. I took some money and a charm bracelet that had been my grandmother's. My mom didn't wear it, but I remembered it on my grandmother's wrist, thinking it was so beautiful. I even had a favourite charm, one I thought was better than all the others.' She raised her left wrist and showed him the bracelet and the charm she had meant. A small, simple angel. 'After my encounter, this was the image I was drawn to.'

'Angels,' said Jonah, trying to hide his scepticism but not quite managing to do so.

Tess picked up on his tone. She lowered her wrist, her other hand covering it. 'It's simplistic, but it's how I felt.'

'And the being within you is the same one I spoke to in the Underwood revival.'

Tess looked at him warily, then at Andreas.

'No,' said Andreas. 'Tess was the first to survive but not the first to try. The first of us, our pioneer, died. A weak heart, it seemed, missed by all our testing; he died during the final resuscitation. The next day, we tried to speak to the being he had bonded with. It had gone. It had died with him, tragic proof that true Unity had been achieved. Once free of their tomb, they're as mortal as we are. Now there are eleven of us blessed with Unity, here to witness the last.'

Annabel spoke to Tess: 'You've had this thing in your head for sixteen months, and you're still only able to guess at what it really wants?'

Tess looked shame-faced. She bowed her head. 'I'm trying,' she said. She glanced at Andreas again. Jonah saw a hint of impatience in his eyes, and a look of failure in hers. 'It's difficult to describe. We're one being now. Memories return, confused and impossible. The being within me is the strongest of them, but it still only comes through in dreams that are hard to understand. It's started to become more clear. I think they came to save us. There was a great shadow over all things, but they found the way to defeat it. They can teach us.'

Jonah took a deep breath and realized that she was desperate for them to believe her, to validate the choice she had made.

Andreas stood from the seat he'd been in. 'Now, we have prep-arations to make. I apologize again for your incarceration, but we had no option. We'll try and make your stay as comfortable as we can.'

'When do you let us go?' said Jonah.

'You'll be held until the Unity group has left the country. The revival will proceed at 3 p.m. If all goes well, we'll be holding a celebration here tonight and leaving the day after tomorrow. You'll be released within twenty-four hours of our departure. I'm sorry it can't be sooner. What role you play after that will be up to you. You can tell whoever you like what went on here. Whether they believe you or not, we'll be far from harm. I suggest you take the opportunity to catch up on the sleep you missed last night. This afternoon, if any of you want to witness the Elder's revival firsthand, please do.' He looked at them in turn.

'Count me in,' Annabel said, wry scepticism in her voice that won another cold look from Andreas.

'I'll give it a miss,' said Never.

Jonah kept silent. Yes, if he wanted to know for sure he would have to see it with his own eyes. Perhaps there *was* a chance that the doctored medication explained it all, that the hope Tess had felt was more than wishful thinking. That what he had seen in Alice Decker wasn't real.

But Eldridge hadn't been in any doubt that it was. Real, evil . . .

And patient.

And if this was the last Unity revival, it also made it the last opportunity to show itself.

*

Soon after Andreas and Tess left, a guard opened the door. 'You, come with me,' he said to Never. 'Time to shower.'

It was the one who'd Tasered him. 'Not unless there's a lock on the door. I don't trust you.'

The guard wouldn't be baited. 'You want to sit in your piss all day, fine by me.'

Jonah and Annabel sat in uneasy silence for the quarter hour until Never returned, his hair wet. He was wearing what looked like surgical scrub pants, carrying a stack of towels.

'They let me take these as makeshift pillows,' he explained. 'They said they'd sort out something better by tonight. I'm guessing we'll be in this room for a while.'

He handed out the towels and killed the room light. With the light spilling in from the window in the door it was far from dark, but at least it wasn't quite so harsh. They each lay on the floor, the stress and exhaustion creeping up on them all.

'Jonah, what's your instinct?' asked Never. 'You really believe this?'

'Maybe they're crazy, but I think they're being open with us and have no intent to hurt anyone. Except themselves. I know what I felt in the Decker revival, and I haven't felt that here. I don't know what to believe now.'

'And what about your, uh, *friend*?' said Annabel.

'Yeah,' said Never. 'How're you coping with that?'

'More to the point,' said Annabel, 'how much do you trust her?'

Jonah thought about it. He didn't know how to feel about Tess. Since he'd first met her, she'd been confident, and always looking out for number one. Now, suddenly, she seemed vulnerable. Did that make her more trustworthy or less? 'All I know is, I have to find out what comes through in that revival. The only way is to watch it happen.'

Annabel nodded. 'So we watch it. Not that we have much else to do. We watch it and hope there are no surprises. But I've been thinking. They say they don't plan on hurting us, but crazy people can get very desperate very quickly. I think we need a backup plan. We need options.'

'What kind of options?' said Jonah.

'How easy do you think it'd be to get us out of here, Never?' she asked, and Never turned his head and grinned at her.

'Escape? Yeah. Right.' Then he saw the look in her eye. His grin dropped. 'You're serious.'

'You're the technical expert, right? You must have some idea how the security could work in a place like this. So give it some thought.'

'You're confusing me with the A-Team. But I'll try.' He sat up, his eyes drifting around the room, ceiling to floor. He stood and walked to the corner farthest from the door and folded his arms. A few minutes later he lay back down and closed his eyes.

'Giving up so fast?' Annabel asked.

'The plan's taking shape, but I'll sleep on it. Like I told Andreas, you can count me out of watching when they bring back number thirteen. Tess thinks angels, Andreas thinks aliens. I'll stay here and suss out our escape route, just in case *Eldridge* is right and we find ourselves dining with the Antichrist.'

'So what's your plan, Houdini?' asked Jonah.

'First,' said Never, 'we have to get out of this locked room. Problem one.'

'And then?'

'We're in an office section of a lab facility. The security in a place like this is designed to keep people *out*, not keep them *in*. It's a normal building, a little more secure, yes, but in the end it has to obey fire regulations.'

'Meaning?' Jonah didn't think he was going to like the next bit.

'If there's a fire, the fire exits open.'

'So we start a *fire*?'

'Christ, no. We might even be able to unlock the doors just by hitting a fire alarm, but *smoke*'s the thing. If we make enough smoke, I'm sure the whole system will kick in before anyone comes to check it out. Whenever it's quietest, three or four in the morning, we sneak out of the room, set off the alarm, run out the nearest exit, and away we go.'

'And how do we get out of the room?' Jonah asked.

'Partitioned office,' said Never, pointing up. 'Air conditioning means a ceiling cavity. We just go over the wall.' He indicated the wall the desks had been pushed against. 'When they took me to have a shower, I paid attention. If I'm right, on the other side of this partition is an empty office. Hopefully it isn't locked, but at worst we'd have to go on a little further to reach the corridor. More exposed, but we could do it.'

'And then we make smoke *how*?'

'Yeah. Working on that. There are rough edges, but these things take time and my brain needs to shut down for a few hours. I'll think some more while you two watch Andreas later.' He looked hard at Jonah. 'But promise me. If it *is* Satan this time, scream loud. I'd like a head start.'

32

Jonah woke suddenly in the semi-darkness of the office, disorientated and scared. He had been dreaming of Lyssa Underwood, the woman sitting up on the gurney and screaming about the burning city as her face became the bloody mess of Alice Decker's.

The clock on the wall showed eleven. Just over four hours of sleep on harsh carpet tiles, and he was feeling it. He stood, wincing as his muscles rearranged themselves. He walked over to the door, looking out through the small window. A guard sat opposite, reading a magazine. Jonah knocked until he had the guard's attention.

By the time he got back from the toilet, Annabel and Never were up.

A request for food and water brought them sandwiches, snacks and soda an hour later.

'And you'll be wanting these back,' the guard said, throwing a plastic bag at Never.

He looked inside. His clothes, cleaned. 'I hope they used non-bio,' he said. 'I'm very sensitive.' He threw a particularly disrespectful grin at the guard, but the guard just grunted and left, locking the office door behind him.

*

The three prisoners sat mostly in silence as the building around them became increasingly busy. Annabel and Jonah had not felt hungry, eating only because they knew it was sensible, while Never more than made up for them, wolfing down almost everything in range.

Jonah shot him a look. 'Have you ever lost your appetite? Even once?'

'I eat when I'm nervous,' Never said. 'And I'm *very* nervous.'

Jonah could see it in his eyes, and he knew his own eyes must look the same.

They were given camp beds and sleeping bags for the night to come, assembling them and avoiding talking about the approaching revival.

When Jonah and Annabel were escorted from their office prison, Never's refusal was received with a shrug from the guard taking them.

'So I heard,' said the guard, handing him a bucket. 'You'll need that. There'll be nobody around to take you to piss.'

'I'll manage,' said Never. 'I'd rather get some more sleep. Your employers are lunatics, you know?'

Just for an instant, Jonah thought there was a twitch of a smile on the guard's face. He wondered how much the guards knew. How much they believed. Whether they did or not, they would be well paid.

Once the door was locked, Never moved the camp beds to make sure they were only just visible through the window in the door. He padded out one sleeping bag with the towels they'd kept, enough to fool a quick glance. He turned the lights out, sat out of sight, then waited fifteen minutes before removing a ceiling panel.

*

Jonah and Annabel were taken to a long, thin observation area that overlooked a large chamber. Two rows of seats faced massive windows. Most of the seats were occupied, the room noisy with excited chatter. Jonah scanned the faces and wondered which of these people had gone through the Unity process – which ones had their secret souls, waiting to be discovered, waiting to reveal their nature. There were twenty seven people in all; four were obviously security, stern faces on imposing bodies. Tess was not there, but the ten others who had survived the Unity process could all be sitting in front of him now, yet none really knowing what it was they had agreed to take on.

A guard went ahead and indicated a seat for him to take, on the front row near the door. Another guard sat to his right, Annabel in the next seat along.

His nightmare from that morning had left him on edge, wanting more than ever to believe Tess's attribution of his experience with Alice Decker to the tampered medication. It would make things so much simpler if Tess was right about everything. Michael Andreas would have his Unity, and Jonah and his friends would go free back to a world that had nothing to fear.

It was a seductive hope. Because if Tess was wrong, what did that mean for her?

He looked down into the chamber. Several assistants went with purpose from place to place; all of the dozen people down there were dressed in green scrubs and surgical masks. He assumed Gideon was there too, but Will Barlow was the only one he recognized. Jonah knew those eyes.

Barlow stood by a padded table on which Michael Andreas lay – pale, naked save for a green surgical gown, unconscious, his eyelids taped down. A monitor to the side of the table showed vital signs. Tubes and lines were inserted in his arms and thighs, pumping the chilled fluids around him that would allow his heart to be stopped and his brain to shut down. He was intubated, meaning it was to be a nonvocal procedure, which Jonah hadn't been expecting. The set-up made him feel queasy, the memory of Lyssa Underwood strong in his mind.

For a moment, Jonah was puzzled by the size of the medical team, the scale of the preparations. But then he realized that Andreas would have to be resuscitated, warmed slowly until his heart restarted. If that failed, more extreme measures might be needed. If made perfect sense to have a full team ready, the area sterile.

Speakers erupted nearby, startling him. 'Ladies and gentlemen,' said Barlow's voice. Jonah's eyes moved to Barlow, noticing the headset he was wearing.

The murmurs died down. 'Ladies and gentlemen, welcome. We are gathered to witness and celebrate this historic day. Those of Unity, you have been through this yourselves. And the rest of our guests, I welcome you with sympathy. Like many here, you are to witness an event you cannot be part of: our final Unity. At once, this is a glorious day and a sad one. There will be no more after this, and for those of us left . . .' Barlow held out his arms. 'It was not to be.'

Jonah glanced around him. Some heads were nodding, sad faces giving away those who had been involved with the hope of Unity and would always be denied it.

'And to those of you who have been graced,' Barlow said, 'your presence alone is a gift to us, and a comfort. You have shown great courage in giving yourselves to this cause, this quest for understanding. Soon we will be gone, hidden, devoted to discovery. Devoted to revelation. When the first contact was made with these *others* that we have embraced, today seemed an impossible dream. But some dreams are fulfilled. And soon we shall see the end of the beginning.'

Barlow's audience applauded. There were tears in most eyes, and shared looks of sincere joy. Jonah's mind couldn't help but flip Barlow's phrase. *The end of the beginning. The beginning of the end.* He scolded himself.

'The time is here,' said Barlow. 'I ask that you remain silent, and patient. Michael is still being prepared. Soon the final cooling stage will begin. It will take twenty minutes. When complete, his heart will stop. Brain activity will cease. After a further fifteen minutes, we will proceed.'

Brain activity will cease, Jonah thought. Dead enough for the doorway to form. Dead enough to open the path through.

There was another ripple of applause. Barlow held up a hand for silence. 'May I introduce to you the person who has taken on the role of Grace, so cruelly lost to us. Finding them wasn't easy . . .' Barlow smiled and laughed as he spoke. The laughter was returned by those watching, and it jarred in Jonah's mind. Victor Eldridge had suggested that the search for a reviver to replace Grace Ferloux was what had led to Hannerman's attack at the conference. If true, it was what had led to Sam being so badly injured.

He thought of Sam, then – a raw pain hit him, not knowing if Sam had been brought out of his coma successfully. The memory of the stabbing came to him, Jason Shepperton's arms flailing against the attack, Sam and Pru looking on in horror. Yet in a moment, Shepperton would enter the chamber, eager for his riches.

'Welcome our reviver,' said Barlow. Pru Dryden came in through a door at the rear of the chamber, dressed in scrubs like the others.

Jonah's mouth fell open. '*Shit* . . .' he found himself saying. He could sense the looks he'd earned, and the guard beside him leaned close and whispered to him to shut up.

He glared as hard as he could at Pru Dryden. So Hannerman had been targeting *her*. Shepperton had put himself in the way. If he did get out of here, Jonah thought, he might have to make an effort to like the guy.

Applause rippled across the observation room. Pru took a seat. Jonah continued to watch her, but she didn't look up to where he sat. He wondered if she'd been advised they were present, knowing she wouldn't have been happy at the news; but then, he didn't expect she planned to go back to forensic revival anyway. He thought of the money involved and what it would mean for her. A few hours of work for a lifetime of financial security for her and her daughter. No questions asked.

The murmurs of excitement in the audience grew again. The

contrast between how everyone else in the room seemed to be feel-ing and his own rising urgency made him reel as he looked into the chamber.

Jonah glanced at Annabel, on the other side of the guard. She glanced back and raised her eyebrows, looking just as tense as he felt.

Jonah looked back down as Tess entered the chamber. She crossed to Michael Andreas and took hold of his hand. She kissed his forehead and stepped back.

'We're starting the final phase now,' said Barlow, talking more to those he was working with than the audience above.

*

Under his breath, Never Geary cursed his stomach.

Getting into the ceiling crawlspace had proved tricky enough, but right now he was jammed tight. A little less food would have made all the difference.

Thick cabling had been fed through on the inside of the ceiling tile supports, further restricting the gap available and limiting which tiles he could try and lift.

When he'd been taken for the shower that morning, he'd tried to keep his bearings. As far as he could tell, the other side of the wall from their prison *was* an empty office. He had no way to be sure if that office's door would be unlocked, but he was optimistic.

At least, he had been. Right now, he was in trouble.

He felt around in the near-dark. The only light was from the open hatch he had come through, but it was hardly enough for him to navigate by.

He grunted a little as he managed to lift the first tile. The office underneath was almost dark, but he could see that he would have to position himself above a desk to the left if he didn't want to fall the whole way to the floor.

He took hold of ceiling supports and pulled, wriggling, feeling the skin on his fingers complain as they gripped the sharp edges of the metal supports. To his relief, he started moving again. Pulling any harder would have been a disaster: he was pretty bloody sure that a swearing Irishman would draw attention, however hard he tried to keep it to a whisper.

As it was, he thought the noise of his breathing had to be audible to anyone within a mile radius.

At last he dropped to the desk with a solid thump that seemed dangerously loud, and stayed still for two full minutes, breathing hard.

Nobody came.

*

Fifty minutes after Jonah had sat down, Pru Dryden started to earn her five million.

Those in the observation room had become restless during the long wait for the condition of Andreas to be optimal for the revival, but the moment Dryden stepped over to the chair by Andreas and took his hand, the atmosphere changed again. Tension spread over all the watchers. Quiet murmurs fell away until there was silence.

He watched Pru with interest, trying to recall the last revival he had viewed first-hand. Reviewing taped footage to assess revivers for additional training was common enough (an uncomfortable image of Eldridge in that alley loomed up at the thought), but the last time he had been present while someone else revived a subject was at least a year before.

Without knowing how difficult the task would be for Pru, Jonah had no expectations of how long it would take. When he first heard the whisper it made him jump.

The whispering was shapeless, coming in short bursts. Pru Dryden looked up. Her eyes moved, it seemed to Jonah, in tandem with the sounds. Jonah glanced at the other observers. Their faces were expectant, but there was nothing to suggest they could hear it.

The whispers grew. Jonah looked at Annabel, but she clearly heard nothing. She was watching Dryden with the pensive expression he himself must have had a few moments before.

Down in the chamber, Will Barlow seemed more alert. He sat tall in his seat. Then he looked to the observation window, right at Jonah, a cold smile in his eyes. Jonah looked away.

And then Pru Dryden spoke:

'I feel it,' she said. A few seconds, then: 'He's ready.'

The words provoked applause.

Barlow stood. 'And now we wait. The Elder will find us.'

They waited. It was barely two minutes, but it seemed so much longer.

And then Jonah felt something he hadn't experienced before. A warmth, like breath, sweet and comforting, passed through him. He heard a rush of air over his ears. He looked around. No one else seemed affected.

'I felt something . . .' he whispered to Annabel, but the feeling – the nature of the feeling – had taken him by surprise. 'It felt . . . *good*. Benevolent.'

Annabel looked puzzled. 'What does that mean?' she whispered, but the guard's patience had run out and he told them to keep quiet. Jonah looked at her and shrugged, shaking his head. *I don't know.* Could he dare hope that Tess was right?

Then Dryden spoke once more: 'Friend?' she said. 'Friend? Are you there?'

Michael Andreas did not speak, did not move – it was a nonvocal revival, of course – but Jonah was astonished to find he could hear the reply nonetheless. *Yes . . . I'm here.* It wasn't Andreas, he knew, although to Jonah it sounded like his voice. He was certain now. This was not the creature he had seen inhabiting Alice Decker. This was something else altogether.

Pru Dryden said: 'Welcome, Friend.' An excited ripple of chatter broke out and settled almost at once.

Thank you, the voice said.

'Is it time?'

Yes. Now. Please.

Pru raised her hand, holding Andreas's, for all to see.

Jonah had no idea what the process entailed, but he saw Pru look to Barlow for confirmation, then her fingers began to open. Jonah was struck with a sudden panic – a professional one. Pru was about to break contact. The revival would end. The impossible thought struck him that Pru had another agenda, and that this was yet another attempt at sabotage.

Pru Dryden's hand opened fully, allowing Andreas's to fall.

The audience gasped, and Jonah gasped too, but the thought of sabotage vanished as the gasps from around him became a cheer. A sudden break in contact, he realized, must somehow be a crucial part of the process.

Applause grew. After a few moments, Barlow urged silence and, when he had it, he spoke. 'The indications are clear,' he said. The audience waited, and Barlow seemed to enjoy keeping them in suspense. 'Unity has been achieved.'

The audience stood and applauded. In all the room, only Jonah, Annabel and the guard between them remained seated.

'I guess you'll be letting us go soon,' called Annabel to the guard, having to raise her voice to be heard.

The guard looked at her with a cynical smile. 'Can't be soon enough for me, lady. Can't be soon enough for me.'

*

The first thing Never had done was move the desk he'd landed on so that it was directly underneath the ceiling tile nearest the wall. That would make the whole process a much quicker up-and-over.

He glanced around the room. It was clearly unused. Like its twin on the other side of the wall, it was a dumping ground for office furniture and other leftovers.

The slats of the window blinds were slightly open. He closed them, then looked out of the narrow slit at the side, fingers wrapped around the door handle. He watched for two minutes without a soul passing by.

He pulled the door. Part of him expected it to be locked, but it opened. He shut it again and smiled. Then he frowned. This was all he'd intended to do – try the door and get back to his prison. He looked up to the ceiling, to the hole where he had slid the tile across. But then he noticed something in the far corner. A phone.

He hurried over and picked up the receiver, not expecting a dial tone but getting one anyway. He tried the first number he thought of: the FRS office.

The rapid pulsed tones that came back were familiar to him. The phones in the forensic lab in Quantico had done the same when you dialled an external number without first getting an outside line. He got the dial tone again, hit nine for the outside line, then swore: a computer voice requested his code. External calls here were ID controlled. It probably wasn't a security measure, he knew – more a financial one, preventing the staff from abusing the system for personal calls – but the effect was the same. The phone was useless.

He glanced around and saw something else that made him smile. Under one table, a shiny PC was calling to him. Its monitor was lying on its back beside it, cabling coiled on top.

Keeping his hopes in check, he pulled it out and started to hook everything up.

It was a long shot, but *if* the machine worked, *if* any of the network ports in the office were connected, *if* he could log in, *if* there was external network access . . . Maybe he could get word out that way.

A lot of *ifs*, but it was worth a try.

At first, the computer sat stubbornly silent when he tried to switch it on, but once he'd found a pair of scissors he could use as a screwdriver, it took him only two minutes to remove the case and get the thing booting again. He crossed his fingers and tried every common admin password he knew, all the ones that made any half-decent IT administrator wince. He got in on the ninth attempt.

He started to investigate how the network was configured, having a look around the machine for any clues to their system. And as he looked, his heart sank. The network wasn't configured at all. The hard drive was pristine, with nothing but the operating system installed. He gave network configuration a shot, trying a few common choices, but with no luck.

The damn thing was just too new.

'Bollocks', he said, and knew it was time to give up. He considered risking a look around nearby offices for other machines but decided he'd been fooling himself. If their phones were set up to prevent abuse, he thought, then chances were good that Web access was restricted too.

He powered the machine down, then was suddenly aware of how much time he'd spent working on it. As the thought hit him, he heard footsteps in the corridor outside the office. He took a cautious peek out the window.

Two guards. Every muscle in Never's body started to tighten.

They stopped a little way down the corridor and started talking about the imminent start of the football season and the first Pittsburgh Steelers game against the Cleveland Browns. Almost holding his breath, Never waited.

The guards changed topic to how much they were looking forward to their share of the celebratory food that night, and how much alcohol they could 'borrow', something which brought a smile to Never's lips in spite of his nerves. No better time to get away than when your guards are half drunk.

'I've got to do an exterior sweep now,' said one. 'I'll see you later.'

'Yeah, OK,' the other replied. 'Time I checked on Geary, anyway.'

His smile plummeting away, Never turned and spotted the shifted ceiling tile in the far corner. He took a deep breath and moved.

*

The applause settled as Barlow addressed them.

'Ladies and gentlemen, champagne has been arranged. We will begin the process of resuscitation now. Over the next forty minutes, Michael's temperature will be brought slowly up, his blood supply restored. Only then will we allow his heart to beat once more. There will be little to see until then. After that, our celebrations will begin upstairs. Michael will be kept unconscious for another hour, then he will be carefully monitored until we're happy that he is fully recovered. Then he'll join you all at midnight, to complete the festivities. Please, first, if you would, some appreciation for my colleagues . . .'
He gestured around the chamber at the medical staff. After the applause, he switched off his microphone and got back to work.

The door to the observation area opened and trays loaded with champagne were carried through. As the drinks were distributed, the room grew noisy with excitement again.

Annabel and Jonah watched the medics busy themselves below, readying Andreas for his careful resurrection. Tess was watching from the side of the chamber, Pru Dryden next to her. Barlow stood in a far corner, unmoving.

'You think this was real, Jonah?' asked Annabel. The guard sitting between them had stood to stretch his legs, and it was the first time they could talk with any privacy since being brought there.

'I could *feel* it, Annabel. Something came through but not what I'd seen before. Not something evil . . .'

He stopped, sensing a noise on the edge of hearing. A whisper, again, as he had heard during the revival.

But this time the whisper became a laugh, distant and cruel. He looked around, alarm on his face.

'What is it?' said Annabel.

'I don't know.'

He knew she sensed nothing. He glanced around. There were no signs that anyone else was sensing it, either. The whisper grew.

He felt a shadow fall across him. He could feel movement, around and beneath.

It's below me, he remembered Ruby Fleming say. The sensation of movement intensified, and he could feel it shoot upwards, and around, then down again. The whispering was horribly loud.

'Oh God . . .' he said. Something else. *Something else had come through.*

Annabel grasped his arm. *'What is it, Jonah?'*

He looked at the people in the room. Not one person seemed alarmed. Not one person seemed distracted. He stood and moved to the glass window. Looking down into the chamber, he saw the look of distress on Pru Dryden's face. She was seeking something out, eyes darting this way and that.

Jonah placed his hand on the glass, and Pru looked at him. They could recognize each other's fear.

The sound grew until he was overwhelmed by it. He sagged, leaning on the glass window and on Annabel for support.

He felt movement again, behind him. Something huge, dark and predatory loomed into his mind, then shot past. He fell to his knees, gasping for air. There was a smell, suddenly. A stench of rot.

Annabel helped him up, and he stared down into the chamber again, desperate to see.

Pru was staring at Andreas's body. Tess was talking to her, concern in her face.

Jonah looked at Andreas. The whispering continued, words within it but hard to distinguish. The words grew louder, until at last he could make them out.

We see you, the words said.

Andreas's hand twitched, clutching repeatedly until the arm fell from the table. One of the medical staff called out and ran across. Others joined him.

All Jonah's strength fell away. The Elder had come through, but something had followed it.

The shadow is here.

His vision darkened. He caught Will Barlow's face, a trace of a

smile, of cold triumph. Barlow's eyes moved up until he was looking right at Jonah.

We see you, the whisper said again.

Jonah fell.

33

'Is he OK?'

It was the guard's voice, impatient rather than concerned. Jonah opened his eyes and tried to stand, panicked.

'Steady!' said Annabel, holding him. 'He fainted. That's all.'

Jonah looked around, disoriented. They were in the corridor now, not the observation room.

'They brought you out,' explained Annabel. 'Didn't care for the disruption.'

Jonah was given a few moments to recover, then he and Annabel were led towards the stairwell to be taken down to their office prison. As they turned a corner, Jonah saw a group of people exit a door. Medical staff, with Tess and Pru Dryden among them, heading in the other direction.

Jonah broke away and ran towards them, the guards too slow to stop him.

'Tess!'

She stopped, clearly tired but not distressed. Pru, on the other hand, looked ill.

'Jonah,' Tess said. 'Please, stay here, I'll talk to you in a moment.' She continued on with the medical staff, talking to them. Jonah caught Pru's eye, though, and she stayed where she was.

'You heard it,' Jonah said to her. 'You sensed it.'

She was pale. She said nothing, lowering her head.

He leaned in and whispered to her: 'Get out of here, Pru. Get out.'

She looked up at him, confusion and fear in her eyes, then walked on.

Tess returned. 'You saw what happened? A reflex movement. No cause for concern.'

'Something was there, Tess. At first, when your Elder came through, I felt something good pass through us all. It was real.'

'And it wasn't malevolent, Jonah.'

'No. It wasn't. I believe you, Tess. I believe what you told me.' She smiled at him, still wary. 'But *after* the revival . . . *something else came through*. The same thing I'd seen before, Tess. The same thing Eldridge warned you about. Couldn't you sense it?'

Tess's smile dropped. 'Enough, Jonah. There was nothing. You're wrong.' She walked away. He didn't think she was lying; she really hadn't felt it. He'd assumed any reviver would have been able to, but he and Pru were the only ones who had. He wondered why. Recent exposure to the BPV variant, perhaps, or maybe the Unity process itself had damaged Tess's abilities?

'Pru Dryden sensed it too,' he called, but Tess wasn't interested. 'Ask her. And watch Andreas, Tess. Watch him.'

Then Will Barlow emerged from the same door. He looked at Jonah, and Jonah could tell: he knew. He knew about it all. Of course he did. Who had guided the process all this time, steering everything to this point? Who had chosen the reviver for the job? It must have been a reserve group, revivers this creature could *use*.

Jonah wondered how long Barlow had been engineering events. The whispering that had plagued Victor Eldridge had surely been embraced by Will Barlow long ago.

Barlow walked on, then turned for a moment, smiling. For once, the smile reached his eyes, and Jonah shivered at the darkness he saw in them.

*

'Christ, Never,' said Annabel as the door was closed and locked behind them. 'What the hell happened to you?'

There was a long angry scrape down Never Geary's neck, dotted with red where the scrape was deep enough to bleed.

'That's nothing,' Never said. 'Get a load of *this*.' He pulled up his shirt. All down one side, the same deep scratches. 'I had to rush back. I almost got caught. It's amazing how much faster you can move if you ignore personal safety. How did *your* entertainment go?'

Jonah looked him in the eye.

'Oh shit,' Never said.

'But why now, Jonah?' said Annabel. 'They've done it so many times. What was different about this one?'

'I don't know,' Jonah said. 'Maybe it needed the Elder to get through. Whatever the reason, I felt the same creature again. And I think it's inside Michael Andreas.'

*

By 6 p.m., Jonah was watching the clock, thinking that Andreas would surely be awake by now. The tension among the three of them was intolerable.

Then at eight, Tess came.

'Michael wants to see you,' she said. Jonah found himself frozen. Annabel got up. 'Just Jonah,' Tess added.

He looked at his friends, and they looked back. Their expressions didn't fill him with confidence: people looking at a condemned man. 'Wish me luck,' he said.

With a guard in tow, Tess took Jonah up to the top floor – the sixth – in an elevator. Jonah raised an eyebrow when they emerged. What he'd seen of the building so far was tailored for use as a working research facility. The top floor was clearly the executive upgrade, luxury on display, ready to impress visitors with the sheer profitability of the whole biotech venture. The corridor they emerged into seemed huge, and was decked out in polished steel and black granite. It was broken up by obsidian double doors, all of which had been latched open. Mirrors at either end gave it the impression of stretching to infinity.

'Did you watch him, Tess?' Jonah asked.

She smiled at him with confidence. 'He's doing well. In every way.'

Jonah was keeping his eyes peeled for any rooms that might have exterior windows, in case he could see how the building was situated. Annabel had known the rough location of the facility, but if they did manage to get out, what they did next depended entirely on what surrounded the building. Busy road nearby, then no problem. Isolated, private location? Not so good. Being on the lowest floor, any glimpses outside they'd managed to steal had shown little but the corner of a parking lot and a wall of trees and shrubs.

Half way along, one spacious room had its doors open. Inside, tables were being loaded with upturned champagne glasses. Huge windows on the far wall caught his eye, a grand piano angled in front of them. Most had their blinds closed, but one gave the glimpse he needed. Buildings. Roads. Traffic. Sparse, but at least the facility wasn't stuck out in the boondocks.

'Champagne, huh?' said Jonah, his voice flat. 'Looks like Unity parties hard.'

'We're saying good-bye to many good friends tonight. Most of the people who've helped us won't be coming to our retreat. And for those of us who are, it's one last fling before we leave our old lives behind for good.'

He gave her a non-committal look, but there was a knot of fear in his stomach. Part of it was the thought of seeing Andreas. Part of it was fear for Tess.

They reached the door at the end of the hall. The guard walking with them stood with purpose to one side of it.

'Please,' said Tess to Jonah. 'Michael's been up talking to us all for some time now, and he needs to get some sleep before tonight.

346

He wanted to see you again and apologize. You don't appreciate how much your negativity hurts him.'

He wondered if she'd told Andreas about Jonah's reaction after the revival. 'I'll be gentle.'

They entered. Andreas was lying fully clothed on top of a bed and stood when they came in.

Will Barlow was standing in the corner. He gave his usual half-smile to Jonah, but Jonah's eyes were fixed on Andreas's. He looked tired, certainly, but Jonah saw nothing *wrong* in those eyes. Nothing lurking. Maybe . . . maybe Tess was right.

'Jonah,' Andreas said, smiling. He held out a hand, but Jonah didn't take it. It might be the only way to know, he thought, but he wasn't ready for that.

'If you'll excuse me, Michael,' said Tess. 'I've got things to sort out for later. Promise me you'll get some rest.'

'I promise,' Andreas said. 'You go on.'

Jonah watched her go, not wanting to be left here on his own. The door shut behind her.

'When do you let us go?' Jonah asked.

Andreas sighed. He seemed nervous and disappointed. 'Can't you see this isn't a *bad* thing, Jonah? There's no reason to be afraid of us.'

'When do you let us go?'

Andreas shook his head. 'All right, all right. Tonight, Unity celebrates completion. At midnight, I'll present myself to the others. We'll be complete as a group for the first time and will let our old selves enjoy the moment, with a drink and a dance. Frankly, though, I'll be begging off early and going to bed. Everyone else in Unity is ten years younger than me and right now I'm feeling it . . .' The fond smile that appeared on Andreas's face was falling on barren soil. Jonah was watching with nothing but suspicion. Andreas sighed again. 'We leave tomorrow. You leave the next day, and you're free to tell whoever you like. Tell them everything.' He sat on the end of his bed and rubbed at his forehead. 'Jonah, I wish

I could explain this to you, just how important these few days have been. How important they *will* be. For everyone.'

'I thought you didn't *know* that yet.'

'We . . . we don't understand the importance yet, Jonah, not fully, but this . . . This is first contact, don't you see? Whatever they have to tell us.'

'First contact. With a dead race.'

'They went to extreme lengths to preserve their knowledge for others. This will change everything, if you could just—'

'Are you done with me?'

Andreas visibly gave up. 'Yes.' He stood and held out his hand again. 'No hard feelings, Jonah. Please.'

Jonah looked at the hand. He didn't glance Barlow's way, but he had an uncomfortable feeling that Barlow was enjoying this.

He reached out and took Andreas's hand in his.

Darkness.

Smoke surrounded him.

The cities are burning, a voice said.

He heard screams. The smoke began to clear.

The sight was shocking. He was in the open, a vast dark wilderness. Wind screeched around him. The sky was black. Far ahead, tall glass pillars, huge pillars that must surely be buildings but like none he'd ever seen, stood wreathed in flame.

He looked down. People running far below him. He couldn't make out their faces, faces that didn't make *sense* somehow.

A great hand reached out and down. The hand was a claw. Whatever it touched, smoke billowed from the contact. The people screamed.

Stretched out on the desolate ground before him was a vast shadow.

He wanted to turn his head and see what was casting it, but then he realized: the shadow was his own. The claw was his own. He opened his mouth and cried out, the roar of triumph enough to make the ground shake.

The shadow has come, a voice said.

Jonah released Andreas's hand. The vision had taken only an instant, he knew. It had been raw and real, and deep fear had come with it. For the voice had been Lyssa Underwood's, and the shadow was the creature that had spoken through Alice Decker.

The final confirmation. Tess was wrong. He looked into Michael Andreas's eyes and the creature was there.

Andreas stared at his own hand, clenching it until the knuckles whitened.

Jonah stepped back. He looked at Will Barlow now, who was awestruck, taking in the change that had come over Andreas.

'Is it . . . *done*?' Barlow asked.

Andreas brought his head up slowly and turned to Barlow. 'I'm *weak*,' he said, almost trying out the words. 'He's strong. He resists, even though he doesn't know it. Patience. Tomorrow. Perhaps sooner. And then always.'

Jonah watched them, frozen, dimly aware that it was Andreas's true self that was being referred to. Barlow knelt, took Andreas's hand and kissed the back of it.

They both turned their eyes to Jonah, eyes filled with contempt and arrogance.

Andreas faltered, then stepped back to sit on the bed.

Jonah felt the door handle at his back. Instinct told him not to turn his back to them, but a deeper instinct was shouting at him to run. 'Whatever you are,' he said, 'you'll be stopped.'

Barlow laughed. 'Really? By what? Tess and her friends? They forgot what they were. Lost and silent in the dark, the eons stripping them of identity. I want to see their faces when they remember.' He stepped forward.

Jonah's fear became terror, his legs threatening to fall from under him. He turned, grabbed the door handle and yanked it open, running out straight into Tess, her hand reaching up to the door.

'Jonah?' she said, startled. 'I was coming back to . . .' She trailed off, looking past him, her face creasing with worry. Jonah turned and saw Andreas slumped on the edge of the bed, half-supported by Will Barlow. Andreas's eyes were open, confused, but the creature had gone from them. For now.

'Help me,' said Barlow to Tess, and she ran to Andreas's aid.

'What –' she started, but Barlow shot a look at Jonah.

'It was Miller. He was *ranting* at him, Tess.'

Tess looked at Jonah, disappointment verging on anger.

'Tess,' Jonah began, 'I have to tell you what—'

'Don't even *start*,' she said, walking through and closing the door in Jonah's face, leaving him in the corridor with the guard.

Jonah went to open it again, but Barlow came out, shutting it fast behind him.

Barlow spoke to the guard at the door. 'Take him back. Lock him up. They talk to nobody, not even you, understand?' He turned to Jonah. 'You should be ashamed, Miller. *Ashamed.*'

And knowing that the guard wasn't looking at him, Will Barlow smiled his triumph at Jonah, and in his mind Jonah could hear again the victory roar of the creature on those blackened waste-lands.

*

When Jonah returned, Annabel half-ran to the door to embrace him. He saw the relief in her eyes, and in Never's. Relief that he had come back at all.

As he told them what had happened, their faces lost colour with every word.

'Andreas – the *real* Andreas – is fighting it,' he said. 'The moment that fight is lost, I think we're out of time. How's your plan, Never?'

'It's all we *have*, is how it is. We wait until the building's at its quietest, say three or four. Then we cross every finger. Jonah, what the fuck is Andreas? The vision you had – was that of what's *going* to happen?'

Jonah thought of the huge glass pillars on fire, and of the faces below him that he couldn't make sense of. 'I think that happened a very long time ago, Never. The cataclysm Andreas spoke of. When their own world was destroyed.'

'"Knowledge preserved",' Annabel said. 'That was how Andreas put it. Warnings for those who would listen. Perhaps the warnings were about this creature.'

'Well,' said Never. 'That's a *brilliant* fucking warning.'

Jonah shook his head. 'They were out there longer than we can imagine. Maybe they were a lighthouse, there to warn others off. But after long enough, after they forgot their own purpose . . .'

'They became a beacon,' said Annabel. 'Drawing us in.'

*

They waited. All Jonah's requests to speak to Tess were ignored.

They turned out their light and pretended to sleep, waiting in fear as midnight approached, the time Andreas would present himself to the Unity group.

'If ever there was ominous timing,' Never said as the hour came and went.

Jonah wondered if Andreas was still himself. *Tomorrow*, the creature had said. *Perhaps sooner. And then always.*

They could hear the guard posted outside their locked door, laughing with other guards; cans of beer opening, relaxing as the end of their odd assignment drew to a close. Payday getting nearer.

At one in the morning, the guards discussed doing building rounds. Every hour on the half hour, they said, and sure enough at one-thirty the guard outside the door left, returning after fifteen minutes. The same thing happened an hour later.

When the guard left at three-thirty they made their move.

They quickly stuffed their sleeping bag decoys. With Never taking the lead, the up-and-over into the neighbouring office was fast and quiet, a feeling of edgy commitment in the air as they took their turns.

The plan was simple enough. They would make their way to a store room Never had noted while being led to the showers, and jury-rig a small fire in a trash can or other container to create as much smoke as they could manage.

They waited until they were certain there was nobody around before moving from the office.

Jonah took the door handle and was about to open it.

'Wait,' whispered Never. Jonah stayed still, listening. A moment later he heard it too. Footsteps. He did as he was told and waited. The office they stood in was dark, and his face was in shadow, but he had a good view of the corridor. A woman walked past, white-coated and purposeful.

'Late worker?' he said. There was something familiar about the woman but he couldn't place her. Striking features. Almost beautiful, but her eyes too close together, her nose too long and thin. He shrugged off the feeling; shrugged off too the mild hint of thirst that followed it.

'I'd assume anyone left in the building is either part of Unity or part of security,' said Annabel.

Jonah waited, then grasped the handle again and opened the door.

It took another minute for Never to lead them to the storage room. 'DANGER', a sign on the door read. 'Storage area. Authorized personnel only. Safety protocols must be observed.' In smaller print below was an extensive list of safety directives and the words *Corrosive, Flammable*. 'Here we go,' Never said, reaching for the handle.

Annabel shook her head. 'Won't it be locked?'

He turned the handle and opened the door a few inches, grinning. 'I've worked in labs before,' he said. 'You only lock doors if stuff gets nicked.' He pushed the door wide.

The store room had ten ranks of ceiling-high open shelving. Behind them, the door closed silently as they made their way along, passing a set of fire extinguishers. Boxes of protective clothing, lab wear and low-tech equipment gave way to electrical and electronic devices. What seemed to be a computer junkyard was along one shelf, and it drew Never's attention for a moment. At the back of the room, one wall was taken up entirely with four huge metal cabinets, labelled with familiar warning symbols, and dozens of containers. In the corner was a small sink with a single faucet and a bottle of saline wash. Above the sink was a notice with instructions on dealing with chemical injuries. Knowing what he was after, Never opened door after door until he found it. Jonah and Annabel stood patiently.

'Right,' said Never, three large bottles at his feet. 'Sorted. We need something to light it with. There may be flint gas lighters around; if not I can get any handy power socket to make all the sparks we need. You two hunt around. I'm going to get something nasty.'

Jonah squinted. 'What do you mean?'

'We want plenty of smoke, but if someone comes along to investigate, we want it acrid. Then maybe they'll not come close enough to see it's just a few bins on fire. Anything corrosive will do. The rest's just detail. Chuck it on carpet, plenty of acrid smoke. Just don't breathe it.' He went to open the next cabinet and the door came off in his hand. He balanced it back in place. 'Oops . . .'

Jonah shook his head. 'Try not to destroy the place.'

'Not my fault if their maintenance people are shit,' Never said, bending down. He gave a little cheer and took a bottle out. 'Formamide,' it said. 'Highly corrosive.' The shelf above had smaller plastic bottles of methylated spirits. 'And one for luck,' he said, taking one of them, and as he did, he swore, pulling back. The bottle of meths fell from his hands, thudding to the ground. Annabel jumped.

'Be careful!' she said.

'There's, ah, something in there.'

Annabel and Jonah stared at him, then leaned down to see where he pointed. Tucked in behind the bottles was a small plastic box, wiring visible through the plastic.

Annabel stood. 'Jesus . . . is that . . . ?'

'It's a box with wires,' said Jonah, his mind racing. 'What do *you* think?'

'Shit,' said Annabel. 'Hannerman must always have had someone on the inside, after all. And if they couldn't stop Unity from going ahead . . .'

Jonah thought about Hannerman's file – an obsessive nature, always having a backup plan. Now that Unity was complete, the only option left was to destroy them all.

'We stick to the plan,' said Never, staring at the device buried in all those bottles of flammable liquid. 'We get the lighters we need, then we set off the fire alarms and make it convincing. They'll evacuate but we'll be well gone. Agreed?'

Jonah nodded, but he was torn. He knew that a big part of him wanted Andreas dead. That if he was honest, it might just have been Tess's presence that was stopping him from torching the building himself. But there was something else. Those with Unity were perhaps the only ones who could ever know what Andreas really was, if only the memories would return to them. Perhaps they were the only ones who could stop him.

'Agreed,' said Annabel. She and Jonah walked to the end of the row of shelves.

Then they heard the storage room door click and squeak gently as it opened.

Annabel and Jonah were standing in plain sight of the door. Jonah raised his hand, palm towards Never. Stay back, the gesture said. Stay still.

The woman Jonah had seen in the corridor entered. *Shit*, he thought. The one that he'd thought looked familiar. The thirst he'd ignored had surely been a warning from Daniel, because he could see it now. *Striking features. Almost beautiful, but her eyes too close together, her nose too long and thin.* Long blonde hair in the picture he'd seen of her, standing beside her brother.

Yes, Hannerman did have someone on the inside, all this time, he thought. *And God knows how she managed to do it.*

The woman was Hannerman's sister. Julia.

When Felix Hannerman had died he had taken himself out of the reach of revival, just as his colleagues had done. But it hadn't been a last, pointless statement of defiance, Jonah realized. He had known he was badly injured, maybe close to death. He couldn't risk being captured or revived. He had killed himself to protect their last hope. His sister. Waiting until all of Unity was in one place.

And just like Jonah and the others, she had waited until the building was at its quietest, its residents least alert. Until they were most vulnerable.

Julia Hannerman saw them. 'Don't move,' she said, her voice timid and wavering.

'Please, Julia. We can help you,' said Jonah. 'Lower the gun.'

34

'Please. I know who you are, Julia. My name is Jonah Miller. They've been keeping us prisoner.'

Julia Hannerman took a step forward to allow the door to close behind her. 'I know. I know everything that goes on here.'

'This is Annabel Harker. You know what happened to her father.'

Julia Hannerman looked down momentarily. *Guilt?* Jonah wondered.

'Please,' Annabel said. 'We just want to get away from here.'

Julia's gun dipped down for a moment, but she raised it again, determination visible on her face. 'This is the only way. They're all here now, all sleeping five floors above. The fire system is disabled. External security overrides are inactive. All the fire exits have been sealed.' With her free hand she reached into a pocket and produced a handful of empty tubes, which she threw at Annabel's feet.

Annabel picked one up. 'Cyanoacrylate,' she said. 'Superglue.' She laughed gently. 'You glued the fucking doors shut?'

'My brother thought of everything,' said Julia Hannerman. 'He was always thorough. Every plan had a backup. Everything covered. I wasn't sent here just to watch, just to find out what they were doing.' She reached into her pocket again and pulled out a small black plastic box, a switch on the front beside a white button. She flicked the switch, and a red light appeared beside it. She put the box to her mouth, pulling out an aerial with her teeth. 'Our goal was to stop their leader from coming through. To allow that could be the end for us all, but with only me left there was no choice. Let it come and burn with the rest of them.'

Jonah's eyes widened. 'I know what you think you're doing, but there are innocent people here. Not just us.'

'Collateral damage. Sacrifice.'

At the words, Jonah could feel anger boiling inside him. That was how Julia Hannerman thought of it, and that was how she thought of Daniel Harker. 'Andreas is the only one we have to stop, Julia.'

'They *all* have to burn. The exit on this corridor is the only way out, and I'm the only one who can open it. I have incendiaries throughout the building. When I'm sure they've done their work, I'll be using that exit so I can stand and gun down anyone who comes through the fire. You keep out of my way, then maybe I'll let you follow. At a distance. But don't think I'm going to reconsider sending those *things* back to hell.'

*

Crouched on the ground, Never had been staying as quiet as he could while he picked at the stopper on the bottle of corrosive formamide by his feet.

He looked over to Jonah, and Jonah nodded: time for a distraction. He removed the lid from the bottle. The floor under the shelving units was clear. He set the bottle on its side, then rolled it under the bottom of the shelves. It kept going, liquid glugging out as it went. Clouds of choking fumes reached Never's eyes and throat. He coughed, taken by surprise at just how severe the effect was.

Julia Hannerman heard the cough, then heard the bottle thunk against the wall near her. She turned, seeing the clouds of white smoke billowing from the floor, caught by the fumes like Never had been. Coughing, she turned back, but Annabel was already bearing down on her, clutching at the gun. It fired, hitting the ceiling, the noise deafening in the enclosed space. Jonah lashed out, his fist connecting with Julia Hannerman's face.

She fell backwards, her head striking the metal shelving. She lay on the floor, one hand in the corrosive liquid, unconscious.

'Christ,' said Annabel. 'Her hand.' The skin on Hannerman's left hand was raw red and starting to blister. Annabel grabbed a bottle of saline wash and paper towels from the sink in the corner and set to work, taking the hand out of the formamide and squirting the saline over it to wash away the corrosive. Meanwhile, Never took a second bottle of saline. He stooped and righted the formamide bottle, carefully replacing the lid. Then he emptied the saline bottle along the length of the spill. The ventilation in the room was keeping on top of the fumes, but it still stung to breathe.

Her work done, Annabel reached under the shelf and picked up Hannerman's gun and remote from where they had fallen. She pocketed the gun and passed the remote to Never. 'Switch that off.'

'Uh . . . what?' asked Never, staring at the remote he was holding. Annabel reached over and flicked back the switch Hannerman had enabled. The red light on the remote disappeared. Wary, Never pushed the aerial back down and slid the remote into his pocket.

Julia Hannerman moaned.

Jonah spotted rolls of duct tape on one shelf and took one. 'She's coming round.'

By the time she had, he'd wrapped half of the tape around her legs and used most of the rest to secure her arms behind her back, around the base of one thick metal shelf leg.

'Don't be stupid,' Julia said. 'Let me go. You know they have to be stopped.'

Annabel looked her in the eye. 'How do we get out of here?'

'This may be the only chance to get them! Andreas and his people are all asleep. I made sure. I drugged as much of the champagne as I dared. Only Andreas's *whore* was awake when I checked, crying to herself in the empty room.' Julia Hannerman smiled, her face twisting with spite. 'I think she must have realized what she *is*.'

Annabel shot a glance at Jonah, and he could see that look for what it was – Annabel was gauging his reaction. She looked back at Hannerman. 'Tell us how to leave. We're taking you with us. *How do we get out?*'

Julia Hannerman said nothing.

'Then fuck you,' Annabel snapped. 'We'll get out ourselves.' She grabbed the remainder of the duct tape and covered Julia Hannerman's mouth, wrapping the roll round the back of her head three times. Then she put her hand in one of Hannerman's jacket pockets, searching. When Hannerman's eyes lit up with anger, Jonah knew Annabel was on to something. She tried the jacket breast pocket and struck gold: out came what looked like a security swipe card.

They hurried down to the isolated fire exit, at the end of a short corridor around a corner. Annabel handed the card to Never. 'Go on,' she said. 'Knowing her brother, we might not have long.'

Jonah stared at her. 'What?'

'You saw how defiant she was.'

'Right . . .' said Never, worry dawning on his face. 'Trussed up and she didn't even try to talk her way out. Still confident. She knows something we don't.'

'Exactly,' said Annabel. 'Everything might just be on a timer. Another backup.'

Tess is still in there, Jonah thought. In an instant he'd made the decision. He ran back toward the centre of the building.

'Wait!' Annabel shouted. 'Jonah!'

'Give me five minutes,' Jonah shouted back to them. 'Then go without me.'

*

Jonah moved quickly but with caution. He took the stairwell to the top floor, two steps at a time, slowing down on the last two flights as his legs started to complain.

He glanced down the corridor. It was the one he'd walked

down, with Tess that afternoon, obsidian doors still latched open and the corridor stretching to infinity. There was nobody around. The only light he could see came from the room they'd been setting up for the celebration. He hurried down to it and looked through the door window. There she was. Alone, in a chair near one of the tables that were loaded with empty bottles and glasses and half-full plates, the lights now dimmed. He opened the door, wincing as the hinge squeaked.

She looked up and wiped tears from her cheeks. 'Jonah?' she said, wide-eyed. 'Something's wrong with Michael. He should have rested for longer. That was why. I told him it was too soon, but . . .'

He pulled the door shut behind him and walked over.

'I'm getting you out of here,' he said, keeping his voice low.

'He . . . he was *confused*, Jonah. The look in his eyes kept changing. And then . . . and then once he turned to me, took my hand and asked me to help him. He looked so scared. He said he was drowning. Why did he say that? We left the room and he looked at me and smiled, and it was so *cold*. Then he just laughed and went back inside . . .' She fell silent.

'Come with me, Tess.'

She shook her head. 'He needs me. He's confused. He's still recovering.'

'Tess, something else came through. It's inside him. But right now, *you need to come*.' He held out his hand. She reached out to take it and then froze, looking over Jonah's shoulder.

'Mr Miller,' said Will Barlow from the doorway. 'I'm afraid the party's over.'

*

Annabel and Never stood by the fire exit, waiting. Annabel didn't know how to feel. She'd watched Jonah run into danger, putting himself at risk for a woman who'd been a key part of this whole damn thing. Right now, she wanted to punch him.

'Why did he go back for her?' she said.

'One thing you should have learned about Jonah by now: he's a principled fucker. It's not usually so fucking infuriating. She's an old friend, massive bitch or not. But you saw the look on his face when Andreas called her in and she explained how it was. Let's just say I don't think you have any competition there. If it helps.'

'It's not like that.'

'So you two keep saying.' He looked at his watch, then shook his head. 'Fuck it. Julia said all the alarms are off. We can at least have the door open and ready.' He swiped the card in the reader by the door. The small LCD display said, 'CODE.'

'Fuck,' said Never.

Annabel looked at him. 'Can't we—'

'What?' said Never, despairing. 'Guess? *Hack in?*'

'I was *going* to say, since the alarms are out . . . can't we just find a window to smash?'

He paused, then grinned. 'I owe you a drink,' he said.

*

'They liked you, Jonah,' said Barlow. He was slurring his words, unsteady on his feet. As he entered he picked up one of the few remaining full champagne glasses, raised it and drank. He pulled the door closed behind him and twisted the latch. 'There was something different about you. Special. They broke *through* to you, you see, when you revived that psychologist. What was her name?'

'Alice. Alice Decker.'

'Yes! They even *spoke* to you. It pleased them. Unexpected, but liberation, however brief, is always glorious. Especially after so long in the darkness. I think they hoped you would prove to be our reviver. They thought if you'd been the one, they would come through strong. Much stronger than they did in the end. But you couldn't take your medicine . . .'

Jonah looked around at Tess. She was still sitting with a deer-in-the-headlights stare.

She spoke. 'Wh . . . what's wrong with Michael? What did you do to him?'

Barlow looked at her pityingly, then sat beside her. 'Oh, Tess, the times we had. You know, ever since you were chosen, I watched you with such care. I didn't know how long it would be before you understood. I tried to talk Michael out of letting you be the second to attempt Unity, especially after I made sure the first didn't survive.' He looked over to Jonah. 'You see, the one you spoke to in Underwood, *it* knew, or soon would. It was close to remembering, close to discovering the truth. One death was easy. More could prove harder, but the next was so much weaker, I thought we'd have plenty of time, and I was right. Of all those who reached Unity and survived, Tess has the strongest within her, and she still doesn't know. But I've been ready to take care of Tess ever since she came through the procedure. Just in case she started to remember and ruin everything. I'm glad I didn't have to, Tess. I want to enjoy you again.'

She stared at Barlow. 'What's inside him? What's inside *me*?'

'Ah! Understanding. Finally. But I'm not supposed to tell. They want to tell you themselves.'

'"They", Barlow?' said Jonah. 'Who are you talking about? The rest of Unity?'

Barlow smiled. 'You know who I mean. You saw it, Jonah. I could tell. When you shook Michael's hand, you felt what it was. We are what we eat, Jonah. They are all they have ever consumed, and they will take you too. *They. It.* All the same. One and many. *Legion*. It will take you, and you will be one with it.'

Jonah took Tess's hand. 'Come on, Tess. We're going.'

Barlow laughed, standing. 'Guess again.'

Jonah stared at this man, a man he'd always disliked because Tess favoured him. 'How long, Will?' he said. 'How long have you been playing lapdog?'

'Longer than you think. And my reward will be eternal. I'll be favoured. Granted every pleasure, while the unworthy suffer.'

Jonah pulled Tess to her feet. 'We're going.'

Barlow put his hand on Tess's shoulder and forced her back into her seat. 'You do what I fucking tell you to do.'

Jonah saw that Barlow's eyes were having trouble focusing. 'I guess you didn't drink much champagne, Tess,' Jonah said. She gave him a puzzled look, but Barlow lifted his glass and looked at it, then flung it across the room.

'What did . . . ?' said Barlow.

Jonah brought his knee up into Barlow's groin with as much force as he could, then pushed him hard to the floor. Barlow did some unworthy suffering of his own for a moment, then lay still. Drunk or drugged, it didn't matter; Barlow was out cold, and Jonah had ticked off a long-held ambition.

'Now,' said Jonah, holding his hand out to Tess. 'We have to get out of here.'

'What about the others?'

'We warn them when we're safely away.'

They moved towards the door, then stopped dead as slow hand-clapping started behind them. As they both turned, Jonah wondered if – hoped – it was Barlow, consciousness somehow regained. The one alternative that occurred to him was so much worse.

'The gallant hero,' said Andreas. He was at the back of the room. Jonah couldn't see him yet, but then he rose from behind the grand piano, hidden in shadow in the dim lights. Jonah realized he'd been there all this time, watching.

Jonah held firm to Tess's hand and took the two strides to the door, twisting the latch. Impossibly, Andreas's hand slammed hard into the door before it was open more than an inch.

Jonah looked from Andreas to where he'd been sitting an instant before, his shock clear for Andreas to see.

Andreas smiled, the cold dark in his eyes unmistakable. This was not Andreas anymore. He turned his head, looking at the fallen Will Barlow. 'Poor Will,' he said. 'He wanted to be the one. But

Andreas has the money, and Will could not be risked. Besides, Will had had to rule himself out of becoming like all the others. He knew what they were, you see. Why would he want one of *those* inside him?'

'Michael . . .' said Tess, trembling. 'Is Michael . . . is he dead?'

'No, Tess,' said Andreas. 'We're all getting to know each other in here.' He tapped his own skull. 'Michael will live within us. Always.' He smiled, the expression on his face terrible. He opened the door with one hand. The other hand shot forward, wrapping itself around Jonah's throat, holding with immense strength. Instantly Jonah had a vision of the blackened terrain, the burning city, the creature howling its pleasure as it picked up handfuls of living flesh and watched it burn.

The vision dissipated as Jonah felt himself thrown. He hit the far wall of the corridor and fell to the ground. Andreas walked towards him, gripping Tess's arm, her face twisted in pain. He looked at Jonah and walked to the nearest of the double doors crossing the hallway, thirty feet farther on.

'Some privacy, I think,' he said, taking a pass card from his pocket and touching it to a reader by the door. The door unlatched and swung shut to seal the corridor. Andreas keyed the pad on the reader, and the green light on the pad turned red.

Jonah quickly glanced at the other end of the corridor, the one that led back to Annabel and Never: still a clear path.

Andreas came back and threw Tess to the floor. He stepped towards Jonah.

'What are you?' Jonah managed, rubbing his painful throat.

'Didn't you listen to Will? I am One and Many. Within us, within *me*, you shall find eternal life. They couldn't kill me then. I took their world and thought them powerless, but they had one last trick. Binding me through sacrifice. One Elder and twelve guardians, each creating a shell to enclose me, another wall on their prison. But they would weaken, in time, and time was my ally. They didn't understand how *old* I am. The eons passed. Ten thousand years. Ten million. Each like a second to me. Endless lifetimes to them. They lost themselves.

'Their thoughts spilled out into the dreams of men. Reflections of the war we'd fought. Echoes of their sacrifice, and of what they had faced and defeated. The Eater of Souls. The Great Shadow. Humankind has known me of old and feared me since the first shamans told their tales in the dark, brutal nights. Every creed had their name for me. Yama. Apophis. Ahriman. Devil. Not until the walls thinned between the realms could I reach out too. Reach out, and *feed*.

'What am I, Jonah Miller? Your scientists argue over how to define life. They ask if a virus is alive, a bacterium, an ant. I give you a definition. Something is only alive if it can experience *pain*. Life *is* pain. Life is *suffering*, until death. Is that not the lesson of evolution? And I am life itself, in its purest form. Within me, life is eternal. Torment without end. There are many that would embrace it. They will have their chance soon. And the rest I take by force.'

He leaned down to Jonah and picked him up by the throat again. Jonah could hear the wind of the blacklands surround him, but he concentrated and managed to block the vision, staying focused on where he really was. Andreas began to squeeze. The grip tightened. Jonah was clutching at Andreas's arm, barely able to breathe now, but that arm was like steel.

'*Leave him alone,*' Tess said, stepping closer. Andreas lashed out at her; she was thrown back through the doors of the function room, falling against a table, glasses smashing on the ground.

Jonah knew he had only seconds of consciousness left.

'MICHAEL!' Tess screamed, and Jonah saw her swing her arm, an empty champagne bottle in her hand. It connected with Andreas's head, the sound a sickening crack, the thick glass stronger than the bone of Andreas's skull.

Tess dropped the bottle and stepped back, hands up to her mouth.

Jonah felt the grip around his neck loosen. Blood began to seep through Andreas's hairline and trickle down his face. Andreas let go, staggered back, fell to his knees.

Feeling like he was still choking, Jonah tried to get his breath back. Tess edged towards Andreas, horror in her eyes. The back of his head was pouring with blood.

'Michael . . .' she said. 'My God, what have I done?'

Andreas looked at her, and Jonah could see from his eyes that the creature had gone.

'Tess . . .' Andreas said. '*Run.*'

Andreas fell forwards to the floor, his eyes closing. Tess stared, but Jonah had recovered enough to know what they needed to do. 'Come on,' he said, and led Tess to the open door, back towards the only way out.

They reached the stairwell, Tess ahead of him. She paused a few steps down and turned.

'Maybe we can help him, Jonah,' she said, desperate. 'Maybe he can resist it.'

Jonah glanced back down the corridor. Andreas lay where he'd fallen, unmoving. Jonah looked at Tess. 'There's nothing we can do for him. We –'

And as he spoke, he sensed movement and glanced back again.

Andreas was beside him. Blood-covered face and wide grin, eyes cold and dark. Jonah stared, unable to move, unable to think.

Andreas reached out suddenly, grabbing them both by the hair, dragging them back to the corridor. He stopped by the doorway and threw them hard. Jonah landed heavily. Winded, he watched Andreas lock the door just as he'd done to the one at the opposite end. No way out.

'Where were we?' Andreas said, putting his hand to the back of his head, bringing it round in front and looking at it. He wiped the blood over his own face and smiled. 'Ah yes,' he said, and grabbed Jonah's throat again, plunging him into the blacklands, the face of Andreas now merging with the face of the dark creature towering above the scorched ground.

'Do you understand, Tess? Do you understand what you *are?*'

Tess's eyes widened with horror.

Andreas looked at her. 'The Elder is within me now, screaming its despair. But I want to leave as many of you alive as I can, to witness your failure as I take this world. You tried to stop me. You were my *jailers*. My *wardens*. I had to wait you out, wait for an eternity, until you lost what you were. Until the walls weakened and I could find the cracks, widen them over the centuries, reach out enough to find someone who would listen. Someone who would *help.*'

'No . . . please . . . please *stop*. You're killing him . . .' Tess stood and took a wary step closer to Andreas. Jonah's shallow breaths were harder and harder to take.

'At last, the Thirteen were found, pitiful and desperate, not knowing anything of themselves, but knowing they had something important that your people needed to be told. Something they couldn't quite recall . . .' Andreas smiled, his eyes cold and amused. 'One by one they abandoned their posts without realizing what they were doing, thinking they had found salvation, freedom from that dark void. Leaving that place meant being tied to mortality again. The sacrifice was annulled. When the last of my jailers left, I was free. I hitched a ride, and now the prison is empty. Here I am.'

'Let him go. *Please* . . .'

Andreas hit out with his other hand, catching Tess on the side of her head and sending her to the floor. She looked up, beaten.

Andreas lifted Jonah off his feet, squeezing tighter and tighter, grey sparks at the edge of Jonah's sight as oblivion crept up on him.

Tess stood. She took a step forward. 'Leave him alone.'

'Look at you, Tess,' said Andreas. 'Within you is the strongest of them, of those Thirteen still left. And even now, even now that you *know*, it still stays dormant. It knows it has lost.'

She stepped forward again. Andreas raised his hand, then paused when he saw the look in her eye. Jonah saw it too. Rage filled her face. 'No,' she said. Something seemed to build within her. Jonah felt the hairs on his arms stand, the air around him alive with static electricity. Tess screamed: *'NO!'*

With the scream came a pulse of sheer force, a visible shockwave spreading out from her. It flung Andreas to the ground, sending him sliding on his back far along the corridor, thumping into the first door he had locked. Jonah collapsed, coughing and gasping for air. Tess stumbled, then her legs gave way and she fell. She managed to lift her head. Down the corridor, Andreas seemed incapacitated. Then Jonah heard him call out.

'Tess . . .'

'Michael?' she said.

'It's too strong. I can't fight it.'

'Michael . . .' Her head dropped down again. She was unconscious.

Jonah hauled himself up to his knees. Andreas had done the same, but he looked impossibly weary. Even at distance, Jonah could see his eyes, see that Michael Andreas was himself again.

And then it started.

35

The glass wouldn't break.

Once Annabel had made the suggestion, they'd hunted for the nearest unlocked room with an exterior window, finding a small office along a short side-corridor near the store room. Yet whatever they tried against it, the thick, double-glazed glass held without a scratch.

'You know,' said Never, 'I get the feeling Julia Hannerman knew this shit was tough.'

There was a sudden noise – the sound Never had been wanting to hear, of glass breaking. But this was coming from somewhere else.

'The store room,' said Annabel, and they ran.

As they opened the door, they took it in quickly – the white-coated woman, moving fast from the base of the shelf; the brown formamide bottle, shattered; a bloody shard of brown glass where Julia Hannerman had been sitting; tape, still stuck to the leg of the metal shelf, a ragged tear where the glass had cut through.

Annabel and Never ran to the end of the shelving after Hannerman, to see her crouch momentarily by the metal cabinets, her white jacket spattered with blood from the wounds she'd inflicted setting herself free. Wisps of smoke were rising from her shoes where they'd been covered in formamide as she'd kicked at the bottle to break it. Both hands were blistering now, especially around the fingers of her right hand.

'Gun!' hissed Never at Annabel. For a moment she didn't grasp what he meant, then she remembered. She took the gun she'd pock-eted and offered it to Never.

'You stay right there,' Never said, waving the gun at Hannerman.

'Shut *up*,' said Julia with contempt. She turned and stood. She was holding the plastic box containing the incendiary device. 'I can trigger this right now and we all go up.'

'But you won't do that,' he said. 'One little room burns, and your targets all get away.'

'I've got a chain of devices through the building. One goes up, they all go. It'll take longer, but trust me. It'll burn the building to a shell. So back off.'

'I'll shoot.'

'No, you won't. I can see it in your eyes.'

He waved the gun in an attempted show of confidence, but it didn't come off. He looked at Annabel and handed the gun back to her. 'You shoot her.'

Julia Hannerman stepped forward. Annabel and Never backed off until they were all out of the store room.

'Seriously,' said Never, nodding at the gun. 'In the leg or some-thing.'

Annabel glared at him and aimed the weapon at Hannerman. 'Julia, this is pointless. We have your remote. Give us the code to the door and we can all leave. We can stop Andreas another way.'

'Further back,' said Hannerman, holding up the incendiary device. They did as they were told.

Julia Hannerman kept stepping away from the store room, back along the corridor, back to the centre of the building. She reached into her other jacket pocket, and as she did it occurred to Never that Annabel hadn't looked in *that* one. As he saw what Julia brought out, he understood the look of fear that had been on Julia's face as Annabel had searched her pockets. He understood what it was Julia knew that they didn't.

There was no timed countdown. Julia was holding another remote.

'Felix tried to get to me for help,' Julia said, still moving backwards, her voice giving away her exhaustion. 'He tried to get to me, then he knew it was too late. But he always had a backup plan. He always carried a spare.' She held up the second remote, grinning, pulling the aerial out with her teeth as she'd done before. 'And so do I.'

Something occurred to Never. Julia Hannerman could have just pulled the remote out and triggered it at any time. Why the threats? Why was she still *moving*?

'Reception,' he said, and he saw a flicker of annoyance on the woman's face. 'If you trigger it from here, the signal won't be strong enough. You probably need to be by the stairs. Maybe even on the same level.' He snatched the gun from Annabel, knowing that when push came to shove, he *was* capable. *Let her see it in my eyes NOW*, he thought. 'My friend is in there. So you put the fucking thing down. *Now.*'

Julia Hannerman smiled. 'You got me,' she said. 'Here will have to do. We can all go together.' Her thumb touched the button on the remote.

The moment it did, the incendiary device she was holding erupted. Annabel and Never flung themselves back, watching in horror as burning liquid covered Hannerman's upper half. She fell screaming as flames engulfed her.

They ran to the store room and grabbed the fire extinguishers, then doused the burning body in foam until the extinguishers were empty, but the fire kept burning. The screaming went on and on. At last, the flames stopped. Julia Hannerman's arm twitched for a moment, then she was still.

Annabel leaned over her. The eyes were wide open, and very dead; the horror in the face said all that needed to be said.

There was one question in Never's mind. He looked to Annabel. 'Was she close enough? Did the other incendiaries go off?'

They listened. Above them, they could hear the answer.

*

Andreas turned his head to look behind him. Jonah followed his gaze. He could see a flickering light in the window in the door Andreas was standing by, and he could hear the screaming start. Andreas moved towards the door, shouting out, taking the security card from his pocket. Suddenly he stopped and backed off as an intense yellow light flared behind the glass panel, painful to look at.

'*No!*' Andreas yelled.

And then he stopped. He took a long breath and hung his head. Slowly he walked to where Jonah was still kneeling.

'I am become death,' said Andreas, his voice hoarse, looking at his hands as if for the first time.

Jonah watched in fear as Andreas's head came back up, waiting for those cold, dark eyes to look at him once more before the end came.

But no. It was still Andreas. The only thing in those eyes was despair.

'I can feel it grow, Jonah,' Andreas said. 'It's taking me and there's nothing I can do. The Elder within me is too weak; all I can sense of it now is desolation. There is no hope. My God, Jonah . . . I wanted to put an end to grief. I thought that whatever they would show us, these beings, it would surely bring us closer to that goal. And now I am become death. The destroyer of worlds.'

A burst of light caught their eye, and they looked along the corridor. Liquid fire began to drip from the ceiling above the far doorway.

'It was frightened,' Andreas said. 'When Tess hit it with the bottle. The Unity process grants mortality, Jonah. It didn't think it would be affected, but it was. I think it can die now. That might not be true for long.'

There was another set of double doors latched open beside them. Andreas went to them and used his card. The doors began to swing closed.

'Look after her,' Andreas said. He set the card on the floor by Jonah and walked to stand on the other side of the closing doors.

The side on which the fire was raging, and getting nearer. 'The code is 5972,' he said. The doors shut and locked.

Jonah stood and walked over to the door, looking through the glass panel in the middle. Andreas was looking back. He nodded, turned and walked towards the inferno.

He knows what has to be done, Jonah thought, not knowing if he could have done the same.

The sound of distant screams was growing, but so was the roar of the fire. Jonah watched. Andreas was halfway to the far doors, one arm raised to shield his eyes from the intensity of it, the white ceiling above him blackening. Jonah heard a curious cracking sound, and suddenly the ceiling erupted, a third of its length collapsing in flame, catching Andreas full-on. The scream was horrifying, as Andreas thrashed at the flames covering him.

Jonah looked up to the ceiling directly above, wondering how long it would hold. He bent and pocketed the card Andreas had left behind.

A deep thump came from somewhere in the building; the lights in the corridor went out, red emergency lighting coming on. Long shadows flickered, cast by the flame.

He stood and put his face close to the glass in the door, looking one last time through the thickening smoke.

Andreas's face appeared suddenly at the glass, fire dripping from it, his hair gone. The creature was in those eyes, staring at Jonah with defiant fury. Jonah froze. They watched each other for long seconds before Andreas started to hit the doors.

Jonah looked at Andreas and at the fire raging behind him. 'Burn,' he said. He began to back away, dragging Tess.

Andreas pounded at the doors in slow, deliberate strikes, packing a terrible force. The doors looked strong, but they shook horribly with each impact. Jonah looked at them, praying they would hold.

The flame was growing behind Andreas as he pounded, surging up the corridor. Jonah kept moving, seeing the doors give a little more each time, sure they would give way completely any moment.

Andreas opened his mouth and roared, the inhuman roar of the victorious beast of the blacklands, growing louder until it drowned out the sound of the doors shaking. They were going to give way. Jonah knew it. *They were going to give way.*

'*Burn!*' Jonah screamed out.

Then a rush of flame engulfed Andreas. The doors shook again and again, but the roar changed, becoming a cry of despair, of pain. Of *defeat*.

'*BURN!*'

Abruptly the sound ceased. The doors shook to a final blow but did not yield. At the window was only fire.

It was over. Jonah stood, breathless and drained.

A cracking sound from above snapped him out of it. He kept pulling Tess.

Behind him, flame broke through the ceiling. They reached the doors at the far end, and Jonah readied the card. Then he looked at the panel. There were no lights on it. Nothing on the display. He tried the card, tapped in 5972. The door was still locked.

'*No,*' he shouted, turning. The fire was getting closer now, the smoke thickening. He crouched to breathe properly. Nowhere to go. Then the door behind him shook with impact. Jonah spun, terrified, looking through the glass panel. *Andreas*, he thought, but instead he saw an Irishman wielding a fire axe. Jonah could have cried.

Two more blows and Never managed to get the axe blade deep enough to push hard on the handle and lever a bigger gap.

'Thought you might need a hand,' Never said. One more attempt, and the door opened wide.

They got to the stairs, Never carrying Tess, Jonah taking the axe. Both floors they passed showed the glow of fire through their stairwell entrance.

'We're going to break out through a window,' Never said. 'Tough fuckers but the axe should do it.'

'Didn't the security card work?' Jonah asked.

'It needed a code. Hannerman's code.'

'I have Andreas's card and his code.'

When they reached the bottom of the stairs they heard a huge crash above them. Jonah glanced up, the stairwell at the top engulfed in flame.

Annabel was waiting. They approached the corridor by the store room. Julia Hannerman's corpse lay there in a pool of extinguisher foam. Jonah stared at the body.

By the fire exit, Jonah swiped Andreas's card, then typed in 5972.

'INVALID'. It took a moment for him to realize it hadn't worked. He tried again, and the same word came up.

He looked at Never.

'She's disabled the exits, mate,' Never said. 'Window's our best chance. This way.'

Back they went, to the room Never and Annabel had found with exterior windows. Setting Tess by the door, Never took the axe and swung back. They all looked away before it hit the window. It thudded into the glass, bouncing back hard, barely scratching it.

Jonah looked through the glass at the cars he could see, at the dark sky with the first signs of dawn. Safety, millimetres away.

Annabel glanced at Jonah in despair as Never swung the axe once more, the roar of the fire getting louder with every second.

'NO!' yelled Never, as it bounced off again. He swung a third time, swearing as a small hole appeared in the glass.

With a hiss, part of the ceiling in the far corner of the room burst out into sparks.

Another swing. The hole widened.

Jonah watched the fire as it encroached. He looked at Annabel and could tell she was thinking the same thing – time had run out.

More of the ceiling came down.

'We have to get out of here,' Jonah shouted, but Never was ignoring him. Another swing. The axe head went through, but the structure of the pane held. 'Come *on*,' Never cried at it, disbelieving, as he found he couldn't pull the axe free.

'Let's go,' Annabel cried, dragging Tess through the doorway. 'Now!'

Beaten, Never let go of the axe. They left the room, shutting the door as the ceiling came down behind it.

Thick black smoke was visible toward the stairwell. There was only one way left to them. Annabel and Never manhandled Tess to the locked fire exit, setting her unconscious body propped against the wall.

'Where's Jonah?' said Annabel, looking back down to the bend in the corridor.

'He was right behind us,' said Never, then he shouted, '*Jonah!*'

They ran to the corner and saw a black curtain of smoke advancing, closer now than the store room door. 'Where the hell is he?' said Annabel.

Seeing Jonah emerge spluttering out of the smoke, Never ran to help. Jonah was dragging something. When Never saw what it was, he stared. Julia Hannerman's body.

'Take her legs,' said Jonah. 'Watch it, she's still hot.'

'You went *back* for her?'

Jonah nodded. 'She's the only one who knows her code.'

As they reached the fire exit again, the nearby *thump* of an explosion came.

'Store room,' guessed Never. Dark smoke was already thickening at the corner they'd just come round.

From his pocket, Jonah took out the blister pack of his trial revival meds. Each of the eight pills was one fifth of the dose he should take for a revival. He swallowed all eight. The medication would take a few minutes to kick in fully, but there was no time to wait. And the last thing he wanted was this woman resident in his mind.

He knelt beside Julia Hannerman's body, holding her right hand, the charred skin crackling under his fingers. Everything depended on how deeply burned she was. The odds weren't in his favour. 'Be ready, Never. I don't know if this will work, and whatever happens it'll be close. Nonvocal, I'll tell you if I get anything. Wish me luck.'

All three of them had their eyes fixed on the advancing smoke. Tess, lying propped by the door, groaned but was still unconscious. 'OK,' said Never. He took Hannerman's card out of his pocket and held it up. 'Ready. But do you really think she'll tell you?'

'No one else is going to get out this way. Maybe she will. But if she doesn't, I have options.'

'What do you mean?'

'You *know* what I mean,' said Jonah.

He could do this. He could bring her back quickly, minutes after death. And then, if the choice was between letting his friends die or sacrificing his principles, it was no choice at all.

He tried to block out what was happening around them, to ignore the increasing heat. Underneath the sound of flame, he was sure he could hear more screaming. He tried to ignore all of it. He pushed it away, focusing, knowing Julia Hannerman was close.

He felt heat, a sudden searing pain across his upper body, and fought the reflex to open his eyes to be sure it was from the revival, and not physical. He held his nerve. Within moments she was there.

'Julia.'

'Felix?'

'No. My name is Jonah Miller. You know who I am. We're at the fire exit. We need your code. Help me.'

'No.'

'We're not involved, Julia. We're innocents. No one else will escape this way, there's too much destruction. Please.'

'*Nobody gets out.*'

There was a self-righteousness in her that made Jonah angry. 'You were going to, though. You'd planned it this way, the last exit that nobody else could reach.' He sensed her contentment. She was proud. 'You'd left it open just for you. We need your code.'

'A number.' She sounded so pleased with herself, and Jonah had to fight hard to control his anger. 'One little number and you'd be safe. But you got in the way. It's your fault I'm dead. So why would I want you to leave?'

'Because we're innocent. And Annabel Harker is here. Your brother was responsible for her father's death. You owe her.'

'No one escapes. Not today.'

There was a finality to her words, and he realized he couldn't avoid doing it. Julia Hannerman would say nothing to help them. He thought of the Baseline documents Sam had given them, the ideas he'd been horrified by. He thought of Pritchard, dead in his car, as the memory of his mother's death took away Jonah's reason and let him pour all his fears and hatred and rage into the dead man, pouring them in until the man screamed.

Jonah tried to summon that feeling again. The anger and loss of his mother's death. The pure, fresh rage of what Felix Hannerman had done to Sam. The fury he shared with Daniel Harker for his needless death. The terror of the heat and smoke and flame around him and his friends.

'What . . ?' she said. 'What's there?'

He wanted a nightmare for Julia Hannerman. He thought of the creature that Will Barlow had summoned, the entity he had first seen a lifetime ago when he revived Alice Decker. The creature that had finally perished in Michael Andreas. He thought of the look in those eyes and of the blackened wastelands. Of the roar of triumph and the stench of evil.

Julia Hannerman was terrified. 'What is that? One of *them*? Oh God, Felix, what *is* that?' She was disorientated now, just as he'd hoped.

'Julia, it's Felix, I'm here,' said Jonah. 'It's one of *them*. It's coming for you. It's coming.'

'Please, Felix! Help me! It's so close!' Jonah pushed hard, a cas-cade of images and sensations. He could feel the terror building in her.

'It's coming for you, Julia. We have to open the door. We have to get out of here.'

'Felix, I don't understand . . .' she cried.

He pushed again, trying to drown her in the terror. He could feel reason stripping away, feel her become unaware even of her own death. She was in darkness, a terrified child, but her brother was with her. Her brother could show her how to get out. He just needed the number. That was all. Just a number. *'Please Felix, I'm frightened!'*

'Tell me the number, Julia,' he said. 'Tell me the code.' She told him through her screams.

He could release her now. He *should*. But his anger had momentum and a purpose: he still had one more question. He sent another barrage: Daniel Harker, tied and blackened. Felix Hannerman, screaming in a burning car. He sent her intense, pure *loss*.

Pure *grief*.

He asked the question, and sensed (or imagined – did it matter which?) Daniel Harker, observing, impassive; unable to disapprove, because he wanted to know too.

The answer came in a rush of image and cold truth, shocking him for a moment.

(*'Jonah!'* called Never. *'Hurry!'*)

He was done with Julia Hannerman. He let her go to whatever awaited her, releasing the charred hand and opening his eyes. The smoke around him was thick, the roar of flame overwhelming; he could hardly see or hear.

'Did you get it?' Never yelled, pulling him to the card reader.

Jonah took Hannerman's card from Never, swiped it, and keyed in the number.

The door opened.

They ran through into open air, stumbling as they went, Annabel and Never dragging Tess by the arms as Jonah looked back to see flame bursting through the black smoke now pouring from the door they had just left.

They ran until they felt they were far enough, to the edge of a parking lot at the side of the facility. They fell to their knees.

There were people on the burning roof screaming.

'Christ,' croaked Never. 'Jesus Christ.'

36

The three of them lay down beside Tess, gasping, their smoke-filled lungs barely able to draw enough breath. Feeling a hard lump dig into his back, Never pulled Hannerman's gun and the original remote detonator from his back pockets. He tossed the gun to one side, and stared at the detonator. Beside him, Tess groaned and began to stir.

'Can't we help anyone?' Never said. 'Isn't there anything we can do?'

Jonah, wheezing, stood beside him and watched the horror before him. 'No,' he said. He could see that Never was crying. He realized he was crying too.

'Listen!' said Annabel, standing. There were sirens. Annabel collapsed in a hail of coughs. Jonah went to help her, wondering if he would ever be able to tell her the answer that Julia Hannerman had given him to that final question. *Why did they leave Daniel Harker to die?*

He caught a glimpse of movement behind him. He looked. So did Annabel. It was Tess, disorientated, standing. Angry, and in tears. Pointing Hannerman's gun at Never with shaking hands.

'*What did you do? What did you do?*' she yelled at Never, who was suddenly aware of the remote he was holding. He let it drop to the ground and held up his hands. He glanced at Jonah, then stepped forward. 'We didn't do this! It was Hannerman's sister. It wasn't *us.*'

'*What have you done?*'

Jonah felt a terrible fear crawl across his heart. Tess was confused, distraught. But she'd seen Never holding a remote detonator, and all of Unity was dying. All but her. And she blamed Never.

'Stop!' Jonah called. He stepped in front of the gun. 'Tess? Please. This wasn't us. Please.'

Tess's arm lowered just a little. 'Where's Michael?'

Jonah shook his head.

'He could have fought it,' she said quietly. 'He could have won. We could have *fixed* it, couldn't we?'

Jonah stepped towards her. 'Please, Tess. Please.'

'You wanted him dead.' She said it decisively and raised the gun again. 'You wanted him *dead*. You can't say you didn't.'

'Please, Tess.' He took another step. 'He did fight it. And he won the only way he could.'

She looked at him, and he saw understanding there. Screams drew her eye to the rooftop. Jonah turned as well. When he turned back, she was running.

He made to follow.

'Let her go,' said Never.

Jonah paused for an instant, but for all her faults, he and Tess shared a bond. He had been lost and alone once, and she had been there to help him. Now, it was his turn to help her. 'I want to make sure she knows she's not alone,' he said, and he went after her.

She was heading through the rows of vehicles in the parking lot, towards the road. Jonah was a few rows back, just about keeping her in sight as she weaved. The lot was broken up by strips of vegetation, young trees and bushy foliage. Tess disappeared through the middle of one, and Jonah froze as he got close and saw her stop and turn to see something on her right, raising the gun again. She was speaking. He crept close enough to hear, ducking by the front of a four-by-four for extra cover. A gap in the greenery gave him line of sight.

'. . . son of a bitch,' she said.

A man in a dark suit came in to view, his back to Jonah. Tess kept the gun trained on him, but from his stance Jonah could tell he was aiming a weapon right back at her.

'Come with me, Tess,' said the man.

'Keep away from me.'

'We've been watching you. Keeping an eye on things. Wanting to know exactly what the hell you people are up to. Don't tell me you're surprised. We officially have you pegged as delusional, but believe me, Tess, contact with *unknowns* is a national security issue like no other.'

'Did you make this happen?'

'The fire? Christ, no. We had enough coverage on Andreas to know something big was going down, that whatever he'd been planning all this time was finally under way. I knew I had to be here, but right now I have no idea what's gone on tonight, just that you're one of the only people to come out of it. Now please, come with me. We'll protect you. We're the only ones you can trust.'

The man slowly moved his hands up, opening them and letting the gun hang loose. He took it by the barrel with his left hand and set it on the ground.

Jonah watched Tess's face. She was considering the offer. *No*, he thought. If Tess went with him, Jonah knew the kind of protection they meant. Under lock and key.

Tess started to lower her gun. Jonah knew he could give her a chance, if he wanted. Indecision, but only for a moment. He knew what Never's opinion would have been: hell of a risk to take for a woman who'd treated you like shit.

He thought back to when he'd taken down Felix Hannerman, the momentum of his charge being all that was needed. He started to run, pushing hard to get his speed up, keeping as quiet as he could. The man only started to turn as he reached him, the shock of recognition on both their faces as Jonah's arms clamped tightly around him. Kendrick hit the asphalt, hard.

'Run, Tess,' Jonah shouted, and Tess was away, the gate to the road visible ahead. He caught movement to his right, and suddenly realized that another man had been there all along, twenty feet away, hidden from his view while he'd been watching Tess and Kendrick face each other down.

The man was reaching for his gun, bringing it up, aiming . . .

Jonah leapt to his feet and stood in the way, holding out a hand, palm up. '*No,*' he shouted.

There was a sound, a crack. He took a breath and it hurt.

The other man lowered his gun, shaking his head, irritated.

Jonah turned to see Tess reach the gate, run across light traffic. Disappear through a thin line of people who had formed, watching the fire engulf the facility.

His legs lost all strength and he fell to his knees, then to his side. The pain grew. He saw his chest. There was blood. He couldn't move, only able to breathe in agonizing shallow hitches.

The second man started towards the gate.

'Leave her,' said Kendrick, kneeling beside Jonah. He looked like he had a bad taste in his mouth. 'We'll pick her up soon enough.'

'What about this one, sir? Do we finish him? Put him out of reach?'

Kendrick looked appalled. 'I know him. He's one of the good guys.' He paused for a second, thinking. 'We take him with us. Whether he lives or dies, I want to know what the hell he was doing here.'

'He knows who you are?'

'Nobody does. We don't exist.' Kendrick raised his arm towards his mouth. 'Pickup at gate B,' he said into his sleeve. Then he listened. His expression changed. 'When? You're sure? We're on our way.' He looked to his subordinate. 'Come on. Change of plan. We leave this one here, see what he tells the police.'

'What happened?'

Kendrick shrugged. 'We got lucky.' One last look at Jonah. 'I guess someone had to be.'

Jonah heard them stride away, unable to tell how much time passed before shouts and footsteps approached.

Annabel and Never sat by him, calling his name, crying and desperate.

'*No*,' Never said. '*Stay awake.*'

Jonah could hear sirens grow louder. There were vehicles now, reaching the building. Fire trucks. Ambulances.

But he felt so tired.

'*Jonah, please hold on.* Help's here. Help's here.' Annabel's voice. Hearing it, Jonah felt regret.

He was tired.

'*Please.*'

It was time to sleep.

37

He was nowhere.

Unaware of his body, yet aware of something around him. Some kind of *space*. Some kind of *void*. He tried to speak, but nothing happened. He felt a pang at the memory of Annabel's voice, at the thought of Never Geary's profound grin. He missed them.

A sliver of fear crept in. He imagined what it would be like to be in this curious place, and have a presence, large and predatory, encircle him as it had done with Eldridge's subject, Ruby. He could almost see it, a huge black shark invisible against the darkness.

But there was nothing here, not now. The fear slipped away. He was calm. He wondered what came next.

A different fear hit then, a sudden vertigo, that perhaps this was all. Unending awareness, stretching out into eternity, just as the Thirteen had endured. The thought was terrifying.

No, he thought. *That was not what the dead report. They don't say they've been thinking, reminiscing for hours or weeks. They say they were aware only for a brief time, just before . . .*

Just before they were revived.

There was a rush of noise and light, too brief to understand. Then darkness again, silence.

He wondered who was doing it. It certainly wouldn't be Pru Dryden. Either she'd been in the building when it went up or – more likely – long gone with her money. Nor would it be Jason Shepperton, vacationing as he recovered from his wounds. Stacy

Oakdale, perhaps, but the likelihood was that it would be someone new, someone he didn't know.

He wondered what they would ask him. He had to be brought back, of course. The situation was too extreme to leave him unquestioned, even if it would achieve nothing. He'd handled many cases himself that had been little more than formalities. Would they want him to verify the story that two other reliable witnesses gave? And what good would the verification be? The heart of their story would be dismissed as the ravings of an obsessed group. Unity may have believed themselves the hosts of ancient souls, but nobody else would.

Brought back to be asked meaningless questions. Brought back to say good-bye.

I don't want to come back, he thought. *Please.*

The pulling became stronger. *This is the moment,* he thought. *Here it comes.*

Fragments of memory came to him. He was sitting in a muddy field, staring at the sky, his dead mother in the car behind him. He was holding Daniel Harker's decayed hand in a cold room. He was seeing Sam's grey face, his jeans soaked in blood. He was running from Alice Decker's revival. He was in Baseline, crying into Tess Neil's handkerchief. He was waking in his apartment to find Tess had left while he slept. He was watching the bus bear down on the car, hearing his mother's quiet voice: *No.*

Please, he thought. *Let me sleep. Let me go.*

Another burst. So much noise. It lasted longer, this time. He felt like he was being dragged. He wanted to stay where he was. Bright light flooded him, and he cried out in silence.

*

He opened his eyes.

He was lying in tall grass, a bright hazy sky above him. It was warm.

He stood, the grass up to his knees. He took in the scene around him, recognition hitting. The field where he'd brought back his mother. It had been a dismal mud slick the last time. His step-father's car was there, battered, rusted, its very presence the give-away that this wasn't real.

'Am I dead?' he said aloud.

'No,' said a voice behind him.

Jonah turned to see Daniel Harker, looking exactly as he'd looked in the jacket photo Jonah remembered, with his long dark coat.

Daniel smiled at him. 'I mean, if *you're* dead, what does that make *me*? Hell, if I'm the figment of somebody's imagination, seems damn unfair if they haven't got the decency to be alive.'

Jonah smiled. 'It's good to finally see you, Daniel. In person.' He held out a hand and they shook. 'I'm sorry, though. About what Julia Hannerman said.'

Daniel shook his head. 'I wanted to know. Not your fault it didn't make good listening.'

Jonah looked around, marvelling at the detail of it all, wondering what this was. Not the preamble to revival, he felt certain of that. It had to be some kind of dream, albeit unlike any he'd ever had. 'It feels so real.'

'Tell me about it,' said Daniel, looking at his own hand with the same expression of amazement.

'Daniel, there was something . . . something Andreas said. Well, the creature that took him. What it said about every victim it had consumed living within it. It reminded me . . .'

'Of remnants. Of me.'

Jonah nodded.

'I don't know what that damn thing was, Jonah, but it's dead now. Gone.'

Jonah said nothing. He didn't know if he believed it.

'I wonder,' said Jonah, running his hand over the top of the grass stems. 'I wonder why *here*? This place.'

'I don't know,' said Daniel. 'But maybe you should make the most of it.' With a nod, he indicated behind Jonah.

He turned and saw her. Uninjured, smiling in a way he'd not seen since his father had died. He stared at her, not daring to believe.

'I don't understand,' he said to Daniel.

'Maybe it's what's left of her, in your mind. The pieces you remember. The natural remnants Graves spoke of. Or maybe it's more than that. I'd like to believe the latter, but I'm not exactly impartial.' Daniel smiled, then tipped his head, urging him on.

Jonah ran to his mother, tears pouring.

They embraced.

'My baby boy,' she said. 'My beautiful boy.'

He wept, holding her as tight as he could.

'When you died, I felt so alone.'

'You're not alone.'

'You mean you're—'

'That's not what I mean.'

She held him and he held her, no thoughts in his head, only the joy of being with her again, whatever it meant. At last, his tears slowed. He broke away so he could look at her again.

'It's time,' she said. 'You have to let me go.'

'I don't want—' he started, but she put a finger to his lips.

'Hush,' she said, smiling at him. She brushed his hair back from his forehead. 'You have to let me go.'

He nodded, then held her again with his eyes closed, gathering himself. He took his arms from around her, and felt her do the same. After a few moments he opened his eyes. She was gone.

He turned.

Daniel was beside him now. 'Think I'm off too,' said Daniel. 'Whatever the hell that means. Oblivion or eternity. Either way, I hope they do cocktails.' They smiled at each other.

'Good luck, Daniel. I hope . . . I hope you get to see Robin again.'

Daniel looked away for a moment, his face emotional. 'Thank

you, Jonah. And good luck to you too. Take care of yourself. And of Annabel.'

Jonah smiled. 'What makes you think I'll get the chance?'

'Oh, I can't guarantee it,' said Daniel. 'But just look around you.'

Jonah turned to look but there was nothing to see. He turned back.

Daniel was gone.

Jonah felt tired. In the hazy sun, he sat, then lay down, overcome by a sudden urge to sleep. He closed his eyes, wondering if he would wake, and where he would find himself if he did.

*

He felt movement under him. Light filtered red through his closed eyelids. The sound of an engine. The rocking of a moving vehicle. There was a mask on his face.

He opened his eyes. A female paramedic was looking at him.

'Try and relax, Jonah,' the paramedic said. 'You're stable. We'll get there soon.'

Jonah felt a hand holding his. He squeezed it. Unable to move his head, he looked as far right as he could. He could see Never, Annabel beside him with her arm outstretched. She squeezed his hand in return.

'Hold on,' said Never. 'Hold on.'

Jonah's mother had been right.

He wasn't alone.

38

Pain and dreams came then, punctuated by darkness; then a gradual climb towards lucidity, until at last he opened his eyes to an empty hospital room.

He groped for his recent past, remembering coming round in hospital after his mother's death and again after the revival of Nikki Wood. He seized at last on Andreas. The fire. Tess.

He asked about his friends and was told both were fine, released after one night in the hospital. Once he had fully stabilized, Jonah had been transferred to VCU Medical Center in Richmond, the hospital where Sam was still being treated.

After a time, a doctor explained the extent of his injuries.

The bullet had hit one of his ribs, bone fragments peppering a lung and causing enough internal bleeding to kill. For the first few days it had looked bleak. After a week, it was still touch and go. Now, it was the third week, and he was out of danger.

Jonah listened on his bed and ached, breathing with care. He could tell he was being pumped with some kind of painkiller, a vague euphoria taking over whenever he lay still for long enough.

'Your heart was untouched,' the doctor told him. 'Considering how much damage there was, you were very lucky.'

The word brought back the last thing Kendrick had said. Jonah wondered what form Kendrick's luck had taken.

The doctor discussed the injuries with him, the long-term

problems that might arise, the importance of making a careful recovery. Jonah found himself tiring, and soon he slept again.

*

More darkness and dreams. When he next woke, it took a moment to realize that the faces before him were real.

'Hey,' he said.

'Hey,' said Sam, sitting by the bed in pyjamas and a robe, pale and thin and fragile. Annabel and Never were there too, standing behind Sam. 'We nearly lost you,' Sam said.

'And you.'

'I was glad when they moved you here, Jonah. Meant I could keep an eye on you. Me and Never have a bet on which of us gets released first.'

'I bet on Sam,' Never said.

Jonah thought of Never the last time he was in the hospital, going around to his apartment and cleaning it up before Jonah was released. The thought reminded him of something else, and worry creased his face.

'What?' asked Sam, sitting up, concerned.

'Has anyone checked on my cat?'

'Marmite's fine,' Never said, laughing. 'I've been taking care of him. After everything that's happened, first thing you ask about is the fucking cat.'

They sat in silence for a moment.

Then Sam stood. 'I need to go and rest,' he said. 'I'll try and come and see you later, OK?'

Jonah watched as Sam lifted a pair of crutches and took slow, painful steps out of the door. His stomach twisted at the sight.

Annabel and Never took positions on either side of his bed. Annabel took his hand.

'You scared us,' she said.

'Has there been any word of Tess since?' Jonah asked.

'None,' said Never. 'And good fucking riddance.'

Annabel leaned closer. 'We assumed it was Tess that shot you. Then we heard that someone had seen the other men there. Nobody has any idea who they were.'

'Kendrick,' said Jonah.

'I wondered if they were from Kendrick.'

'One of them *was* Kendrick. They'd managed to find out something about what Andreas was doing and wanted to know exactly what was revealed. He said they'd been there to watch. The fire took them by surprise.' The image of the inferno loomed up in his mind. 'How many people died? Did anyone else get out?'

'Maybe thirty people dead,' said Never. 'The intensity was so bad, it might be impossible to know for sure. There were two regular building security guards who both got clear, and one of the six security staff Andreas had brought for the occasion got out, but badly injured. Nobody else survived. Some bodies have been recovered, some identified.'

'Anything on Pru Dryden? Barlow? Andreas?'

'Pru was already at home. She must have left right away. Nothing on Barlow, but Michael Andreas's remains were identified a few days ago. Dental records. DNA check pending.'

Jonah thought of the heat, of the flames, and closed his eyes. Thirty people dead, but Andreas gone too. He hoped Michael's sacrifice was worth it, that he'd been right about the creature's mortality.

A thought struck him. 'Were any of them . . . Jesus, was *Andreas* . . .'

'Revived?' said Never.

Jonah nodded. He'd barely been able to think it, let alone say it, but the thought must have crossed Never's mind too.

'No. I guess that was why Hannerman chose fire. By the time they were recovered, none of the remains stood a chance of revival.'

'Thirty people, and Michael Andreas is dead. I don't know how to feel about that.'

'Put it out of your head, mate. What's done is done.'

Jonah nodded, knowing damn well that he'd give it plenty of thought in the weeks and years to come.

'So how have people been taking it?' he said. 'What have you gone public with? Just the interrogation methods or Unity as well?'

Annabel and Never shared a look.

'Well, that's the thing,' Annabel said. 'The police will want to get your side of things, and we need to get our stories straight.'

'What do you mean? We just tell them all we know.'

'We can't go public with Unity, Jonah. I need time to nail it. If we went public now, it'd be ridiculed. Sources would clam up.'

'What have you told them, then?'

'We kept to Andreas's own cover story. Turns out he'd said that he was having a private function for a select group of friends and investors. I said I'd been invited as a mark of respect to my father. I was allowed to bring two friends. You and Never.'

Jonah couldn't believe what he was hearing. 'What, is the fire supposed to have been accidental? Didn't they speak to Pru?'

'They don't know Pru was there,' she said. 'As for the fire, some documents were sent to the *New York Times* a few days ago, claiming responsibility and laying out the reasons. They seem genuine. It may indicate that others were involved, although maybe only as far as holding on to a letter, mailing it if they didn't hear from them by a specific date.'

'What did it say?'

'It didn't give their sources, but it set out what they thought Andreas was doing. Bringing evil into the world. It said they were preparing for war in case they failed to stop it. If you want a taste of how the truth would be received, you only have to look at the response their polemic got.'

'Not pretty?'

'You could say that,' said Never. 'Everybody thinks they were a bug-shit crazy outfit of paranoid nut-jobs who murdered one of America's all-time greatest geniuses.'

'So when the police come, I tell them I was at a *party*?'

'More or less,' Annabel said. 'Anything awkward, say you don't remember.'

'Do they know about Tess?'

'They know a woman escaped the fire, not who she was. Your shooting was put down as just another part of the attack. For Christ's sake, plead ignorance about Kendrick's ID.'

'And what about what Kendrick was doing, Annabel? Murder for interrogation? The documents Sam gave us? Have you kept quiet about that?'

'It'll have to be up to you, Jonah. I don't think people will have trouble believing it, but if we want to bring it into the open, we have to do it right. I need those documents, if you still have them.'

Jonah nodded. But there was one condition. 'Only if people can't see how it's done. Any documents that describe that, I'm still going to burn them.'

'Deal. As for Unity, it'll take time. There are people who knew what they were doing, and with Michael Andreas and the others dead, I hope they'll be more willing to talk on record. But the hard part is how to do it so it's not just written off as lunacy. Face it, Jonah, even the best damn piece I could write might just be ignored. Let's just say I don't think it would bag me the cover of *Time*. And there's something else you have to face: if the world ever *does* believe us, revival will be in the firing line. The Afterlifers will have a much stronger position.'

'Revival isn't the problem.'

'I hate to say so,' she said, 'but people will see it as *exactly* the problem.'

He stayed silent. She was right. He knew that revival itself carried no risk. Even if anything else *had* remained, it would take a group as obsessed as Unity to bring it through. Only the revival of a living subject could open those doors to them. He thought of the healed scar on Tess's scalp, and the fresher one on Andreas's. Without those extreme preparations, even if something *did* come across, it could not stay long. There was nothing to fear from revival alone. He knew this in his heart.

Convincing anyone else would be a different thing altogether.

He nodded slowly. It was something he would have to face. In time.

Right now, though, he needed to talk to Annabel alone. He caught Never's eye and looked to the door. His friend's eyes widened as the lightbulb went off, and he nodded.

'I'm . . . going to get some coffee,' Never said. 'You want anything, Annabel?'

She declined, and Never went out of the room.

Annabel looked Jonah over, and he looked back, uncomfortable at the inspection. She took his hand. Her eyes were wet, her voice unsteady. 'You look good,' she said. 'Considering.'

'No. I look like shit. And you look tired.'

'Yeah. Haven't really slept properly in weeks. I'm going back to London soon, and when I do I'll probably sleep for a straight week before I'll be fit for work.'

As she spoke, Jonah felt his heart sink. She was moving back into her own world, her own life.

'Are you OK?' she asked as this hint of despair rippled over Jonah's face.

Jonah forced a smile. 'I was just remembering when I . . .' he said, catching himself. *When I had my name on the cover of* Time, he had been about to say. Some of Daniel's memories would always remain, he thought, but the idea didn't worry him anymore. It had stopped being like having another person in his head. The memories felt second-hand now, events read rather than lived. 'I remember when I saw your dad's *Time* cover,' he said. 'Long ago.'

'Last *month* seems long ago.'

Jonah nodded and tried to sit up a little, wincing at the stab he felt. 'It was six months before my mom died, before I found out what I am. I remember being so . . . excited, I guess. That there was some magic left, some mystery. I remember talking to my mom about it, and she was the same. My stepfather was away, and we had a whole weekend where things were just so *right* . . .' He drifted into silence. He looked at her, his expression grim. 'Annabel, when I revived Julia Hannerman. When she gave me the code . . .'

'You don't need to talk about it, Jonah. You had to do it.'

'Even so, I'll always feel sick about what I did. But that's not what I mean. I asked her something else. I asked her why your father died. Why they left him.'

Annabel stared at him, dumbfounded.

'She didn't tell me, not as such. The knowledge of it poured out of her, sudden and complete.'

He paused, feeling the pressure of the expectation on Annabel's face.

'*And?*' she said.

'They were preparing to move location. One night they went on a reconnaissance trip. On the way out, they realized they were being followed. They shook the tail, but they had a dilemma. Was their hideout already compromised? Should they go back and get Daniel, or was it too risky? If they didn't, they knew it was a death sentence. Daniel wouldn't be found, but they'd gain the extra days they needed. They took a vote. That was the way they were organized. Felix Hannerman may have acted like a leader, but when it came to decisions everyone was equal, and however the vote came out they would abide by it. So they voted. It was split. Two for, two against, Felix Hannerman with the deciding vote. He voted to leave him.'

Annabel nodded, and they sat in silence for a while before she spoke. 'Thank you.'

'I wasn't sure if—'

'It's better to know, Jonah. It's better to know.'

Jonah nodded, wondering if he'd done the right thing. It had been a small lie, after all, and the truth was so much more brutal.

The final vote *had* been split, two for, two against, but with one abstention. Felix Hannerman had already voted to leave Daniel. No. The final vote hadn't been his. When they'd first organized themselves, they'd agreed how a tied vote would be decided, and that was how Hannerman resolved the issue.

The thing that had condemned Daniel Harker to die had been the toss of a coin, and she didn't need to know that.

'So,' Jonah said. 'You're heading back to England.'

She sighed and nodded. 'Yeah. Friday.' Two days. It hit Jonah harder than the pain.

'That soon?'

'I'll be back here in a few weeks. Things to sort out. I have dual nationality, makes it easier. And I have a home here now. But I think I might spend some time hiding. Dad used to joke he only spent a few weeks hiding because of depression – the rest of the time he hid because he liked it. I always thought he was just saying it to make me feel better, but now . . . I think I know what he meant.'

Jonah smiled, stopping himself from making any kind of comment. If he knew Annabel, she'd quickly tire of hiding. It was the greatest difference between them. He thought of his apartment, of getting home and locking the door. And of how much he looked forward to it.

'Did they tell you when you'd be able to leave the hospital?' she asked.

'Another week. Then I'll be at home for a month.'

'And back to work after that?'

'Back to work?' Back to the FRS, after all this? He hadn't given it any thought. But then, he didn't need to think.

'What else would I do?' he said, smiling.

*

When his apartment doorbell rang and Jonah heard who it was, he was overjoyed and horrified at once. He knew exactly what state his apartment was in. He buzzed Annabel up and spent the forty seconds' grace failing to make a dent.

'You could have given me fair warning!' he said as he opened the door, smiling. They hugged.

'Got in this morning. Thought I'd surprise you.'

'You did.' He waved her through. 'Just toss some of the junk off the sofa. I would've tidied up if I'd known.'

'I figured you'd put yourself out. That's why I didn't call.' She set down a package she was carrying and pondered the room with a wry smile. 'It's a mess, huh? You've been home, what, two weeks?'

'Takes skill to make mess this complete in so short a time.'

Annabel started to move a bathrobe piled on one end of the sofa. A shrill complaint stopped her, and Marmite's head appeared from within. Annabel laughed. 'Hello, you.' Marmite watched her warily. She tickled the sleepy cat's chin and won him over.

'He's a bit playful at the moment, he might—'

'Ow!' Annabel tried to pull her hand away, Marmite holding tight, claws out and gnawing her knuckles. When he let go, she couldn't resist tickling his belly until he attacked again.

'Yeah, he might do that. Can I get you a coffee?'

'I'm only here for a few minutes. I just wanted to see how you were doing. Didn't want to intrude, I know you like to hibernate.'

Jonah smiled, but he was a little red-faced. 'I admit I'm not great company. Too many painkillers, too tired. So how was home? London home, that is.'

'Busy. Loved it. Here-home is good too, though. Still weird to think I own it.' Marmite pawed at her hand again but got no response. Dejected, he hopped down from the sofa and padded off to the kitchen.

'Are you giving up work? Travelling the world?' Jonah looked at her with eyebrows raised and a playful smile. She grinned.

'You know damn well I'm not. Got a story to write. I'll be travelling, yeah, but work travel.' She handed over the package she'd brought. 'Look, I don't know if you want it, but I thought you might, after what you said. And I know Dad would want you to have it.'

He unwrapped it: Daniel's framed *Time* cover. Jonah smiled, remembering the excitement he'd felt the first time he'd seen it. Sharing that feeling with his mom. 'Yes. Thanks. Thank you.' He reached out, his fingers touching hers as he took it. For a long moment, they shared a look.

And then Annabel stood and strode over to the front door. 'I really have to get going.'

'Already?' he said, standing, trying to sound aloof rather than desperate for her company.

'Busy girl. Anyway, I'll be back soon.' She leaned in close, Jonah flinching back as her head came towards his.

'You need to work on that.' She smiled. Then she kissed his cheek. The touch was bliss.

'Long-time habit. Hard to break.'

'Maybe I can help. Another kiss, say? Have to have dinner or something first, mind.' She smiled at him, but there was something in her manner that took Jonah a moment to identify because it was so unlike her: she seemed nervous. 'How about it?'

Jonah was lost for words, finding Annabel's nerves infectious. A smile tried to break out on his face, even so.

Annabel continued, 'So what do you say?'

He shook his head. 'I'm not really up for a night out yet . . .'

'Oh, come on, a meal? Just a meal? This week? Before I go back?'

'I don't know, Annabel. I'm just not—'

She raised her hand. 'At least say you'll think about it, huh?'

He looked at her for a moment. 'Maybe,' he said.

Annabel smiled. She moved close again, Jonah concentrating so hard on not flinching that she managed to take him by surprise. She kissed him full on the mouth, sending his mind into enough of a spin that he kissed back.

'I guess you *really* owe me dinner now,' she said. 'I'll call you tomorrow.'

Jonah closed the door behind her as she left. Marmite appeared again, pleading for food. 'I'm coming,' he told the cat, but he let the palm of his hand rest on the door for a moment, thinking about Annabel, still feeling the touch of her lips on his. Wondering if he had the courage to really let someone get close at last.

Maybe, he'd said.

It was a start.

EPILOGUE

'Do we have it?' Kendrick asked. He knew they did. He could tell by the sourness in their eyes. His bosses were getting old, he thought. Old and tired, and fully aware of it. Priestly's face was dry and lined, her grey hair thinning; Wellman's paunch robbed him of the hard edge he'd once had. They'd been watching with contempt for years as Kendrick's star rose.

Wellman and Priestly shared a look. Priestly nodded her head, and Wellman reached into his jacket pocket.

'Here,' said Wellman. He handed over a white envelope. Kendrick opened it without hesitation, and Wellman's eyes widened.

'Hang on!' he said, but beside him Priestley shook her head.

'Don't, Howard. He can open it.'

The three sat in what was known as the 'conference suite', a drab, cramped little box of a room. Wellman and Priestley hated being there, Kendrick knew. They felt it was a tainted place. They liked to keep their distance from the dirty work. It let them maintain their little pretence that as part of keeping their country safe, what they did was entirely just, and none of it left a stain.

Kendrick found such hypocrisy intolerable. You could believe it was necessary, yes. But not that it was *just*. Not if you were using that word with any degree of honour.

And it always left a stain.

That was exactly why he'd insisted that they met him there in person.

Kendrick read the letter. It was, word for word, as he'd requested: two one-sided pages, signature near the top of the second page. The signature made him smile. It showed they meant business.

Wellman raised an eyebrow, amused by Kendrick's open delight. Kendrick's eyes narrowed at once, but he allowed himself to marvel at the signature again. 'How much did they tell him?'

'Enough,' said Priestly.

'Waste of time anyway,' said Wellman. Kendrick watched him until the old man's face reddened and his failing eyes looked down. These people, these dinosaurs, had been in charge of his career for so long. They'd dismissed his proposals so often. What leeway they'd allowed him in this matter had, he thought, been under the expectation of failure and ridicule.

He would relish this victory.

'Let's see, shall we?' Kendrick said. He stood quickly enough to make Priestly start.

'Yes,' she said. 'Let's.' There was unguarded scepticism in her voice, Kendrick noted. No doubt they resented him going above their heads.

There were four guards waiting. They escorted them down the corridor through three sets of externally controlled gates, until they reached the door numbered 438. One guard unlocked the door and remained outside while the rest of the group entered.

Kendrick smiled at the number on the door as he passed. The facility cells were numbered at random, giving a false impression of size to any detainees. In reality, there were only five.

Through the door was an observation window and another door where the guards took up position. Wellman and Priestly stood away from the window, uncomfortable. They looked anxious to avoid seeing the prisoner. Kendrick walked to the glass and looked inside. Unlike the rest of the building, it was pristine. Harsh, white and bare. A mat on the floor for sleeping, a steel toilet. A white table, a white chair, both bolted to the ground. And a man in the chair, dressed in orange coveralls, long thick chains around his ankles and wrists. Three additional chairs at the other side of the table.

Kendrick watched the prisoner. Everything about his treatment was blatant intimidation, crass but usually effective. The man was looking back at him, Kendrick thought, then he reminded himself that the glass was one-way. But still. The man was looking at him. Kendrick felt his inner calm twitch a little.

'When you're ready, ma'am,' said a guard to Priestly. 'One guard will go in with you all.'

Priestly opened her mouth to reply. Kendrick replied instead: 'It'll just be me, thank you. And no guards.' Priestly glared at him but restrained herself.

'One of us must go in with you, sir,' said the guard. 'That's how we do things.'

'You'll be doing things differently today.' Kendrick met the guard's stony eyes with his own. He was used to out-staring.

The guard looked to Priestly, who gave the smallest of nods.

Kendrick entered and made a point of taking the two spare chairs over to the wall, glancing at the mirrored glass when done. He sat, and only then did he look at the man.

The gaze was intimidating. Kendrick was impressed, and returned his own.

The man hadn't spoken a word since being brought here. He'd asked for nothing and had made no complaints. He had eaten what he'd been given and had exercised in any way he could. Kendrick had been assured the man was in great pain, but there was no indication of it. The burns were extensive, raw and seeping, but healing well. 'With unusual scope and rapidity,' was the phrase used in the latest report, but they all knew it was far more than unusual. It was *impossible*. He had kept himself alive and strong, and done nothing more for the seven weeks he had been there.

Kendrick's team had intercepted the man. Unnoticed in the chaos, they had taken their prize away in their own bogus ambulance. And in the days that had followed, they had covered their tracks well, done everything that had needed to be done, ensured the right errors were made. They still had people well positioned.

Kendrick looked away from the prisoner's gaze, judging the time was right. Better now to make the man feel confident than to intimidate him. If, indeed, intimidation would have been possible.

He knew little of what had happened before the fire, but he was sure of one thing: Andreas had achieved his goal and had been preparing to retreat. Whatever information they would then learn from the beings they had been courting, it would have been beyond the reach of Kendrick. That was something he found unacceptable.

Getting his hands on any of the key members of Andreas's group had been the sanctioned plan. Kendrick suspected Wellman and Priestly had given the go-head only because they believed such testimony would show just how *wrong* Kendrick was.

In the event, he had improvised, his bosses horrified by the action he'd taken, but the damage was done now.

Of course, they had known what kind of man Andreas was – principled, benevolent. They had managed to gather a few scraps of information on what Andreas intended, information that had been key in the scepticism Kendrick had encountered: laughter at the ludicrous optimism of a new age for humanity.

But after all the years when they had thought Kendrick deluded as to what Andreas had been attempting, they had changed their minds when they saw how well their prisoner was recovering from evidently fatal injuries.

They had gone from dismissing it all as lunacy to regarding it as a huge risk to national security – a risk they knew they couldn't understand. Kendrick's bosses didn't like things they couldn't understand. And if they didn't like something, they buried it. Kendrick wondered how long they would permit the man to be kept like this before having him disposed of. Years, perhaps, but he doubted it. Not long, he thought. Not long before word spread and loose ends would be cut off, perhaps including Kendrick himself.

Yet they still wanted information. Lots of it. But intimidation had failed, and what good is torture when your subject feels no pain? Kill him and find what you can in the revival, that was what Wellman and Priestly were thinking, though they'd not said as much. Even if they learned nothing in the process, at least it would be over. Then forget the whole sorry event and grind Kendrick into the *dirt* . . .

The only other way was to get the prisoner to cooperate.

'Good morning,' said Kendrick. The man glared back. Kendrick could sense his superiors watching with pleasure, knowing that Kendrick would fail, knowing that nothing and no one had yet coaxed this man to speak even a single word. 'I hope you're being treated well. I apologize if anything's been . . . unsatisfactory.'

The man said nothing, but Kendrick detected a hint of amusement just around the eyes. He held the envelope up. 'I have this. You may be interested.' He removed the paper from within, the two one-sided sheets. The signature on the last, with a space for the man's own. He placed the sheets on the table, a pen beside them.

The man's gaze didn't leave Kendrick's eyes, and for a moment Kendrick wondered if he'd misjudged things. For a moment, he sensed his victory slip. Perhaps the man would rather die than tell them anything.

And then, the man's eyes flicked down. He moved his arms, chains rattling through metal loops on the floor, the noise shocking against the silence. He picked up the paper and started to read. Kendrick watched his face, expressionless until the last sheet, seeing the signature. Definite amusement now.

The letter promised protection, support, resources. Show us what you know, it said. Show us why we should treat you as an ally, not a threat. Earn our trust and you'll have all the freedom you want.

The man set the paper down and watched Kendrick with interest. Kendrick knew he was being weighed.

And then the man reached for the pen and signed. Kendrick was elated, knowing the anger and frustration of those watching him succeed.

Information. Information was what Kendrick *did*. Information was *power*.

And now he would be in control of information nobody else could possibly have. From here on, the prisoner was his responsibility. Everything that resulted would be credited to him. His career would be stratospheric.

'I think we can be of mutual use, don't you?' Kendrick said.

The creature with the face of Michael Andreas looked up and smiled.